The Respite of Ghosts
A Psychological Thriller

by Van Douglas

Hell is empty and all the devils are here.
William Shakespeare, *The Tempest*

The Choosing

The Surgery

This was not the first time she watched herself from outside. From early childhood she treasured her power to stand across the room and watch herself talk and play and cry.

She thought it a great gift, being able to look at yourself as if you were another person. But she kept it secret for fear that her father would say it was only a game she played in her mind. It became part of the detachment that gave her schoolgirl poems their sweet, poignant detail. As a young woman she decided that, even if it was a game, playing external witness to the painful moments of her own life made it easier to cope with all the sadness.

On this occasion she was hovering in the air above the bustling surgical theatre, her mind full of a soft white light. The light was magical and comforting, but she could not see beyond it, into her soul. She could only see outward into the world.

She had been to this place before. She was quite sure of that. How could she forget the sterility of it? How could she forget the stainless steel equipment and white tile and the dehumanizing antiseptic smell? And then there were the gauges and instruments, the digital readouts, and the fast moving lines silently announcing the condition of the patient's body. She was quite sure she had experienced the fear of this place before.

She saw herself on the operating table, covered in white sheets. Only her face and, of course, her skull, were visible. The top of her skull had been sawed carefully in sections that were placed in a receptacle on the table beside her body. The precisely carved fragments of bone were flecked with dots of her blood.

Her brain, a pulsing mass of red and yellow and blue, was being prodded and inspected by trained hands wrapped in thin surgical gloves. Through the transparent gloves she could see the wedding band worn by the distinguished doctor in charge of her surgery. She smiled at the fringe of thin gray hair sticking out of the surgical cap that covered most of his balding head. He was her husband.

Though she heard no sound, she could imagine the authority in his voice. He was directing all of the nurses and doctors arrayed around the operating table, but most especially the nurse handing him instruments at his command. The young nurse exchanged knowing glances with her master, the great surgeon, as if to say that all in the operating theatre shared his commitment to the valuable life now literally in his hands. Floating above it all, the disembodied spirit felt his love.

Despite this, the disembodied spirit was losing interest in the details of the scene below. Instead, she conjured memories of an Irish afternoon.

She longed to be there again, embraced by the magic in the clear blue sky, away from this place with its sharp gleaming instruments and antiseptic smell. She remembered the final lines of a poem she wrote as a child, a poem that her mother loved to hear her recite—*Lift me up to the sky; 'tis clear and bright like my good Lord's smile. Take me where sadness floats away, When my own special breezes lift me up for a while.*

Her wish was to be among the clouds. Not alone but with the children, the Little One and the Precious One. She could see her Little One with his pale baby skin and red hair. She could see the Precious One's beautiful brown eyes and her innocent teenage smile. They would be up in the clouds with her. Eyes closed, she savored the image. But when her eyes opened, she was suddenly mindful again of the scene taking place in the operating theatre right below her.

The nurses and physicians spoke and nodded as they went about their work. In the bright light she could see how blood clotted ever so slightly into a purple gel at the places where her brain oozed onto the white gauze. Sadness began to well up in her as she watched the wavy lines measuring life in the helpless body lying with half a skull.

Suddenly the smooth waves on the monitors turned jagged and the doctors shouted in jargon and clambered about for different instruments. There was so much frantic activity now. Instead of making her more afraid, the hustle and bustle deepened her sadness. She wept at the thought of being violated by the cold room and the cold people in it. She saw it all as an act of violence. She began to shout, "Don't look at those monitors. Look at me! That is my brain. That is the place where my heart and my mind and my memories live." But of course, no one heard her.

The great surgeon and his minions in the operating theatre were focused on the brain inside the skull attached to the body that lay before them. They were focused on the jagged lines on the monitors. Her heart and mind were not of any concern at the moment.

Watching the doctors and nurses and the frenetic dancing of their lines with waning interest, the disembodied spirit floating above them grew calm. She was nurtured by her vision of the Little One and the Precious One away from all of this, with her up in the clouds. Her spirit understood what the nurses and the doctors in their white scrubs did not. Her spirit knew that their toil and their science would not prevail unless she, floating there, could somehow conjure the magic that lives up in the skies.

The Crash

The squall had come with a sudden violence, blue-white lightening and claps of thunder followed by marching sheets of rain. Just as quickly it was gone, leaving behind a sweltering Miami night. On the hood of the red Porsche, diamond beads of water shimmered as the driver revved the engine to a roar, a measure of his anger.

As the thunder boomed off into the distance, wispy clouds trailing after the storm dropped a steady rain onto his black leather seats and into his coal-black eyes. He was rushing and there was no time to put the top up on his convertible. Teeth clenched, rage growing, he stared at the business card his fist pressed to the steering wheel. With only a glance at the pathetic cargo passed out next to him, he pressed the gas pedal to the floor and slammed the gearshift into first.

Just down the street, a luxury Sedan glistened silver in the streetlights. The pretty driver, wearing sunglasses at night as she always did, tied her golden hair back in a knot and finished applying lipstick in the mirror. She added a final candy-colored swipe to banish the aftertaste of the martinis she'd had for her dinner.

"Beautiful," she assured her reflection, pouting her lips as if to practice a kiss for her latest boyfriend. She tapped her accelerator firmly without looking or thinking at all, and her car zoomed out of the parking lot and onto the rain-slick pavement of the bustling thoroughfare.

She was still looking in the mirror when she slammed broadside into the streak of shining red metal that had careened into her path. The driver of the sleek Porsche had his foot pressed full against the gas pedal when the silver Mercedes smashed his passenger side with massive force.

Her father bought her the brand new 1980 Mercedes because it had one of the heaviest diesel engines on the road. Now its massive engine was a weapon slamming into the Porsche like a wrecking ball smashing plaster.

The impact wrenched his leg from its socket. The unbearable pain did not register until the screech of tires from wheels locked in place penetrated his rage. What followed was a sickening cacophony of human wailing and metal scraping metal as the larger Mercedes locked a gnarled death grip onto the convertible and its passengers. The heavy car's momentum propelled both vehicles into the oncoming traffic of the opposite lane.

The old gent speeding down the other lane in his battered pickup was on the way home from a convenience store run for beer and smokes. Puffing a cheap cigar, he was singing along to the Gospel music off a barely audible AM radio station. He gasped in disbelief when he saw the twisted insect of red and silver metal rolling into his path. His lit cigar dropped onto the crotch of his jeans as he flashed his headlights and yanked his steering wheel hard right in an effort to swerve away from the looming menace.

Heartbeats later the bumper of the pickup truck rode up onto the hood of the low-slung convertible, shattering its windshield and removing from the Porsche's driver the last shred of conceit he possessed moments earlier. The force of this crash corkscrewed the girl's Mercedes until it, like the Porsche, was facing toward oncoming traffic. The blonde in sunglasses had quickly plunged into confused panic, sobbing but not understanding what was taking place. She was pinned against leather by the seatbelt she reflexively fastened just before she applied that final touch of lipstick.

With jigsaw momentum the three vehicles swerved on the slick asphalt until finally the jumble of mangled steel rolled to a halt in a pool of water and oil and dangling chrome. The shattered engines sputtered and hissed above the shouting of the crowd gathering on the sidewalks and the moaning inside the wreckage.

Bleeding from a gash on his face, the impeccably dressed man at the wheel of the Porsche gasped for breath. His refined sensibilities were assaulted by the acrid smells of engine oil and tires and rainwater evaporating up from asphalt. This, he could not prevent.

Blood filled his eyes and throat as he wept. "Merciful Allah! Please, this cannot be true. This did not happen. No. Merciful Allah! No!" His brain began succumbing to the shock and the trauma and the loss of blood. His mind, by equal measure, sunk slowly into a stupor and a dulled realization that all he possessed just minutes ago, including, possibly, his very life, was lost to him now.

His last conscious thought was a wish that the radiant dots he saw through his blood were Angels of Allah's mercy, but even in his shock he knew that they were really the headlights of the other vehicles and the multi-colored indicators of his Porsche's elaborate dashboard. As his eyes grew heavier the points of light blurred and finally merged into one soft glow. A wailing of sirens announced the arrival of the paramedics who quickly lifted him onto a gurney and whisked him into an ambulance. Two broken bodies remained in his convertible to be attended to later by others.

The Tryst

The hotel room was by no means cheap. In his bragging tone he had assured her of that, making a point of showing her the room reservation on his cell phone.

But the moment he pushed the door open for her, she knew it was not the luxurious accommodation he thought he had purchased to please her. The curtains were slightly but noticeably out of kilter. The stippled rose-colored wallpaper was faded. It reeked quietly of stale perfume and cigarettes and Lysol sprayed after many guests and many cleanings. Reflexively, she glanced at the time on the elegant watch dangling from her wrist. As soon as she arrived in this place, she was ready to leave.

The bed itself retained a certain odor of use, of bodies sweating and fornicating and sleeping there. The original purpose that brought these two into the bed was much the same as that of countless pairs before them. But something had changed, and the headboard rattled and the bed coils squealed from the force of the bodies thrashing in a violent struggle.

The young woman slung across the bed was, inside of her alarm and panic, vaguely aware of the odor of the bed and the smell of the man leaning over her. He was aware of nothing but the kicks and shrieks of his prey. Like an animal, he barred his teeth and focused every sense on the woman he was subduing.

A flush painted crimson streaks up and down the light brown skin of the woman's elegant neck. As her upper torso writhed to oppose the force of his hand on her throat, her breasts peaked out of the satin negligee she bought just hours before as a special surprise for him. Feeling his other hand sliding a cold metal object down her abdomen toward her legs, she pounded the sinew of his shoulders with renewed vigor and gasped, "No, not this time. No. No."

Wild eyes flaring at her defiance, he leaned on his elbow to get a better grip on her neck. His thick black hair, tightly cropped in a military style, was a sponge of perspiration. When a drop of sweat trickled from his forehead onto her cheek, she tried with all her strength to pull herself away. She couldn't. He was too strong. And then she became aware of the cold steel of a gun sliding upward, between her legs. She had felt it before. She knew what it meant.

She reared up and kicked furiously. "No!" Unprepared for her escalating resistance, he paused to stare into her eyes. Louder still she screamed again, "No."

Each time before, she indulged his game of policeman's gun-turned-sex-toy as the Hindu Goddess Mohini would, an enchantress taking pleasure in her power over the will of a man. This time was different. Now her heart summoned Goddess Mohini, not as an accomplice in an erotic charade, but rather as a mighty female incarnation of Vishnu, the creator of the universe.

Yes, Mohini, her favorite Goddess, could madden her lovers with her beauty, the scent of her skin, her wiles. But the goal now was not to please a lover. The goal was to prevail against the terrible enemy squeezing the life from her throat.

When he relaxed his grip on his service automatic to devote both hands to the task of choking her, the thrashing of her hips tossed the weapon onto her belly. He glanced down at the blue-gray metal against her pretty skin, but her fingertips flailing for the gun robbed it of its erotic meaning. Only subduing her mattered now.

In the midst of the violence between them, the gun, as if endowed by that moment with a mind of its own, discharged one, then another nine millimeter round. The booming reports deafened her. Sparks and fire flew out of the muzzle and suddenly there was blood and gore everywhere. On the sheets. On her. On the man. Even the stippled rose-colored wallpaper ten feet away was splattered with flesh and blood.

It was a moment later or an eternity later—she couldn't be quite sure—when she noticed that the hands were gone from her throat. Now blood and gelatinous flesh covered her face and torso. She thought she glimpsed a chunk of flesh clinging to the fashionable watch dangling from her wrist. As time passed the ghastly sight of her body dripping with blood began to fade, and she saw the beautiful smile of her Goddess Mohini bathed in light somewhere in the distance.

"Come," the soft voice and many arms of Mohini bade her. "Come and be safe. You will be safe here with me. Come to me." Soon, what felt like a hundred fingers caressed the bare skin of her back, lifting her off the bed and away from a place of betrayal and violence and death.

The Inferno

There it stood, as it had since the Great Depression, a tinderbox of wood and cedar shingle. The warehouse reeked of rusted pipes and rats long dead in rafters. There was also the odor of old sacks of heartland wheat tainted by mildew and over-ripe decay. And now there was another smell, the smell of a fresh fire consuming all in its path.

The shining fire engines roared up, red lights spinning and sirens heard in farmhouses miles away on the Kansas flatland. With wide-eyed expectation mixed with fear, the volunteer firemen hanging onto chrome handrails watched their hook-and-ladder close on the blaze.

The widest eyes of all belonged to a bookish young man with red hair. The smell of smoke and the sight of flames lapping into the night sky triggered a little boy's dread that made him regret the conversation he had with his father just minutes ago. He regretted comparing his life to the legend of Faust, who sold his soul to the Devil in exchange for knowledge. He regretted his conceit when he said the religion he learned in church and the science he learned in medical school did not equip him to understand God. Most of all, he regretted confiding to his father that sometimes Satan and demons would come to him in dreams.

Needing to say something to someone, though not expecting an answer, the young man leaned toward the tall thin farmer clad in baggy firefighter gear and hanging next to him on the truck. "Maybe that's how Dante pictured *The Inferno*," he shouted, releasing an arm to point at the fire.

Even if the lanky fellow had heard him above the din of the sirens, the young man's sophisticated sarcasm about Christianity would have been lost on the countrified audience. No matter. He bantered on with this fellow like he had just bantered with his dad.

"Hell isn't described in the Bible very much. Did you know that? It was Dante's *Divine Comedy*. Heard of it? Purgatory, the Deadly Sins, all of that? Think maybe Dante was a volunteer fireman back in medieval times?"

The other man smiled without understanding a single word. Plus, unlike his young friend, he'd fought a big fire before and was too lost in his thoughts about the real inferno up ahead to care what the rookie next to him was saying.

The clamor and confusion were high drama for the Midwestern town on this hot summer night. A full moon shown down on the onlookers milling about and chattering and pointing at the flames. When a big man with flaxen hair jumped out of the red Chief's sedan and yelled, "Back, please, stand back," everyone within earshot responded to his command. They knew him. They knew he was in charge.

The big man sauntered alone toward the warehouse, smiling as the heat of the blaze reached his face. Watching the flames lap at the pale white moon, he paused, as he often did, to admire the beauty and the power of fire.

He looked the brown structure up and down and then glanced over his shoulder at the volunteer fire brigade ready to enter the building. He walked back to join his men. With uncharacteristic hesitation he muttered to his lieutenant, "This 'ol place has been vacant since the depression took hold in the early thirties. It's sat empty for damn near twenty years. If nobody has used it for that whole time I guess nobody would mind if I let it burn to the ground."

But it didn't seem right to him to be at the scene with equipment and men and do nothing. Plus his son was there, home from medical school in Chicago. The boy had joined the volunteer fire company in high school and grew through early manhood in the large shadow of his father. To the consternation of father and son, the only thing they did together in The Company was sit in the firehouse whiling away time as they had been doing just minutes before.

Here was a chance for them to fight a big hot one with a good-sized crowd looking on. In a volley of shouted orders and pointed fingers, the Chief began deploying men and equipment to the fire. And then he suited up to go in himself.

Yanking his headgear into place, he told his lieutenant, "My boy says he doesn't understand the Lord's plan for his life. So I should go in there with him and teach him some things?" An exchange of glances acknowledged that the Chief of even a small volunteer fire company should not be climbing a ladder to join a fire line.

Soon the young man and his father, the Chief, and the other firefighters were silhouettes inside the gray billowing smoke that filled the warehouse. The young man's hands shook with a tension he had never experienced as he watched the firefighter ten feet down the line wait stoically for the order to begin dousing the floor and walls with the powerful hose.

Before the command came, a wall of flames shot up through the very floor where they stood and began rushing toward them. It was the fearsome tidal wave of fire and air and heat and noise known as a backdraft. Their helmets and asbestos suits would prove to be no help at all.

In the briefest of instants the son watched his father's thick hair and rugged face burst into flame, the molten jaw expelling fire and an inaudible scream as it fell to the ground. The next man in the fire line was the tall fellow on the hook-and-ladder who couldn't hear the joke about Dante as a volunteer fireman. He was also quickly engulfed by the fire. His boots and hair ignited simultaneously and burned toward the middle, melting him like a candle in a matter of seconds.

The fire was moving at an angle from left to right, such that the young man was last to catch fire. The roaring red-orange tidal wave burned the rafters out beneath him, and he tumbled downward to the floor below. He landed with a dull thud on a sack of rotting wheat. The shock of the fall stunned him, but, sensing that the flesh on his face was burning, he had the presence of mind to roll his body on the burlap to extinguish the flame.

Believing he was dreaming again of being cast into hell to live among demons, he cried out to his father. He imagined the Chief throwing him over his shoulder in a fireman's carry and running out of the fire and smoke back into the cloudless prairie night. He moved his lips to say, "If you can't help me Chief, can you get Jesus to do it for you?" His fading thought was there was no hope of reaching safety without the help of someone more powerful than himself.

The Cave

It is said that a gun can make all men equal. Had they fought using their rifles, separated by a hundred meters of dusty air, it would still have been a deadly match. But it would have been a better match. Fighting hand to hand, rolling in the dirt like ancient Greek wrestlers, the two were by no means evenly matched.

One was a man, full grown, well fed, trained by a powerful modern army. He had sophistication and experience gained in another country far away. The other was a boy, perhaps fifteen. Had he been interrogated, the boy could not have said with certainty how old he was, because he had been an orphan since days after his birth. There was no record of his birth. There would be no record of his death.

The boy was trembling in a large hole nature carved out of the white rock hills overlooking a desert valley. Below, convoys of army trucks and tanks reeking of diesel fuel were belching smoke and grinding gears. There were several such entrances to a honeycomb of caves that shepherds used for shelter centuries ago. The man, a lieutenant, had volunteered for the risky mission of searching the caves to gather intelligence on enemy positions in the hills above the primary fields of battle.

They sighted each other when the lieutenant, rifle at the ready, took a step into the cave to inspect it. The boy held up his World War I carbine and, arms trembling, tried without success to point it at his enemy. The lieutenant aimed his vastly superior automatic rifle carefully and squeezed off two rounds. Both hit their target, the right ankle of the boy. Writhing in pain, the boy tossed his rifle haplessly toward the enemy entering his hideout. It clattered against the wall and landed on the ground near the entrance

After days of killing anonymous foes in an effort not to be killed, the young officer saw a welcome opportunity for an act of kindness. Smiling to reassure the boy, he went over and, crouching down, inspected the wounds. He offered the boy his canteen, but the boy waved it away with a hateful look that said your water is unclean.

Suddenly the boy wrapped his skinny arms around the big neck of the lieutenant and, shouting wildly, managed to wrestle the larger man to the dusty, rock-strewn ground. They rolled and tumbled as each tried to gain control of the other, grunting and shouting and frightened.

The man quickly overpowered the boy and choked him into submission. He shined his flashlight into the corner of the cave and saw a crate of rags among the disorganized stacks of ammunition, medical supplies, and gasoline cans. Seeing that there was enough cloth to bind the boy's arms and also apply a tourniquet, he decided to let him live. He would leave him here, even let the supplies stay intact, because his mission was only to gain intelligence. Killing the boy was not required.

Kneeling beside the boy's ankle, the stench of his prisoner's breath and uniform was so powerful that the lieutenant was breathing through his mouth as he began to treat the wound. He sat his flashlight on the ground where it rolled to rest, casting a broadening swatch of light across the floor.

The dagger. They both saw it at the same time. From the corners of their eyes both saw the ornate dagger on the ground. It was barely an arm's length away. The lieutenant saw from the darting of his prisoner's eyes that the boy knew it was there, and he imagined that it belonged to the father or uncle who sent this child into this battle. For a span of heartbeats they both stared at the dagger, then the boy sprang to life and crawled furiously across the dirt and reached it first. With a shriek he plunged the rusted blade into the young officer's wrist sending blood squirting onto the sand.

Almost as loud as the boy's shriek was the sickening sound of his nose breaking when the lieutenant punched him with deadly force. Well trained in hand to hand combat, the lieutenant grabbed the dagger from his mortal enemy's hand before the boy's head thudded to the ground. Blood from the lieutenant's wrist poured into the face of his victim as the lieutenant leaned his knee on the chest of the lesser creature and cut the boy's throat.

When he heard the clatter of weapons and footsteps coming, not from the front of the cave where he had entered, but from another entrance in the back, he reached for his rifle. His heart, pounding now with adrenaline, was full of faith in the God of his father, the God who brought him to this place of killing.

And thou shalt be secure, because there is hope;
yea, thou shalt…take thy rest in safety.
(Job 11: 18)

The Respite

The room is eerily still, save the murmur of the Atlantic surf buffeting the sand just outside the imposing window. Despite the butterscotch sunlight pouring in to paint the office's lofty ceiling and elegant furnishings, there is a tense and melancholy cast to the moment.

By furtive glances the three patients inspect each other warily, eyes darting, heads not moving at all. The psychiatrist observes them from across the polished desk of his spacious office. Finally he speaks to banish the darkening mood.

"Psychiatry can be pretty depressing." He smiles, hoping someone would laugh at his ironic joke, as attempting to cure depression is the stock and trade of his profession. Instead he sees no reaction at all. "The reason it's depressing is that the mind can be like an old Gothic mansion with bad memories haunting the rooms and taking over the place from time to time.

"I chose each of you to participate in my psychotherapy group. One definition of psycho-therapy could be mind-therapy. Although my technique focuses on the mind and the memories it holds, I tell my patients we are here to treat their souls. Many don't even believe in the soul when they begin here. But all who are cured believe in it when they leave. Do each of you believe that you have a soul?"

Silence.

"No one answered, so let's assume you all believe you have a soul. So let me try a different question. Does your body possess a soul, or does your soul possess your body—meaning, your soul is capable of existing in numerous forms?"

Dr. Isaac Abraham is neither surprised nor deterred by their confused looks, this being, to his mind, among the great questions of the ages.

"Regardless of what you believed about souls and religion and all of those things when you entered this place, from this moment forward I am asking you to believe what I am about to say.

"Each soul begins its existence unblemished. In this life the soul is battered, torn, sullied in so many ways. But the eternal soul is never corrupted. Only the earthly embodiment of it. We will rid you of this corruption. Your soul must be purified, so that it may spend eternity as it began—unblemished."

Peering down at his timeworn hands, Dr. Abraham draws a careful breath. "Thus, healing is the goal. Some religions speak of redemption and forgiveness. The healing I speak of does not forgive, but rather it restores. This is better. To be pristine once more. This is what we will accomplish together."

A wry grin appears as the confident authority of his voice brightens the mood. "You will be a very interesting group. Your shared experience is that each of you is a trauma survivor. You are here to share a respite in your journeys, a chance to be still and renewed. Otherwise you are completely different one from the other. Does everyone agree with that?"

No reply.

"So far, I've explained how the group therapy will work. Each of you shared some facts about yourselves," Dr. Abraham says. "So now what I'd like is a reaction from you. Do you feel that you are like each other, or different?"

Silence.

The psychiatrist tries humor and a fatherly smile. "I'm not supposed to do the talking, you know. That is your job!"

The patients smile stiffly but still do not speak.

"Let's try this. Let's delve into the differences among you. Why are each of you here? For the same reason or for different reasons? Let's find out." His eyes sweep clockwise from left to right like the second hand on a stopwatch that is running very fast. "Mohammed, please go first. Why are you here?"

To Dr. Abraham's left, sitting erect, mannequin-like, is a well-tailored black business suit containing the person of Mohammed Irani. He is a handsome, broad-shouldered man with piercing coal-black eyes trained straight ahead as if studying a mirage on a distant horizon. His thick hair, once a deep, textured black, is now grey. Prematurely. His mustache, also a pallid grey, imparts an ashen cast to his lips and his mouth. A deep scar runs from just above his left eye across his cheek to his neck.

Mohammed bears other scars, hidden from untrained eyes. But Dr. Abraham knows that Mohammed's posture and body movements are constrained by the motor loss he suffered and the limb that he lost in a tragic automobile accident. Dr. Abraham understands why Mohammed sits silently, ramrod stiff, like a captured soldier refusing to speak.

"I'll put the question this way, Mohammed: What can I cure you of? Describe the malady, imagine the cure."

Mohammed finally looks Dr. Abraham in the eye but says nothing.

"It's a difficult question, isn't it? Think of healing as having a distressing condition taken away. What condition can I remove from you? Tell me the word on your mind right now. Quickly."

"The word in my mind at this moment is rage," Mohammed says in a deep voice.

"Rage. You want me to remove your rage. Is that correct?"

"Yes."

Dr. Abraham's eyes fall next on Shyi Lee Huang, striking a youthful, haughty pose. Well turned-out in an open-neck red business dress and high heel shoes, she, like Mohammed, avoids looking at the others in the room. Her brown eyes and jet-black hair gleam in the brilliant sunlight enveloping the office. Shyi Lee calls herself Joy, telling people that the English translation of her Chinese name is intense happiness and joy.

"Joy, you do the same. Tell me how I can heal you."

Joy remains silent, eyes trained sideways toward the large window. She is a pretty woman; some, according to their taste, would say beautiful. She wears a stylish wristwatch on a braided gold chain that fits loosely about her wrist, the pearly white clock face dangling seductively about her hand. A matching braided necklace, by contrast, fits tightly about her neck at the collarbone.

The locket attached to the necklace bears an elegant gold rendering of a Hindu goddess with a beautiful face and many arms. Joy is a blur of motion—smirking, frowning, waving her hands and shaking her head—yet her goddess of many arms simply rests serenely against Joy's soft brown skin and smiles out at the world.

Again, untrained eyes see no mark of Joy's trauma. Indeed, her body bears none. But the effects of her trauma are not hidden from her healer. It is her behavior, her seething anger and her wariness of others that reveals to Dr. Abraham that this is a woman who has been abused by people who she should have been able to trust.

"Joy?"

"I am thinking."

"About what?"

"Your question, Dr. Abraham."

"And what else?"

Refusing to meet his eyes she chose not to answer.

Dr. Abraham stares at Joy. "For now, don't think about how your condition came to be. Think about how I can heal you."

"I am not sure you can heal me."

"That's a good answer," Dr. Abraham says, looking not at Joy but rather at Mohammed to acknowledge that he knows Mohammed holds similar doubts. "Be assured that I can heal you. Telling the truth will heal you. So you must begin, Joy. Tell me the word on your mind right now."

Joy shakes her head no, turning her gaze out the window again.

"Please look at me," Dr. Abraham demands, pointing two gnarled fingers at his own watery eyes. "What word is on your mind?"

Joy's eyes lock onto his. "Two words! Fear! Shame!" she shouts. "Please make me stop being afraid and ashamed."

"I will try my very best Joy."

Dr. Abraham shifts his gaze to Mary Josephson, who is smiling a soft, enigmatic smile that invites comparison to the Mona Lisa. "And you, Mary? How can I heal you?"

Mary tries to form a thought. She seems weak and sick, and even the untrained eyes of Joy and Mohammed sense that Mary's countenance bears the mark of the disease she is fighting. But they do not know the details. Yet.

Eventually they will know how a teenage bride who wrote love poems to the sky—a lithe, sensuous Irish beauty with strawberry hair down to her waist and the haunting blue eyes of an angel—has been pounded and wrought by disease and depression into the plump, dowdy gal with swollen ankles sitting in the room today.

Despite having been shaved and cut many times, her red-blonde hair stubbornly retains a measure of its girlish curl. Yet dressed in the kind of loose-fitting slacks and blouse the elderly wear to the shopping malls near Miami, Mary presents herself as a dowager. Her cherubic, freckled face, plump from the weight she's battled to keep through her many bouts with cancer, rounds out the persona of a woman grown old before her time. Her eyes tear as she looks into the distance. "I can't say I understand what healin' means, Dr. Abraham."

"That's fine, Mary. Just tell me what condition can I take away? What word is on your mind?"

In a soft voice Mary replies, "Sad. Ahm so sad all of the time. Please take away my sadness."

"We shall try, Mary, together."

Dr. Abraham leans back in his chair and speaks toward the vaulted ceiling. "One wants their healer to take away their rage, and another their fear and shame, and another sadness. So different," Dr. Abraham says, eyes still cast upward.

Dr. Abraham scans the three patients again, this time allowing his eye to linger on the empty chair between Mary and Joy. The upholstery is a luxurious, thick red cloth that stands in beautiful contrast to the highly polished mahogany back. The back of the empty chair is more ornate, higher than the others. He stares for a moment as if he is surprised to see it vacant, then continues.

"And of course your backgrounds are different," the psychiatrist says. "Many of my therapy groups consist of Americans, usually Christians, or more precisely atheists and Pagans who were raised as Christians and continue to masquerade as such. There is a sprinkling of liberal Jews, which is to say non-believing Jews. You as a group are all over the map, literally.

"Mary has told us that she is from Ireland, raised in a strict Roman Catholic home. Correct, Mary?"

Locked inside the cocoon of her thoughts, where her word sadness has unleashed memories of loved ones lost and trusts violated, Mary's blue eyes are as vacant as the cloudless sky outside the window. Seeing this, Dr. Abraham does not wait for an answer.

"And Mohammed moved here many years ago from Iran but still professes to be a devout Muslim. Am I correct?"

"Yes. I am obedient to Allah, as was my father."

"And Joy, born in Hong Kong, was a Buddhist but has turned to the Hindu faith. She—"

"Let me correct you. My father was a Buddhist. I was never a Buddhist. Since the day I was born my soul yearned to be reunited with the creator. My soul is my essence, it is who I am and it is what I do. This is what a Hindu believes."

Dr. Abraham looks at Mary, then Mohammed, then pointedly at Joy. "So you believe in the soul."

"Yes. It is the unchanging me that continues through time. Buddhists like my father do not believe in such a soul. They do not even worship a God. I listened to my father drone on about suppressing desire and the middle path. It made me sick sometimes."

"Then why did you listen?"

"I listened to his lies because I wanted to please him. Then one day I saw he was wrong. That day my adopted Hindu parents showed me their many Gods. I now know that desire increases your Karma as your soul passes through one life after another, growing more perfect with each incarnation."

She looks at Mary and then Mohammed. "Only Hindus embrace the beauty of pleasure, which is why Muslims and Christians and Jews wage their endless wars instead."

Mohammed, a man of impeccable manners, turns his body in his chair and glares at her hatefully. Her eyes lock onto his in a fierce and full stare, acknowledging the mutual antipathy that took root the moment they met.

Dr. Abraham asks, "Mohammed, did you object to Joy's remark just now? If so, please tell us why."

"I am a man who keeps his own counsel, Dr. Abraham."

"Perhaps elsewhere that's true, but when you are with me you must say your thoughts out loud. So speak, please."

"Very well then," Mohammed sneers, looking Joy up and down with a false sense of familiarity. "Concerning this woman Shyi Lee who calls herself Joy, I just met her, this is true. But instantly, I disapprove of her demeanor. Her beliefs. Every word she says. What is more... it is her voice itself. It is the coarse, sing-song voice of a sassy Asian whore in the filthy American movies I so despise."

With a taunting laugh Joy strokes her fingertips on her bare legs, staring Mohammed up and down as he had done to her. Exaggerating her Chinese accent she says, "Hey Joe-black-suit-red-tie, fifty dolla I spend time you! Good Joe? Only fifty dolla to make Joe happy first time in life maybe?"

"Dr. Abraham, she has proven my point!" Mohammed shouts, clenching his fists. He looks at the vacant-eyed Mary. "Are you not disgusted by this too, Mary?"

Mohammed's question summons a confused Mary out of her stupor and into the moment. "This isn't makin' any of any of us feel better, not me at least. How did we get onto this, Dr. Abraham?"

"I'm not quite sure,' Dr. Abraham replies. "I wanted to talk about how different we are, using religion as an example."

Mary looks at Dr. Abraham. "Why does that matter? Should we know your religion, Dr. Abraham?"

"I'm thinking Jewish," Joy smirks.

"You think I'm Jewish, eh? Did the name give me away? The beard? Was that the clue?"

After a thoughtful pause, Dr. Abraham says, "Perhaps I'm a bit like you, Joy. I was born a Jew but have rejected the notion that the Hebrews are God's chosen people. My hypocritical Miami Jew-of-a-stepfather believed his birthright made him special in the eyes of God but did not even bother to keep Kosher. His talk was trash."

The eyes of his patients widen with surprise, shock in Mary's case, as Dr. Abraham hoped. He smiles. "First Mohammed judges a woman he hardly knows, then Joy pretends she's a whore, and now your old psychiatrist sounds like a street punk.

"Do my words startle you? Pagans and atheists masquerading as Christians? A hypocritical Miami Jew talking trash? Harsh words to be sure. No matter. I simply spoke what I was thinking. I may not even believe what I said, but... we have the luxury to do that here. In fact, we are obliged to tell each other what is in our minds, so that we ourselves can hear it. That is how healing takes place. Agreed?"

Nodding their agreement like preschoolers in their little semi-circle of chairs, the patients stare across an ornate wooden desk at their healer—a man with a massive head and full grey beard, a face that would belong to an ancient Hebrew patriarch, were it not trimmed to suit the style of a wealthy Miami psychiatrist. "We're finishing a bit early for an initial session, but I am tired, and I am sure you are all exhausted as well. Are there any questions?"

Their healer looks across the polished wood that is the border between his power and their weakness. He knows that the human eyes and mouth are the places where inner tension is revealed, and he is not surprised to see it on all of their faces today. This is the effect of the difficult first session of group therapy.

"If there are no questions, I will see if you understand my therapeutic technique. My technique is based on two exercises which I call the Memory Book and the Portal.

"For the technique to work, you must believe that it is possible that the four of us may be here, together, until the end of time. Please understand that time can bend and warp here. Most important, you must understand that your healing results from the truth you tell each other in this place. Do you know what that requires?"

The patients look at one another, saying nothing.

"It requires that you come prepared to fling your Memory Book open for all of us to share.

"One other point. As you move forward, your Memory Book will reveal battles and enemies. Even on the small stage of a single life, villains strut and epic battles are waged. Take us out of this room to meet your villains in the places you encountered them. Take us out of this room to witness your battles, battles that you are still fighting, battles that brought you here because they are not over."

Lips quivering, Mary says, "Dr. Abraham, I haven't an enemy in the world. This cancer is my enemy. Were it not for this cancer I wouldn't be fightin' any battles."

"Are you sure? In your life there are no villains at all? There is nobody who you wish you never met?"

"Indeed nay."

Mohammed smirks. "I am like her. I have no battles to fight."

"Truly?" Dr. Abraham looks over his shoulder at a copy of the Koran on the credenza. It is an antique, the words written in beautiful flowing Arabic. He opens it to a certain passage, holds it in front of Mohammed, then carefully replaces it on the shelf. "No battles? No enemies? Doesn't this book teach us that obedience to God involves Jihad, a constant struggle against not believing and temptation and those who would tempt you?S"

Mohammed offers no reply.

Staring at Mohammed, Joy says, "Di Ren," then rattles off a series of words in Chinese. She stares at Mary next, repeating the words in Chinese. Dr. Abraham nods approvingly. He knows the answer but nonetheless asks, "What was that all about, Joy?"

"The point is that, depending on the context, there are the many different words that can mean enemy in Chinese. That's because our enemies can come in many forms. Unlike Mohammed and Mary, I know very well who my enemies and lovers have been and which times one person has been both."

"A good way to end the session. We are done for now." Dr. Abraham's voice trails off as he catches his breath.

Ignoring the patients he exhorted so passionately a moment before, in silence he reaches around to his intricately carved mahogany credenza. Tall and imposing, it's many shelves brim with richly bound texts from many religions, sheaves of notes on paper the texture of parchment, and small archaeological artifacts arranged in a surprisingly haphazard manner, more like an old hermit's bric-a-brac than a wealthy psychiatrist's collection of antiquities.

On a shelf, at shoulder height, two items occupy a place of prominence. The first is a shining Arabian dagger of silver and gold, its blade pitted and worn by many years of use.

Next to it is a platter of drinking glasses arranged in a circle around an ornate earthenware pitcher filled with water. The lid is capped by a ceramic lotus leaf, faded now but once a brilliant green. The body of the vessel is a relief in blue and tan and orange. It shows a smiling Buddha at peace among vines and leaves. It appears to be very old, an artifact. His arm trembles slightly with the weight of the vessel as he carefully lifts the lotus flower lid and pours the clear liquid into a glass filled with ice.

Like marionettes awaiting a tug at their strings, his patients neither move nor speak as they watch their healer drink deeply from his glass.

2.

Dr. Abraham enters his office to see Mohammed, Joy, Mary and the empty chair facing him. The scene would be a snapshot of their first time together, were it not for Joy. Now she is wearing a blue dress cut longer than the red business dress she wore for the first session.

Otherwise, all appear as they did before: Mohammed in his black suit and red tie, Mary in her ill-fitting blue slacks and blouse with the strings on the sleeve that can be tied in a bow, and he in his canary-colored cardigan.

"Hello again."

Mary says hello. Joy and Mohammed nod their greeting. "So far we've talked in generalities. I explained how psychotherapy works, the power of the subconscious mind, how each person can be their worst judge and jury. For the most part you have revealed the kind of unimportant facts you would tell a stranger standing in line at the market."

The psychiatrist smiles from the corner of his mouth where a small droplet of saliva glistens. "Now you depart on a journey with one unavoidable destination—a full accounting of your life, scene by scene. Memories are very private things. Some memories we even conceal from ourselves, or at least try to conceal. That was one of Sigmund Freud's goals in psychoanalysis: To probe the subconscious for repressed memories.

"Nothing matters any more but your Memory Books. Are you ready to start opening your Memory Books?"
Silence.

"First we'll do an easy warm-up. We'll limber up like a tennis star." In jest he awkwardly sways his stiff shoulders side to side. "I will go clockwise, left to right, starting with Mohammed. Mohammed, what is your earliest memory?"

Mohammed's eyes brighten. "I remember walking with my father and uncle to the mosque. I was walking between the two of them, sometimes getting a step or two ahead so I could look up into their faces. It was a warm spring evening, an evening full of soft breezes and the aromas of cooking as we walked the narrow streets to the mosque.

"The comforting sound of the call to prayer rings in my ear even at this moment. It grew stronger as we neared the holy place. I remember how tall and handsome my father and uncle were. I remember the beautiful white and blue tiles lining the walls of the mosque. Inside of that place, the whole world seemed warm and safe and peaceful."

"Thank you Mohammed. Joy, what is your earliest memory?"

After a pause she says, "I do not have one."

"Of course you do." The tiredness in Dr. Abraham's raspy voice seems to console Joy. "It's the earliest recollection of your life."

She casts her eyes to the ceiling. After a long pause she admits, "I do not remember much from my childhood."

"Try," the physician says. "The memory may be distant, perhaps something you would rather forget. Just say what comes to your mind right now. Tell us what is in your thoughts right at this second."

"I am thinking about a childhood nightmare that I still have from time to time."

Dr. Abraham jots a note. "A nightmare?"

"Yes." Joy looks down, a meek frown painting her face.

"Tell us about the nightmare."

"I would rather not."

"You must," Dr. Abraham insists. "That is why you are here."

After a small sigh Joy says, "I recall a bad dream. It was a recurring dream that I started having when I was very young."

"How young?"

Joy presses her eyes closed. "I don't remember."

"Try."

"It may have started when I was three or four."

"Describe the dream."

"I can't really remember."

"Perhaps you will remember if you just let the words come out. Try to describe a place."

"I was sleeping in my bed. It was dark. My parents were not home. I woke up and there was a man in a uniform beside me. My little bed was pressed against a wall so I was between him and the wall. I could barely move.

"The man's face was so close to mine that I could feel his stale cigarette breath enter my mouth. My nightshirt was lifted up. He was staring at my breasts, rubbing his hands on my knees, my stomach, all over me. I kept my eyes closed pretending to sleep."

"In this recurring dream, were you afraid? Do you recall how it felt?"

"I had the dream different times and still have it. I think I was afraid at times, but not always. I think I was more afraid as I got older."

"That is the earliest memory you can recall right now, Joy?"

"Yes. My mind is empty except for this memory in my bed."

"Thank you. I know that was difficult. And now you, Mary. Tell us your—"

"Is Joy finished, Dr. Abraham?" Mary asks in her soft voice, casting a sideways glance at Joy's down-turned face.

"For now, yes."

Mary offers a sheepish smile. "But my memory is different from Joy's. Mine is happy."

"That is quite alright. Open your Memory Book for us."

Mary smiles her Mona Lisa smile. "I remember a walk with me mam in the springtime, with the hills greenin' up and the sun smilin' from high in the sky. My mam and father and I took a ride into the country in his car. He stayed behind while mam and I took a long walk, just the two of us. My mam loved all children to be sure. And I love them, like her.

"The sky was totally a clear blue. I think that is why blue is my favorite color. We walked fer hours under that perfect blue sky. Every once in a while she would stop and take my hand and tell me jokes about leprechauns. We would pretend to look for them behind trees."

Dr. Abraham scratches a note then asks, "Did your mother believe in leprechauns?"

"Indeed not."

Her psychiatrist does not look up from his notes. "Magic, then?"

"We talked about magic that very day, 'tis true. She surprised me when she talked of it so, just like your question just now surprised me, Dr. Abraham."

"What did your mother say about magic?"

"She lifted me up in her arms and pointed at the sky and said, 'Mary, I will tell you what my mother told me. Magic sits in the blue sky every day just waiting for us to wish for it.' I remember watching her holding me, like she and I were on a cinema screen."

Dr. Abraham jots a note. "You were watching yourself from the outside? Does that happen often?"

"Nay, not often. That day was the first time I remember it happening."

"Interesting. Your mother sounds very special. Tell us more about her. Is she in good health? Does she visit you?"

Mary's smile fades. "She visits me in my prayers. The Good Lord called me mam to his side not long after this day ahm telling about. That day she told me she would be goin' to the Lord's side."

"Thank you Mary. This walk took place in your native Ireland?"

"Of course. 'Tis no other place with hills that green, with air that fresh, with skies so blue. Only Ireland."

Dr. Abraham jerks his shoulders again in his awkward impression of an athlete warming up. "We're a little loose now, so let us try something more difficult. I want each of you to select some object in this office and turn it into a symbol that tells your life story. This time I will go counterclockwise. Mary, your turn first."

Mary looks sideways to Joy and Mohammed. "Ye want us to pick something in this room that tells our whole life story?"

"Just try to connect what you see in the here and now to important things that happened in the past."

Mary's eyes scan the room and come to rest on the huge window that runs floor to ceiling the entire length of the wall. "The window symbolizes the happiness I have sought all my life. The window lets the light pour in and makes this doctor's office feel… magical."

Mary glances sideways at Joy, like she is coaching the younger woman on how to be a medical patient. "This room feels like a place where people with souls arrive to be healed instead of a place where only yer body is inspected and cut up and then stitched up again. It…"

Mary stops talking as her concentration fades. Dr. Abraham speaks up. "Mary, it's true, our healing here is done by words. No pills dropped into your mouth, no tubes inserted into your body, no scalpels cutting slices out of your flesh. Words are our scalpel; we wield them with precision here. Thank you, Mary. Joy, you are next."

"What am I supposed to do?"

"Pick an object in this office that can act as a symbol of your life. Look around the room. Take your time."

She leans forward in her chair, craning her neck, exaggerating the uselessness of the exercise. Just as she utters the words, "Nothing in this room has anything to do with my past," she looks at the floor.

"O-M-G! The carpet," she announces triumphantly.

Dr. Abraham smiles with curiosity. "O-M-G?"

"Short for Oh My God," she explains.

"I've learned something new, Joy. Describe the carpet, then explain how it symbolizes your life."

"I used to sell rare carpets. This one is rare and beautiful. The knotting and deep shades of purple and beige and blue tell me it was made by hand in India long ago. Whoever decorated your office had an excellent eye for color and design."

"How so? I decorated my office, so please praise me lavishly."

Joy waves her fingertip at the carpet. "You've perfectly matched the carpet to the scale of the room. The office is about thirty feet long and twenty feet wide. The floor tiles are large, a cream-colored stone in a diagonal pattern. The walls and the lofted ceiling are of the same stone. A very unusual treatment."

"Yes, the stone is unusual. But describe the carpet. Why does it symbolize your life?"

"Your carpet and your exquisitely crafted furniture sit at the closed end of your office. Speaking for myself, I enter your office confused and alone, but by the time I reach the carpet I feel connected."

"Maybe I'm reading too much into this, Joy, but you seem to be saying that the carpet symbolizes a sought-after intimacy."

"Intimacy and, also, I would say, safety."

"Interesting. Why do you think that is, Joy?"

"The carpet reminds me of Mr. and Mrs. Patel. Their store always had a thick aroma of carpet and Indian cooking and it made me feel safe and intimate with them. From the first time Mr. Patel…"

Joy stares at the beautiful carpet and, like Mary, stops talking.

"Are you finished, Joy?"

"I have taken more than my time."

"There is no time limit. I am sure we will learn more about the Patels. Could you perhaps tell us a bit right now, by way of a sneak preview one might say?"

Joy peers impishly into the eyes of her shrink. "A preview of Mr. and Mrs. Patel? They are short carpet merchants who hired me to work in their store. They took me in and brought me here from Hong Kong. They taught me everything I know about life."

"A nice preview, Joy. Thank you. Mohammed, it is your turn."

Mohammed is ready. "Your desk could be a symbol of my life, Dr. Abraham."

"Describe the desk. Explain your symbolism."

"If I may reply impulsively to you Dr. Abraham, as you are trying to teach us to do, I am tempted to say simply that the desk stands for tradition. And authority."

"In what way?"

"I deal in antiques, so I know your desk is old, as are these chairs and your credenza. To describe your desk is to say it is large, the size of a dining room table. It is deeply varnished, a black-brown. The elaborate inlaid designs on the sides were crafted painstakingly long ago. Men who loved beauty created the furnishings in this place."

"And what does the desk symbolize to you?"

"The desk symbolizes my father and my family traditions."

"He owned a desk like mine?"

"Yes. My father once showed me an old picture of his great grandfather sitting behind a desk nearly identical to yours. It was in the Second Empire style in vogue after World War Two."

Mohammed, eager to display his knowledge of antiques, elaborates on the desk. "The style is mentioned in Sartre's play *No Exit,* the play where people are trapped in a finely furnished room. Many wealthy Europeans made offers for the desk but my father refused. Finally he sold it to come to America. This caused him great sadness."

Dr. Abraham offers his wry smile. "Unlike that very depressing play, in our story together each of you can in fact exit. But that is for later. For now, Mohammed, open your Memory Book. Tell Mary and Joy about your father."

Mohammed has a far-away look in his eyes. "My father was a wise and educated man. But he was a stern man also, a man very quick to discipline his wife and his children. My memory is of a moment when he was very stern. It was late at night. I was a young man trying to be a good Muslim in America. But occasionally I failed. Once I skipped prayers. My father punished me very harshly. "

Dr. Abraham asks, "And how did he discipline you? With a rod perhaps?"

"I do not care to say. But I shall tell you this. When my tears stopped, my father told me that one must cling to tradition even in America. He showed me a faded black and white photograph of the desk that his father and his father's father had owned. He had to remember that desk from the picture he showed me, and this helped him remain faithful to tradition and Allah."

Dr. Abraham slides his hands across the desk toward Mohammed, opening his palms upward like a fragile photograph was resting on his fingertips. "So a tattered photograph had the power to sustain your father's faith. I'm surprised your family was not able to bring to America anything of comparable significance."

"Well in fact there was one thing my father still possessed. It was a certain ancient bowl."

Dr. Abraham nods. "Does the bowl have significance for your life? Please describe it for us."

Mohammed resists. "If I have answered your question I prefer not to speak further."

Dr. Abraham draws a slow breath. "Fair enough. Thank you Mohammed, and of course Joy and Mary. That wasn't as difficult as it seemed at first, was it?"

"No, 'twasn't at all," Mary giggles, acting the schoolgirl. "And also Dr. Abraham, don't it seem a delight how the symbols in the room are such wonderful things?"

A salesman's enthusiasm enters Dr. Abraham's voice. "Please say more, Mary."

Looking out the window, she replies. "Well, Ahm feelin' that your window stands for magic and beauty. Joy says your carpet means feelin' safe and bein' with people. And Mohammed says your desk stands for tradition and authority. I just think we're all tired and this is a place where we can rest." Mary looks at her fellow patients. "'Tis true, those are all good things, aren't they?"

"They are indeed," Mohammed replies.

Joy nods in agreement.

"Well thank you Mary," Dr. Abraham smiles. "Such a nice thought. You've said that this is a fitting place for a respite, a pause on our journeys."

He draws a breath. "And so, now we are warmed up. I want you to truly open your Memory Book to the rest of us, with whom you will spend eternity. I want you to say three specific words, 'Let me take you to a place where…' then open your Memory Book. The reason I use the term Memory Book is that our entire life is written in our memory. It's all there for us to bring back, if we allow it. So many people are there. Your friends, those you loved, the enemies some of you claim not to have. Take us to meet them. Who volunteers to go first?"

Noting the skepticism in the eyes of Joy and Mohammed, Dr. Abraham turns to Mary. "Mary, you seem eager to get started. Would you like to be first?"

"I would be very pleased to do that. I will even read my story. I typed it out on my computer and printed it." Passing out copies, she asks," Is that a'right, Dr. Abraham?"

"It's never been done here before, let's see how it works."

Studying the neatly printed pages, Mohammed asks, "You wrote this on a computer? And printed it?"

"Ahm not well-educated but I can do lots on my computer, Mohammed."

"He did not mean offense, Mary," Dr. Abraham says. "Perhaps he did not know a computer could do such a thing. Now I want you to say the words, 'Come with me,'" then begin telling whatever story about yourself you choose to tell. Mary?"

Eagerly Mary says, "Let me take you to a beautiful night in Ireland. I want all of ye to meet a beautiful lass doomed to live in a world that was cold. Fate married me into that life due to the misfortunes of my father. When I finish my story you might think I blame things on me father. Not true."

Mary looks at Mohammed. "My father is a good man. When me mum died it broke his heart. He is a devout Catholic who believed from the bottom of his heart that it was possible to live a good life among fellow Irishmen, the Protestants. He said they were people he could do business with even though history deprived them of the True Church and the blessings of the Holy Father in Rome who is the heir to—"

Dr. Abraham waves his hand toward Mary. "Mary, please tell the story of your life."

He looks around at the circle of patients, addressing them all. "This other matter, the Pope, the religious wars in Europe, or Arabia, or wherever, is of no consequence to us here. It is just another example of how the minds of men can contrive gods to conspire with them for evil. To the detriment of souls.

"So Mary, just go ahead and read your story aloud. And please, as I have asked each of you, tell the story with so much detail that you take all of us out of this place. Take us to where it happened. Can you do that, Mary?"

"Indeed so." Mary sits perfectly erect and begins reading.

The true story of Mary begins on a night when a host of bright, shimmering stars peered down at her from the purple-black sky over the countryside north of Belfast. Let me take you there right now. Is that how you want us to say it?

"Yes, that is perfect for now, Mary," Dr. Abraham says. "Please continue."

This was the night when the young Mary Fitzpatrick finally understood that her marriage to the man walking next to her had been arranged like a business deal. Robert Fitzpatrick asked Mary's father for her hand over drinks in a pub while both fathers—they were business associates—drank and laughed about what a good deal it would be for Mary. Mary never felt she had a choice.

And so tonight she secretly searched the stars for the magic that would set her free and let her find true love. But all that happened when she looked up was that the wind snapped bitterly at her face. Her eyes were full of tears from the wind and her thoughts. So she bent her head and trudged up the long, stone-strewn pathway.

Robert's father's house, brooding black-grey with yellow lights on the crest of the hill, was finally within reach. Robert glared over his shoulder at Mary following several paces behind.

"Faster, Mary. This cold is bitin' me ass."

The moon, half-full against the cloudless sky, cast a soft light on Mary's face. A different man might have seen some beauty there, or at least noticed the tears. Robert only saw Mary walking up the hill too slowly. "Would you catch up, Mary? Me ass is freezing."

Mary kicked her feet at the loose stones for a few shuffling quicksteps until she pulled abreast. "There."

Robert clutched his woolen gloves together as he glared sidewise at his wife. His voice bore the slight but unmistakable brogue that even the most educated of the Irish mold around their words. "Yer a beauty, Mary but if ya didn't have that smile and long red hair I'd send ya back to your father right now. Make him get ya some schoolin' and marry a good Catholic warehouse man.

"Tonight father and mother will be talkin' about our going to America, Mary. But no mention of our surprise until after my father ushers in the New Year. And don't mention the headaches either."

A sharp gust of wind blew into their faces. Reflexively, Mary clutched at her muffler. "If I get one tonight, I can just lie down somewhere."

Mary watched Robert's cold breath issue a fog about his face and shoulders. The fog changed shape and size as the words rattled out of his mouth. "It's New Year's Eve. Just like he's done every year, tonight my father will be spouting off about how the Irish should have backed the Nazis. How the Americans are ruining the world. Why they should ban American books so that only James Joyce will be read at Irish universities."

"What's that got to do with us? What does James Joyce have to do with this cancer that's eatin' at my brain?"

Mary's tone was pitiful and sincere at the same time. For a split-second, Robert almost responded to Mary's sadness. But not tonight. Robert was too busy feeling pity for Robert as he readied himself to bear the yoke of his father's insufferable egotism and pessimism. Mary's pain, well, Robert would take note of it later. Father came first tonight.

"Mary, it's just a fact. Father hates America. It's bad enough that I'm going there for a year—and to work for their space program, no less. It's bad enough that he hates Dr. Josephson for going there to practice medicine. But they're not ready to hear about your cancer at all, let alone that you are goin' to be seein' Dr. Josephson in Florida. Not tonight."

Joy waves her hand in the air. Cocking her head she says, "Mary, may I ask you a question?"

"Of course."

"You just mentioned a Dr. Josephson. Your name in the story is Mary Fitzpatrick. Now it is Josephson, right? Is—"

Mary looks straight ahead. "Indeed. Larry Josephson is my second husband."

Dr. Abraham nods. "Thank you for answering Joy's question, please continue reading."

Robert shuffled his feet against the stone and rang the bell. Light and warm air rushed out as the door opened and his mother appeared. Greetings rang out from inside. "It's Robert," the voice of some uncle or cousin shouted.

"And Mary, our family's beautiful Mona Lisa," his mother added with her own shout. Robert's mother was a good-hearted woman who doted on her husband, spoiled her treasured only child, and was fully prepared to spoil his wife. Robert had told his mother that his new wife looked like the Mona Lisa. It turned out that Robert's mother thought the Mona Lisa was a portrait of the virgin mother.

Robert's father put down his drink and walked heavily toward the foyer. Mary and Robert stood awkwardly until his father reached around and pushed on the heavy door a final time; as if to tell Robert he hadn't closed it quite properly.

"There, closed," his father said.

Robert gave him a polite but penetrating look.

"Got to close it total, lad. Heat costs money."

Robert shrugged.

"Bitter cold, coldest in years," the elder Fitzpatrick offered.

The father, a big man with whitish skin ruddy tonight with drink, helped Mary out of her heavy coat. As the coat came off, Robert's mother secretly scanned Mary's tummy for evidence of the grandson she wanted so badly. Mary noted the inspection but avoided her mother-in-law's inquisitive eyes.

Robert introduced Mary around the crowded rooms. He and his mother said more about the heirloom wedding ring on Mary's finger — how the stone may once have belonged to the King of England—than they said about the new bride herself. He then deposited his Mona Lisa safely among the womenfolk.

Robert's mother told the ladies about Mary and Robert's upcoming trip to America. A pleasant and happy-minded talker, she even managed to work Mary's virginity at marriage into the conversation without mention of Mary's Catholic upbringing. "Tis how it should be, a man should have a virgin for a wife," the mother said to nods of agreement.

Grinning mischievously, Joy waves her hand in the air again. "Mary, were you really a virgin when you got married?"

"I was indeed."

"I'm interested in the heirloom ring," Dr. Abraham says. "Do you still have it?"

Her eyes tear up. "No. It was just a ring. And I haven't much to say about it."

Dr. Abraham studies his patient. "The ring seemed significant to Robert's family."

"I've nothing to say about it now."

"As you wish, Mary. You have done a good job of taking us to the house that night. Take us back now."

Mary smiled at the praise she and Robert received for their small triumph over modern life's temptations. For what seemed to be an eternity, Mary sipped dutifully at the fruit punch, craving a beer or even an Irish whisky. She stood stoically, smiling when she could, as the older ladies made gossip in the kitchen and the parlor. Two toddlers were making their last tired rounds among the women, and Mary tried her hand at acting motherly toward them. "Need some of your own," Robert's mother winked. Mary just smiled.

Robert dominated the conversation among the men. He moved from one circle to the next, gravitating away from his father and toward the younger ones who smoked and drank on the porch in the cold dark.

A whirl of activity and sound had commenced with the arrival of Robert and his new wife Mary. But the evening lapsed into tedium.

There is really a limit to how much alcohol and food a person can consume before becoming flat and tired. Robert's oldest uncle, a skinny old bloke in his eighties, nodded off and spilled his drink. He rubbed his pants at the crotch where the drink spilled, then fell asleep again, head cocked against the seat back. Occasional snores and snorts issued from his mouth. Soon everyone was taking secret glances at their watch or the big clock on the mantle. Mercifully, midnight was drawing nearer.

At 11:55, the traditional time, the elder Fitzpatrick strode ceremoniously to the fireplace and pulled an old but well-kept shotgun from above the mantle. He took a deep pull on his Irish whiskey and headed outside with his shotgun. "We'll ring in the New Year as we always do," he announced. Robert beckoned with his eyes for Mary to join the men following his father outside.

Three loud, booming shotgun reports later, the elder Fitzpatrick headed back into the house with fatalistic smile. Robert stayed outside, leaning against the cold stonewall of the house, his teeth chattering involuntarily in the cold. "Now it's time," he said, heading into the warm house. Mary followed him like a puppy into the living room. "I have an announcement," Robert shouted, placing his hand on Mary's shoulder. When all eyes were on him he said, "What you all know is that I am moving to America for work. What none of you know, because I am announcing it now is that my wife is pregnant. The baby is due in June."

The men shouted and hooted, led by the elder Fitzpatrick, who promptly offered a toast. "To my grandson, finally a-comin' this year. Truly," he said, raising his glass, "'tis going to be a great new year."

The womenfolk beamed and gathered around Mary. When Robert's mother whispered to Mary, "You and the Lord have made me very happy," Mary suddenly got one of her crashing headaches. Her head throbbed so badly that her eyes hurt. She felt nauseated. She beckoned to Robert, standing with his father and uncle near the fireplace. "I need to go lie down," she whispered into his ear when he finally crossed the room to where she was standing.

He took Mary's arm and said to his mother. "Mona Lisa is feeling a bit queasy." Soon Robert was walking Mary upstairs to his childhood bedroom. It was cramped and dark and cold. Before she could get under the covers they had a terrible argument.

Alternating her eyes between her papers and Dr. Abraham, Mary says, "He went stompin' and I—rather, Mary—

let me keep reading this as it is written… Never mind, I know this part by heart. I rewrote it many, many times. I could hear his heavy boots boundin' down the narrow wooden stairs. His boots were so big and loud. It was a dreadful sound, echoing in the stairwell of that old stone house. I ended up simply lying there in the dark by myself until—"

A tear begins welling up in Mary's eye. "I'll be stoppin' here," she says, yanking the page she was reading from out of the stapled story. She rips the sheet of paper in half, rolls it up into a tight ball, and then tosses it on the floor in front of her feet.

Mary's physician furrows his brow and scowls. "You may rip up your paper, but do not throw anything on the carpet in this room."

"Sorry," Mary says.

Dr. Abraham points at the wad of paper. "Pick it up."

Joy begins to reach down for the ball of paper.

"Not you, Joy. Mary. Please pick up the paper you just threw on my carpet."

Leaning over to pick up the ball of paper at Joy's feet, Mary tries to smile apologetically but instead clenches the paper in her hand and begins to sob. "Let me take you to the place I lived my life? Is that how we are supposed to begin these stories? I'll take you to a place where I lost a child. Robert never forgave me for that. But later he was satisfied. Later Robert's mother and father got the grandson they wanted. Ahm done talking now."

Her psychiatrist's chair creaks as he leans back to study her. "How did you say goodbye to Robert's parents?"

"I don't remember."

"Are you sure? Please try to remember."

"No."

"I'm surprised you don't remember, since you said you rewrote this section many times."

"That's the story of another person, another Mary, and it isn't even the true story. I'll get to fixin' it later. Next week I will have a truer story."

Dr. Abraham raises his voice. "More true, Mary? More true?" He mentions Mary's name, yet he is staring at Mohammed, who rears back in his chair as if propelled backwards by the force of his physician's look. "No. Something is either true or false. Let us all understand that. Mary, I demand that you tell the truth."

Mary closes her eyes and says, "The truth is that the argument lasted a long time. When we went downstairs all the guests had left. Robert's father was drunk asleep in the same chair where his uncle was snoring away earlier. His mother was in the kitchen. You could hear her clanging the dishes. Then…"

When Mary's voice trails off, Dr. Abraham says, "Then what? What happened next?"

"I – I mean Mary – started toward the kitchen to help her finish cleaning up. Robert grabbed my wrist and yanked me over to the fireplace like a disobedient child.

"The fire was dying. The room was cold. He reached up above the mantel and got his father's shotgun down from the rack. He had an awful look on his face. 'Twas hateful. He snarled through his teeth, 'An old Fitzpatrick family legend says they once shot bloody Papists with this old piece.' He pushed the big cold shotgun toward my face. Then he said, 'Maybe it will happen again. Maybe soon.'"

Joy interrupts. "And this man is your husband? What kind of thing is that for a husband to say?"

Mary's jaws tighten, recalling the anger of the moment. "I pulled his damn ring off my finger straight away and said, ''Tis as good a day as any. Ahm takin' your damn ring off so you won't have to be prying' it off my dead hand.' He smiled that cold smile of his then pushed the shotgun back onto the rack. 'Can't be shooting a pregnant lass with cancer in this house, what with maybe the cancer will do the job for me,' he said. Then he looked me in the eye. 'Ya know, Mary, Ahm just now wonderin' if you didn't bring it on yourself. All of this that you're putin' me through, maybe you brought it on both of us.'

"How did you react to that?" Dr. Abraham asks. Joy stares intently at Mary.

"React? I just went cold, 'tis all. We went into the kitchen, said goodbye to his mother, and we left. From that day on, try as I might not to, I hated him and his family."

Dr. Abraham nods approvingly. He looks at Joy and Mohammed. "Mary has done well, wouldn't you agree? I felt the cold air and the dying fireplace. I heard the hatefulness in Robert's voice. Would you like a drink of water Mary?"

"Please."

Dr. Abraham's hands shake slightly as he reaches around to his credenza where the ornate water pitcher sits. The patients, especially Mohammed with his eye for the craftsmanship of antiquity, have each become secretly intrigued by its elaborate design, its heft even, but say nothing; they simply watch as he pours a tall glass of water for Mary.

She drinks deeply, the soft sound of the water washing down her throat overtaking all other sounds. Her fellow patients do not move while she drinks, but Dr. Abraham does. He eases himself from his chair, exiting without a word.

3.

Their next time together begins with Dr. Abraham jotting notes on his yellow pad. A fleck of sunlight twinkling on the tip of his pen catches Mohammed's eye and pulls his mind, which had been wandering about in his painful memories, back into the room.

"Mohammed, would you like to go next?"

Mohammed remains silent so everyone is certain he attends the therapy reluctantly Then in his deep voice he says, "If I must, yes. But I do not need a computer to help me. I prefer simply to speak."

Dr. Abraham's watery eyes study Mohammed, the empty chair, the other patients like a judge about to render a verdict. "That's fine. So now, Mary and Joy, Mohammed is going to take us out of this room and into the places he's lived his life."

"I will begin as you requested, Dr. Abraham, by saying, 'Let me take you to my antique shop."

Pausing to shift the weight off his prosthetic leg, he glances at Joy in her dress with the bare arms and legs that would assault the sensibilities of any devout Muslim. Suddenly energized by the difference between him and her, he forgets, at least for a time, his reservations about Dr. Abraham's method. "My antique shop is, of course, nothing like the rug merchant's store Joy has described. Rather, it is elegantly furnished in every way."

"Mohammed, shouldn't ya confine your story to your life," Mary asks, nodding toward Joy. "Ah don't think you should be commentin' on Joy's shop."

"Perhaps you are right," Mohammed replies, satisfied his point had been made. "My shop has a large window facing out onto a shopping promenade bustling with wealthy shoppers. You are here with me, surrounded by antiques. Follow my steps for a single day, and you will share my love of beauty and my profession, a dealer in rare antiquities. To succeed in such a business you must be a disciplined businessman, but what really matters is one's understanding of beauty."

"And how does one understand beauty?" Dr. Abraham asks.

"To understand beauty you must somehow feel it. To say something is beautiful is to describe a feeling not a thought. One must appreciate texture and form and color. One must be able to discern the origin and rarity of a piece but, more importantly, one must appreciate the beauty and fragility of it.

"And even more important still, one must understand that the person who desires to own an antiquity, let us say a rare vase, comes to feel that their very happiness depends only on having that one rare, beautiful thing. They become enamored by it. They will pay any price to own it."

"And you have observed how a thing becomes truly priceless." Dr. Abraham pauses. "Are you talking about your customers or about yourself? Can it be true of you? Have you ever been so enamored by something that you would pay any price to possess it?"

With a wince noticed only by Dr. Abraham, Mohammed ignores the question and changes the subject. "Iran, the country where I was born, is despised now perhaps but once was a place of grandeur. From my native country and other places, I purchased things that are very rare, very old, and very valuable. And then I sell them for even more. I am a millionaire many times over," Mohammed continues. "And here in America, that sentence tells my father's life story and mine as well."

"So your father's life and yours are intertwined."

"Yes. I was born in Tehran. My father was a professor of history born to a prominent family. Iran was a turbulent place even in my father's time, intrigue swirling around the wealthy and the powerful. He and his brother reached the decision to come to the University of Miami to research and teach. This is when I moved to your country.

"I grew up a Muslim in America, the son of a respected professor."

Dr. Abraham looks directly into Mohammed's eyes and says, "Your Memory Book is very full of your father, isn't it?"

"Full, indeed."

"And why would that be, Mohammed?"

"For a Muslim boy, your father is your world. Your father sees to it that you adhere to the teaching. He sees to it that the other people who influence you are teaching the right lessons. My father was a student of history and a pious man. He started our family antique business from nothing and made us very rich. The business began with one very precious bowl, a truly ancient artifact. He brought it from our home in Iran and never sold it, although he would make a grand, elaborate display of showing it to potential buyers as if it were for sale. 'I shall never sell it,' he would say to me."

Joy peers into Mohammed's eyes. "So your father would deceive his customers, then."

"In a manner of speaking, perhaps. That is of no consequence. He sat that beautiful piece in a little room in our apartment among some other items he did eventually sell. It was a cramped room not much larger than a closet with a small window where he hung a beautiful gold and brown curtain that my mother made by hand.

"From that little room in our apartment Irani and Sons Antiquities grew into a fine gallery located in one of the most prestigious shopping districts in Miami."

Looking out at the beach he gestures with his arms, "We now have a fine show room with windows as large as this. But in my office there is a smaller window and there still hangs the curtain my mother made. When I was a teenager my father would tell me that the time he spent away from me with the business was an investment like dollars, so that I would be an even wealthier man than he. When he died, I inherited everything he built. When I die…"

Mohammed feels a stab of pain in his plastic prosthetic leg. He knows that pain is impossible. He knows that there is no leg to feel. Still, there is the sensation of pain. Grimacing through clenched teeth, he says, "Dr. Abraham, I prefer to stop talking now."

"May I ask why?"

"In part—and for the first time I will admit this—it is because I am not sure where I am. I am disoriented and it becomes worse when I speak in this place. But I respectfully ask that you honor my wish."

"Of course we will. Thank you Mohammed. You are next, Joy."

"I am not—"

"You are not ready?" The smile Dr. Abraham gave Mohammed turns to a scowl.

"No."

"Joy, you are very conscious of time. Time may or may not stretch off into infinity for us. No matter. Do not waste our time. Mohammed and Mary have opened their Memory Books. You must do the same unless you think you have special privileges here. Do you?"

"No, I don't."

"Then we'd all like for you to speak. And please begin with those three specific words."

"Very well, let me take you to Hong Kong, the place where a shy little girl was born and grew up alone. I am now a woman but I am also that little girl."

Confused, Mary asks, "You grew up an orphan?"

"No. In fact, both of my parents are alive to this day, but it makes very little difference in my life because we were not close. I always felt alone in their home. Maybe it was because they focused on my stepbrothers."

"Tell us about these stepbrothers," Dr. Abraham says.

"My father called them his real family. He told me that I was a mistake."

"How did that make you feel, Joy?"

"I felt nothing. Two of my stepbrothers were grown up and out on their own. The youngest lived with us. He was a policeman, about ten years older than me. All my father cared about was that my mother took care of his sons when they were little. He married her because his wife died and he needed help raising his sons. I don't think he loved her, and I think he just wished I never happened."

Joy looks side-to-side at Mary and Mohammed. "Want to meet me? Picture a little girl who woke up alone one morning in a small bed in a small room with dirty green walls. She wandered into the room where her mother and father slept and through the window saw her mother shouting and waving her arms around at another lady."

The Respite of Ghosts   45

Mary is paying close attention to Joy's story. "You were a little girl you say. How old?"

"Twelve. As if that mattered."

After a pause, Joy continues. "Let me just tell this story. I noticed her nail polish on the small bureau. Looking out the window constantly to make sure she wasn't coming, I sat on their bed and carefully painted my nails, hands and feet. It was on a whim. They were a kind of orange-red. To me as a girl, they seemed very pretty and grown-up.

"I went down the hall to the bathroom and closed the door. The light from the bare bulb dangling from the ceiling was harsh. So I reached up and unscrewed it, then opened the door to let some light come in. I slowly unbuttoned the blouse I slept in. I touched myself all over, paying attention to how my hands looked different with the polish. It felt nice."

Joy winks mischievously at Mohammed, and continues. "When I decided that I looked like a woman, I gave myself a round of applause. I kept clapping for the girl I saw in the mirror until... I heard my stepbrother come into the apartment..." Joy's mind drifts off, her voice along with it.

Dr. Abraham cocks his eyebrow with interest. "Is there more to tell us about the time you spent looking in the mirror?"

"Not really."

Dr. Abraham jots a note, then says, "Very well. Please continue your story. Tell us small details.."

"As I walked out of the little apartment of my mother and my father, incredible loneliness was in the pit of my stomach. The streets and the crowd and the noise seemed to have a will of their own. They were mocking me.

"And then I happened to glance in the window of a shop. It was a confused sort of place where oriental rugs of many colors and textures competed for my eye. I thought I would be safe inside."

"When I opened the door there was a bell hooked to it and it rang a loud but melodic ring. I walked into the shop and looked at all the rugs for what seemed like minutes. Suddenly a man stepped out of a room far in the back. He had shaggy grey eyebrows and wild grey hair and a potbelly filling a white shirt hanging over his belt."

Mohammed takes an interest in the description of a Hong Kong merchant. "Were you nervous? Did he intimidate you? A little girl in a strange place should be—"

"I was not afraid at all. He looked me up and down with a smile then asked if he could help me. He spoke English, asked the question in English but with the accent the people from India have. It sounds like their tongue is too large or something. I have an accent too, but his is different. In English I said yes, he could help me by giving me a job.

"Mr. Patel, a short man, stood almost eye to eye with me. I could smell the strong spices of his cooking on his breath. 'And why do you want a job?' he asked, looking me up and down.

"I stood there without speaking."

"Why couldn't you answer him?"

"I did not know why I wanted a job. I just said, 'To make money.'

"He broke into hearty laughter and patted my head. 'There is not a better reason in the world than that reason,' he said. He called for his wife to come.

"She sort of shuffled out of the office, a short woman with henna-colored hair, wearing a brightly colored tunic and a thick jeweled ankle bracelet and a pair of red sequined slippers. A pretty plump little lady with cheerful, beautiful dimples, she took a place by his side and he said, 'Perhaps we have found our shop girl.' Then Mrs. Patel looked me up and down just as he had done moments earlier.

"He looked into my eyes and, inspecting me head to toe one more time, said, 'You are a pretty Chinese girl. What is your name?'

"I told him my name was Shyi Lee Han.

"He looked sideways at his wife. She gave me a smile with her plump little face and said, 'That is not a good name for business. Your name Shyi Lee means joy, so we will call you Joy.'"

Jotting a note, Dr. Abraham asks, "And so it was Mrs. Patel who named you Joy? How did you react when she suggested this new name?"

"I said yes with a happy smile. But maybe my smile was not so happy because then Mrs. Patel asked me the strangest question. 'My dear, you look a little bit upset. Are you having trouble at home? Are you having some trouble with the boys perhaps?' Mrs. Patel cocked her eyebrow up when she asked, then looked into my eyes waiting for my answer."

Joy falls silent, peering pensively out the window at a beach day that is cloudier than most. Despite the intermittent gusts of summer wind, the palm trees are very still.

She sees Dr. Abraham cocking his eye much as Mrs. Patel did. "And what was your answer?"

"I said I have no problems with boys at all. I stay away from the boys. I am a virgin."

Joy glances side to side at Mary and Mohammed, anticipating the question they might ask. "It was a lie"

"Why did you feel the need to lie," Mary asks.

"Because I believed I needed to say that to get the job. I felt sick in my heart because it was the biggest lie I have told in my life, but Mr. Patel said nothing about my answer. He excused himself and headed back to his office, Mrs. Patel shuffling behind in her red slippers. A minute or two later he came back, smiled and said, 'Come tomorrow afternoon, and we will give you a try.'

"When I came back the next day, I stood on the busy street teeming with jabbering strangers. I began feeling like destiny had brought me to this small shop with a little blue and white sign in English and Chinese: FINE RUGS. A. PATEL, PROPRIETOR."

"And so, did you think you could do this job the Patels gave you?" Mohammed is fascinated by the idea of Joy selling precious merchandise.

"Yes."

Mohammed inquires again. "And why?"

"I was drawn to Mr. Patel and his wife. As human beings they were, still are, larger than life. They are Hindu. They had all sorts of pictures of elephants and other deities everywhere in the shop. Every wall had some kind of slightly faded, slightly tattered picture of half-humans and blue women with many arms and elephants."

Joy sweeps her hand toward the floor, leaning slightly so that the tips of her nails touch the deep-piled carpet. "But mainly on the floor were huge piles of beautiful Persian rugs, and hanging from the walls were beautiful rugs, and the store smelled densely of tapestry and carpet and incense.

"That first day he told me I would be his shop girl, a salesperson who would greet the customers and show them the basic selection. In less than an hour I was doing as Mr. Patel taught me."

Once more, Mohammed. "Who was your first customer?"

"A husband and wife, tall, fat Americans with grey hair and Bermuda shorts, walked in the store. I said hello and then followed them around. They walked up to a pile of small oriental carpets. When the man raised his voice because he was surprised by the high price on the tag, Mr. Patel came out of the backroom. He left his lair with its pictures of elephants and women with many arms and all sorts of strange deities to sell a carpet. He sauntered toward me and the Americans.

"So here we were in his store crowded with and smelling of carpet, the two tall fat Americans, a skinny little shop girl named Joy, and Mr. Patel with his wild hair. He said, 'I heard my assistant tell you the price, but you are not interested in the carpet?' The American man said, 'Nice carpet, but the price is too high.'

"Then Mr. Patel said, 'This carpet is new, like a virgin. Like this lovely young girl here, virginal, pure, yours alone after you purchase it. You are Americans and you do not understand that in my culture a virgin brings a high dowry. Just as a Hindu virgin brings a high bride-price, so too must this carpet bring a high price.' Looking the tall man up and down, Mr. Patel said 'What price must I offer for you to buy this carpet? Buy it so my shop girl can at least have one sale today.'

"Didn't you feel like he was using you?" Mary asks.

"I was really a little girl, still a child, but I understood immediately his trick. When he mentioned his shop girl, me, I bowed my head and looked shy. I ran my fingers through my long black hair, looking at the floor. Then he pretended that my being there calmed him down and he haggled to get a good price for the carpet.

Jotting a note, Dr. Abraham asks, "The Americans bought the carpet?"

Joy grins triumphantly. "Yes. The lady said to me, 'Stay pure, child, that is how God intended it as they walked out of the store with a carpet they did not plan to buy. That is how I made my first sale, pretending to be a virgin."

Mohammed looks over at Joy. "You are proud of this deception?"

"It gave them more pleasure in owning the carpet. At any rate, I became the Patels' child. Mrs. Patel would comfort me. She would hold me in her pudgy arms when she saw that I was upset. I would cry, and I remember my tears on her skin, which smelled of her cooking. If a teacher had yelled at me, some girl in my class had been mean, all of the things girls that age would get upset about, Mrs. Patel would listen and hold me in her arms. She helped me grow up."

"Tell us more about how she helped you grow up," Joy's shrink says.

"She let me talk about my period. She seemed to know that my real mother did not talk to me about my womanhood at all. Mrs. Patel explained womanhood to me the way a Hindu sees it."

"For example?"

"There were deities on the wall of their office. Mostly they were pictures of Vishnu. I especially liked the one picture of Mohini, a female avatar of Lord Vishnu. I loved her beautiful face, her many arms.

"One night Mrs. Patel came in and saw me staring at Mohini. 'Isn't she beautiful, an enchantress, yes, a model for all women. She wears the holy thread meant only for Brahmin men,' Mrs. Patel said with a wink, running her stubby fingertips across the picture of Mohini. 'For me as a young girl Mohini put a lie to what the men say, that God is a man. End that one lie and the world will be better.'

"Right then, I decided I was a Hindu. I loved the idea that God has appeared at different times in different ways, sometimes male, sometimes female. Why would God have genitals at all, really? Maybe I am the only one in this room who thinks this, but it's stupid to think God is a man or a woman. That would limit God."

The physician interrupts. "As a young girl you made this dramatic decision about your faith?"

"Yes, I did."

"What did your parents say? Did you tell them?"

"No. They didn't care what I believed. But one night I made my mother and father sit with me at our little table. I brought them together and told them that the Patels were moving to America and invited me to come. My father nodded and looked out the window. He never looked at me. And then out of the blue he quoted Confucius."

"I remember as if it just happened. My father said, 'Confucius tells us that in the world there are many different roads but the destination is the same. There are a hundred deliberations, but the result is one. Do as you must, Shyi Lee Han. Go where you must.' Then he got up from the table and walked out of that cramped little apartment."

Mary breaks in. "'Tis all he said? What did your mum say?"

"When my father got up from the table she and I sat together not saying anything. Then she said, 'It is good that you leave now. Your brother will miss you. I will miss you.' From that point on, the Patels were my family. Mrs. Patel had paperwork strewn all over their office, but they got it all submitted and after a lot of effort I moved to America with Mr. And Mrs. Patel and—"

Joy stops to look at her watch. "My time is beyond up, isn't it?"

Suddenly Dr. Abraham rears back in his big leather chair. "Joy, please do not talk about the time when you are in this place."

In a loud voice he demands, "Please look around my office and tell me if you see a clock. There are none here. I am correct, yes?"

"Yes."

"And so therefore time does not matter here. I, not a clock, am in charge of time here. I decide what it means. Do you understand?"

Joy looks away and says, "Yes."

The expression on Dr. Abraham's face changes. Again his flaccid jaw and watery eyes are those of a weary, patient father. He addresses his group as if the scolding moments ago never took place. "I would like to pay all of you a compliment.

In the psychiatry business, there is an old saying that everybody has a story tell. It means if you give a child or an adult a chance to talk about their lives, every one of them can tell you about triumphs, defeats, loves, hates, disappointments, all of that.

"But it takes special effort for one person to have another person feel what they felt. You are trying to do that. So thank you for taking us to your childhood, Joy. I could visualize your father staring blankly into the air quoting Confucius."

Out of the corner of his eye, Dr. Abraham sees that Mohammed's lips are quivering. "Mohammed, is there something wrong? I hope Joy did not offend you just now."

Mohammed steels his expression. "She did not offend me, Dr. Abraham. She is reading from her Memory Book according to your rules, which I, for now, am accepting. The reaction you saw is caused perhaps by the fact that my father despised the teaching of Confucius and Buddha."

Dr. Abraham jots a note. "And did he tell you why?"

"Most assuredly. My father was an educated and pious man. He was quite certain that there is in fact only one path. Obedience to the letter of Allah's teaching as revealed to the Prophet. How I wish that it was true as Joy says, that there are many paths. Perhaps it is wrong for me to wish this. But just now, I wanted it to be true."

Joy looks at the man in the black suit, with his formal demeanor and impeccable manners, and she senses that he has, perhaps for the first time, listened to what she said. "Thank you, sir. That is the honesty I need. If we're stuck here together like Dr. Shrink says we are—and you and I both know we're not—that kind of honesty would nurture me."

Mohammed smiles and tries a joke. "Please, not sir. I am Mohammed."

Dr. Abraham cannot conceal his pleasure at this unexpected exchange between Mohammed and Joy. "On that very positive note, let me say that if there are no questions, we are done for now."

4.

Walking across the room toward the semi-circle of chairs, Mary is taken aback by the surreal silhouette of her psychiatrist against the muted grey light of a stormy Miami day. Stroking his beard and holding his large head cocked to the right, he seems totally absorbed in the scene outside.

Moments ago it was a cloudless, breezy, perfect beach day with the sunlight infusing the greens and browns of the palm trees with a glistening blue-white sheen. But a tropical squall has moved over the beach, darkening the sky and painting the horizon with an ominous glow.

His motions convey an odd sense that time stands still in this place until he orders it to move forward, like he presses the STOP and PLAY and fast forward buttons on a DVD player to control the pace of scenes, conversations, events.

He moves slowly to his desk, watching from the corner of his eye as Mary's dowdy brown penny loafers shuffle across the tile floor to the oriental carpet and then to her chair. "Hello, Mary," he says. "I hope you are looking forward to our time together today. I plan to devote it exclusively to you."

She takes her seat without answering, making a ceremony of placing a large blue mesh beach bag adorned by embroidered sunflowers next to her chair. Sheets of rain begin lashing at the window the moment she sits down.

Her psychiatrist adjusts his yellow sweater across his shoulders. "So it has been decided?"

"Yes."

"When?"

"As early as the day after tomorrow." A solitary tear wells up in her eye then trickles down the round contour of her cheek. "Dr. Abraham, Ahm tryin' so, so very hard not to get depressed again. And now on top of the depression, Ahm confused. Ahm not understandin' what is happenin' in here and I worry so much about the children. I love 'em so."

"Children plural. Do you mean your son and also Carmella. Do I understand correctly?"

"Aye. Both. She is like a precious child to me. I love them both with all my heart. What would happen to them without me?"

Her physician's voice is more raspy than usual. "I understand your anxiety about them and of course yourself. Perhaps today's discussion will help."

"I dearly hope so."

"Will you tell Joy and Mohammed, or should I?"

She looks down at her blue mesh beach bag. A tear falls from her cheek onto the deep pile of Dr. Abraham's oriental carpet. "I'll be tellin' them. When Ahm ready."

Mohammed and Joy appear at the threshold simultaneously, as if the psychiatrist had clapped his hands bidding them to enter. They take their seats in the semi-circle, ignoring each other, save for silent nods of greeting.

After darting about the room, Mary's still wary gaze settles on the face of her psychiatrist.

"May we start with my story today, Dr. Abraham? I've cleared up my thoughts and I want to continue."

"Please do," her psychiatrist replies.

She reaches into the blue mesh beach bag beside her chair and proceeds to hand out printed copies of her story. The cover page bears the title MARY'S STORY in a huge font with capital letters. It has a photograph of four people on the beach under a palm tree.

In the center of the photograph stands Mary, wearing a bright, flowery bandana that matches her beach shift. She looks younger than her forty years. In her arms is a toddler with fair, pink skin and bright blue eyes and a wild mane of red hair. Standing next to her on one side is a Latino teenager, smiling radiantly and wearing a bikini and dark sunglasses. And standing to her right is a tall, balding, be-speckled and bookish-looking man of about sixty.

"Ta-da," she says. "This is a revised version of my story. Just lookin' at this picture makes me feel better."

Joy waves her hand, "Before she begins, can I ask Mary a question?" Without waiting for Dr. Abraham's response, she turns to Mary, "Why did you write your story in the third person? I found it odd. You say Mary did this, Mary said that. Then after your brain surgery it's I did this, I did that."

Mary frowns as if an unpleasant thought is crossing her mind. "Can't say. 'Tis all there is to it. But I can say today my Book is full of happy, magical things," Mary says. "Let me take all of you to the place where I met Carmella Alvarado. She is the person who changed my life. As you will see later in my story, she became like a child and a sister and a best friend all at once.

A confused look passes across Mary's eyes. "Let me take you to a place where Mary was living with Robert. It was Cocoa Beach Florida. He was working for NASA and Robert Junior had just turned two—I kept calling him the Little One even as he got bigger. The cancer she was fighting in Ireland went into remission after the first surgery with Dr. Josephson in America, but now, fifteen years later, it was back. So with that introduction, let me read—"

Joy turns to Mary. "I hate to keep bothering you with questions. Your little one as you call him is two years old. How old is the child you were pregnant with in Ireland? He or she would be fifteen or sixteen, right? Is it a boy or girl?"

"I lost the pregnancy in Ireland." Mary's reply is stone-faced. "So please let me take you all to my happy place."

Dr. Laurence Josephson introduced Carmella to Mary. Among the many things I will tell you about that man, beyond a doubt his greatest gift to me is that he brought Carmella into my life.

Mary and Dr. Josephson were in his office. He said, "In a couple of minutes you're going to meet Carmella Alvarado. Carmella's parents moved to Tampa from Spain. They were rather wealthy. Her father died in a plane crash five years ago and then, the very next year, her mother was diagnosed with cancer and passed away.

"Carmella is fifteen and alone in the world. She's having trouble making ends meet. You need help, and I personally recommend her as an aide. As a young adolescent she cared for her own mother who, like you, fought bravely against brain cancer. Her mother fought long and hard but lost. You, Mary, are waging that fight now."

At exactly that moment the door opened and a beautiful girl with long black hair walked in the room. She was dressed in a pink and white candy-striper uniform. Mary was struck with the grace and poise and, well, the beauty of the girl. This was a truly precious creature. It was like love at first sight but the kind of love a mother has for a child.

The introduction was very matter-of-fact. "This is Carmella Alvarado. I have arranged for her to stay with you and Robert and the baby from time to time. Today I'd like for you to give her a ride to your house and show her around, then help her figure out the best way to get there using public transportation."

In the car Carmella said nothing until Mary pulled into the driveway. "You have a pretty house, Mrs. Fitzpatrick."

Feeling upbeat, Mary beeped the horn with a big smile on her face. "Be right back," Mary said as she slid out of her seat. "You stay here, and we'll see if Robert is around." Mary literally skipped along the short cement walk that led from the driveway to the front door, peering in the bay window on the way. Pushing open the creaking, faded green front door, she called her husband's name.

Soon Robert appeared holding their son.

"Carmella, this is Dr. Robert Fitzpatrick and our son Robert Junior. We call him our Little One, He means everything to us."

Carmella reached out to hold the groggy and half-asleep baby like she was his big sister. It was a perfect moment. My Precious One and my Little One were together for the first time.

The psychiatrist, leafing through the pages of the printed story, interrupts. "Let me clarify something, Mary. In this version of your document, it appears that you've skipped over your relationship with Robert and his family and how you felt they were not supportive of you when you were sick. Am I correct?"

Mary is pleased that he notices. "Yes, Dr. Abraham, I have deleted that entire section."

Mary sighs, wondering what his tired eyes see as he leafs through her revised story. Finally her psychiatrist asks, "Do you use a laptop or a desktop computer?"

Mary is surprised by the question and judges by the look on their faces that Joy and Mohammed seem to wonder, as she does, why her psychiatrist would ask her about her computer.

"I use a laptop. Why do you ask?"

"I ask because I'm trying to visualize you when you made this important change to your life story. Can you help me with that? Take me there. Can you take me to the moment?"

"I was stretched across the bed in my PJs tappin' away at the keyboard of my laptop. I had checked on the Little One.

He was sleepin' groggy like he does with his thumb in the corner of his mouth. My husband was in the shower. I know that the document is getting big so I just said, to dickens with it, this part of my life don't count."

"Why not?"

"It's behind me and God has forgiven me for… if there is something to be forgiven, God has forgiven me. When I deleted it I went downstairs and got myself a glass of wine. I felt like you feel after you clean out an old closet and reward yourself with a nice glass of wine. I felt good."

"Do you know why you felt good?"

"I think I do."

Her psychiatrist smiles. "Can you tell us why? I'm sure Joy and Mohammed share my interest in why."

"I guess it's because Robert and his family are not really part of my eternity. They were a detour standing between my destination and me. That's what the Confucius quote showed me."

Mary's psychiatrist cocks his brow. "Detour? That seems like a harsh way to talk about people in your life."

Hands clasped in her lap, Mary lowers her head. Eyes closed, she mutters to the ground. "Ireland has many small roads. Two-lane roads. It seems like there are always groups of men working on the roads. You encounter these detour signs and you have to drive miles out of your way until you are on the right road again. My life started that way, with a detour."

Mary raises her head and looks at Joy. "That was my discovery after our last session. I have come to believe that God grants to every soul the power to determine their everlasting life. It's not exactly what the Church teaches, but it's not contradictory either."

Mohammed's leg muscles ache with a dull stiffness. He shifts his weight in the chair, then asks, "I understand so little about you and your laptop. But isn't your first husband the father of your son?"

Mohammed's, baritone voice and the formal way he constructs his speech make Mary feel that Mohammed's question was put to her by a lawyer and that she is on trial. She pauses to compose her answer.

"Yes, true, I had his son. But my real husband and I are raising the boy. He is our son now. Robert left me and I left him. I'm writing this story for this therapy to prepare for eternity. My eternity is about leaving that awful cold place. Eternity is about magic and my blue sky moods with the sun shining on everything and Carmella and my son and my husband the famous surgeon who's tryin' to save my life. Robert is nothing for me now. Nothing."

Mohammed makes passing eye contact with Joy as he peers past her to look into Mary's eyes. "You speak constantly about JJ and Carmella but Robert seems to mean nothing at all. You feel no… sentimentality?"

"No."

"Thank you for your candor, Mary," her psychiatrist says. "Please continue." Mary places the tip of her pudgy finger on the place in the manuscript where she plans to begin reading. Her hand is shaking slightly.

The day was here: The surgery. Mary's head ached so badly that tears welled up in her eyes if she moved her head or neck in any sudden motion. Thus far today, God had not been kind to her, he had set her head to pounding, and her heart as well.

Carmella insisted on taking the bus to Mary's house and riding to the hospital. When finally it was time to go, Carmella held Mary's hand tightly with the powerful, aching, fearful love that she probably felt for her own mother, as the two walked silently out of the bungalow and climbed into the car. Carmella got in the back and Mary in the front. Carmella looked so lonely and frightened that Mary decided to get in the back seat with her. Robert seemed surprised but said nothing.

A tear welled up again in Carmella's eye when Mary joined her in the back seat of Robert's big Mercedes. She tied the bow on the sleeve of Mary's blue blouse, then rested her head there. "Can I tell you what I think will happen to you today—I mean, if it is not too painful for you, Miss Mary. It will help me if you let me try to explain it," Carmella asked Mary.

"Of course," Mary smiled.

"Dr. Josephson will take out as much of your tumor as possible without damaging the other healthy brain tissue. Online it says the surgeon tries to remove ninety percent of a tumor. They want to get your entire tumor, but even partial removal of the tumor can improve how you feel and maybe the awful headaches will go completely away."

*Mary stared at the little teenager who was really just a dear child.
"You seem to know an awfully lot. Do you know the name of my
operation?"*

"Craniotomy. Did I describe things right?"

*"Yes," Mary said. Staring out the window at the passing traffic,
Mary's voice dulled to a monotone. "Dr. Josephson will make an incision
into my scalp. Goodbye hair, what's left of it. Then several holes are made
in my skull. A bone saw is used to join the holes together to create a flap of
bone. Then the bone flap will be removed to expose my brain. Then he and
his team will take a deep breath and remove as much of the tumor as
possible.*

*"It's hard work and can take hours. Eventually they think they
are done. After the tumor has been partially or completely removed, the
bone flap is replaced and secured using fine wire. Recovery from the
procedure may take as long as eight weeks."*

*Wide-eyed from the description of holes being drilled into skulls and bone
flaps being removed, Carmella rested her head on Mary's shoulder.*

*Mary touched her lips to Carmella's forehead, savoring the scent
of the child's luxurious hair just as she had savored the scent of her son
when she bade him farewell by his crib.*

Mary's psychiatrist interrupts. "Mary, can you tell us
why this story about your ride to the hospital seems to be
mostly about Carmella?"

Mary says nothing. Lost in thought, she stares upward
like the answer was etched onto Dr. Abraham's ceiling in
ancient hieroglyphics. "I can't explain it, except to repeat that in
my heart I call Carmella the Precious One," she says finally.

"Perhaps you could describe her to us? Does she
resemble someone you knew in the past?"

"Carmella is so very petite and pretty. She has these
large brown eyes and that perfect skin and deep brown hair that
is so, so curly. I'm white as a ghost and won't go into the
sunlight on a bet, as you can all see. I love her skin."

Mary's psychiatrist looks at the picture on the cover of
MARY'S STORY. "She is quite pretty, indeed. But that was
not my question. My question was: Have you known anyone
like her?"

Suddenly Mary feels as if she has breathed silence into
the entire room. There are no sounds. Even the ocean outside
is still.

Mary's psychiatrist jots a note and waits.

"The closest thing to Carmella—when you say like Carmella, do you mean in terms of physical resemblance?"

Her psychiatrist tugs at one of his cardigan buttons. "In any way."

Mary nods. "The closest in appearance, I guess you'd say, was a graduate student friend of Robert's. He was a Spaniard with dark eyes and high cheekbones and beautiful skin, like Carmella."

Her psychiatrist jots a note and then asks, "What was he like as a person? Did he resemble Carmella in other ways?"

Mary feels as if Mohammed and Joy are peering into her soul. She avoids looking at them. She decides to try a joke, "To be honest, that was almost twenty years ago and maybe the part of my mind that remembers those days got lost in surgery."

All in the room force a smile. The psychiatrist makes a note on his yellow pad and then says, "Sorry for the interruption. Please continue."

Mary breaks into tears. Bowing her head and weeping, she says, "It was strange how the thought came to me out of nowhere that day in a car in Florida, America.

"But suddenly I couldn't stop thinking about the fact that my father's brother, my uncle, killed a Protestant man in Dublin. That was the turning point where my father's business went bad. After that, only Robert's father would do business with our company. And that was because Robert wanted me to marry him, even if it was going to be a way for my father to avoid bankruptcy."

Joy is startled by this revelation. "Who did your uncle kill? What happened?"

"He killed a college boy from London in a fight in a Dublin bar. The Brit was a student on holiday from London. There were two of 'em sittin' at the bar. A telly was playin' news footage about the Pope. The British lad looked at the Pope on the screen up above the bar and makes that sign with his finger that means... I think you all know what that finger means.

"My uncle was drunk, like he always was. He rushed both boys, knockin' one of 'em off his bar stool. The Brit's head struck the side of the bar on the way down in some cockeyed way that twisted and broke his neck. The lad died instantly."

Joy is shocked. "So your uncle killed a college student for giving the finger to a picture of the Pope on the television. Just for going like this?" Joy sticks up the middle finger of her hand, wagging it first at Mohammed and then at Dr. Abraham. "This gesture? Like if I gave Dr. Shrink here the finger?" She whirls in her seat. "Or Mohammed?"

"Yes."

Joy shakes her head, looking at Dr. Abraham. "Dr. Shrink, why do men kill each other in the name of God? Why would God want men to kill each other in his name? Isn't there already enough suffering built into life itself?"

A weary look on his face, Dr. Abraham stretches his arms out in a wide motion. Slowly, theatrically, he brings his hands together in front of him as if clasped in prayer. "Suffering and struggle are part of the natural order of things.

"I remember late at night my mother would weep bitter tears for those who died in innocence at Hiroshima. She talked about the little children who were vaporized by the atomic blast because their fathers were at war with a country far away. She grieved as much for them as she did for my father, I sometimes believed. Even as a little boy, I grieved for children and babies who were turned to dust.

"But do not be deceived. Many people—many souls— do indeed bring about their own suffering."

The aging psychiatrist releases his hands from in front of him and allows them to come to rest on his desk. "Perhaps we four are such hapless souls, having been the cause of our own deepest wounds. Can it be that the burden is lighter for those innocents who suffer at the hands of other men? Or acts of nature? Or simply tragic happenstance? Can it be that we in this room bear a greater burden of guilt and shame? Perhaps we are here together to relieve each other of this special burden."

He sighs a labored breath and casts his eyes toward the lofted ceiling. "I speculate. But this much I do know. We are here to be healed, not to suffer further. Let us maintain our concentration. So let us continue with Mary's story."

Mary pats her manuscript affectionately. "No need to read further Dr. Abraham. I often think that I did in fact die in my first surgery. Not only that, I think I was a witness to my own death. Many people believe they rise above their own bodies and watch themselves go under the scalpel. I'm one of those people. Maybe that's why I like writing in the third person, like I was somebody different watching myself."

"You seem alternatively eager then hesitant to talk about this experience," her psychiatrist says softly. "Why is that?"

Tears well up in her eyes. "I wish I could say. I tried to sit at my computer and write this story of my life, but everything is so... jumbled and confused. After kissing the Little One goodbye and riding in the Mercedes with Carmella, I'm not sure what really happened in my life."

Mary's psychiatrist nods with fatherly understanding. "This can be expected sometimes, Mary. Let me encourage you simply to talk. Even if you talk with your eyes closed. Perhaps closing your eyes will help."

Obediently, Mary closes her eyes like she is praying. "At first I was normal and watched Carmella and Robert say goodbye to me. Carmella's cheeks were swollen with crying. Her cute teenager makeup was streaked and runny like a Halloween mask. She kept making it worse by pushing her tears away from her eyes with her fingertips. My last words came from my heart: 'Carmella, you are my beautiful girl.'

"Robert had his usual sarcastic smirk on his face. That smirk, like somewhere in his soul he is laughin' at you—I don't believe he could control it. My last words to him were: 'I will be fine.' Soon I was alone in a hospital bed. A special nurse in a long white lab coat came bustling into the room.

"She said, 'Dr. Josephson has asked me to work directly with you, Mrs. Josephson. You are lucky to be married to such a fine man.' She was a tall, pretty blonde with her long hair tied in a bow. What I would give to have my hair again, I thought. Talkin' about the weather in an accent like from Tennessee or Georgia or the Carolinas, she held my hand and patted my shoulder when the time came for me to go to surgery.

"Next thing I remember, Dr. Laurence Josephson whispered into my ear, 'Remember, Mary, the brain itself feels no pain.' He was my surgeon then, not my husband. But even then, somehow, his voice comforted me.

"I was sedated. I know it is not possible, but nevertheless I believe I watched when the time finally came for him to make the incision into my scalp. Red blood issued immediately from the gash he was makin'. A surgeon's scalpel is so very sharp. My blood was so very red and thick like ketchup."

"Could you hear?" Mary's psychiatrist asks.

"There was some chatter I couldn't understand. I figured it was the doctors and nurses reviewing the process one last time. Then a doctor assisting him used a drill-like tool to make holes in my skull. The drill made a loud, whining noise. Whirrr, whirr. Whirrr-schreeetch when it hit something hard. It was the same noise a household drill makes when you drill a hole in a piece of hardwood. A sort of smoke came up from my skull. I could smell my skull bone smoldering. It smelled like when the dentist is drilling a cavity. It was so horrible. But I smiled to myself, saying, 'the brain feels no pain.'

"I saw Larry's big hands marking my skull, directing his team and their drills and scalpels and special instruments for breaking the skull bone. The bone saw... it is an ugly, scary-looking thing. I watched them use a bone saw to join the holes together to create a flap of bone. Then the bone flap was removed and there, red and pink and white and pulsatin', was my brain.

"Then he and his team, each person, seemed to take a deep breath before he went into my brain to remove as much of the tumor as possible. There was a sucking machine. The doctors used their scalpels and all manner of precision devices. For hours I just floated above the scene watching myself struggle for life."

Dr. Abraham smiles sympathetically as a cue for Mary to finish. "Thank you, Mary," he says. "Anything else?"

"Yes," Mary says. "I'm clearin' my thoughts."

"Take your time."

"When I first awoke after the surgery my vision was blurred. My mind was a jumble. I was in incredible pain. It wasn't my brain itself, of course, but the surrounding tissue that was causing the pain. I can try to describe how horrible it was using words, but an eternity of trying will not communicate the feeling. Dr. Josephson and Carmella and Robert came in and out of my room and, I guess, in and out of my mind. Or maybe it was vice versa. When my mind finally cleared, I don't think I knew who I was. "

Dr. Abraham jots a note. "Now do you know who you are?"

"I think so."

"That is a good answer, Mary. Is there more?"

"I lived through the operation—I'm assumin'." Mary offers a wistful smile, lips slightly parted, eyes far away. "But it never seemed to be over; there was always some sort of treatment to take. Anyhow, let me continue. Now the story is in the first person, like Joy said. Another person has replaced the Mary I wrote about before. That person is the one you are looking at now. Here is the story of the new Mary."

Larry Josephson is a brilliant physician, but he is also a gregarious man. He likes to drink and swear in what he fancies to be a traditional Irish style. Dr. Josephson was finishing up my first post-surgery visit when, out of nowhere, he said, "Baby Robert is lucky to have a mother like you. Seeing you two makes me wish I hadn't been too busy with medicine to marry and bring children into the world."

I replied, "That is a shame, if you do not mind me saying so, Dr. Josephson. Children are a miracle of God. Today, just a smile from the Little One put me in such a great mood. Those little Irish smiles of his are a delight for me. It's like they're...magic."

"So you believe in magic?"

I wanted to make sure he knew I wasn't some starry-eyed little Irish girl who still believed in leprechauns and other nonsense.

"Of course not. What I meant was—"

I stopped in mid-sentence, unsure of my point. He looked closely at me and noticed the embarrassment.

"Finish the thought, Mary."

"What I meant was that—it's a feeling. Maybe I do believe in magic. It's a small feeling, but it's a good feeling. I leave here feeling better even when the news is bad. Like today's news will be, because I know I'm losing weight."

"We'd expect weight loss under any circumstances. I'm concerned. As you must know because we're bouncing you on and off of

that scale so often, we keep a close eye on your weight. But I expected some weight loss."

I held my hand in front of my face and looked at the small freckles. Heaving a huge sigh I said, "My hands look better when I get a little skinny." I felt the need to cry.

Dr. Josephson put his pen down and patted my hand.

"That was a very big sigh."

"I sigh a lot."

Dr. Josephson nodded in agreement. He smiled. "It's a habit you got from your mother. She was always sighing. Now that I think of it, your father does it too—especially when he's had a pint or two."

I smiled and nodded my head in agreement.

Dr. Josephson saw that I didn't want to talk about my parents. "Anyhow, both of your parents sighed. So I would expect it from the daughter, too."

"You keep talking about things you expect, Dr. Josephson. Maybe it would be worthwhile if you just told me what you're expecting to happen."

"It depends on whether or not you go into remis—"

"I know that. I mean, what do you expect me to do? What should I do other than shave my head and put up with the awful treatments?"

He picked up his pen, handed it to me then turned over the form he had been writing on. The back of the sheet was blank. He tapped his finger on the blank sheet of paper.

"You mentioned magic a minute ago. Write down your definition of magic."

I took the pen and wrote the first thing that came to mind. I read my definition aloud: "You say something happens by magic when you can't explain it any other way."

"Perfect, Mary, perfect."

I looked at the paper in silence. A small tear sat on my cheek.

"All I expect you to do, Mary, is believe in magic. Your mother did. Your father does. I'd say it was an Irish thing, but the Seminole Indians down here in Florida swear that magic can heal."

"You mean it? You believe in magic."

"Yes. We give these cancer treatments to thousands of people and some do better than others. All of the science can't explain it. We use terms like psychonurologicalimmunology—do you know how many letters

are in that word, Mary? —but we can't explain why some people do better. So it must be magic."

"I'm not a child. I'm a grown woman and I know I am not brilliant or educated but I am not stupid or foolish either."

Dr. Josephson smiled that kindly smile of his. "Of course you are not stupid Mary. Neither am I. But I mean what I'm saying." He tapped his finger on the definition I had penned neatly on the paper. "Think about it, Mary. Having worked with many patients, I know that they must feel to heal."

"That sounds like a rap song, not something coming from a doctor."

He touched my hand with an affection I had not felt from him before. "To feel is a good thing. To have faith is a good thing. And there is nothing wrong with the word magic. Lots of people believe in magic, you know. They have since time began." When he said that, I—

"Thank you Mary," her psychiatrist says, surprising her with the finality of his interruption. "Let's stop for now. Water?"

"Yes, thank you."

Dr. Abraham nods in his fatherly way, reaching for his earthenware pitcher. The patients watch as Dr. Abraham, hand shaking slightly, pours a tall glass of water for Mary. Outside, a line of clouds sweeps south across the beach hiding the sun and darkening the room. Both sound and movement seem to cease. Time has stopped pressing forward.

5.

The patients are in good spirits, chattering like school children returning from recess. Mary's story about her surgeon's faith in magic has captured their imagination. Yes, they all agree, there is a positive force in the universe capable of producing happy outcomes inexplicably. Even Mohammed in his orthodoxy agrees that magic seems to be a good word to describe that force.

Dr. Abraham enters the room smiling, jotting a note on his yellow pad as he walks to his desk. The sound is loud like a comedian's impression of the noise a pen makes when marking an everyday pad. "Joy? Are you ready to take us someplace in your life?"

Waving her arm like she was going somewhere and beckoning the others to follow her, she says, "Yo! Come on everybody. Let me take you to a place where I spent a lot of time. Night clubs. One in particular. Let's get out of this dreary place. I'm bored. The quiet is killing me. Let's go clubbing. Come see me dressed in a see-through blouse and tight skirt, like a slut. Let me take you to a loud and confused bar at a confused time in my life when I met a loud and confused cop. The cop—"

Joy interrupts herself to look at Mary. "If I had printed my story from the computer like Mary did, my story would have a picture of a cop on it. Maybe not this cop I'm going to talk about, but rather a gener... Dr. Abraham, I know the Chinese word but I'm looking for the word in English. It sounds like general but means they are all the same. Like all aspirin are the same."

"Is generic the word you are looking for?"

"Yes. Generic. The cover of my story would have a generic, faceless cop wearing a hat. It would be—"

Dr. Abraham's watery brown eyes brighten with curiosity. He interrupts Joy to ask, "A generic cop. Interesting idea. What would your cover look like if it had a generic cop?"

Joy tugs the locket tight to her neck. "What would a generic cop look like? There would be a hat, there would be a gun—maybe not a gun, they don't always wear guns—there would be a blue uniform that any person can shove themselves into."

Dr. Abraham's eyes are still bright. His voice is, for the moment at least, strong, full of interest and curiosity. "Let me interrupt you for one more second, Joy, and please know that you will have ample time to speak, but I want to ask the others a question. The question will sound silly. I'll ask Mary first. Mary, will there be police in your eternity?"

A vacant-eyed Mary does not reply.

Seeing this, her psychiatrist asks his question different ways. "Will you need police for anything? Does the Church teach anything about police?"

Mary's jaw tightens as she considers her answer. "I rightly don't know."

"Let me ask the question another way. Of all the different occupations—doctors, lawyers, police, teachers, accountants like Joy here with us, priests, whatever—will there be any of those people in your eternity?"

"Yes, doctors and priests." There was a little girl's certainty in her voice.

"Why doctors and priests?"

"Because even for eternity in heaven rules will be rules, the people will feel pain and... no, never mind. Eternity will be magical so I got it wrong, won't be a need for them. Dr. Abraham, I can't answer your question. Please don't ask it another way, either."

A tear wells up in the corner of her eye. "When you confuse me, I start believin' we are all dead and that this is a dream I had before I died. Please stop askin' that question."

His fatherly voice replies, "I won't ask again Mary, you tried. And you, Mohammed?"

"I am like Mary. The question makes no sense to me. I have nothing against police, I will say that. A very brave and strong policeman pulled me from my car and gave me mouth to mouth resuscitation and stopped the bleeding where my leg was... But I cannot answer the question."

Joy scoots to the edge of her chair. "I can answer the question. There will be no cops in eternity. Or doctors. There will be no sign of rank or station. No pain. No suffering. Only

---

joy at knowing that the karmic wheel has come to rest. Only unshackled souls united with their creator."

Her voice is high. It is her rata-tat-tat voice. "But especially the cops. Their karma will be paid, and they will be free."

Dr. Abraham smiles. "What will the cops be free from?"

"Thinking they know right from wrong, but knowing nothing at all. They will be free of that bondage."

"I like that answer, Joy. Continue with your story, the floor is yours. I interrupted you."

"Anyway, the cop that ruined my life was a weird combination of people inside one body. As a cop, he was a straight shooter, a Boy Scout-type almost. Like my Buddhist brother back in Hong Kong. Both were cops who claimed to do everything by the book. They both used the expression 'by the book.' What frigging book these guys talking about? That's a question I will ask myself for eternity."

Joy tugs absently at her locket. "Never mind. Back to the cop that ruined my life here in America. As a lover, I found out quickly, he could act diabolically."

Joy's shrink cocks his brow. "May I interrupt you yet again, Joy? I just want to be sure we all understand what you just said."

Joy shrugs, tugging pointedly at her watch.

"First, it was just a bit confusing, who you were referring to? Help us understand. Your brother in Hong Kong was a policeman?"

"He was my half-brother, a child of my father's first marriage. But yes, he was a cop in Hong Kong."

"Incidentally, Joy, it's OK to call him your brother. Lots of families skip the half and step stuff."

"He was my half-brother."

"Very well, and you say he was a straight-shooter, a Boy Scout-type, just like the cop that ruined your life?"

"Yes."

"What made him a straight shooter?"

Joy's eyes pan the vaulted ceiling. "He was rigid. Maybe it was because my step father, his father, hit him. Maybe it was his dedication to Buddhism. Buddhists don't believe in

God, he would say. He would tell me that the Four Noble Truths—that life is emptiness and suffering, that craving causes suffering, that to end suffering you must destroy craving, that the Eightfold Path can destroy craving—were really one truth. Life is a struggle."

Mohammed interjects. "Without obedience to God life is a struggle."

Joy looks sideways at Mohammed. "You know, you may be right. When I met the Patels and saw all the Hindu deities, it freed me from my stepbrother's depressing lack of a God. But I never forgot what he taught me about the Buddhist way. He would try to simplify it so I would understand. To him, the Four Noble Truths boiled down to one truth. Life is suffering, so get used to it. Same way, Buddha's Eightfold path boiled down to one idea."

Joy holds her hands in front of her and begins counting on her fingertips. "He'd grin and recite the eight things—right view, right intention, right speech, action, livelihood, effort, mindfulness, concentration—that's all eight, right? He said it all boiled down to one thing—concentrate and shoot straight. Then would pretend to aim his pistol."

"How old were you when he told you these things and showed you his pistol?"

"I don't remember. I haven't thought about any of this for the longest time. I had forgotten it. But the pistol… it wasn't his police pistol but another one I think he may have gotten on the black market or something. It was very shiny. I was a little girl, I know, but he would not let me touch it. As I grew older and was more of a young woman, I would reach for it but he would pull it away. I could look but not touch when it came to his gun."

Dr. Abraham nods as if the story told him something important about Joy. "But your half-brother was not the cop that ruined your life. That cop is the one you met here in America, the one you are getting ready to talk about, correct?"

Joy looks at the palm trees swaying outside the window and shrugs.

Receiving no answer, the psychiatrist jots a note then asks a different question. "So let's stick with the cop here in America. Now, your expression 'diabolical fiend' intrigued me. That's an interesting phrase coming from a woman who wants to use her words precisely. Why do you say that?"

Joy presses her fingertips tightly to her lips. "Why call him a fiend? He told me how he tricked his dates—he said he never had a girlfriend, only dates—in strange ways. He lured them into little erotic traps. He said he had the power to trap a woman into doing things she swore she would never do. He could get a woman to submit gladly to his weird ideas. I know he got me to do what he asked. He said he was a one-man cult, the cult of Dennis the Menace. That is what he claimed, my friend the cop."

Smiling a wry smile, Dr. Abraham asks, "Just now you said 'my friend the cop.' Did you mean to say 'my fiend the cop?' When you said friend, that is what they call a Freudian slip, unless you actually meant friend."

"He was both. He was a fiend for sure. And I think he was a friend, too."

Despite her defiant tone, a blush paints red into the wheat-colored skin of her neck and cheeks. The physician detects a tear welling up in her eye. He pauses for a moment and says, "I've sidetracked your story. Take us clubbing again."

"So I'm in this crowded, noisy Miami Beach bar where I used to go to meet cops. It's the type of bar where women can come and play a role. Respectable chicks like me— accountants, lawyers, computer programmers—show up in high heels and dresses like negligees with everything hanging out. The black guys call us posers. It's ghetto talk, but it fits. You're posing as something you really aren't. Any guy feels free to look you over like you were a dancer at a strip bar. A guy in those bars will come up and stare right at your cleavage. No fear."

Mary looks puzzled. "And you meet men like this?"

Looking out the window, Joy's eyes sparkle with reflected sunlight. Her voice rises in her rata-tat-tat cadence. "That, in fact, is how we met. I was walking out of the bar, fooling with a long, dangling belly button piercing of a little silver gun. I had on a red bare midriff top. He was sauntering in, talking on his cell phone.

"The moment he saw me he stopped dead in his tracks and shoved his cell into his pocket. He leaned toward me and said, 'Mind if I take a look down there?' I looked at my watch and said, 'You don't have enough time.' He said, 'I will if you head back in there for one more drink, beautiful.'

"I told him no. We stood there for a second looking at each other. People were coming in and out of the doorway, bumping our shoulders, but we just stood there in the noise and the crowd. There was something about him. From the very first moment there was something about him.

"I said but maybe you can walk me to my car if you answer one question Are you a cop?" He said yes and asked how I knew. 'The haircut,' I said."

Then I said to him in an exaggerated Asian whore accent Mohammed hates, 'You in luck Joe I only date cops.' I could see the surprise on his face when I said it. I took a pen from my purse and wrote down my cell number without him even asking for it. I said that's for later, for now you can walk me to my car.

"He made a joke of following two steps behind me as we walked toward my car. He said, 'I obey like a puppy dog, don't I?' Then he stepped in front of me. 'But how about you, gorgeous? You know how to obey like a puppy?'

"He looked me up and down then looked straight into my eyes waiting for an answer. 'I obey when I feel like it,' I said. He looked me in the eye again. 'What if we go to my truck, then?' I did."

"You got into the truck of a stranger without hesitation?" her shrink asks. "No hesitation at all?"

"None. When I climbed in Dennis gave me a boyish peck on the cheek. Soft. Like you'd kiss a baby. It was not the kind of first kiss I ever got from a cop before."

Dr. Abraham smiles. "Tell us what kind of first kiss you usually get from a cop."

"They're in a hurry. They jam their tongue in your mouth or maybe feel you up right away. I've had cops slide their hand between my legs the first time they kissed me. Some of them think because I'm Asian that somehow turns wherever I am into a massage parlor."

"But this kiss was different?"

"Yes. It was a peck on the cheek. I liked it. I also liked it when he grabbed me and pulled me toward him and kissed me again. It was still soft. Then he slammed the seat back as far is it would go and tilted the steering wheel out of his way. He bowed like an actor on a stage and said, 'Meet Dennis the Menace.' Then he kissed me on the hand.

"I asked him what the name meant. 'There was a cartoon character by that name, although I really wasn't like him. From when I was little,' he said, 'they called me Dennis the Menace. No matter what game I played, I fought like hell. My father taught me that I had to win every time. He'd beat the shit out of me if he came home drunk and I told him my baseball team lost. Heaven forbid if I told him I lost one of the fights I was always getting into in high school.'

"I asked Dennis, 'You mean literally beat you up? Hit you with his fists?'

"He said, 'Yep. It was just my old man's way. He drove a truck and he'd get drunk after a long haul. He'd call my mother on the phone and she would tell him how my baseball team did. I was a pitcher. If he knew I'd lost a game, he'd slap me around. So after a while I would honestly believe I had to win every time. Not just some times. Every time. My father taught me that life's a bitch and then you die.' When Dennis said that, in my heart it felt exactly like my stepbrother was saying the Four Noble Truths are only one truth, that life is suffering. I leaned into his face and kissed him."

Stroking his beard, Joy's shrink jots another note. "So within minutes of meeting this stranger he tells you about his father and shows he was capable of affection. Wasn't that pretty fast?"

Joy nods. "Yes. Let me keep telling this story. So I said, 'Hey mista Dennis Menace,' trying to sound like an Asian massage parlor chick, 'I virgin so don't be rough with me. That secret but I tell you.'

"Dennis leaned away from me and told me I was lying.

"I said I wasn't. I waited until he looked me over—you can get these guys to follow your eyes down your body if you make sure they are paying attention—and then I said, 'Check my piercing. My brother is a cop in Hong Kong.'

"He got so happy when he heard that. He said, 'Chicks in the bars hate cops for no reason. When they need a flat fixed on the road or when they need some first aid or when they think somebody is followin' them, that's different.' Soon we were doing real kisses."

Inexplicably, Dr. Abraham addresses the empty chair. "So Joy is leaving a Miami bar, meets a stranger who tells her his life story, then she lies to him and says she's a virgin, then they exchange real kisses. What are real kisses, Joy?"

Joy's eyes become mischievous. "Let me ask you the question for a change, Dr. Shrink. Have you ever kissed a girl? Have you ever kissed your mother? That is the difference."

For a passing instant, Dr. Abraham seems confused. He sets his ornate pen on the desk. "Are you saying a real kiss is not for your mother?"

Joy doesn't understand the question. "All I wanted to say was that the kisses were exciting me, you know, sexually."

Dr. Abraham flicks his hand dismissively. "Please continue."

"He yanked me toward him and said, 'What if I ask you to take your clothes off?' He whispered the suggestion in my ear, kissed it, then leaned away to gauge my reaction. I found myself considering the idea.

"I can't believe you would even consider doing something like that, having just met him," Mary offers.

"Normally I wouldn't, but there was something about this cop. He had a hold on me. I acted like it was out of the question, which it was. I wouldn't do it in a million years. At least that's what I thought when he first asked me. Then he looked up at the stars. 'Why not? Are you a prude? Are you afraid of cops? But never mind. I have lots of chicks undressing for me all the time in all different places, but I guess they ain't in the habit of disrespectin' cops. But maybe you ain't dissin' on cops. Maybe you are a virgin.'

"If that was a trap, I fell for it. He kept looking at the sky, then he looked at his watch and said he had to go. For whatever reason, I pointed back toward the club and said, 'Somebody could walk by or drive by and see us.'

"Our eyes made brief contact. Then he said something strange, something like, 'What if I was attacking you? We can pretend that I am. Then you wouldn't be embarrassed if somebody drove up.'

"I shrugged 'Why would I want to pretend you're attacking me?'

"He grinned at me with that diabolical grin that I was just getting to know. 'Some women like to pretend. They like to play victim. Want to play victim, dear Virgin Joy? Do you want to play some games with Dennis the Menace?'

"I didn't know what he was talking about. 'Play victim? What does that mean, Dennis? I'm not experienced. I'm a virgin.' So there is that lie again, but this time I was glad I told it.

"He had a big grin on his face. 'By pretending to be my victim, you can let yourself do things you might secretly want to do. Surrender your virginity, maybe...'

"Suddenly he leaned over into the back seat, tossing around a jacket and some other things. When he leaned back forward, he had a gun in his hand. I gasped at the sight of the thing.

"He laughed. 'Here, see, I can even point my piece at you.' He clicked some button to make the magazine of bullets fall out, then he pointed his service automatic at my head, not four or five inches from my eyes. I had never seen a real automatic before. It was a metallic steel black and blue color. That's how I would describe it. Slowly he touched it to my cheek. The metal felt cold. I have to admit it aroused me."

Joy looks at Mohammed and Mary. "I know this is a strange thing, but I am telling it as it happened."

"And that's the purpose, Joy, continue," her shrink says without looking up from his notes.

"He slowly lifted the muzzle off my cheek. He slid the gun along my bare midriff and down to my thigh. Touching it to my thigh, his eyes grew as wide as saucers. He whispered, 'Sexy, huh?'

"It was a strange moment. My thoughts were jumbled. I told myself if the gun was empty, it's just a weird sex toy. Still, if Dennis hadn't been so good looking, if he wasn't saying those dangerous things with the pretty Tom Cruise grin on his face, I might have freaked out. Instead I looked him in the eye and said, 'You're crazy, Dennis.' He smiled, 'Now do you know why everybody calls me Dennis the Menace?'

"Suddenly he put the gun on the floor and started joking as if nothing had happened. 'I probably am more ridiculous than crazy. I saw the gun thing on an X-rated video. The chick seemed to get excited, but those movies are fake. Since I have a gun, I thought I'd try it. I wanted to make-pretend scare you.'

"I said something like 'No explanation needed, Dennis, I'll play along. What are you ordering me to do?'

"He locked his eyes on mine. 'Are you sure you want to play this game?'

"When I said, 'I like games' he picked the gun up and pressed it against my cheek again. 'I'm ordering you to get naked.'

"I smirked at the silliness of it. 'Do it, bitch,' he shouted, brandishing the gun.

"I stared at him wondering why I was letting him call me awful names and do this.

"He laughed. 'The game is that I really do scare you. Like it?'

"I'll admit it here in this room. I did like the brief, strange thrill of it. Dennis pressed his face right into mine. He rubbed the gun against my thigh. The cold metal gave me a chill. It did feel erotic in a strange, perverted way. Then he shouted in what cops call their command voice: 'Do It!'

"I started to take my blouse off, then said, 'Wait. Not here. Let's go to your place, then maybe I will do it.' Dennis leaned back in the driver's seat grinning the self-satisfied grin the devil himself would grin knowing he was about to despoil a virgin. Am I being vivid enough, doctor?"

"You're being very vivid. Thank you." Dr. Abraham jots a note. Without looking up he asks, "Have you ever told anyone this story before?"

"No."

"Not even to Mrs. Patel?"

"No."

"But you are telling the strangers in this room."

"Why not? Isn't that is the point of being here? Plus I'm probably dead and therefore we have time. Eternity, right?"

Mary and Mohammed had been listening in stunned silence. But this remark draws a nervous smile from Mohammed.

"Yes we have time Joy," Mohammed says. "But don't get caught up in what your cop would call a head-game. We are not dead," he concludes, looking defiantly at Dr. Abraham.

Dr. Abraham ignores Mohammed. "Continue, Joy."

"I remember exactly what I said next. I rubbed his forearm gently and put my lips near his ear so he could hear me whisper. 'But remember, Dennis, I'm a virgin.'

"With that I got out of his truck, got in my car, then followed his truck to the run-down apartment complex where he lived. He made a point of waving his gun toward me as I got out of my car in front of his building. He kept it in one hand. With the other hand he pulled me—nothing dramatic or too strong, but he made sure I felt the sensation of being pulled—into his apartment and then into his bedroom, squeezing my hand more tightly as we went through each door and finally up to the bed.

"Then he squeezed my hand very hard and tossed the gun onto the disheveled bundle of covers. I undressed standing there. I did it slowly, then like a little girl I threw myself onto the pile of covers where the gun was. And... Dr. Shrink, I don't think these details will matter."

"Actually, I'm interested in one detail. Did he point the gun at you when he got into bed?"

"No," Joy says, eyes glimmering. "After I got undressed I picked it up from the bed and pointed it at him. I figured it was unloaded but I just wanted to hold the gun. I waved it at him and told him to undress. I said I was in charge and he had to let me stare at him getting naked. When I shouted, 'Do it,' he did exactly what I told him to do. When he was naked, I threw the gun on the floor and reached out for his hand."

Joy looks over at Mary. "Maybe you can understand this, maybe you can't, Mary. This guy was drop-dead gorgeous from head to toe. He was a short, muscular guy. He had this Tom Cruise sort of smile that was always pinned to his face, no matter what he was doing or saying. He had this mane of thick black cop-haircut hair on the top of his head and not a single hair anywhere else. We made love right then. I was passive, or at least I tried to be."

Without looking up from his notes, Dr. Abraham asks, "Was it a good or bad experience? Do you wish you hadn't done it?"

Joy clutches her necklace, fighting tears welling up in her eyes. "I wish I hadn't done it. I wish I never met him. But... the experience? I enjoyed it. I hate myself for it, but I... had an orgasm... my first ever."

The psychiatrist scribbles a series of notes, not looking up. Then he turns his back and reaches for the earthenware pitcher on his credenza. He pours a tall glass of ice water. "That's enough for now, Joy. Would you like a drink of water?"

"Yes, please." Joy takes the water glass from Dr. Abraham. She drinks slowly, muttering to Mary, "I'm savoring the clean taste of Dr. Abraham's water. Doesn't it taste so clean?"

Dr. Abraham pulls himself erect and pours a glass of water for himself, drinking greedily. He says, "Joy and Mohammed, would you excuse us now? I would like to speak to Mary in my private study. Mary, would you please follow me?"

He rises from his leather chair. Gait unsteady, he shuffles slowly toward his door. Startled, Mary bolts out of her chair. "Should I just follow—"

Her body is trembling and so is her voice. "Will I be comin' back? Should I take this?"

Mary leans over to pick up the blue mesh bag beside her chair when Dr. Abraham says, "No need for the bag. Just come with me."

Joy and Mohammed exchange a series of glances until Mohammed nods yes, acknowledging their shared confusion and perhaps envy of Mary as she disappears into Dr. Abraham's private chamber.

6.

Their time together resumes in an unexpected way, with Joy and Mohammed sitting in their chairs, statues in a silent garden, staring past Dr. Abraham's massive desk toward the Blue Door. The door finally opens to reveal Mary, in blue slacks and blouse as always, though thinner than before. Mohammed and Joy blink into wakefulness to watch Mary step through the door and take her seat, her blue eyes lowered, studying the carpet as she steps past her physician's desk.

Dr. Abraham follows close behind Mary, steadying her elbow momentarily as she takes her seat. He walks toward his window, legs moving stiffly and head tilted back, cocked at an odd angle. Without looking at his patients, he says, "Mary and I just had a good talk, but now Mohammed is the center of our attention!"

He abruptly turns from the window then walks stiffly to his chair, the glossy black leather receiving him with a ceremony of creaks. "Mohammed, you look well today." Noting that his comment draws Joy's attention to Mohammed, Dr. Abraham eyes her as he speaks to him. "Please open your Memory Book for Joy and Mary."

"Thank you for the compliment, Dr. Abraham. The story I will tell started with an antiquity that belonged to my family for centuries. I mentioned this bowl when we opened our Memory Books for the first time."

Dr. Abraham's gnarled hands tap his desk. "We remember your father and the bowl. Perhaps now is the time to describe this bowl. What made it so beautiful? What made it so precious? Describe it like it was sitting on my desk at this moment and Joy, Mary and I are your discerning clients."

"An interesting challenge, Dr. Abraham. I accept it gladly."

Mohammed gestures palm up with his left hand, almost touching his physician's desk. "Let me take you to the room where I kept a locked wooden box—an artifact in its own right—that held our most precious pieces. Let me open the box so I may show you this bowl. I will lift it our carefully so you

---

can see it. It is large, eight inches wide and four inches deep."
He sweeps his hand around and down to outline the bowl.

"The handiwork is exquisite. Long ago it was painted and fired and glazed to the most exacting standard. The beautiful glaze reflects the light in subtle ways, but most particularly candlelight. My father and I together would sit by candle light and look at the bowl, sometimes with dates or other fruit resting inside it, as he said sons and fathers had sat together for generations before us."

Seeming to savor the moment, Mohammed, his head slightly bowed, smiles contritely at Dr. Abraham. "The artifact is painted in an Islamic motif called knot work. The knots are painted in subtle hues of blue and tan against a white glazed background. The knots were intricate and beautiful, with one very large one in the middle of the bowl. To an American it might look like brown and green ivy covering a trellis. But to a Muslim it is a beautiful, traditional design."

Addressing Mohammed but alternating his gaze between Joy and Mary, Dr. Abraham says, "Excellent. I can almost visualize it. May I show you something, Mohammed?"

"Of course."

Dr. Abraham turns to the credenza and carefully hands the dagger on display there to Mohamed. "You will of course recognize this type of weapon."

Mohammed inspects the weapon. "Do you have the sheath, Dr. Abraham?"

"No, I do not."

"No matter. I can tell by the hilt of this weapon that it is an arab dagger, a Janbiya they are often called. It is of ancient design but I can determine by the steel of the blade it was manufactured in modern times. How did you acquire it?"

"That doesn't matter," Dr. Abraham replies, staring at it before returning it to the credenza. "I thought you might be interested in the similarities between this dagger and the bowl you describe. The elaborate design and so forth."

Mohammed nods. "Yes. Interesting. But that is a weapon. And more, it is worn and flawed. The bowl I speak of was in perfect condition, a rare and beautiful antiquity. It was to be a gift for my son Zayd. My son had an apartment, more exactly a condominium that I purchased for him."

"Tell us about your relationship with your son," Dr. Abraham says.

"No matter what I did for him, he rebelled. He dropped out of university. He was a confused young man. The more I tried to set him on the right path, the more he rebelled. He brought great strife into my family, began turning my wife—her name is, was, Nia—against me."

"How?"

"In her eyes, I had done all of the wrong things with him. For that reason, she suggested that I give him something of great value to me. He had complained to her, in a way he should not have—he should have come to me—that buying the condo did not convey my confidence in him. He told his mother that it was a shallow gift. His mother agreed with him. Because I am so rich, she said, it was an empty, shallow, loveless gift to my son.

"As circumstance would have it, one day he called and asked that Nia and I come see him. He had an anger in his voice that I had begun to notice more and more."

Dr. Abraham looks carefully into Mohammed's eyes. "You were noticing a growing anger? Did you know why?"

Averting his physician's gaze, Mohammed mutters, "No. But when he called I thought perhaps Nia is right. Perhaps I should make this gift to Zayd. He is the heir to all the family possesses. So the two of us took the gift, the antique bowl, to his home, just north of Miami. It was during the workday, just before 4 pm. We did not call first, part of me hoping that he would not be there."

Dr. Abraham cocks his brow. "If you were going there at his request, why would you hope he was not there?"

Mohammed looks up into the vaulted ceiling. "I had great trouble talking to him. He had willfulness in his eyes; they could pierce your heart like daggers. I wanted the bowl to speak in my stead. Zayd knew the history of the piece. He already knew of its great value. There would be no need for me to explain more than the card we took, which said, '*HERE IS A SYMBOL, MY SON, OF YOUR ANCIENT AND HONORED HERITAGE.*'"

Mohammed scanned the eyes of his fellow patients, avoiding those of the doctor. "There was a horrible confrontation with my son. Strong alcoholic drink played a part."

Mohammed waits for a reaction, a sign of interest, from Mary or Joy. But they sit passively. "To a devout Muslim, alcohol is swill. Poison. Do you know why Anwar Sadat was assassinated? One reason why the Islamic fundamentalists gunned down the President of Egypt was because he was photographed drinking alcohol with an American. This may or may not be true, but it is said that one reason was this photograph with alcohol. Alcohol is strictly forbidden in Islam."

Dr. Abraham asks, "Why is alcohol important for your story ?"

"My son was a confused young man. Yes, it is true that we allowed him to be raised in America. But we taught him the strict rules of Islam."

The psychiatrist jots a note and then asks, "What rules did you teach your son?"

Mohammed casts his eyes around the room then continues in his mellow, beautiful voice. "There are what are called the Five Pillars of Islam, as each of you may know."

The psychiatrist furrows his brow. "Assume that we know nothing of Islam. Explain what you taught your son."

"I must say it again? I taught him the Pillars of Islam."

"And they are?"

"First, and of utmost importance, is the recitation of the words 'There is no god but Allah, and Muhammad is his messenger.'"

Mohammed's healer leans forward and says softly, "Recite the words as you learned them. Recall the day from your Memory Book when you and your father and your uncle walked to the mosque on that beautiful evening."

Mohammed exhales slowly, casting his eyes toward the vaulted ceiling. "*La ilah illa Allah Muhammad rasul Allah.*"

Dr. Abraham nods in approval. "And now continue. You were telling us about your son."

"Zayd observed the other Pillars of Islam. He said his daily prayers. He gave to the poor. He observed Ramadan with the proper fasting. These are the Pillars of Islam."

Dr. Abraham tugs at a button of his yellow cardigan and says softly, "And the hajj, the pilgrimage to Mecca, is that not also considered to be one of the Pillars of Islam?"

"Yes, and we made the pilgrimage as a family when he was twelve. It was a trip back to our ancestral homeland, and I spared no expense. We stayed at the finest accommodations, ate the finest traditional food at those times when we were allowed to eat."

"So you taught him well. But something must have been amiss. Did he misunderstand one of the Pillars of Islam perhaps?"

"Yes. As a young boy he was part of our community, our devout community. But at his university, something went wrong. He seemed to misunderstand the admonition to give to the poor. He came to think that our duty was somehow to serve the poor. Almost a kind of communist idea, like wealth was somehow evil. Our greatest folly, surely I know this now, was that we did not forbid him to have friends who were not Muslim. He had one friend in particular, a very beautiful American girl. He—"

Dr. Abraham interrupts, his yellow notepad and antique fountain pen poised to take notes. "Why would it be folly to allow him to become friends with Americans?"

"The folly was to allow him to spend so much time with non-believers."

"But Mohammed," Dr. Abraham says, "are you not now in a room full of non-believers?"

Mohammed shakes his head furiously. "Yes, that is true. But I am mature and wise and none of you can lead me down your false paths."

"I can't believe what you just said," Joy shouts, bolting up from her chair.

A pinkish streak appears on her neck beneath her wheat-colored skin. "Did you hear what he just said, Dr. Shrink? He said that for eternity, he will turn a deaf ear to our beliefs. He refuses to change."

"Would you like to respond to that, Mohammed?" The psychiatrist is looking at Joy.

Mohammed's lip turns up in a spiteful sneer. "My reply is that I am not here to spend eternity with this woman. I am alive and this is the office of a well-respected physician who has instructed me to tell my story so that my mind can be healed."

Joy sits down, hiking her skirt slightly. Making a point of looking closely at the scar running down Mohammed's cheek, she crosses her legs and points her fashionable high heels in Mohammed's direction. "So Dr. Shrink, Mohammed and I agree that we don't want to be together except for these fifty-five minutes, of which much has been spent with him hemming and hawing about a bowl."

Dr. Abraham mutters, jotting notes. "Let's allow Mohammed to continue. I believe you were talking about a non-Muslim girl."

"Yes. This girl, this girl who ruined all our lives, he met this girl in college. Her name is Gloria."

"And what is this girl like?"

Mohammed sits in silence.

"What is she like? Please tell us, if she is an important part of your story."

"She has large, radiant black eyes and raven hair, very much like his mother's. This Gloria could pass for a beautiful Iranian woman, even by her bearing. But she is a Cuban who came to America as a child. Although her family was once wealthy, she had no morals. She is evil."

"In what way?" the physician asks.

Glancing reflexively from the corner of his eye at Joy, Mohammed says forcefully, "She is haughty. She manipulates men with charm. This is wrong."

Dr. Abraham leans forward. "Mohammed, I want you to forget about right and wrong for a moment. Use all of your energy to take us out of this room to the place where this confrontation occurred."

"Picture a prosperous man and his well-dressed wife standing awkwardly in the elevator. My father made a ceremony of handing me the bowl when he was old and weak, but he wore his best business suit for the occasion. So at my request Nia dressed in a black business dress, and I was wearing this suit in fact.

"Not looking at each other, this man and woman are walking down the corridor to the apartment I bought for him. When we opened the door to his condo my wife and I were overwhelmed by a foul smell like the odor of animals in a barn. We found Zayd asleep on his sofa, wearing only his underwear. It was shameful. His shirt and pants were lying on the floor, covered with vomit. We thought he was alone.

"'He is drunk. Our son is drunk and sick with alcohol,' I said to my wife. 'He has stripped and thrown his clothes on the floor because he was too drunk to clean it. Wake him up,' I told her.

"Nia, my wife, said, 'First I will clean this up.' She grabbed a towel from the kitchen and, having wrapped it around her hand like a glove, used it to pick up his clothes and started toward the bathroom, which has a small washer and dryer in it.

"I yanked the foul-smelling clothes from her hand. I said his clothes are now garbage and went to throw them down the garbage chute.

"When I returned to his apartment Zayd was stirring. My wife had cleaned his face and chest. He moved slowly on the sofa, listless, still coughing. Nia and I simply sat at his dining table, saying nothing.

"An hour passed before he finally came to. It was the longest hour of my life, or so I thought then, staring at the heir to my line befouled by drink. I felt incredible shame for him. For me. For his mother.

"When he began to wake up, he glared at me. Wobbling to straighten himself, he got up off the sofa. 'I am sick,' he said.

"His mother handed him water. He drank it like a homeless Miami street bum in a stupor, spilling water down his cheek. He looked me in the eye. 'Please do not look so closely at me. Yes, I am sick.'

"I asked him, 'What did you drink?'

"He glared at me in silence as before. There was a look of spite, even hatred for me, in his eyes. I should admit that my son and I had our—how would you say—disagreements. Looking back, I must say that our disagreements went unspoken until that horrible day of the accident. That day, through his stupor he slurred, 'My father, you bestow nothing but trinkets upon me. My very name humbles me.'

"I became angry and said, 'Your name is beautiful, revered.'

"He smirked. 'Perhaps, but for me it is an allusion to a slave child, already grown, given to the Prophet Muhammad by Lady Khadijad, the Prophet's blessed wife. By my very name, at birth, you saw me as a burden. You are so absorbed in yourself that you know nothing of me.'

"I said, 'Zayd, you are mistaken.'

'Am I?' he shouted. He was wobbling on his legs. His mother grimaced, her beautiful black eyes red with tears. 'He is still a boy, husband. Be lenient with him. I beg this of you.'

"She braced him up against the wall. In his eyes was that spiteful, willful look that could anger me so. He sneered at me and he said, 'Lenient, Mother? Of what concern am I to him anyway. Father, you spend days and nights selling objects. Fatigued and angry inside your mind, you walk through the door and begin giving orders to me and my mother like you were a general in the army.'

"I do not give orders.

"Zayd sneered. 'Mother. Tell him.'

"When he saw that his mother would say nothing, he kept talking. His breath was foul. His words were slurred. 'She is afraid of you. No wonder. You are tired, irritable most times. Your mind is elsewhere. You are eaten up with your hatred of the Americans and their liquor and their bathing suits and their pornography. But you take their money. You smile at them in your elegant shop and listen to their stories. And then you take more money from them.'

"I said, 'And I wash my hands after each transaction with them, as I taught you to do, as my father taught me. You know this, Zayd.'

"He looked at his mother and said, 'See what a hypocrite this man is? You believe all that matters in the world are things and money. No, father. Love is what matters. Gloria taught me that.'

"I looked him straight in the eye. 'I wanted to teach you how to succeed here in America. There is much to be gained here in America.'

"He looked at his mother, and to me he said, 'You did not teach me to thrive in America. You did not teach me anything but rigid rules that tell me what I should not do. You did not impart wisdom to me. Instead, you taught me your greed. Gloria taught me more in one night in her bed than you taught me in a lifetime at our supper table.'

"Again, I looked him in the eye. 'Where do you get these ideas?'

"To this he said, 'Gloria said good fathers spend quiet time at home, just playing. They read a story to their babies and put their children to bed. You did none of these things, Father.'

"I watched him hold his hand up to his mouth and almost retch again. He was disgusting, but he kept talking. 'And it is fathers like you who are often shocked at how little they actually know of what's going on in the lives of their sons. They fail to realize that being involved in their sons' lives means paying attention to the small details. That was you, father. You did not know me at all.'

"I shouted 'How dare you talk to me in this manner!'

"Nia asked me to lower my voice. She tried to move between me and Zayd. I pushed her away.

"He saw her stumble to gain her balance and said, 'See the kind of man you are? And then you ask how dare I speak this way? Why shouldn't I? Let me repeat myself. You are no better than the Americans you say are so lazy in their morals. See how you treat your wife, my mother? Like an object. Fathers like you do not understand that loving a son means paying attention to the small details.'

"'What details?' I asked.

"Now his eyes seemed to grow clear for a moment. 'Details you ask, Father? Like what Gloria means to me. How soft her heart is, how she listens to me. You did not know me at all. Until now. Now you see me. I am drunk. I am with a woman that you may regard as a whore. By the definition of many men, she is indeed a harlot. So be it.'

"My anger was growing toward him."

"I can tell that just from the anger in your voice right now," Mohammed's physician observes. "You were probably angry before you even left your own home. Is that possible?"

"Perhaps."

Mohammed sees that Joy and Mary are staring intently into his eyes. "In any event," Mohammed continues, "my wife saw this, but she spoke to him instead. 'Zayd, perhaps your father and I should leave. We can give you this some other time.'

"He glared at the antique bowl in her hands.

"'What is this?' he asked. 'More trinkets?' He seized the bowl from his mother's hand. 'I do not want any more trinkets.' He looked sideways at me but spoke to his mother. 'Tell him to take it back.'

"He tossed the bowl at me, and I was barely able to reach out in time for it to strike my hands and fall to the floor. The floor was thickly carpeted, so the bowl, though delicate, did not break. It was not broken or even chipped. I picked the bowl up off the floor and inspected it carefully. We, the three of us, looked to see that yes, the bowl was not damaged. Still, I felt this incredible anger.

"'If I am to receive your ire, my father, let me deserve it,' he said. 'Gloria, come out here,' he called back toward his bedroom. 'Gloria. Gloria. Gloria.' There was no answer to his calls.

"He staggered and stumbled toward his bedroom. Instinctively, his mother and I followed him. In the room there was a naked girl, passed out on his bed. She was sprawled spread-eagle, so very shameful. But that was not enough.

"To compound his shame and ours, the girl had a towel on her head fashioned loosely to resemble the hijab Muslim women wear on their head for modesty. I was mortified by the sight, as was my wife.

"My son stumbled back into the living room. 'I am sorry, Mother,' he said. Then he looked me in the eye. He picked my precious bowl off the table and said, 'Here is what your slave-boy son thinks of your family trinkets. He held the bowl above his head then threw it against the wall. It shattered into small pieces and shards that fell to the floor. It had survived for centuries, literally centuries, in my family, his family. And he did this thing."

Mohammed jerks his head back and forth violently and thumps his chest. "My son, my very flesh, did this horrible thing!" Embarrassed by the unintended display of passion, he leans back slowly until his aching muscles come to rest against the uncomfortable back of the mahogany chair. "Forgive me. I am done for now."

Thrusting her head back haughtily, Joy steals a glance at her watch. "We have more time. Continue your story." After a pause she says, "Maybe it will help you."

Mohammed straightens the cuffs of his business suit. "No. I am finished. It is time that I stopped."

A sympathetic look on his face, Dr. Abraham looks deeply into Mohammed's eyes. But there is a tone of censure in his words. "Mohammed, time does not count here. I'm surprised that I must keep reminding my patients of the premise of our therapy."

With a forced smile he says, "So please, continue to open your Memory Books. There is no choice."

Mohammed sneers at his physician. "Most assuredly there is, and I choose not to reveal any more details of my life."

Dr. Abraham leans back in his chair. "We did so well so far but now your defiant tone surprises me. Did you defy your father in such a tone?"

"You are not my father. This is not eternity. And your little warm-up exercises were fine because they revealed nothing. But I will not divulge anything more because I still have a question about your method, Dr. Abraham."

"And what do you question, Mohammed?"

Unexpectedly, Mohammed struggles up from his chair, swaying like a toddler about to take his first steps. Striving mightily to conceal the final adjustment his hip makes to properly align his prosthetic leg, he grimaces and glares at Dr. Abraham.

"No need to stand, Mohammed," the physician says in a cavalier tone. "Just tell us what it is that you doubt."

"I am standing because there is a part of me that is fully prepared to leave."

"Is that so?"

"Yes, doctor, it is. I came to you for your technique of recovering patients from trauma suffered in automobile accidents. Your technique for causing the mind to heal just as the body heals."

"That is correct. But Mohammed, what is your question? Are you stalling for time because you did not prepare to tell your story as I instructed, or are you confused about something?"

Jerking his shoulders back, Mohammed says, "I am not stalling. My question is why must the three of us pretend that we will be here for eternity? Did we not put this matter to rest in our very first session?"

Dr. Abraham shrugs. "Did we? Tell me what was said."

"You asked each of us if it was possible for a Muslim and a Christian and a Hindu and a Jew to share their eternal lives. We all said no. Yet you insist that we play this charade. How will this heal any of us?"

"Right now you do not understand how the process will work, Mohammed." Dr. Abraham leans back into his thick leather chair. It moans and creaks under his weight.

"What each of you believe at the beginning of our time together about yourself or about God or eternity is irrelevant. What anyone else taught any of you about life or death prior to coming here is also irrelevant. Perhaps it is even the case that there is a conspiracy of minds and Gods set out to baffle us in life. Could that be? Could it be that your thoughts torment you and your God has decided to let the torment continue?

There is no reply. Dr. Abraham leans forward. "Actually, it doesn't matter. All that matters is what you believe when we perform the Portal exercise. Do you each understand this?"

Dr. Abraham studies the gathering storm outside the window. "Life? Do we really know what it means? Do you, Mary?"

"Most days I feel like I don't understand life at all."

"You do not, Mary. Thank you for your honesty. And Death? Who dares to claim full knowledge of it? I speak of the true knowledge of afterlife. Not stories you believe because they were passed down to you by people you trust. Do any of you claim true knowledge? Joy?"

Silence.

"Mohammed?"

Silence.

"Death is a mystery. Nothing we know about it is important. We know only what happens to the body. Decay. Rot. The predictable decomposition of organic matter. But that is not important, is it? What we want to know is, what becomes of the soul? Or is there really such a thing as the soul? This is a mystery, a source of speculation."

Joy shifts in her chair, agitated, crossing and uncrossing her legs, until finally she also stands up. "This is too confusing."

The physician looks out at the darkening sky where a solitary shaft of sunlight pierces the billowing clouds to illuminate a small patch of water. "I don't know what is confusing. Let me explain our therapeutic premise one more time. Perhaps we are together for eternity. Perhaps we are simply playing silly mind games in a psychiatrist's office.

"Either way, we are here to be healed. You must let others see into your soul by opening your Memory Book."

Joy begins to sit down in the empty chair.

"Not there. In fact, Joy, I would prefer that you not touch that chair. That goes for all of you. Is that understood?"

When Joy takes her seat, all eyes are on Mohammed. "And you, Mohammed."

"I stand because I am prepared to leave."

Dr. Abraham bolts up out of his chair. "Very well then, let me walk you to the door." He struts from behind his desk, shoulders thrown back, almost a soldier's bearing compared to the bent over old man sitting behind his desk moments before. "Follow me. Come this way."

Mohammed, stunned, follows his physician. When they reach the door both men pause, then Dr. Abraham positions himself between Mohammed and the door, grasping the antique knob. "Are you prepared for what will happen when I open this door?"

"How dare you threaten me, you old man."

"I am threatening you? Is that so, Mohammed? If I am threatening you, then surely you can take your fist and punch me in this old man's face."

Dr. Abraham faces off against his patient then pointedly looks down at his hands, drawing Mohammed eyes to his clenched fists. "I will fight you right here and now. But first tell me who you are fighting. Your father, or your son? For surely this rage I see in your eyes is not directed at the old man who stands between you and what is outside of this room."

After a pause, Dr. Abraham shouts. "Who are you fighting, your son, or is it your father? Or perhaps Allah himself. Who is it? Who?"

Mohammed begins to weep.

"Please come back. Please rejoin the others. I will pour you a glass of water. Would you like a drink of water?"

Mohammed nods yes. When both men have returned to their places, Dr. Abraham fills a tall glass from the ornate pitcher on the credenza. Mohammed drinks.

7.

Dr. Abraham watches the patients arrive one at a time. He takes note that Mohammed and Mary are dressed as they were the last time, in contrast to Joy—wardrobe always changing—who is now sporting a woman's black pantsuit, not unlike Mohammed's except that it is tailored in a military style.

In silence they take their places like seabirds landing on wooden pylons. One pylon jutting from the waves is still empty. Staring at the empty seat, he addresses Mary. "Please continue your story, Mary. Open your Memory Book for us."

"Shouldn't Mohammed take center stage again today? He is strugglin', Dr. Abraham. He's startin' to tell his painful memories. Plus, I have already taken several turns to read."

"We do not take turns here, Mary," her psychiatrist snaps. "We tell our individual stories, that is true. But there is really just one story to tell. It is like the patchwork quilts your mother made in Ireland. There are many patches, just as there children pluralare many souls. But there is a single quilt of souls seeking solace. The quilt is eternal and as large as creation. So please continue."

"Aye then." Nodding eagerly, she lifts her copy of MARY'S STORY from her lap.

Let me take you to my house on the first Saturday back from the hospital. I awoke to the bright sunlight streaming in my window. I awoke simply glad to be alive. Breathing, seeing, smelling, I made a vow to myself and God that if I did only one thing in the time God had granted me, it would be to make dinner for the Little One and Carmella.

By the afternoon, I found myself feeling strong. I was bustling about in the kitchen like a complete, healthy woman. Carmella was due over at six o'clock. RJ was sitting in his highchair, banging a rattle and goo-gooing like little ones do. His red hair seemed to shine in the daylight that poured in the window. The day was shaping up to be wonderful.

Even Robert was cooperating. He watched tennis on the telly and drank beer all day. He left me alone. He was taking a nap. He was welcome to join us for dinner. He had been invited.

When Robert woke from his nap he came in and leaned in the doorway to the kitchen. He was slurring his words. "Mary, I haven't seen your diamond ring for a while. Have you?"

The question took me by surprise. *"No, I haven't."* I went back to the sizzling frying pans with the thinly sliced chicken and beef and onions. But now my hand was shaking and I could hardly hold the pan.

"So?"

"So? What do you mean, Robert?"

"So, don't you wonder where the ring is?"

I kept my back to Robert. I picked up the pan with two hands and concentrated on the chicken. But I couldn't hold it. It slammed back onto the burner. I turned to face Robert but said nothing.

He was groggy and unshaven. *"Do you know where the ring is?"*

"Not right at this moment I don't, Robert. I'm fixing our dinner. Are you going to make the sangria?" I looked him up and down and suddenly in disgust said, *"No mind. Carmella can do it."*

He shrugged. *"Fine with me. 'Tis a fittin' job for your little helper, making such a festive drink."*

I looked at him again. *"You can if you want. The apples and oranges are already sliced. Over there. This time I got real Spanish wine and real Spanish brandy. Carmella says the sangria tastes better if the wine is from—"*

Robert interrupted. It was his peevish tone. *"Mary, for Christ's sake, I'm asking you about your diamond ring."*

I didn't even want to hear Robert's voice in the midst of my loud and smelly and merry cooking. *"I told you months ago I was going to stop wearing it. It didn't fit or maybe it was because of the treatments—I don't know."*

"I know you stopped wearing it. But have you seen it?"

"I stopped wearing it, that's all I know."

"Your voice has that shaking sound Mary like when you're telling me a lie. Where did you put the ring?"

Robert's questions finally had the desired effect of making me stop what I was doing. *"I'm not sure, Robert."*

"It was a family treasure, in the family for generations. My parents honored you when they let me give it to you. So ye may want to think about where ya put it."

I looked directly at him. *"You don't have to remind me that the ring was a family treasure. But you could explain to me why we are talking about this right now. Why must we discuss the ring at this very moment?"*

"Too busy cooking to worry 'bout my ring I bought 'ye? Your wedding ring?"

"I thought it was in the closet in that little jewelry box, but I don't know."

"You mean that black box with the velvet lining?"

"That's the one, Robert, yes. I thought I put the ring there."

"Well, it's not there."

"How do you know? Did you look?"

Robert, his tall frame leaning on the frame of the narrow doorway, shifted his weight from one foot to another. "Yes, I did just now."

"Why are you looking in there now?"

He drummed his fingers on the kitchen wall. "Because I haven't seen the ring in a while, that's the reason."

I spun my eyes around the little kitchen. The pans were popping to signal that the meats were ready, the sangria was waiting to be made, and the salad was not quite finished. I could be dead before the year was out. My Carmella and this meal were part of the magic that would keep me alive. Robert and his ring—I always noticed how he called it his ring, even after he gave it to me—were not part of the magic. I made a decision.

"Well, Robert, it will just have to wait. I'm sure it's somewhere. I want to get this meal ready."

"If the meal is more important than my ring—"

"Robert. I'm finishing up—"

"Well, don't include me. Ahh! jest get ma' shower and be leavin'. I am meeting some friends down—"

I slammed the pan of beef and onions onto the range. "Why don't you just be goin' then."

Mary's soft voice falls silent. The surf can be heard crashing against the sand. "Five minutes later I heard the front door slam shut. When Carmella arrived and came into the kitchen, she asked where Mr. Robert was. I remember my answer to her. 'He just walked out slamming the door behind him and maybe he won't come back. It doesn't matter because today is for me and you and RJ.'

"The three of us had a great dinner. Carmella made the sangria. The Little One ate his meats a bit at a time, Carmella helping him. She smiled at me with each bite. We took our walk on the beach. God gave me the day I dreamed of. And as for Robert Fitzpatrick, I never saw him again."

Mary sighs with finality.

Mohammed shifts his weight awkwardly in the chair and turns slightly toward Mary. "How did you get by financially and raise the child, with the burden, I am sure, of your medical bills and the treatments and so forth?"

Mary nods to the question. "I got no help from Father, who was now bankrupt. A letter occasionally was his contribution. There was some insurance money. Carmella helped for a while, and as I got to know Dr. Laurence Josephson more and more he became not just a doctor but also a prop of sorts.

"Larry loved my baby. He began paying the fees to Carmella's agency when it was clear that Robert had left me. For weeks the police looked for Robert. My wedding ring was in fact missing. They were constantly questioning Carmella about her friends and even held her overnight for questioning. They thought if she stole it, the threat of a night in jail might bring a confession. It didn't, of course. But there were always police in their poor-fitting suits comin' to the house.

"As if that wasn't enough, another line of investigation was pursued, not by the local police, but by the FBI. The issue there was that his laptop computer with sensitive files of some sort or another was missin'. All of this was very mysterious and hush-hush. They would come to the house in black government sedans and take electronic measurements.

Mohammed interjects, "How do you know this Carmella didn't take your ring? I've known women who will do unspeakable things for money."

"Aye. But you do not know my Precious One and that was not a possibility. It was a terrible time for my family. Adjusting to Robert being gone. Dealing with the police. Neither the ring nor the computer was ever found. There was absolutely no trace of Robert. That leased Mercedes he so loved was found unlocked in the parking lot of a Chinese restaurant. No sign of foul play, no sign of Robert. I was surprised at how soon the calls slowed and the investigation appeared to wind down. Then the calls suddenly stopped altogether, as if the case had moved from active to non-active status.

"On the heels of my surgery, it all seemed so very strange. It was as if some black magic spell had taken him away."

Dr. Abraham leans forward in this chair, adjusting his arms under the yellow cardigan sweater draped over his shoulders. "Having told us about Dr. Josephson's magic, Mary, perhaps the concept of magic, even black magic, should be avoided with reference to Robert's loss. Or do you disagree?"

Mary offered Dr. Abraham her cherubic smile. "Of course. I was just tryin' to say that there seems to be no understandin' it, no explainin' it. But life must go on. With cancer, you don't want to see a day, even an hour, wasted. As soon as it was legally permissible, I had the Little One's name changed to Joshua, Josh for short. He is now Joshua Josephson, not Robert Fitzpatrick, Jr. He belongs to me. On Josh's sixth birthday, Larry popped the question. The three of us and Carmella were on a ski trip in Vail."

Mary touches her fingertips to the picture of her second husband on the cover of her story.

"Larry is thirty years older than me, but I don't care. I said aye right away, which I believe was a surprise to him. He threw his arms around me and kissed my forehead. I said, 'Now we're a family.' Carmella rushed over with JJ. We embraced in a family hug and then I leaned my weight into Larry. Carmella saw what I was doing and we pushed Larry into the snow then all four of us tumbled about."

Leaning forward so she can look directly at Mary, Joy asks, "What did your fine local priest have to say about all of this?"

Mary nods. "I don't mind discussin' it. The Church teaches that once a marriage is a sacramental marriage, there may never be another, unless one of the partners should die. The annulment process is an investigation to determine whether the marriage was a sacrament from the very first day.

At this point Joy asks, "Did you ever consider that your subconscious mind wished Robert would die so you could get your marriage to Robert annulled?"

Mary replies, "I got my marriage to Robert annulled based on the fact that the wedding wasn't performed in a Catholic Church."

Joy studies Mary's face.

Mary sees this, but she does not return her gaze. "There were many other reasons. Robert made me use birth control and also convinced me…"

Mary's eyes flutter, and she pauses before saying, "That's another story, what he said I must do one awful day in that cold house of his father's."

Mary scans the eyes of her audience, face flush with embarrassment, as she reveals the intimate details of the sins she has committed. "So now I have told my story. The night Robert announced my pregnancy, the day I met Carmella, the day Robert left me and vanished. So my story stops here, it stops with the total completeness of my life with the Little One and Carmella and Larry."

Now Mohammed takes his turn looking into Mary's face wanting to see into her soul. In his baritone voice, that lawyer-like tone he asks, "For the sake of our honesty in this room, do you not agree that the outcome of this story is perhaps the outcome that you wished for? It is as if in fantasy or by magic, perhaps even black magic, you now have your beautiful life away from Robert and memories of his father's cold house."

Mary nods. "Aye. You are right. In fact, when I was editing my story on my bed that night I wondered, really wondered, if that moment was in eternity. Perhaps our eternal life, our heaven, is where we rewrite the life that we actually lead to be the one we wanted to lead. That moment on my bed, I thought I had in fact died on Larry's operating table."

Joy and Mohammed sit motionless, eyes riveted on Mary's. "It is true. I thought that the sound of the shower was really the sound of the spigots in the operating theatre and Larry was rinsing his hands having lost me to death on his table.

"And perhaps I will spend my eternal life on some operating room table. I thought I would never have to face it again, until… until last week, when I found out that I had to go in again for surgery. Larry was the one who had to tell me. The cancer is back hauntin' me."

Tears well up in Mary's eyes. With a small sob she says, "Ahm done for now."

The news that Mary must once again undergo surgery sets off a flurry of furtive glances between Mohammed and Joy. The psychiatrist jots a note on his yellow pad, sighing.

Suddenly Mary's Mona Lisa smile is gone and anger fills her eyes and her voice. "So I have told everybody in my eternity that Ahm going for surgery yet again. Aren't you going to ask me how that makes me feel, Dr. Abraham? My Dear Lord, my God in Heaven, do you know how that makes me feel?"

She makes a fist and scans the ceiling and walls of his chamber like she is looking for Christ himself so that she can wave her fist and shout her lungs out at him. "It makes me feel like a prisoner who can never be free. I'm a prisoner of sadness and pain. Sadness in my soul. Pain in this goddamn head of mine! A prisoner of never-endin' pain."

Mary puts her face in her hands. Her face, her shoulders, her hands, every part of her is quivering. Joy and Mohammed both reach over to pat her shoulder, their fingertips touching inadvertently on Mary's trembling back. Mohammed pulls himself upright to stare blankly toward the horizon. .

Dr. Abraham offers Mary a glass of water.

"May I have some water also," Joy asks. Mohammed sees this and says, "I would like some also."

"We are making progress." Dr. Abraham smiles as his patients drink deeply. He knows that they have crossed a bridge in his treatment. "You are beginning to understand Mary's sadness as if it were your own. At the Portal you will grasp the eternal truth that the rage and guilt and fear that you each described in our first session are the same poison. They boil in our souls until we pour the poison out. If we resolve to do it, it is as effortless as pouring a cool glass of water as I just did for each of you."

8.

Checking her watch like an old-time train conductor waiting for a locomotive to puff into the station, Joy confirms that she has arrived ten minutes early.

Before stepping through the White Door, she lets her fingertips linger on the cool brass knob. She looks again at her watch and opens the door. She can't understand why she doesn't just give in to Dr. Abraham's insistence that time doesn't matter. At the very least it seems warped and bent.

Turning the knob, Joy feels a palpable rush of anxiety mixed with confusion, as if she is dreaming about waking up from a dream. It happens every time she enters her shrink's office. She tells herself it's probably because the picture window throws such a bright light into the office. This time she is taken aback by the sight of her shrink standing next to her chair in the middle of the semi-circle. He is leaning casually against the ornate mahogany back of the chair where Joy sits like he has been waiting for hours.

Dr. Abraham sees her body reflexively lurch back, the startled look in her eyes. "Sorry, Joy, I did not mean to startle you just now."

"You didn't," Joy says, ignoring the pounding of her heart. She locks eyes with her shrink as she walks across the room. Finally she sits, her bearing, haughty shoulders thrust back, eyes ahead, the style of a runway model.

Her shrink removes his hand from the back of her chair, steps back, then looks deeply into her eyes. "Glad to have a few minutes alone so I can see if you have any questions. Incidentally, that blue outfit looks good on you. Each time I see you your young lady's wardrobe offers a different color, but the green today may be my favorite."

"Thank you. I do have a question. Will Mary be here?"

"Yes. But what does that matter to you?"

"I can't exactly tell what is going on with Mary. Did she need brain surgery again or is she just confused about what has already happened?"

Leaning down, Dr. Abraham whispers into Joy's ear. "She muddles her story a bit, doesn't she?" His eyes dart toward the

White Door; Joy's follow. "Mary and Mohammed are arriving now. What do you see, Joy? Tell me quickly."

Joy rata-tat-tats nervously. "Mary looks weak and unsettled." She smiles at Mary but nods coldly at Mohammed as they cross the room.

Her shrink's mouth touches Joy's ear as he whispers. "And Mohammed? Tell me quickly, Joy, what do you see?"

This time Joy whispers her answer. "He's touching his scar and tapping his tie, like he always does. He tries to hide his limp, like he's ashamed of his fake leg. He—"

Joy can hear his labored breath as Dr. Abraham touches her shoulder to direct her face to look into his. "And your Dr. Shrink? Tell me quickly, what do you see when you look at me?"

Her skin turns crimson.

"Tell me what you see. Describe the Dr. Shrink you see."

"My shrink looks almost as gaunt and weak as Mary. His eyes are sunken and brown around the edges. His skin seems pale, lacking sun on it. His beard, so elegantly groomed when I first met him, now looks shaggy. It's like as if he has decided to copy the wild look of some Old Testament Jew, like in the movies."

"So much honesty," Dr. Abraham sighs as he walks, back slightly bent, behind his desk. "You will surely be healed."

Once all are seated, Dr. Abraham's eyes linger, as they often do, on the tall back of the empty chair. "And Mary, how are you feeling?"

Mary is wearing her blue shirt and blue slacks and brown penny loafers as always, but now there is a bright bandana over her head and sunglasses to conceal puffiness and darkness under her eyes. "I feel alive," Mary says. "I feel grateful, and more thoughtful than ever about surviving. I want—"a tear wells up in her eyes "—to hear the other stories. I thought about death and that it is true; we may already be together forever."

Dr. Abraham jots a note on his yellow pad then asks, "Did you have an out-of-body experience during surgery again, as you did the first time?"

"Truth be told, I never really know what I'm experiencin'," Mary rears back, like a hostile witness on trial.

"Very well," her psychiatrist says, "perhaps we will have Joy open her Memory Book. Joy?"

Touching her watch and then her locket like a baseball coach taps his hat and his sleeve to give signals, Joy looks into the eyes of her shrink. "Before I start, I want to say something to Mary and Mohammed. I am an accountant and Dennis is a cop.

"One reason Dennis and I got along so well is that cops are more like accountants than anybody realizes. With cops and accountants, things are black or white, true or false. Sir, a cop will say, you were doing fifty-five in a thirty mile-an-hour zone and that fact will be a black or white fact. An accountant will say Ma'am, you did not comply with Section XYZ of the tax code, and it will be true. Again, it's black or white. The facts are the facts, no matter what you say."

Her eyes pierce Mohammed's. "That's where both of you totally misunderstand God."

Mohammed's shoulders jerk convulsively, thrusting his body forward in the chair. Awkwardly he rights himself on the tip of his seat, throws his shoulders back, and glares at Joy. "Do not dare question my knowledge of God." He looks at Dr. Abraham. "Dr. Abraham, I will not permit this."

Casting a sideways glance at the man in the black suit sitting next to her, she pointedly ignores his protest. "Do you know why I say you do not understand God, Mohammed?"

He glares in silence.

"Do you know? You don't. You are foolish."

Joy turns her head and casts her haughty look at Mary. "Do you know why you do not understand God, Mary?"

"Not really," Mary says sharply.

Like a parent tiring of a pointless quarrel among his children, Dr. Abraham says wearily, "Joy, instead of trying to anger Mohammed and Mary, you should help them understand. Be part of their healing. Tell Mohammed what he does not understand about God."

"I will, Mohammed, but first you must tell me just one simple fact. How fast were you going?"

Mohammed looks at Dr. Abraham.

Dr. Abraham jots a note on his pad and says, "Mohammed, it's your decision whether to answer Joy or not. You are not obligated to answer."

Joy stares into Mohammed's eyes, bent upon stoking the anger already radiating from them.

"I will answer you! The police report said ninety-three miles-per-hour in a thirty-mile zone," Mohammed shouts.

Joy pans her eyes from Mohammed to Mary and then addresses the palm trees and the hot sun and the ocean on the other side of the shrink's window. "Neither of you understand that God always knows all. For God, the facts are the facts. God knows if you did not obey the speed limit. God is all-knowing."

She points her finger at Mohammed. "Your God, Mohammed, may be merciful or not, I don't know, but if he is God then he must be all-knowing. Omniscient. God knows the exact speed of your car, the exact amount of pain and suffering that occurred that night. It's a fact of the universe, for all time."

Clutching his left thigh for balance, Mohammed thrusts his body out of his chair and gathers himself awkwardly to a standing pose.

Joy holds her ground as he takes two halting steps toward her.

Suddenly he stabs his finger toward Joy. "Must I listen to this, Doctor?"

"Let me answer," Joy says. "Yes, yes, until the end of time. That's our shrink's ground rule. Even if you banish this little slut—I know that is what you think I am—from your eternity, my words will ring in your ears, for I speak an eternal truth. You were going ninety-three miles an hour. Eternal truth. I don't know what happened in that accident, I don't know who might have been killed or maimed, but God knows. That is an eternal truth."

Mohammed slams his hands together and lurches toward the door. Stretching awkwardly, he grasps the knob. Over his shoulder he shouts, "This, Doctor, is an atrocity. Good day."

Joy, still not satisfied, clatters across the tile and leans her body against the door so Mohammed can't open it. Abruptly her self-satisfied grin fades and tears fill her eyes.

"Aren't you afraid to leave here without Dr. Abraham's permission? I know I am. Aren't you?"

"Perhaps I am."

"Good. Then go back over there, Mohammed. Sit or stand and listen to MY story. Turn around on that plastic leg and be a man."

Sobbing and then moaning, tears blot her vision. "And you too, Mary, please listen to me. Somebody help me. Please listen. I need to be heard. Dead or alive or who knows, you do have time to listen to me."

Joy rips the watchband from her wrist—a show of significant strength—and throws it across the room where it bounces off the huge window. "Goddamn time, anyway. We have eternity."

Mohammed takes his hand from the knob and moves. They face off toe-to-toe. Their eyes are locked.

"I will listen to your story, and I will find the words to multiply your eternal grief one thousand times as you, just now, have multiplied mine."

Through red eyes she sobs, "Challenge accepted. And you, Mary, divorced your husband because you hated him, not because you hated his family. You hated him from the beginning but had stretched out and secretly gritted your teeth and pretended to have sex with him anyway. I never did pretend like that. No paper you buy from the Pope that says you were deceived or did not understand will hide that fact from God."

Joy walks over to the huge window and picks her watch up from the floor. "My lucky day," she mutters toward Dr. Abraham, "the clasp is still working."

Dangling her watch from her wrist, Joy walks behind her shrink's desk. She stands directly behind him, staring down at his shoulders, which seem narrow and hunched when he is viewed from behind. "You don't seem so big and so wise from this angle. I'd say old and weak and confused is what you look like from here right now."

He is unperturbed by her presence, watching instead how Mary and Mohammed respond to Joy's behavior.

She walks around to the front of the desk and sits on it. "So now I have told you that you can hide nothing from God. And now, let me tell you both the difference between you and me. I have never done anything wrong that I didn't do on purpose. That's right. I admit it before God. All that I did, I did on purpose."

"Joy, why not open your Memory Book and let us not judge, but simply understand, what you have done?"

"Very well. You folks hungry, in the mood for Indian cuisine? Let me take you to a restaurant. It was a special night in my life. Maybe the most special.

"I've taken you to the place where I met the Patels. I've taken you to the place where I've met Dennis. Now you're at the place where they meet him.

"The run-up to the event began when Mrs. Patel called me and asked me to come to her condo. After she had fixed some tea she said, 'My dear Joy, I know Mr. Patel has told you that Hindus believe life has specific stages: youth when you are a student; adulthood when you build your household; then retirement and an old age where you devote yourself to spiritual things. That is where we are now in our life. For this, Mr. Patel and I are moving back to India.'

"I asked why not Hong Kong and was surprised when she said, 'We do not belong in Hong Kong. We want to die in the place we belong. We were both born in India, near Bhopal.'

"I pretended not to care, saying something like I knew it would happen sooner or later. When she asked if I wanted to come with them, I said I wanted to stay in America. 'I have a career and a boyfriend,' I told her.

"Mrs. Patel asked me about Dennis, and I explained that it was an unusual sort of relationship. He wasn't educated, all of that, but that I felt good most of the time I was with him. I said something like, 'He makes me feel safe and wanted. Like you and Mr. Patel. Different but a little bit the same.'

"She touched my shoulder and asked me if I wanted to get married while they were still in America. 'Usually Hindu marriages are arranged by parents,' she said. 'You have no parents here. We have no children. Therefore we will help you marry this fellow you call Dennis the Menace.'

"I took a deep breath and told her I would not, could not, marry Dennis. Not now, maybe never. I was not ready to raise the children of Dennis the Menace.

"She said, 'You are indeed a sensible girl. To bring a new life into this world is a serious matter indeed. So that is fine, my child. We will do the closest thing possible. We will have a party for you and this man. We will make it our going away party for when we go home to India, but also a betrothal party for you, if you would like.'

"She saw the surprised look on my face. 'Trust me, child, it will be a pretty ceremony only. Our friends will be there and they will understand.'

"That night I called Dennis to explain her idea. Hindu boys and girls can be betrothed even at infancy, with no set time to get married. 'Your father is dead and mine is dead to me,' I told Dennis, 'So Mr. Patel is sort of empowered to decide for both of us.' Once I convinced him that nothing was expected now, not even a dowry, he began to like the idea.

"And now Mohammed and Mary, let me take you to the party. It was held in a beautiful garden outside of a little Indian restaurant. A warm breeze was blowing in from the beach. You can see lights shining up into the palm trees and beautiful floral arrangements everywhere. Can you see the fires to honor each of the ten principal Hindu Gods? About thirty of the Patel's Hindu friends were there, older men and women all dressed in traditional Indian ensembles. Don't you like love colors?"

Mary looks at Dr. Abraham. "Can I answer Joy's question. I love colors."

"Thank you Mary," Joy says. "So, when Dennis and I arrived, Mrs. Patel threw her arms around me and sobbed and sobbed and sobbed. 'This is my baby,' she told her friends. 'Good fortune brought her to our shop in Hong Kong. We have made her our daughter. Tonight is a special night for her and for us! Help us celebrate!'

"Mrs. Patel looked at my hands and ankles and admired here handiwork: the traditional henna tattoos of a bride. They were the swirling symbols of deities that Mrs. Patel painted on her skin with loving care. 'You are so beautiful, my child,' she whispered, touching my cheek with her lips. She held my hand up for her friends to see. 'Look at the beautiful patterns.'

"I whispered to her, 'There is something on my mind today, on my pretend betrothal day.' 'We will talk,' she said. After all the greetings and the attention on me and Dennis, who enjoyed every minute of it, I asked Dennis to excuse us.

"Mr. Patel and Mrs. Patel and I stepped I onto a narrow stone path that lead through lush shrubs toward the parking lot. The air smelled of the ocean mixed with the aroma of Indian cooking at the restaurant in the distance. The aroma brought back the feeling I had the day I met them.

"Suddenly I felt such a great love for those two I could hardly breathe. I whispered into Mr. Patel's ear. 'I want to tell you something. The day you asked me if I was a virgin, I lied. I was not.'

"Mr. Patel laughed and said to his wife, 'Our little Joy was not a virgin.' They both laughed. She said, 'It did not matter if you were or not. We knew in an instant that you had the pure heart of a virgin. That is all that counts.'

"Mrs. Patel hugged me again. 'Now bring us your Dennis the Menace.'"

Dr. Abraham jots on his yellow pad. "So Joy, on your final night with the Patels you told them your secret. How did that make you feel?"

"They didn't care."

"I'm sorry Joy, I believe I asked how did that make you feel. What was your inner experience?"

"Me? It made me feel... I just loved the Patels even more. They accepted my nature. They loved me.

"But let me continue my story. Dennis did a lot of things on the Internet. Some of it was silly and gross, like his porno sites. But he had become very serious about avatars on the Internet. Does everybody know what that is?"

"I surely do not," Mohammed says.

Dr. Abraham, seeing that Mary is staring into space and not listening, says, "Explain for us, Joy."

"In Hindu mythology an avatar is a physical embodiment of a god. Vishnu appeared as many creatures, male and female. On the net, an avatar is sort of an alternative self. You can have a composite picture made of a person you will be on the net. It can be a different personality from yours; it can be a man if you are a woman. Dennis had several avatars. He was different people."

Staring at his hands, Dr. Abraham does not look up when he asks, "Was Dennis a woman on the Internet?"

"No. He was basically three guys: A cop, more or less himself; a de-frocked priest; and a truck driver. He showed me the pictures on the Internet. It was strange. But anyhow, on the way to the party Dennis kept saying the idea of avatars comes from Hindu mythology. He said that an avatar is the bodily manifestation of an immortal being, 'It's the opposite of a ghost. It's where the ghost controls the human while it is alive.'

"So when it came time for Mr. Patel to talk to Dennis, the three of us—me, Dennis, and Mr. Patel—were standing in a corner, sort of an awkward thing. I smiled when I looked at Dennis with his muscles and his tight haircut, not being any taller than Mr. Patel with his wild grey hair and potbelly and stooped-over shoulders.

"Mr. Patel took a deep breath. 'People complain that Hindu customs vary so much from place to place and time to time that some people say there are no set customs. For me, this is a good thing because the Gods celebrate what is in our heart at a moment in time.

"'The essential part of a betrothal is that I am empowered to give my beautiful Joy to you. And you, Dennis must treasure this gift as much as I do. Do you treasure our beautiful Joy?'

"I saw tears in his eyes for the first time. His lips trembled. He looked Mr. Patel in the eye. "I do, sir, I do promise to treasure her. Now, and when the time comes for us to be married.

"Mr. Patel said, 'In this time and place, you Joy, and Dennis are betrothed with my blessing.'

"We kissed, then stood there smiling at each other. Then Mr. Patel said, 'So now you are betrothed in the Hindu style. Do you understand our beliefs at all, Dennis?' Dennis blushed and stuttered for the first time ever in front of me. He said, 'I'm interested in avatars on the Internet and sort of got into Hindu scripture, though I don't really understand it. But I have read the Hindu Bible.'

"Mr. Patel smiled at me and then Dennis.It was his look of mischief. 'I guess I need to get that book, the Hindu Bible, because I've never read it.'

"Dennis looked surprised. 'You haven't read the Bhagavad-Gita?'

"Mr. Patel's big eyes lit up with mischief. 'You have?'

"Dennis nodded, then said,, 'Well, I've read parts of it. On the Internet.'

"Mr. Patel's bushy eyebrows went up in the little upside down V that came together on his forehead between his eyes. He smiled at Dennis and said, 'My son, the Bhagavad-Gita is not really a bible. It's a series of verses about an upcoming battle. It is really about the battle of life itself.

"Mr. Patel squeezed my hand and looked at Dennis' face like every girl must dream that their father would look at a husband to be. It was a stern look but full of love—love for me was brimming in his eyes. 'Dennis, my young friend, when she was still a girl in my eyes, Joy here spent hour after hour with me in our shop. There we would sit in my cramped little office or out on the floor with our beautiful carpets of amber and violet and blue and gold. I explained to Joy all sorts of things, karma, reincarnation, many mysterious ideas.

"He pointed up at the clear, starry sky. 'I do not have the time to do the same for you, so may I do something else? I will explain the universe as a silly little story about policemen and judges and the stars in the sky. Forgive the silliness. It will make it easier to explain dharma and karma. The more you know these ideas the more you will treasure Joy.

"Mr. Patel put his hands on our shoulders. 'Think of God as a countless host of policemen inhabiting the universe like the countless stars in the sky. Using words from TV, the cops are busting every person, every day for not behaving according to their dharma, their duty.

"'Now my friend Dennis the Menace, for a traditional Hindu dharma means a particular kind of duty, duty according to your station in what Americans call a caste system. In America, you are taught that all men are created equal. Traditional Hindus do not believe this. The cops in the sky understand how you see your duty, and they judge your deeds accordingly. Each soul is judged according to the duty it fulfills in its lives.

"'Now to the concept of karma and reincarnation and all of that. Americans and Europeans try to understand it, like the Beatles song about instant Karma. Usually they do not figure it out. Can you guess why, Dennis the Menace?'

"'Dennis looked around the crowded room at all of the chattering Indian women and men. 'Because it's from India.'

"'Mr. Patel clapped his hands together and grabbed Dennis by the shoulder. 'Joy, you have found yourself a smart man, this cop Dennis the Menace. You are exactly right. Americans get confused by Krishnas throwing flower petals and dancing in their bare feet and Yogis walking on beds of nails and all sorts of symbols of Indian culture that have nothing to do with karma or the universe.

"'I have a simple way to look at it—as you pass through many lives, many incarnations, karma dictates that you are what you are until you become what you will be. Your good deeds and bad follow you until you discover what you have done because of what you are doing. Finally those cops in the sky who have busted you so many times say to the judge, this one is becoming perfect. It is time to set this soul of yours free. This is all very mysterious, yes?'

"Dennis just looked at him.

"His bushy eyebrows made the V again. 'Am I just a crazy Indian rug salesman?'"

Leaning forward excitedly in her chair, Joy looks into Mary's eyes then Mohammed's to be sure they are listening carefully. Her voice is high pitched; the rata-tat-tat cadence conveys a joyousness she has not displayed before. "Do you know what Dennis said?"

Mary smiles. "I couldn't guess."

"To my surprise and delight, Dennis looked him in the eye and gave this answer: 'Crazy rug salesman? No. The opposite. You raised Joy. And I love her.'

"Mr. Patel looked at us standing next to each other. He gave Dennis a pat on the shoulder and me a kiss on the cheek. Then he shouted in the direction of Mrs. Patel. 'Some day this girl and boy will be bride and groom.' He pulled our heads together and whispered, 'We must get back to the party. Forget about all of this for now, my beloved Joy and her groom. Forget about blue goddesses with many arms and deities that look like elephants and enjoy our friends and our food and our drink.'

"We danced the Hindu dances. He dipped and swirled as he tried to do the traditional movements inside a crowded circle of old Indian ladies in their bright dresses and ankle bracelets of flowers. The evening had magic, the kind your mother told you about, Mary. But eventually it was time for the party to end. After some tears and long goodbyes and promises to write, I found myself in Dennis's truck."

Dr. Abraham hands Joy a glass of water. "Thank you so much Joy. You took us there with very vivid words. I believe you deserve a rest now."

"Not yet," Joy shoots back. "Let me tell everybody what happened in his truck."

Surprised, her shrink says, "Go on, we are listening."

"Once on the road, I got very quiet. Dennis said, 'What if we did get married? Maybe it would be possible for us to get married in India.' That was not my Dennis the Menace talking. It was a Miami cop falling in love with an accountant from Hong Kong. Not a good idea. 'Can I look at your gun,' I asked, wanting to summon the old Dennis the Menace back.

"He reached into the backseat and pulled his gun out of the holster. Then, abruptly, he put it back.

"I asked him why he stopped. Can anybody guess what he said?"

Mary and Mohammed and even Dr. Abraham have puzzled looks on their faces.

"He said, 'I stopped because I want us to be a normal… couple. There, I admitted it. I want to marry you. I want to stop being Dennis the Menace. Even before tonight, I'd been thinking about it. I know you have a college degree and whatever. I'm just a cop. You need a man who makes real money and can put you and the kids in a big Mac mansion and all of that. Guess what? Maybe I can. There's some security gigs out in Vegas that people I know are talking about. Lots more money there, he said. 'I can get a degree going part-time during the day, because most of the work is at night.' He went on and on about how we were going to be normal."

Tears come to Joy's eyes. "When we got back to his place, we made soft, pretty love. The kind that real lovers make. We said we loved each other."

"Thank you Joy," the psychiatrist smiles, pouring water. "You definitely deserve this now."

She nods her acceptance, tugging her choker slightly away from her skin, as if to allow her to drink more easily. "This water is so very cool on my throat."

Joy's shrink nods. "Water is life. Joy, perhaps I could speak to you in my private office." Rising slowly, his tired voice says, "Mary and Mohammed, please be comfortable. We will return quite soon."

Joy walks around Dr. Abraham's massive desk. When the door closes, Mohammed looks at Mary. "First he met privately with you and now he is meeting with Joy. What is the meaning of this? What did you talk about?"

Rising from her chair, Mary smiles her Mona Lisa smile. "It was private, Mohammed. We said many things. As for me, I'll be leavin' you now."

9.

Mohammed and Mary are staring ahead like travelers on a train clattering down an endless dark tunnel, their thoughts dark also, untouched by the bright blue sky and ocean outside Dr. Abraham's window. Their reveries are broken when Joy opens the Blue Door behind the desk and takes her usual seat between Mary and the empty chair. She is smiling, though her face is flushed.

Mary looks at her with concern. "Are you alright?"

"Yes, of course. We are all going to be—"

Just then Dr. Abraham steps through the Blue Door. He moves slowly to his desk, sits, then gazes at his time-worn hands. He touches his knuckle to the corner of his mouth, and offers in his raspy voice, "And so, the four of us are together again." He looks at Mohammed, "Joy and I, and I am sure Mary as well, are eager to hear more of your story."

"I do not wish to speak today. I have already revealed too much."

Brow furrowed, his physician shrugs. "Is that so? Tell me what you have revealed?"

"I revealed the irresponsible speed of my car, my son's drunkenness, the disgusting display of his girlfriend Gloria, many details of my story. The other facts of the story are far too painful for me even to recall, much less speak of."

"I'm certain that the facts are very painful. But that is why you are here. To be healed of your pain, your rage, you have agreed to tell your story."

Now the sonorous, measured sound of Mohammed's voice, that lawyer's voice, is matched by the words he chooses. "Perhaps that was the agreement, but I no longer can abide by it."

Yanking absently at a button of his cardigan with one hand, and jotting a note with another, Dr. Abraham does not look up. "Then I shall have to ask you to leave."

Mohammed nervously taps the knot of his tie. "Are you serious, Dr. Abraham?"

"Yes," Dr. Abraham says, lifting his eyes toward the massive White Door at the back of the office. "You may leave here as you came in."

Mohammed looks toward the door. He is silent. Joy and Mary turn their shoulders as Mohammed did to look at the door, and then quickly turn to face Dr. Abraham. The moment is awash in silence, as if all of creation awaits Mohammed's words.

"Very well then, come with me, let me take you to the parking lot outside my son's condominium. Watch me very carefully as I put the convertible top down so Nia and I could load my drunken son into my Porsche. We struggled with Zayd's weight until finally he and his mother were wedged together on the passenger seat. A bad storm passed through and light rain still fell, but I did not put the top back up. I was too angry to care.

"In fact, my anger was too great for me to bear. Blood was dripping from the cut above my eye, mixing with raindrops. I ignored the rain. The pavement in Miami smells of tar when it is wet with a soaking rain. The water stands defiantly in small eddies inside the road where constant traffic has made small track-shaped rivulets where water gathers when the street is soaking wet. You can see this if you look closely as you walk down the street. However, if you are driving, this escapes your notice. The traction of tires against the road weakens, unknown to the driver."

"Why are you telling us about the street? Did the street cause your anger, make you speed off in a rage?" Dr. Abraham asks.

Mohammed looks into Dr. Abraham's eyes. "I make excuses, perhaps. That is what Joy is thinking, true?"

Dr. Abraham interrupts the ensuing silence. "Joy?"

"The deed is done," Joy smirks, her almond-shaped eyes glistening as they stare at Mohammed. "So I don't know why excuses would matter."

"Please do not look at me like that, Joy."

"Tell your story, Mohammed. How I look at you doesn't matter either."

Mohammed taps at the knot of his tie. "I shifted into first gear and literally banged through to fourth gear, accelerating my car to the highest speed possible. I pulled out of the parking lot and made a right onto Ocean Boulevard.

"My tires were screeching, the engine was whining, my wife was begging me to slow down. 'Go slow. Please. Your eye is full of blood—can you even see? You must be careful. We are all here together,' she said.

"Just as she was speaking, it happened. Suddenly, a large car, a Mercedes, pulled out of one of the driveways. I found out later that the driver was drunk. A drunken American girl caused it all."

Mohammed suddenly leans forward. "I am mistaken. Gloria caused it all. This other drunken American girl was not the true cause. She was not even injured."

Dr. Abraham is watching Mohammed intently. "Stay focused on what happened to you and your family. The drunken girl is not relevant anymore/

Mohammed's eyes are far away, examining the wood grain of the Blue Door behind Dr. Abraham's desk as if the wood had been crafted by an ancient artisan. "What I knew at that moment was that a big silver car with the weight of a truck banged into the side of my car. It was really that driver's mistake. The drunk pulled out without looking."

As if understanding what Dr. Abraham is thinking, Mohammed says, "But so what? What does matter is that she struck the passenger side of my car with incredible force. The impact propelled my car into the lane of oncoming traffic and a second vehicle—it was a truck, I can see it now with my eyes—tried to swerve to avoid us but could not.

"Before I became unconscious, I remember the sound of my wife gasping, moaning my name. 'Mohammed, I am dying,' she said. There was this horrible sound of metal shearing off. It was a crunching, crashing sound that simply cannot be described. The police believe my son never fully woke from his drunken stupor. When at first we were hit on the side, he called for his mother. His heavy body tumbled when we were first hit, and I believe his shoulders were lodged under the dashboard of the passenger side.

"There was a horrible lurching of his mother's head, her body, as the car was hit first from the side and then from the front. I believe, but I am not sure, I saw a piece of the windshield plunge into her neck. The blood gushed everywhere. On me, on Zayd, it sprayed and gushed everywhere. Dear God, this was my beloved Nia. She is destroyed. Destroyed.

"God understands the pain I felt in my heart. I know now that I am a righteous man because I was able to see visions of God during the time I believed I was dead. Unlike the wicked, I did not see visions of hell. I was taught that my soul entered a soul sleep until Judgment Day. But it appears I was not dead, and I awoke before judgment."

Dr. Abraham cocks his eye. "How do you know you are not being judged right now, right here?"

Mohammed looks his physician deeply in the eyes. "Because I am among infidels."

Although he is looking in Mary's direction, Mohammed's eyes, fixed and vacant, betray that he is talking to himself now. It's as if nobody is present but him. "I am a human being," he says, "created in God's image, composed of a body of clay and a spirit that can communicate with God. I believe that the crash sent me to a place where only my spirit mattered. A brilliant light pulled me to a place where I no longer heard the awful sounds of the crash and the pitiful sounds of my wife and son dying beside me."

Mohammed continues to talk only to himself. There are others in the room, and they are listening, not as an audience being addressed by a speaker, but more as eavesdroppers to another person's private conversation with his most intimate confidant. "My soul resided briefly somewhere between the darkness of our physical being and the light of the eternal. That is all I know. I do not understand where I am now."

"Thank you," Mohammed's physician says. "May I explain something to Mary and Joy?"

Mohammed nods agreement.

Dr. Abraham casts his soft, watery brown eyes on Joy and Mary. "The word is Barzakh. Barzakh is the period of time between death and the end of time. Some believe that souls reside there until the Day of Judgment and resurrection."

Mary peers past Joy to Mohammed. "So it's sort of limbo? Is that what it is? And if the four of us are actually dead, could we be there now?"

Mohammed's eyes spring to life as he says, "Perhaps we would be there if we were dead. But despite the ideas of our physician, we all know that we are not dead."

Dr. Abraham jots a note on his yellow pad. "Are you sure, Mohammed? Is it not true that the inter-world of Barzakh somewhat resembles dreaming? Joy, did you not once say to me that these sessions seem like a dream?"

Joy nods. "Yes, I did."

"And Mary, did you not also say that—"

Mohammed's deep voice rises in anger. "Please stop this kind of comparison, doctor. Barzakh is not a dream. It is where the soul of the dead is liberated from all of the bodily layers. It is a place where the soul can awaken and become aware of its true nature."

Dr. Abraham looks at Mary. "I will take your point Mohammed if you allow me one more comparison. May I?"

Mohammed's upper lip curls with an anger that he is trying hard to control. "Must you?"

Dr. Abraham cocks his brow. "In fact, yes, I must. The inter-world period would remind the typical American of the limbo some Christians talk about."

Mohammed's voice is impatient, harsh. "I cannot say what others believe. But no matter if the day of resurrection lasts countless of thousands of years or just an instant of time, on that day my soul—and my wife's, and my son's— will find eternal life in paradise."

"Will you encounter the Madhi, the rightly guided one during his reign in the last days? How about the prophet Jesus when he ushers in the final judgment? Mary and Mohammed, the scriptures you claim to believe both describe the role of Jesus. Would you expect Jesus to appear here in my chamber?"

Joy looks at her watch, looks up at Dr. Abraham, and looks down again at her watch. Gazing at the face of it she says, "How long are we going to spend dwelling on these myths about how the world will begin and end? Are you really asking us if Jesus will appear here, Dr. Shrink? Or are you just proving a point that the Koran mentions Jesus?"

"Is that true, Dr. Abraham?" Mary asks.

Joy answers Mary's question. "Of course Muslims and Christians and Jews believe many of the same myths. Mr. Patel told me that," Joy says.

"But right now I want to know more about his accident. I want to hear how the cars collided." Sliding toward the edge of her chair, Joy looks at Dr. Abraham.

"Did Mohammed ever see pictures of the wreck? Sometimes they make the driver look at the pictures they take at the scene of fatal accidents. Dennis once showed me a collection he had of pictures of fatal crashes. Cops take them with their own cameras and show them around.

"Dennis said nothing smells stranger than a bad accident scene. You see the broken glass and the tire marks and the bodies of people sometimes, but he said there is this weird combination of smells. Gasoline, burning rubber from where the tires skidded, sometimes you smell that the upholstery burned. Even the rainwater on the street smells strange after an accident. He told me this when he was showing me his disgusting, gory pictures. He—"

The psychiatrist leans forward across his desk and holds his hand in front of Joy's face. "Stop." In a stern voice he says, "Joy, why are you interrupting with this ghastly talk about accident scenes?"

"I'm not sure. Probably because the point of this is that accidents are gruesome. We shouldn't be distracted by this guesswork about the afterlife. It seems to me—"

"I have another theory for why you are interrupting. You want attention. Like a little baby. Is that what you wanted just now when you interrupted? Is that why you did it? So that you would get attention?"

Still perched near the edge of her chair, Joy crosses her legs. "No. I want to hear about Mohammed. Not Islam. So—"

Jotting a note, the physician says, "Show us your watch, Joy."

"What?"

The psychiatrist leans forward to look at Joy's watch. "You keep making a point of looking at your watch. It is very pretty with the thin gold chain and the pearly watch face.

"Mohammed and Mary, I'm sure you would agree that Joy's watch is part of her feminine mystique. Maybe the group hasn't given Joy's watch enough attention. Maybe the group hasn't given Joy enough attention. Let's fix that. Hold your hand out and show Mohammed and Mary your watch."

Surprise in her eyes, Joy says, "I'm not going to do that." She glares at Dr. Shrink.

The psychiatrist ignores her, looking instead at the papers on his desk. After a moment he shakes his head and says, "Yes you will. I require it."

Joy leans back in her chair with such force that the front mahogany legs raise off the tufted oriental carpet and she loses her balance. "No."

"Very well, I must ask you to leave," he says sternly.

"What? Are you serious?" she asks, perplexed.

"Yes."

"I think you are serious."

The psychiatrist jerks his massive head up and toward the door. "Of course I am serious. Leave. Go. Exit through the White Door right now and never come back. Or do as I have asked and show Mohammed and Mary your watch."

Mary and Mohammed look away. Joy and the psychiatrist lock eyes. The silence lasts and lasts and lasts as Joy keeps looking at the door, out the window, and then at her shrink.

Finally, Joy thrusts her wrist toward Mohammed's face, then Mary's. "This is stupid. See, this is my watch."

The psychiatrist sits up straight in his chair and nods approvingly at Joy. "And why is the watch so important, Joy?"

"I don't know."

"I'll accept that. Who gave it to you?"

"My brother."

"And where did he get it?"

"He stole it from my mother. He gave it to me the night before I left Hong Kong to come to America."

"What did he say when he gave it to you?"

"I don't remember."

"Try."

"I don't—"

"Joy, if you are going to stay here with me and Mohammed and Mary, you simply must do as I say. Please try to remember what your brother, he was your half-brother of course, said when he handed you the watch."

Defiantly, Joy fights tears until she finally says, "Let me take you to a place where he held me in his arms and said, I will think of you for all time.' That is what he said to me."

Jotting notes in his illegible scribble, the psychiatrist says, "Thank you. Memories of your family are difficult for you. But let me make one more request of you before our discussion resumes where you interrupted it. Will you promise to obey my request?"

"I need to know what it is first," Joy says through a sob. Her accent is suddenly very heavy.

"No. You must promise to do it because I have asked you."

Lips pursed petulantly, Joy fights back sobs. "I will do as you ask, oh mighty Dr. Shrink."

"While Mohammed is speaking, do not look at your watch. While Mary is speaking, do not look at your watch. And while I am speaking, do not look at your watch. Is that understood?" Joy cannot stifle the haughty look on her face. "Yes."

In his raspy voice, Dr. Abraham continues to discuss religion as if the interchange with Joy never happened. "As in the Judgment Day scenarios of other Middle Eastern religions, the dead are resurrected and the dead are judged. The Islamic Paradise, al-Jannah, is…"

Dr. Abraham interrupts himself. He pointedly stares out onto the beach. "It is nice to have this window for us to look out during our sessions. Let's all look out the window together."

Confused, the patients turn their heads toward the window. "Describe the beach, Mary."

Mary speaks slowly in her softest, prettiest voice. "I can do that. The beach is a delightful place with pretty pastels of blue and green, the thick green plants and the beautiful palm trees, the white sun-kissed clouds in the sky, the sound of the waves, the feel of the warm sun on our skin. The—"

"Thank you, Mary," Dr. Abraham says. "The place al-Jannah may be like that, a delightful garden reserved for those favored by God. Did you go there, Mohammed?" Dr. Abraham asks.

"I do not know."

"Are you there now, Mohammed?"

"No. I have said that many times."

"Indeed you have." Dr. Abraham's tired eyes and lips wrinkle in a wry smile. "I think that if you had gone to such a wonderful place, you would remember. Perhaps you went to hell instead. Did you? Can you describe it for us?"

"I did not go there and of course I cannot describe it, doctor."

Dr. Abraham shrugs. "Let me describe An-Nar, then. It is where the soul's punishment consists of being far from God. To be far from God is considered to be the worst chastisement in virtually all religions that focus upon deities including, my dear Joy, Hinduism. Do any of you feel close to God right now?

"Mohammed?"

Mohammed strokes his mustache and shakes his head. "No. I do not."

"Mary?"

Mary shakes her head balefully. "No."

As Joy looks at the patients on either side of her, studying them, she stiffens her posture in her chair. "I am not sure."

"Joy is so honest, admitting that she is uncertain. Would you care to go to Mohammed's Hell for a while? Joy? Mary?"

The psychiatrist takes a breath, then reaches for the copy of the Koran on his credenza. "The Koran does provide some vivid descriptions of hell, the Pilgrimage for example. 'Garments of fire shall be cut, and there shall be poured over their heads boiling water whereby whatsoever is in their bellies and their skins shall be melted; for them await hooked iron rods; as often as they desire in their anguish to come forth from it, they shall be restored into it, and taste the chastisement of the burning.'

"Gruesome stuff. Like an accident scene." Dr. Abraham looks into the eyes of each patient. "But suppose it is not the body but rather the mind alone that is tormented in hell. Is that possible?"

Eyes downcast, the three say nothing.

"Mohammed, suppose this is hell and Joy's words, the very sound of her voice, are going to torment you forever. No fire, no iron rods, just the sound of her voice."

Mohammed heaves a great sigh. "This is nonsense. This is blasphemy."

"But don't some Muslims believe that if a believer entered Hell, after a while his imperfections could be burned away, Mohammed? Could it be that Joy is doing that for you? So many things could be true about eternity. Time and therefore eternity are scientific concepts, on the other hand heaven and hell may only be myths dreamed up by Pagans and perpetuated by fools and shamans and charlatans," Dr. Abraham shrugs, carefully placing the mysterious writing back in his drawer.

Joy's rata-tat-tat talking fills the room. "I am totally confused by what just happened."

The corner of Dr. Abraham's lip turns up as if he is trying to smile but cannot. "What happened that confused you?"

"Why are you are trying to convince Mary and Mohammed that they are dead?"

"I'm citing Islamic scripture. That is all I'm doing." Dr. Abraham scans all three faces before him to get their attention. "Let me remind all of you that I am not a priest or minister or rabbi or mullah or anything of the sort. I'm a psychiatrist. I am not trying to understand your religion. I'm trying to understand your mind.

"I was wondering if Mohammed remembers what happened immediately after his accident. But perhaps it sounds to you like I'm probing his beliefs about eternity. So let's turn our attention to you, Joy. Do you feel like you might be dead and here for eternity? Don't tell me what you think. Tell me what you feel."

"I am the youngest one here, I am single, and my story so far is all about sex. Dr. Abraham, suppose for a second that you are God and this is eternity and we keep reliving our lives here in this room."

Joy tosses her head from side to side, looking first at Mohammed and then at Mary and back to Mohammed again. Finally, she stares directly at Dr. Abraham. "That is possible, right, Dr. Abraham? Inside this fantasy premise that we are here for eternity, it is possible that you are God. Yes?"

"God or perhaps an embodiment of God, if you believe God is omnipresent and takes on various forms as a Hindu might believe. Yes, that is possible."

Joy nods in satisfaction. "Good. So this is eternity; you are an incarnation of God, and you are letting me talk about sex. It is obvious that each and every one of us has sinned, even if all we knew about each other was what we have said in our stories so far. But we seem to keep going anyway. So let me ask a silly question: Since nothing seems to be wrong, does that mean I can have sex for eternity?"

"Absolutely," Dr. Abraham says, his voice suddenly full of playful energy.

Joy absent-mindedly tugs at her choker and says, "Erotic for eternity. I guess that is my desire. Want to know why? Here's part of the reason." Handing her Blackberry to Mohammed, she says, "I brought a picture of Dennis."

Mohammed looks at the screen. Seeing Mohammed's confusion, Dr. Abraham thrusts out his hand. "Please hand that to me instead, Joy. Give it to me right now."

She obeys. Dr. Abraham takes the phone and tosses it in a desk drawer. "If you want to show pictures, do it the way Mary did. Printed on paper. We're all used to that now."

He looks at Mohammed. "For now let's follow the path Mohammed took after his horrible accident. He is not sure what happened, he is not sure what is happening now, but he believes he spent an interlude of some sort in another place. True, Mohammed?"

"Yes."

"Let's talk about that other place. For the moment, let us call it eternity. Joy, didn't you just say you want to spend eternity having sex?"

"Yes."

"Is that truly what you dream of for your eternity? Dream of in the sense of wish for? Are you really wishing to have intercourse over and over again for eternity?"

Joy looks her shrink in the eye. "Of course not every minute literally. And you know that, Dr. Shrink."

"You're right, your shrink knows that." Joy's shrink cocks his brow inquisitively. "Then tell us: What do you wish your eternity will be like? Take us there."

Joy begins sobbing, "I want to be held in the arms of someone who will keep me safe. Forever. Safe."

"And who will be the person to hold you?"

Eyes closed, Joy shakes her head.

"You don't know, do you Joy?"

"No." Sobbing, she continues to shake her head.

"Your shrink knows that, too. Joy, I want you to say the word that is in your mind right now. Do not think. I am not asking you any question. Just say the word on your mind at this instant. Say it."

"Vishnu."

"Very good. Now what words are on your mind?"

"The all-powerful one. The power of the universe will make me safe."

Mary begins sobbing.

Mohammed bites his lip.

Dr. Abraham allows silence to sit in the room until he says, "Thank you, Joy. I think Mary and Mohammed share your need for a powerful force to keep their eternity safe.

"In fact let me ask you, Mohammed. What do you wish your eternity will be like?"

"I cannot answer such a question, doctor."

"Why not?"

"It is far too complex."

"Do you expect eternity to be complex? What does complexity even mean when we talk about eternity?"

Mohammed stares sullenly into a distant place outside of the room. "I do not know. Once again you are posing silly riddles, Dr. Abraham."

"You are over-analyzing my question, Mohammed. Respond from your heart. To say it another way and more precisely, allow your soul to speak."

"Doctor, my soul does not speak directly except unto God."

"Very well. Just say single words if that will help. And so I ask you again: What do you wish your eternity will be like?"

"Dr. Abraham, I cannot answer. I am trying to answer, but I cannot."

"Is it because you are not sure who you will spend it with?"

"Perhaps that is part of it."

Watching, Mohammed puts his head into his hands. Dr. Abraham speaks in the softest voice he can muster, "I understand. When I ask people who they would wish to spend eternity with, it often causes confusion and even anguish. This is because of the troublesome fact that the people do not belong together, they—"

Mohammed interrupts. "How do you mean that they do not belong together?"

"They do not belong together in the sense that on this earth they would never be brought together for any reason. Perhaps that is true in your case, Mohammed. So let us approach this from a different direction. All I want in your answer is adjectives. Let me ask the question this way: How will eternity feel? Do not think about your answer. Start talking. How will eternity feel?"

"Warm."

"Tell me more."

"Safe. Quiet. Peaceful. Full of beauty."

"Are you describing a place where your rage will be gone? That is what you are here to be cured of, isn't that what you said? Rage?"

"Yes. I want to be rid of this rage."

"And that will take you to a tranquil place where you are at peace with yourself and the world. Perhaps like the mosque you recalled from your earliest memory?"

"Exactly like that."

"And now Mary, you have had lots of time and you've heard the other answers. Open your book of dreams for us. What is your dream for eternity? What do you wish your eternity will be like?"

"I loved Mohammed's answer. I want to be warm and safe and quiet. Oh, so very quiet and peaceful. I also want to be surrounded by beauty in a place where I can make things happen magically. I pray that there will be no more pain for me, no more surgery. And 'tis true what you are about to remind me, no more sadness. No more guilt. But for me, there is no confusion about whom I will spend eternity with. I want to spend it with my Little One and my Precious One. To be with those two up in the safe clouds, only we three, that is what I dream of."

"Ah, that is interesting. Thank you, Mary. And Mohammed. And Joy. Now, do the three of you wonder what my answer would be? Aren't you curious about my ruminations on eternity?"

He looks at Mohammed. "Mohammed, all of you, aren't you curious about what your physician dreams of .Don't you wonder how your shrink wants to spend his eternity? Then ask me, Mohammed.''"

They all lean forward like children about to ask a teacher a question, but Mohammed speaks first. "Let me ask the question the way you finally put it to me, Dr. Abraham. How will eternity feel?"

Dr. Abraham looks out his huge window at the beautiful ocean lapping against the beach. "I want to spend eternity in a place where I am warm. Safe. Quiet. Peaceful. I want it to be a place full of beauty."

Mohammed smiles. "Perhaps like the mosque I recalled from my earliest memory?"

"Very much so, Mohammed, except in my case when I say I want it to be a place full of beauty, I mean a place where my beautiful mother is with me again."

10.

Outside it is a bright and windy day and the hot air is full of the scent of the ocean, salty and clean. After some time passes, Dr. Abraham jots a brief note, puts his ornate gold and silver pen down, and looks at Joy. "We are making progress, each one of you. And so today, our time belongs to Joy," he says in a cheery voice. "So Joy, please continue to share your Memory Book as you have begun to do so generously."

"Thank you," Joy says. She hands Mary, Dr. Abraham, and Mohammed a document. "This little book is just like Mary's but the title isn't Joy's Story. The title is Generic Cops."

There are two images on the cover. At the top is a picture of a muscular, tan, pleasant-looking man in baggy blue swim trunks with a loud floral print and a tight, sleeveless white tank top.

She points at the picture on Mohammed's copy. "If you can ignore that wife-beater tee-shirt, your competition in heaven looks pretty good."

The shoulders of Mohammed's black suit shrug grudgingly. His brow furrows as he studies the picture. "He is a handsome young man, a bit like… my son. Ah, in any event, to be handsome is a blessing. Your Dennis is a lucky man for that, at least."

"And speaking of lucky, the picture below is my brother—the one that Dennis reminds me of. He does look like a real Chinaman in this photo, and the uniform looks ridiculous."

Joy rests her hand on Mary's knee and shows the pictures of Dennis and her brother to Mary, who smiles broadly. "I can see the resemblance between the two of them. They both have nice smiles, big shoulders, sort of macho in a way."

Watching the exchange between Mary and Joy, Dr. Abraham smiles. "So this is the brother who stole your mother's watch so you could have it in America, I assume. What is his name?"

"Wa Cho."

"Why did he have to steal the watch? Why didn't your mother give it to you?"

"After that day I put on the makeup and began working for the Patels and practically living with them, things got—well, I guess you could say my parents disowned me. I couldn't bear going back to their apartment.

"By that point, Wa Cho was the only one speaking to me. He felt sorry for me, maybe blamed himself for the way my parents treated me. He and I had a love-hate relationship, but we stayed in contact with each other. We exchanged letters, sometimes even spoke on the phone."

"I see. Very well, please tell us more of your story, Joy."

"Where should I start?"

"Start anywhere," Joy's shrink instructs her. "Start with Wa Cho."

"No. Wa Cho is a story unto himself. But he is in Hong Kong and that life is behind me." Joy stares intently at the cover of 'Generic Cops.' "And now let me take everyone to the place where my life changed for eternity." She begins to read from the document:

Let me take you to a place, it's really a time and place, where Dennis and I had been dating for almost a year. That's the longest relationship I have ever had with a man. He called me one day at work and invited me to go with him to Las Vegas. "Know it's sudden," he said. "I got some friends there, and I want them to meet you. Maybe we can even get married while we are out there."

We actually talked about getting married. Dennis put it as What if scenarios, I guess you'd call them. What if I won twenty grand, What if there was a Hindu wedding chapel with all the Gods and flowers and all of that right there in Vegas. Maybe we can call the Patels and put them on a speaker phone or some way for all of us to talk.'

I said, "What if there is no twenty grand? What if we don't get married, then what were we going to do?"

"We're going to meet my buddies, then gamble, then hang out just you and me. You've seen the commercials for Vegas, right? What happens here stays here? We'll make something happen."

I said yes, right on the spot. I had never been to Vegas, and I had never met any of Dennis's friends. We flew on an airplane. Dennis called them the bus with wings. We took the first flight and got there in the morning. I think it was 7:15 a.m.

Dennis rented some big, ugly truck. The truck smelled of cigarettes, like the odor in a bar after it closes. I made him stop to get an air freshener. Soon we had a Joe Camel air freshener dangling from the mirror. He said we were going to take a ride in the desert. I assumed it involved some sexual adventure he wanted to have. I figured he'd tie me up in the hot sun or something.

As we crossed the desert, the pinkish blue sky appeared over the approaching dry hills and mountains. Dennis patted me on the knee then pointed in the general direction of the brightening sky. "I'm heading up to a spot out east of Vegas first. Gotta see a buddy, a man about a horse as you might say. Then we'll be zoomin' to Las Vegas just as fast as I can get us there."

I gave him a peck on the cheek. "That was a nice kiss. We're gettin' more and more normal, don't you notice that?"

"I don't know what normal means, Dennis. But if you mean we are getting to know each other, then yes."

"It's not all about sex is what I mean. Since I met the Patels and we had the engagement party, I'm changin'. I might even convert to Hinduism."

"I'm tired of being a Pagan. Not like the white supremacy dudes in jail," he nodded with the Tom Cruise smile, "but a Pagan like not believing in Jesus and all of that. My mother was a Jesus freak and my father pretended to be, but it was all crap. So I am going to convert to Hinduism. You did it, right?"

"Not really. Mr. Patel said all I needed to do is worship a deity and follow the dietary laws. Do you really think you could be a vegetarian, Dennis?"

"Not sure. All I'm saying is that I want to be with you and like you, and I want us to be normal."

And believe me, "I can tell you I am serious about movin' to Vegas. I'm finished with Miami. I decided last week. That's why we're coming out here. I want to see if you like it."

The stop out in the desert consisted of a mysterious rendezvous— Dennis hopped out of the truck, jogged into a run-down shack. When I say run-down, I mean it. It had broken windows and an old junked car and sofa in the front, like in a movie. He went inside for what seemed like a long time, then came out laughing and then hopped back into the truck and drove off, squealing wheels..

"That took a while," I said.

He patted my knee. *"Shoulda had those guys come out to meet you, but once they came out and saw you I probably couldn't get rid of 'em."*

"Who are they?"

"Used to be Miami cops. Now they're doin' contract security work, mostly for the casinos. Make twice what they made as cops, plus all kinds of extras—chicks and so forth. The chicks ain't in my game plan, I swear, Joy. But the money is. And I'll go to school out here and get a degree. We're goin' to India for a real wedding at Mr. and Mrs. Patel's house. That's no bullshit."

Oddly, he seemed weak when he was being serious and sincere, and it almost was a turn-off. I liked the wild stuff. Still, I wrapped my arm around his neck and said, "Don't worry about that for now. Let's enjoy this little vacation."

It was about noon when we arrived in Las Vegas. We had reservations at Bally's, Dennis's favorite Casino. We settled into the room, with me hanging two dresses neatly in the closet, Dennis playing absently with the TV controls. "Great cable up here. Pay-per-view X-rated, whole nine yards" he said. "But this is even better." Dennis pulled out a wad of what looked to be 20 or more $100 bills. "I'll probably lose it all."
I eyed the money warily. "You don't make that much money."

"I told you I'm changin' things around for my little Joy. But right now I'm here to gamble."

Glancing at the watch dangling from her wrist, Joy says, "Dr. Abraham, can I interrupt my reading to say something that just came to my mind? He—"

"Of course," Dr. Abraham says.

"Dennis would joke about death. He said most cops joke about death, especially at accident scenes where they see people mangled up."

Dr. Abraham notices Mohammed closing his eyes momentarily at the mention of accident scenes. Joy does not.

"So—and I guess I never saw the coincidence in this, because this happened on the last day we were together," she pauses a moment. Joy becomes animated and her voice takes on a faster, higher-pitched rata-tat-tat cadence. "He took me into this big noisy betting room with horse races and boxing matches and football games playing on TVs all around. There was a big scoreboard with red and green and yellow lights that covered all the walls and had names of horses and teams and people also.

"Then he said, 'Vegas is like being inside a pinball machine, all lights and buzzers and noise and bouncing around. I told you that heaven would be Vegas, right? See that scoreboard? See that guy over there in the cashier window? When you die you go to Vegas and Saint Peter is in a cashier window with a long grey beard and a long white robe and little laptop computer. You tell St. Pete who you are then he runs a program that sorts all of the names of people you have known in your life.'

"He grabbed my arm and pointed up at the scoreboard. 'A scoreboard just like that lights up with the names of the people you will be with forever. I'll know for sure I'm in hell if my father's name shows up on the scoreboard,' he said.

"Dennis had wild eyes when he got excited for any reason. They were wide as saucers now. 'After you know you're going to hell, the pain gets worse and worse each time a new name comes on the little scoreboard. St. Pete, I gotta put up with these bastards day after day for eternity? Goddamn, dis is hell, AIN'T IT?' He said it with his fake hillbilly... accent, I think that's the word I want. Dennis could make me laugh."

Dr. Abraham smiles. "Well, that is a truly creative vision of the afterlife." Smiling more broadly, he adds, "And I thought I knew them all."

In her loud, rata-tat-tat voice Joy says, "It made sense to me when he said it. Hell is where you spend eternity with people you can't bear to be with. Heaven is when you never have to be with those people."

Joy makes a point of looking at Mary. "Do you know what else Dennis said to me that day? He said until he met me he figured he'd go to hell or if he got to heaven he would be alone. Then he wrapped his arm around me and said, 'I'm changing my ways because I want to see St. Pete's scoreboard with only one word on it—Joy.' He gave me the sweetest kiss." Holding her fingertips to her lips, Joy fights back a sob. "He picked me up and twirled me around toward the scoreboard and said, 'Instead of that scoreboard up there with all the names and bets, the only word on St. Pete's scoreboard would be Joy. All of the TVs will have the same picture of your beautiful face.' Dennis said that. So let me begin reading again."

Mohammed, Mary, and of course you Dr. Abraham, let me ask you a question. Ever been to a casino?" Without waiting for an answer, Joy says, "Let me take you to one. It's big and noisy and lights are going off, and gambling is stupid so the place has the feel of a circus where clowns are machines robbing people of their money. Let me read.

I watched him for a while before wandering off to shop. "Be back around six," I said. I charged a new negligee, assuming, correctly, that it excited him. It was a low-cut red teddy theme with tap pants, something I felt confident Dennis would like.

After a nap and a shower, I changed into the shortest skirt I had, then rejoined Dennis in the casino. After trekking around for ten minutes I spotted him chain-smoking cigarettes and playing black jack. Across from Dennis stood a rather heavyset dealer, stuffed into an undersized white tuxedo shirt.

When I walked up to Dennis, he smiled and put his arm around me, kissing me on the forehead. I bit him on his shoulder – he was wearing an upscale version of the wife-beater tee-shirt he's wearing in the picture. "Winning?"

"I'm not losing. For me, that's the same as winning. Have you played anything?"

"I played the slot machines for a while. I guess a couple hours of shopping and slots is enough excitement for one day."

"I hope not," he whispered. "I have some excitement planned." He looked at the dealer. "Hit me." The dealer nodded obediently and slid the queen of spades onto Dennis's pile, where it joined the five of diamonds and nine of clubs. "Busted," Dennis shrugged. "Hope my luck improves in our room. Let's go."

I was hoping for some dinner but — well — Dennis would probably want to go out later. As we made our way back to the hotel room, he focused his attention on me and began kissing me on the neck, embracing me as we waited for the elevator. Dennis made it clear he was expecting some sex, so as soon as we got into the room, I excused myself and took my new outfit into the bathroom. I emerged soon after in the hot, hot, hot red negligee.

I walked over to the bed where Dennis was sprawled with his shirt, shoes and socks strewn on the floor beside him. I always liked the look of his bare, muscular chest, and without planning to, I leaned over and kissed him softly on the lips.I stood back and let Dennis give me a once over. "I bought this today as a treat for you."

Dennis was flattered and appreciative. "I can't believe you did that for Dennis the Menace."

I smiled at him. "Well, I did."

"Guess what? I bought a treat for you, too."

He gave me his Tom Cruise smile and pecked me on the cheek like he did on our date at the beach. He did have a Dennis the Menace child in him that could be sweet and soft as well as mischievous. He pulled out a small box with wrapping paper from India. And in the box was—"

Joy stops. She softly touches the locket on her necklace. "This. It is the Goddess Mohini, one of the avatars of Vishnu." She holds her face toward Mary and then Mohammed and finally toward her shrink so they can see the intricate gold handiwork.

"Dennis had secretly conspired with the Patels to buy it for me. It was unbelievably sweet. And a surprise. We were definitely falling in love."

A tear wells up in Joy's eye. "Love? How could I be so wrong! You'll see when I keep reading."

"Please," Joy's shrink says to her.

After I looked at the gift and kissed him, his voice became hesitant. "I brought another treat, too. But I can't decide if I should give it to you."

"What is it?" I didn't have a clue. My first guess was a sex toy. A vibrator, cherry-flavored condoms, something like that.

"Before I give it to you, you have to swear that the treat will be our little secret."

Now my voice grew hesitant. "As long as it's legal and doesn't leave marks." I tried to smile.

"No marks. But not legal either."

"Then I don't know, Dennis. I'm a certified public accountant. I'm on a green card. One illegal slip, and they'll ship me back to Hong Kong."

"It's up to you."

"What is it?" My curiosity, as always, was getting the best of me.

"Our secret. It has to be our secret."

"At least tell me first."

Dennis reached into his pocket and pulled out a small plastic bag. I recognized the white powder. My neck streaked scarlet through my wheat-colored skin.

"Coke. That's cocaine. Dennis, you're a police officer. What on earth—"

"It's a treat, a rare treat. Believe me, Joy, I'm not a cokehead. I just got this stuff this morning. Like I said, my friends do security work out here and they said, dude, you gotta do just a little bit of coke out here, it's like an initiation. They made arrangements to get this great room at a price I can handle. While you were shopping, I was partyin' with those guys, maybe we did a couple of lines. I partied with them a little. Give some to your lady, they said. That's what I'm doin' Joy. You can do some coke with me, or not. It's up to you."

He got up from the bed and walked over to the low-slung, honey-colored chest of drawers that ran the length of the room. He began taking his pants off. "Mind?" He asked after the fact.

Silently, I watched him strip to his jockey shorts. He kicked his pants in the direction of the chair next to the bed, where they landed in a heap, then prepared two lines of coke, glancing occasionally at his reflection in the mirror. I saw that he was hard. His chest was crimson with excitement.

Already, just thinking about it, I felt that weird sexual rush. I could feel a bit of wetness on my new negligee when he glanced over his shoulder at me. "Just a little. Only one line each. I've got it ready. Just one line each. At least come over and watch me do mine."

I moved beside him, touching his shoulder. I thought about all the stories I'd heard back in Hong Kong, the one-time opium capital of the world, about sex when you're high on cocaine. I watched the line of white powder disappear.

"Never hurts to try anything once," I said, then did my first ever line of cocaine.

The effect was immediate. He took my hand, and we walked back over to the bed.

"I'm only doing one line, ok?" I said.

"One line is plenty."

I bit him playfully on his shoulder. He didn't say anything. We sat on the bed for what seemed like a long time. Finally he beckoned for me to slide over next to him, which I did. He laid me down slowly, kissing my lips. He moved his kisses from my mouth to my neck to my stomach, to my thigh. Then he parted my legs.

He pulled off his shorts, moved onto me, and entered me. "We'll keep your things on," he whispered.

"Good, feels good," I answered, also in a whisper.

Dennis sensed the responsiveness of my arms, the tension in my legs. We moved faster and faster together.

Suddenly, somewhere inside of the moment, I got distracted worrying about my green card. Strange, so strange, that I should think of how hard Mrs. Patel had worked to bring me to America. I decided that neither the high nor the sex had been worth the risk.

Dennis seemed to sense that something had happened in my mind. He breathed a short sigh and slowed his thrusts for a minute or so. But he was gradually lost again in his own desire.

That's when I asked him to stop. I whispered at first. "I want to stop. Please."

He stopped for a split second then started again.

This time I shouted for him to stop. "I said STOP."

"What?" he said.

"Stop," I said. "Stop right now."

"No way, I'm about to get off."

I remembered some things from long ago, when I was a little girl, and suddenly I went cold. I wiggled and kicked, trying to get my knee into his groin if I could. Anything to make it all end. But instead of making him stop what he was doing to me, it made him more excited. So then I rolled from side to side and thumped my fists on his neck and finally he couldn't stay inside of me. Finally we both rolled over on our backs and lay there, separated by a foot or two of Las Vegas hotel bed.

"If you need more date-rape drama, I can give it to you," he said. He got up, crossed the room, and got his gun. "This is an automatic, and it's loaded. See."

He showed me the bullets in the magazine.

I kicked it, taunting, "So what?" For some reason I just kicked it. It fell out of his hand to the floor. I could smell his sweat, I could hear his panting, I could see the anger in his eyes.

Joy looks up from her story and says to Mary, "Then, for some strange reason, he started looking for his underwear on the floor." Looking at Dr. Abraham, she continues, "I'll stop my story there."

"No," the psychiatrist says, "please continue."

"I don't want to say any more just now. Let me tell this in episodes like Mary is doing. You're letting Mohammed take his time and tell his story the way he wants. Why can't I?"

"Because right now your shrink insists you continue to the finish," Dr. Abraham's gravel voice shouts. "It is time you tell your story."

"I'm embarrassed and ashamed, and this is making it worse. You know that, Dr. ...Abraham. See? I showed you respect. I will try to stop calling you Dr. Shrink. I do respect you. Please respect me." Joy turns her head to Mohammed and then to Mary. "I won't tell this story until you convince me that we are actually dead. Then it won't matter."

Dr. Abraham rises up in his chair and glares at Joy. "You must tell it now."

Silence in the room.

"Very well," Joy says. She looks at the screen as if planning to continue reading, then suddenly throws her document on the floor. "I don't want to read this."

The shrink looked at her with his watery eyes. "Then tell us."

"No."

"You must."

Joy looks at her watch. "My time is up."

"We have eternity," the shrink says. "Tell us the story in your own words. Just now you threw that little computer on the floor because you know you cannot really hide behind it. Not in this place. You know that, don't you Joy?"

"Yes."

"So therefore do not read your story. Tell it. Tell it from your heart. From your very soul. Make us feel it. Take all of us there. Can you?"

The rasping voice of Joy's shrink is as loud as she has ever heard it. "Your shrink is a tired old man. I can barely speak. Make me feel it. It is better for you if all of us in this room feel the fear and the anguish and the pain. Make all of us the victim of what happened to you."

Joy sits erect. Tears glisten in her eyes. She focuses her thoughts. "Like I said, for some strange reason Dennis started looking for his underwear on the floor. He dropped to the floor with a thud and started feeling around, on his hands and knees. I grabbed the gun off the floor, pointing it at him. 'Hey, rape-date, lookie here. Who has the gun now, oh mighty

Dennis the Menace? Is it Joy the former virgin?' He told me to give him the gun."

"Did you?" Dr. Abraham says.

"Yes."

Her shrink cocks his brow. "And then?"

"He threw my body back onto the bed. He held the gun in one hand and put his other hand on my neck. Then, I felt something cool on my abdomen and then on my vagina. He was stroking me with the gun. He dragged it across my breasts. The metal was cold. Then he started to put it inside of me.

"I said take your hands off and I'll do myself. He handed me the gun and said 'No problem,' making me think that the whole rape scene thing was over. But then he grabbed my neck and started shaking me, pushing me back down on the bed. He had done it before, so I—"

A tear sits in Joy's eye. She falls silent.

"You must continue," Dr. Abraham says softly.

"But I, I… I don't know what to say next."

The psychiatrist nods a fatherly acknowledgment of what Joy was trying to do. "Let me help. Dennis and you were passionate. When two people make love to fulfill their passion, the moment is very intense. It is like two wrestlers tumbling in sweaty disarray in an effort to subdue their opponent, and thereby subdue themselves. Dennis had many flaws but a lack of passion was not among them, was it, Joy?"

"No."

Dr. Abraham looks down at his hands. "Even when the two of you weren't doing your silly bondage thing, making love to him was like fighting with him. Is that true, Joy?"

Tears fill Joy's eyes. Her voice grows soft again. "Yes, yes. It was like fighting. He would press me so tight, kiss me so hard, look so far into my eyes, I felt like I had to retaliate. Sometimes we did punch each other."

"Somehow you understood the violence as play acting? Is that how it worked?"

"And it always worked out except that time with the cocaine. For eternity I will hate every man who has ever given cocaine to another human being. It is a horrible thing. The man in the shack who sold Dennis the cocaine that day will roast in eternity's worst hell. He killed Dennis. He killed me, too, if I am dead.

"When Dennis and I were in that cocaine stupor, a tether—I think that is the right word for something that holds a boat to the dock—was broken. He looked down at me holding the gun between my legs. Without warning, he yelled 'You slut' then began to choke me very hard.

"He was throttling my neck. I could feel the locket he gave me digging into my skin. The delicate arms of Mohini were digging into my flesh and making my neck bleed. I thought to myself that this cop with all the muscles isn't just playing sex games. He is crushing my windpipe. I was gasping for breath, flaying my legs in fear and anger too. I thought he was killing me. Maybe he did.

"We played choking games before. Maybe I shouldn't have gotten angry or scared, but I'm not sure what happened to me. He was forcing me down on the bed with all his might, this big, muscular cop who told me he was invincible. He was cutting my air off. I was gasping.

"He seemed to forget about the gun. I slid my one hand under his body until I felt the metal and slapped my hand around until suddenly it seemed to put itself in my hand. I pointed the gun toward his stomach. I pulled the trigger."

Mohammed and Mary look out the window.

"I don't know if I'm alive or dead but if I'm alive it means that I was completely delirious with fear but still managed to shoot him. He reached down to clutch his stomach and sort of rolled over, and I fired again and again toward his head until I shot him there.

"There was blood and parts of his brain everywhere, the bed, the walls, on my abdomen, in my hair, on my breasts. It's true. I killed him. I murdered Dennis the Menace with his own gun. And then, I think, I thought, I don't know what word to use, but I think I used the gun to kill myself."

Mary bolts up from her chair crying, sinking her teeth into her knuckles. She takes two steps toward the window, looks at Joy, then sits back down. She sobs uncontrollably, fists clenched in her teeth.

Mohammed watched the two women stoically, casting his eyes to the floor. He could say nothing.

A breeze rustles against the huge window looking out on the beach. But otherwise, there is a silence that seems endless. Moments pass.

Finally, Dr. Abraham scans the semi-circle of patients, taking the measure of the souls in the room. He also clears his throat, then says, "Thank you, Joy. Your story was vivid and honest." He smiles a wan smile and hands her a glass of ice water.

"I am ready for a long drink," Joy sobs gratefully. Her eyes are streaked red. Her deep black mascara is damp and blotted at the corners of her eyes. As she drinks, time and motion seem to stop.

11.

The patients enter the chamber to discover their healer leaning on the fourth chair talking as if somebody is sitting in it. He has a wild-eyed look, so different from his appearance when the four of them first met. Is he becoming ill? Is he absorbing their rage and guilt and fear? The patients cannot tell.

Only the rushing breezes outside the window can be heard for a time until Dr. Abraham's voice disturbs the quiet. "Joy's honesty has inspired me to tell my story.

"Let me take you to the place my life was lived. You are entering the world of the Hebrews, God's chosen people. My father was a Jew, living at a time disastrous for Jews but, as my mother told me many times, not unique for their suffering. This was the era where they were nearly exterminated by the Nazis and later harassed by petty warfare with the Arabs.

"My mother was a Jew but less-so; she used to tell me, as if it is possible to be less of something that is a Jew—" his eyes pan the room—"or a Christian or a Muslim or a Hindu.

"My real father died a brave hero by all reports. He was a United States Marine, killed in battle while storming an island in the Pacific. You've seen the nineteen forties vintage pictures of bodies floating in the surf on a beautiful island. There are palm trees in the background, as beautiful as the ones outside our window. Except fire and plumes of smoke loom up behind the palms, and the tide carries dead carcasses onto the shore toward them. One of those was my father.

"My stepfather once told me, 'had he been fighting in Europe where a Jew should have been fighting, my father would have lived.' Even as a child I bristled at the audacity of a man who did not serve at all. In anger one day my stepfather said to me, 'Had your real father come home to your mother, the burden of raising you would have not been mine. It is a heavy burden.' He despised my real father on principle for having served and died in the Pacific.

"My mother was a beauty. I remember her big sad eyes and big sad breasts. I was born here in Miami, not five miles from here, at the very instant, so she claimed, that the atomic bomb fell on Hiroshima. She was alone with a newborn and then a toddler until she married for a second time. I can only assume that she did it so that I would be fed and have a home. Food was often scarce, I dimly recall.

"My stepfather proudly described himself as an observant Jew. This meant he observed the ancient dietary laws and other customs, to the extent that is actually possible in the modern world. Perhaps he married her out of pity or charity or because of her beauty. A Jewish woman as beautiful as my mother would have been unattainable for him otherwise.

"Whatever the reason for their marriage, even my young eyes could see that there was no love between them. He would shout at her, glare at her, citing the Talmud and the Rabbi and accusing her of things. On purpose he would use Jewish that I was learning, but she didn't understand.

"During this period of my life—I do not know when—there was a dreadful incident. Food was scarce before she married again, and my mother breast fed me long after the time we consider it proper today, perhaps long after the time. Again I do not recall clearly when her breasts would produce milk. In the far reaches of my childish memories I recall the languid luxury of it, both for her and me. One day he came upon us unexpectedly. It was a bright afternoon, and terrible things happen that I do not remember. There were shouts, tears. I cried, as did my mother.

"A period of time passed after that incident. But I do not recall how much time. After years of reflection and psychotherapy, I cannot recall any details of the incident or exactly when it happened. Sometime later, as a child of seven I remember her saying, 'I am done with this Miami Jew' and watching her pack two suitcases.

"We left as soon as my stepfather pulled his car away from the house." Dr. Abraham looks across his desk. "Please come with me to that morning. The sun was still coming up as my mother lumbered down the street with two big suitcases, having to stop every so often to rest. We waited for the bus without speaking. She kept looking around, and even I knew our departure was a secret and that she was afraid of something. I remember watching her struggling to get the suitcases onto the bus that took us from the nice Jewish neighborhood in Miami across the bridge to Miami Beach, a very different place.

"We lived in one room in a boarding house of some kind that had a bathroom on the same floor that we shared with other boarders. She made a living as a maid and also teaching English to Cuban immigrants at the YMCA.

My mother spoke fluent Spanish. She would smile and claim that she was a descendant of the Spanish Jews who were burned at the stake by the Catholic Church during the Spanish Inquisition, but I never found out if this was true. In fact, I never found out if she was actually a Jewess by birth.

"We slept in the same bed with a flimsy cotton sheet over us in the heat. Me and my mother, with those big sad eyes and breasts.

Before bedtime on the hot nights, we'd drink water together in a ritual I didn't quite understand. We'd drink from this old battered pitcher on my credenza. Let me get it...

With great difficulty he lifts it. He holds it so close to his eyes, his face, that it touches his cheek.

"She found it in the ashcan of a house she cleaned. To them it was trash, but for her the lush vines and trees and placid Buddha somehow were a symbol of my father's sacrifice far away. It was her greatest worldly treasure she would say— except for me. When we drifted off to sleep she would caress me, hold me so close, and kiss my forehead. She would tell me that I was the greatest treasure.

"Mohammed, you have your antique bowl. Yes?"

Mohammed nods.

"And Joy, you have your beautiful watch. Please hold your hand out so that we may all see it."

Joy obliges.

"Oh yes and of course there is the locket. Joy, would it be impolite if I invite Mary and Mohammed to take a close look at the locket?"

"No."

Thank you Joy."

Mary and Mohammed rise from their chairs to look at the beautiful piece on Joy's beautiful neck.

"And Mary, there was a ring. It meant a great deal.

"For me, that pitcher and the water it contains is the treasure."

Having told his story while gazing out the window, Dr. Abraham scans the faces of his patients. His face is contorted as if years of pain are finally exacting their measure of him.

"I am done for today," he says. He rises abruptly from his seat and leaves the room, breathless, shoulders slumped. The large Blue Door closes behind him.

Joy has a tear in her eye. "That man may be God like he said to Mohammed, but even if he is, he is so sad," she says to Mary, who nods her agreement.

Mary manages a Mona Lisa smile, but there are tears forming again in her eyes. "Every one of us is so sad."

Suddenly the door opens and he returns, ignoring his patients and talking at the window as if he had not interrupted his own soliloquy.

"My mother kept a picture of my real father on our little dresser. Later I learned that she had a picture of my stepfather that she never took out of her suitcase.

"She died suddenly on her maid job. It was in the evening, and I slept alone, so frightened. The first time in my life. I drank water from her pitcher, as if that would bring her back. When I awoke, I was alone. I was hungry. I was afraid to leave the bed. It was almost dark when the police came into our room with a rabbi and a very fat, bald man who said he was my father. He looked like the man we ran away from five years earlier.

"He had known where we were and did nothing to help. What did I do to deserve this neglect? And my mother? What did she do to deserve it?"

The room is silent.

"Perhaps it was because the Miami Jew caught me at my mother's breast, and found it abominable."

Dr. Isaac Abraham's careworn eyes peer down at his trembling hands. "The Torah says little or nothing about the afterlife. They say it was because the Egyptians who held the Jews in bondage were so obsessed with the afterlife. But if we four are together until the end of time inside of eternity, then you will meet my mother. And perhaps—and I say this with shame—you will see us together in the sun, me suckling at her breast."

After a silence, Dr. Abraham says, "Perhaps I shock you. Still, I wish to continue my life story. Is that acceptable?"

All nod yes.

"In 1967 I joined the Israeli Army. I joined on the very day I finished medical school. I had a copy made of my real father's picture in his blue Marine Corp uniform. I had a copy made of my favorite picture of me and my mother. For reasons that I did not fully understand until I went into psychiatry, I showed the picture of me and my mother to the sturdy young Israeli lieutenant who was present for my signature. 'I am doing this to walk in my father's footsteps, but more importantly, to please her,' I told him. A tear came to my eye. He looked puzzled but made no reply. Those pictures are the only possessions I took from America to Israel.

"My departure for Israel was not as I had planned it. The plan I originally crafted in my mind was vivid and detailed. It had the feel of a retribution fantasy. My plan was to visit the grave of my mother, to remember the sweetness of her eyes and her soul and yes, her breasts that sustained my life in its infancy. I had selected special prayers that I would say in Hebrew. I would hold the pictures of my mother and my father and say such special, mournful prayers.

"Then I would gather my wits and drive to the Miami airport. From the airport I would call my stepfather the Miami Jew, bid a perfunctory goodbye, then board the plane to Tel Aviv never to communicate with him or my stepbrother again. My plan was to die fighting for Israel. In this way I would atone for the guilt my stepfather placed upon the head of my real father, fighting for America in the Pacific instead of saving the Jews in Europe. More important, my soul would be released to be reunited with my real father and mother.

"What happened instead was that my stepfather learned of my enlistment from a friend whose son had also enlisted. After years of neglect and cold indifference, suddenly I was the apple of my stepfather's eye. The bald and rotund Miami Jew was now calling me 'my son' and telling all of his friends about how his brave son was off to fight for Israel. He threw a big farewell party.

"His real son, my stepbrother, had suddenly receded into the background. After toiling through his young manhood at his father's failing clothing business, he had now become inferior. His name was Alan. I want all of you to visualize him snarling at me from across the room at the farewell party. Appearing as a dashing figure in my Israeli Army uniform, as I am sure my father appeared as a United States Marine, I was the center of attention. I was dark and lithe and thin—hard for you to believe now, as you deal with an old man with swollen cheeks and eyes and gnarled hands.

"Alan, like his father, was portly, sponge-like. The father called Alan and me together and said to Alan, 'At least God has given me a second son who has the genes to be a soldier in defense of God's Great Nation Israel.' On that fateful day, I could see the envy sitting hard in Alan's deep-set eyes.

"I will not recount every detail of my every experience in the wars with the Arabs."

Seeing Mohammed's downcast look, Dr. Abraham clears his throat. "Excuse me, Mohammed, for using that term. I hope you believe me when I say I do not divide the human race into parts with words like Arabs or Chinamen. But I am telling the story of my life on the earth and that is the phrase that comes to my mind.

"As a soldier in those battles, I killed men who were absolute strangers to me. I would take aim and from, say, 100 feet, shoot a man dead. I did it at least four times—four times I verified that the man I shot was dead. Yet, for me, on balance, they did not deserve to die. The Jews dying at the time did not deserve to die either. Nobody did.

"But I killed and killed again." Dr. Abraham pans the eyes of his patients, listening in rapt attention. "So it turns out that this mamma's boy of a Jew is a cold-hearted murderer. That, dear patients, is my sin."

Dr. Abraham looks into the blank faces of his patients sitting quietly in their little semi-circle. "What a motley crew we are. I, the physician, am a murderer. Am I the worst kind of killer? I invite each of you, and of course God Almighty, to judge.

"Not once but several times I crawled in the jangled rubble of a bombed-out village under a white-hot desert sun, held up a rifle, swept the sweat from my eyes, took nervous aim, then launched a fusillade of bullets big enough to pierce the side of a truck into the body of a man who I had never met. Am I the worst kind of sinner, one who kills another man because somebody else has ordered him to do it?

"Or is Joy the worst kind of sinner? A self-described slut—"

Dr. Abraham peers gently into Joy's eyes. "Is that not true?"

Casting her eyes to the floor, Joy nods in assent. "I call myself a slut, yes." Raising her eyes and glancing side to side at Mohammed and Mary, Joy mutters, "But I do not believe that is a sin."

"And perhaps it is not. But you did say, Joy, that murder is a sin. And you, Joy, killed your lover."

Dr. Abraham's eyes scan the semi-circle of patients. "Stand up, Joy." Joy stands.

The aging physician stretches his palm in Joy's direction. His hand, indeed his whole arm, is trembling. His shoulders wobble under the yellow cardigan sweater. His voice trembles also. "This woman killed a man. She and the man she killed had known each other for more than a year. They had dined together, walked together, made love together.

" Still, this man whose picture we all have seen wrapped his muscular hands around her fragile windpipe and shook her head so violently that she began to lose consciousness. As he gripped tighter and the breath fled her body, she knew that this, surely, was the prelude to death by strangulation. Did you not know that you were about to be choked to death, Joy?"

"Yes."

"At the last possible moment this woman removed his hands with the best method she could find, a bullet from his own gun, fired into his head. She was so far gone that she never really understood what had happened, never understood that her bullet exploded her lover's brain into shards of flesh and bone."

Mohammed holds his shoulders erect and stiff as Dr. Abraham's gaze falls upon him. "Would you stand, Mohammed?"

Mohammed slowly pulls himself erect, leaning his left hand on the back of the chair so as to better control his right leg, the leg that used to be human but is now a piece of plastic and wire.

"Mohammed kills by accident," Dr. Abraham says. "It was an accident so far as the world uses that term. But was there more? Neglect perhaps. How does God Almighty judge that? Do we know, Mohammed?"

Mohammed sits erect. "Of course we know. The judgment is harsh?

"How can you be certain?"

"I cannot be."

"Yes. We cannot know what God does or will do, except as an invention of our mind. But perhaps there is more to the story, more to be discovered in the Portal Exercise."

Then Dr. Abraham looks at Mary. He seems to be exhausted, and his jaw and eyes are set firm in an expression so stern that it scares her. She begins to rise from her chair, but he shakes his head to stop her.

"Did Mary murder? Based on what she has told us, she has killed only in her heart and mind. She wanted to kill her first husband. How does God Almighty judge sins of intention? Or is there more to the story?"

Suddenly Dr. Abraham coughs so hard that his eyes seem to roll to the back of his head. The unexpected and gruesome display draws the notice of his patients. As a sickening stream of thick, glistening mucus trails down from his nose, all three recoil slightly at the sight, leaning back in their chairs in unison.

Noticing this, Dr. Abraham straightens his slumping body and pushes it out of his chair.

"Please pardon this disgusting display. My body is fading."

He bolts toward his private entrance. Over his back he says, "We have said a great deal today. We have finished this phase of the therapy as I planned that we would."

Mary tries to catch his attention with her eyes, but her physician has turned his head to his private door. He is leaving. And so she speaks, "Dr. Abraham, can I have a moment of your time to tell you something about my story?"

He coughs into his hand and responds in his raspy voice. "This session is over. But there is still much time to go."

Mona Lisa's stoic lips are quivering. "But, my crying is back and today's session might make it wor—"

"Mary, you must wait," her physician says.

Mary looks out the window at the beautiful palm trees swaying softly. "But Dr. Abraham, listen to what Ahm tellin' you. Why do I cry so on a beautiful day like today? I can no longer wait to understand. My cancer is gone but I cry all day. I lay alone in bed and sob. I cry in the kitchen as I make the Little One's peanut butter and jelly sandwiches."

"You will have to cry some more, but you will not weep forever. We will meet again in an instant. I believe it is time to open the Portal."

Thus knowing oneself to be transcendental to
material senses, mind and intelligence, one should
control the lower self by the higher self and thus—by
spiritual strength—conquer this insatiable enemy
known as lust.
The Bhagavad-Gita 3: 43

The Portal

THE PLACE TEEMS with energy. Outside the window, palm trees sway dramatically in the summer wind. On the opposite wall, a newly installed line of photographs are vibrant with color, as if life were emanating from the beautiful scenes of wheat fields and mountains and scrubby plants blooming on the desert floor.

The White Door opens and closes three times as each patient enters the room with their hopes, their fears, their matters, their hearts, all which need to be resolved. The common element to all of their imaginings about what will happen next is Dr. Abraham's promise that a mysterious Portal exercise would somehow be a final act of healing.

Joy enters demurely, soft smile, downcast eyes, a shy school girl walking into class for the very first time. The sun pouring in through the window bathes her dress and simple sandals in an aurora of light.

The only chair in the room is the one with the high mahogany back that was always empty. She is not sure what to make of this, so she spends her time studying the photographs.

Each picture is large, three feet wide, running floor-to-ceiling like the window. The pictures are framed with the same bleached pine that frames the window, inviting the eye to make the photographs as lifelike as the beach outside.

A picture of snow-covered mountains that disappear into wispy clouds is closest to the desk. The mountains are jagged brown and gray with snow and ice in crevices. The next picture, in the middle of the three, is a wheat field. Amber grain runs off to the distance until meeting a cloudy sky portending rain. The third picture is a desert scene shot with the camera on the ground. Small rocks and struggling plants look skyward against dust and sand that stretches toward the horizon. A placard on the wall reads:

Photography by Isaac Abraham. The Himalayan Mountain image was shot from a Buddhist monastery to capture the frigid serenity of the place.
I took the photo of the American plains at the entrance to a rural Baptist church. The endless expanse of wheat and the rain in the distance are gifts of creation the parishioners see when they enter their place of worship.
The desert is the Holy Land. The camera is on the ground at the scene of a battle to capture the perspective of a fallen soldier drawing his last breath.

Joy stands so close to the wheat field scene that the aroma of wheat seems to reach her senses. Having never seen such a place in her life, Joy is fascinated by the luxurious thickness of the wheat. The dark wall of storm clouds in the background loom up like mountains, purple and brown with flecks of light.

Next Mohammed struts into the room like a young man. He acts as if his prosthetic leg is as limber and strong as the natural leg he lost in his accident. He too walks up to the pictures.

"These are new." He applies his discerning taste to the new objects. "I especially favor the desert landscape," he tells Joy. "It captures the strength of the plants that manage to thrive with so little water and so much heat."

Her smile is bright and confident. Mary enters the room and joins the conversation. "Dr. Abraham's new pictures are delightful," she offers after a few moments of study. "He captured the essence of the scenes like he captures the essence of our thoughts."

Suddenly Dr. Abraham's private door flies open, a stranger bursts into the room. He is wearing the lab coat of a doctor. It is stark white, almost brilliant. The garment is starched and stiff, as are the white trousers he is wearing.

Joy, then Mohammed, then Mary turn their heads and look into each other's eyes as if the other knows who this person is and what his entrance means. Fear flashes in their eyes, retreats, and then returns as they all stare at the strange man in white. The presence of a stranger breaks the comfortable, languid mood of the discussion about their healer's art.

The young doctor looks like Satan in the flesh, except the horns and hooves are missing. There is something very wrong with the skin on his face. It looks as if a thin coat of flesh-colored plastic has been applied to his cheeks and his forehead, removing his eyebrows in the process. He is completely bald, causing great emphasis on his eyes. The whites of his eyes are streaked with red, the rims lined with crimson flesh. He has a broad smile with gleaming teeth. It is the smile of a fiend. He exudes boundless energy, completely opposite to the careworn countenance of Dr. Abraham.

Clearly, this new man has news to share, but he waits for Dr. Abraham's patients to abandon their study of Dr. Abraham's beautiful landscapes. They seem to take the seats they first chose at random but now seem part of an immutable cosmic order. But there is only one chair now.

"I am here to collect the ransom that your gods and your minds demand for your release from this place. Do you even understand that you must pay this ransom? Do you understand that the currency for payment is truth? I doubt it. Please stand where your seat used to sit."

When all of the eyes in the semi-circle of patients are upon him, he steps from behind Dr. Abraham's massive desk and sits in the solitary chair. "This seat was for me, but I chose not to come 'til now. I wanted to wait until you and the good doctor Abraham grew tired of talking about the little wind-up doll villains in your life. Now get ready to deal with everybody's worst enemy. I am the ugly truth, your eternal foe. And I... am... in... your... face!"

He jumps up from the chair, turns his body, and saunters backwards to Mary. After standing for a moment with his back to her, suddenly he whirls around and thrusts his face into Mary's. "Boo!" he shouts.

He takes two steps, stands in front of Joy, then shouts, "Boo! It's Halloween! Trick or treat. No, wait... trick or truth!"

Two steps more, and he is in front of Mohammed. He turns to walk away, then spins around and shouts "Boo!" into Mohammed's face.

With a self-satisfied grin, he returns behind the desk. "Please look closely at the skin on my face. What does it look like to you? Some people say plastic, some say putty. Surgeons try to make the pigment pink like real flesh, but I'm thinkin' it looks like grey putty. "I have no hair on my head, no eyebrows. It looks like I'm wearing a woman's bathing cap The skin around my eyes isn't right either. Nope. It looks like I've got big red rims around my eyes. Yes?"

The patients say nothing.

"Look at me," he insists. "I won't talk any more until all of your eyes are focused on my face."

When the patients comply, he continues. "I'm hideous, frightening to behold—at first.

"In fairly short order, my face goes from being frightening to being sickening. Sickening like a spot where you know somebody puked and it's been cleaned up, but the stain is still there to remind you.

"And then finally, I don't scare you or make you feel like vomiting, I just look ugly.

"We'll be together for what will seem like… well, an eternity, so I'll have a chance to go from frightening to sickening to just plain ugly, before your very eyes. Tell me, Mary, has it happened yet? Are you still frightened, or do I simply make you sick when you look at me?"

Mary recoils at the question. "I'm still scaring Mary," he says. His tone is mean, triumphant.

He leans his face across the desk toward the other two patients. "Joy? Mohammed? Scary, sickening or ugly—which am I?" To their silence he shrugs, "All three, because I am the truth, and the truth is ugly. The truth is scary. The truth is sickening. You will all know that soon because the truth will set you free, but you must face it first."

The man in the lab coat sits in his chair then gets up and walks over to Dr. Abraham's desk. "They called me Junior when I was a boy but now I am Faust. You may call me Doctor Faust if you want to because I am in fact a medical doctor. But I prefer plain Faust." The patients look away.

"Remember when Dr. Abraham told you he sometimes has a colleague join him for the final session of healing? You may have been expecting another weary, bearded, vacant-eyed physician, but guess what? I am that colleague. However—and there is no easy way to tell you this—I will conduct this session without him. I will do it alone. I guess you could say that the group is under new management—my management. I look young for the part, a medical student to that old coot Dr. Abraham's

"But here's more about me. I'm the incarnation of the German legend of a guy who made a pact with the devil. I'm an illusionist and a magician with the power to do what Dr. Abraham couldn't. Under my management, things will be very different from what you expected a couple minutes ago. Let me tell you what is different. Anybody want to guess?"

He greets their silence with a challenge, "If you don't talk, you have to listen to me. Who wants to guess what will be different?"

"I'll do the talking then. First, time will be different. Despite what the ol' doc said to the contrary, under his management time seemed to be allotted in chunks with Dr. Abraham as time-keeper. Like this place was a video on a screen and he had a remote control that started and stopped action. Not anymore. Time means nothing now. We will be at this as long as it takes. You will see.

"And for right now at least, words are not important. I know Dr. Abraham likes that Bible passage, *In the beginning was the Word, and the Word was with God, and the Word was God.* Unlike Dr. Abraham, I myself don't see a reason for a lot of yakity-shmakity like you all got used to in here.

"I don't care about words. I misuse them on purpose and I love to watch the confusion that I create. I know he told you that words heal here, and that is partially true—as he said, there are no scalpels or pills or bandages in this place.

"But in my therapy, if you could call it that, it is not the words that heal but the emotions. And by the way, you will all begin to notice that your accents are just about gone now. No Irish lass Mary, no Asian gal Joy. You stay the same Mohammed, as your English is impeccable. Like you.

"Any who... Do you know the difference between when a word conjures an idea versus when it conjures an emotion?"

Silence.

"Hmm, a very unresponsive bunch. Let's try an exercise. Ready? I am really an ugly-lookin' dude. My skin is a strange-lookin' white and my face looks as if I've wrapped it in plastic like you would do with a sliced-up melon. Worse yet, I ain't got no hair. See that?"

The patients remain silent, but there is a grimace on each of their faces.

"You're not talking, but at least you reacted, right? Just a couple more tries. Everybody ready? Joy, you're a lying slut. We already knew that, but Mary, you too are also a slut and a liar. And Mohammed, the millionaire several times over, you're a murderer. That's right. You and Joy both.

"Think you can gimp on over to the window here, Mohammed?"

Mohammed moves across the room unsteadily. Smirking, the physician points a finger at the window. "Stand right next to it, please."

When Mohammed complies, the man in the white coat takes the cord that controls the blinds and drapes it around Mohammed's neck. "You beat a man senseless—your own son, no less—then got him killed in a car crash. These days they call it vehicular homicide. Back in the good ol' wild west cowboy days in the part of the good ol' U S of A. where I come from, the sheriff would have hung you from the nearest tree."

When Faust yanks on the cord, Mohammed tenses and rears back like a man about to be hung.

"That's a sample of my therapeutic technique," Faust says. "What do you folks think?"

Mary holds her gaze to the ground.

Joy looks at her watch and mutters, "This is a total waste of time."

The man in the starched white coat jerks his head in Joy's direction. "Finally, a reaction! None other than our painted-and-dolled-up Asian slut here. You say 'waste of time,' Shyi Lee Huang? Waste of time? Probably, since the only reaction I'm getting is what I can read in your lying, sinning faces. But I just said we got all the time in the world. Eternity, right? And by the way, do you all like my white trash country boy accent? I'm an educated man of course, but I'm white trash too! That should help make sure you feel words sting and burn as never before. Am I making sense?"

Silence.

"Will one of you please admit it? Will somebody admit that they just want to get this over with and feel all the horrible things they've been hiding away in their minds?"

Eyes seeming to glow, the new physician grabs his lips with his hands and presses them tightly closed. Then he sticks out his tongue and yanks it. "Cat got your tongues?"

Joy takes two aggressive steps toward Faust. "Tell us, why are you really here in his office, his home. Is he dead? Have you harmed him somehow?"

Faust laughs derisively and claps his hands together. "Moi? How would I have harmed him?"

Joy, who came to the chamber to be cured of her fear, exhibits none as she rubs her fingertips on the chair that Dr. Abraham forbade her to touch. "How do we know that you are not a patient so demented that you were unable to come here and take your seat?"

Faust looks at her thoughtfully. "You will soon know that I could never harm that old man. All of us together—you three, me, him—we could have been a team of life coaches for each other. But truth is needed for that, and all any of you did was lie. Lies of omission are lies nonetheless.

"It is you and people like you that have destroyed him. He absorbed your rage and sadness and shame. Your refusal to tell the truth became like an acid eating away at his very being.

"As for this place, it is mine now. It was bequeathed by him to me. Everything else is the same, by the way, and you can feel free to stay here as if there were no exit."

Mohammed tugs at his tie and interrupts before Joy can speak again. "Where is he then?"

"It does not matter to you now," the young doctor says.

Mary bursts into tears but manages to say through sobs, "Oh, God, let this be a trick! Let this be one of his therapeutic techniques! Let this be a joke! Do not let it be true that we no longer have Dr. Abraham."

Dr. Faust glares at Mary. "I've read all of Dr. Abraham's notes. They're mine now, came with the territory." He reaches over to the tall credenza behind the desk and picks up a thick leather book. The three patients watch him place it on the desk and open it.

A slight musky odor fills the room as he begins leafing through what appear to be hundreds of sheets of Dr. Abraham's notes, except the sheets now look like they should stink of moldy parchment or rotten papyrus. "These are written in Hebrew of course, but I can anticipate what each of you will—"

Joy, eyeing the sheaves of yellowed paper suspiciously, interrupts. "Even if those are his notes, they cannot tell the whole story. They cannot tell you what is in my heart even if you are the demon you appear to be."

"Demon? Satan more specifically, fo' the Muslims and Christians in 'dee house—y'all like that little rap music thang?"

He jerks his body like a rapper then stands at attention like a soldier. "Yes, I have been told that. But when people say I look like the devil, I wonder if that means they have actually seen Satan with their own eyes? The Catholic Church still performs exorcisms, of course, so perhaps you, Mary, have seen Satan with your own eyes. Have you?"

Mary looks at Joy when she answers his question: "Of course not."

"Then if I am Satan, this would be the first time we met, at least with me taking this particular form," the new doctor says. He smiles a wry smile as he observes the tension on the faces of the little semi-circle of patients.

"I joke of course. But perhaps the real issue for Joy is that she was getting used to looking at Dr. Abraham and his beard. Perhaps you all had become comfortable with his Michelangelo visage resembling Moses or maybe even God on the ceiling of the Sistine Chapel in Rome.

"You know the kind of picture I am talking about? God is a handsome old fella. And then here I come, the new guy so to speak, with my bald head and my fiery eyes. Even Joy, who believes gods and goddesses manifest themselves in various forms, can't bear to look at me. Am I that ugly? Do I look like a man who is half-turtle?"

Faust sneers at Joy. "Mr. Patel took you for a walk in his cramped little carpet merchant's office and showed you the avatars of Vishnu, the keeper of order. Half-man, half-turtle. Half-man, half-boar. All of that. Well, perhaps I am an avatar of Shiva the destroyer. A hideous man, destroyed, bent on destruction."

Strutting back and forth in front of his patients like they were army privates lined up for inspection, he says, "No matter how you look at it, I'm a poor substitute for Dr. Abraham, true? Joy? Mohammed? Mary? Is somebody going to answer me?"

Joy casts a piercing look at the new doctor. "Yes, you are a poor substitute for Dr. Abraham, but not because of how you look. It is how you are treating us. You have nothing to offer us."

"Nothing to offer? And why would that be? The three of you were very impressed with Dr. Abraham, and I can see why that would be so. He knows the scripture. He knows Sigmund Freud and Carl Jung. He knows the modern stuff too, like Skinner's theories of positive reinforcement. That's how he trained you to spill your guts and tell your horrible secrets to each other just so you'd get a drink of water for a reward, like a pigeon in a research lab pecks a disk to get a pellet of food.

"He knows group dynamics, of course. He's too much of a charlatan to level with you and tell you that you were just another group going through a predictable cycle of forming, storming, norming, performing and—the absolutely most special event—adjourning.

"You may all come to believe that I am some sort of huckster or cheap magician, and you may be right. But it may also be the case that I am just part of the conspiracy, just like Dr. Abraham."

"Conspiracy? Like in politics or crime? What are you talking about?" Mohammed asks.

Faust grins. "A conspiracy is the act of secretly planning to do something that is harmful or illegal. Remember when he said early on that maybe there is a conspiracy of minds and Gods, the effect of which is to keep us fearful and hopeful and confused. That's what I am talking about, friends."

"Maybe that's what The Portal is about. The end of your eternity together. Or is it? As the conspiracy's chief agent among you, he neglected to tell you. You're all confused. Afraid. Pardon this uncharitable description, but Faust says you're all just… plain…clueless."

The new doctor studies the big White Door in the back of the room. "I will admit The Portal is awesome—in theory. But the Memory Book? Not so much. A psychiatric social worker in a south Miami mental ward for welfare patients could step a group through superficial drills like the Memory Book..

"Ah, the dreary, stupefying slow Memory Book method. As a woman who counts minutes and pennies, I am surprised these things impressed you, Joy. Or you, Mohammed, the millionaire. Or you, Mary, the wife of a famous cancer doctor who also happens to believe in magic."

Dr. Looks-Like-Satan leers at Joy.

You exude special strength." Making a point of scanning up and down Joy's bare legs with his wild blood-shot eyes, he says, "Nice sandals, nice ankle bracelet, nice locket. The goddess Mohini on that seductively tight choker around your pretty neck. Like it. But the watch, not so much. What makes you think your time is so precious?"

"I consider time to be precious because when you run out of it you depart that life." Joy addresses Mary and Mohammed. "I say we stand here and do nothing. I still wonder if this is a trick."

"No trick," he sighs. "Not that I cannot do tricks. For example, look out the window at the beach. The sound of the surf and the breeze are pretty melodies. Ahhh.

"Now let's look at the wall across from the window. Please, everyone look at the wall. Aren't Dr. Abraham's photographs vivid and life-like, like the stories about your lives that you really haven't told yet? Look at the places in the pictures on the wall, the snow-covered mountains snuggled in the clean wispy clouds, the seemingly endless field of abundant amber wheat, the desert with the scrubby red flowers struggling to survive. If you use your imagination, they can be real too, just like the beach outside.

Mohammed and Mary and Joy will not look at the wall across from the window. Instead, they defy their new healer and look out the window as if to reassure themselves that the beach is real, that the palm trees are moving, that the surf is still crashing outside the window.

Dr. Looks-Like-Satan falls silent with the patients.

"We are wasting time," Joy finally says, glaring disdainfully at her watch on its dangling gold chain.

"We are indeed, but we have eternity. I will say nothing more until all three of you look at the pictures on that wall. I must perform this trick for you before time can move forward again."

First Mohammed and then, as if by silent agreement, Mary and Joy turn their heads to look at the pictures on the wall.

"Thank you," Dr. Looks-Like-Satan says. "Listen and look at the pictures. Can you now hear, not only the surf and soft breeze of the ocean outside the window, but also hear wind blowing through the mountains and the hollow ringing of a still night in the desert?"

He tugs at the sleeve of his white lab coat. "And wait. This is interesting. Please look outside the window for a moment. Have the palm trees stopped moving? Do we have only a picture of the beach now? I think so. It's as if the scene out the window is a large photograph of a beach, a beautiful likeness, of course, as are all of Dr. Abraham's photographs.

"And, how odd. Suddenly the photographs on the wall are becoming the real scenery.

"See the rain rushing you in Kansas? Hear it beating on the window that used to be a picture?

"See the dust kicking up from a windstorm on the desert?

"See the black darkness settle on the Himalayas? There are no humans out there, and therefore no light.

"Can't you see that they are no longer pictures? Can you grasp the power of my trickery? Am I a great illusionist, or what?"

Mohammed waves his fist in the air. "I speak for myself at least when I say I do not believe these amusement park special effects mean anything. We are not here to be tricked, but rather to learn about ourselves. Dr. Abraham understood me. And finally, I was coming to understand myself. I will not continue with you; you are a young pup. You cannot know anything of life or of death."

Wiping her eyes with the back of her hand, Mary sobs. "Mohammed is right. We aren't here to be tricked."

Joy, composed, peers at her watch dangling from its beautiful gold chain. Her voice is even, the rata-tat-tat absent. "Our time is valuable."

Dr. Looks-Like-Satan breathes an audible sigh and says, "Let me assure you that this is not a trick or a joke or a therapeutic technique. And let me also assure you of something else. Everything you have said in this place, Joy, I already know."

Joy glares at him pointedly. Dr. Looks-like-Satan stares back at her until her eyes avert.

Having by his eyes achieved mastery of Joy, he says, "Perhaps each of you can tell me how you feel right now."

Silence.

"Very well, I'll keep yakkin'. The pictures on the wall are meant to tell you that in this place, you can make anything seem real. You're very good at that, aren't you, Mary. That child you lost was not Robert's; it was of that Spanish student you loved. You knew that, and Robert sensed it. In your mind, that child came back as Carmella. Yes?"

Mary's eyes fill with confused tears.

Dr. Looks-Like-Satan ignores her. "And you, Mohammed, brought in a picture of a bowl and not your wife and your son. No matter. Because of you, all of them have been destroyed. How shameful."

Mohammed stands in silence.

"And Joy's picture of Dennis and her picture of her brother. Is there a story in those pictures, Joy?"

"Yes, there is quite a story as a matter of fact. Do you know it, Dr. Satan? Can you possibly know—"

Joy's head jerks upward toward the violent claps of thunder that are suddenly booming in the sky above. Outside the window, a rolling wall of grey-black clouds billows up from the ocean and races onto the beach. She cannot stop shuddering.

"Scared, darlin'?"

"Yes."

Mary, closest to the window, gasps at the sight of the storm. "My God, the weather has never done this," she says, turning to the other patients. "This is so sad. Nothing is the same."

"Sad? You are sad again, Mary?"

Weeping pitifully, Mary does not answer.

Mohammed shakes his fist at Faust. "How dare you do this to them. Have you no pity?"

"Pissed, big fella?"

"I'm outraged."

"Rage? Perfect!" Faust shouts, jumping up on his chair. "You all want to talk about your fear and your sadness and your rage. Wrong subject." He thrusts his arms out like he is about to be handcuffed. "Shame and Sin. That's what I wanna talk about. Those are the shackles I will force you to break! That's the only way we can get outta here! Let's get to it!"

Faust jumps down from the chair. "You may ask, what is sin? Through sin, guilt is incurred. And according to guilt, punishment is meted out. God can forgive sin.

"Joy? What did your parents teach you about sin?"

"My father never talked about sin."

"Really? Why not?"

"I don't know," Joy snaps.

"Speculate, Beautiful."

"Maybe as a Buddhist or Confucian he figures there is no God to sin against. I never cared. My biological father gave me nothing."

"Well, even if you didn't care or listen to the man whose DNA is in your body, he had a point. You don't need God to make you feel guilty. Or sad. Or afraid. Or enraged. Other people can teach you to feel that way."

He stands in front of Mohammed. "Think about that, big fella."

Next he stands in front of Mary. "You too, Mona Lisa."

Then he stands in front of Joy. "Okay, then how about your erstwhile parents, the squat little furry huggable Hindu teddy bears the Patels?"

"Don't mock them."

"Can't answer my question?"

"Mr. Patel would smile when he told me the stories of the worldly excesses of the Hindu gods and say that the concept of sin is not required in order for there to be Karma. Our human failure to achieve perfection in a particular life is what makes Karma necessary."

Faust tugs the lapel of his white lab coat like a cowboy tugging at his vest. "Did you feel guilt at any time about anything?"

"Yes, but I refuse to tell you."

When Joy said the word refuse, the noise of the rain pelting the window begins to drown out even Faust's loud voice. Grey gobs of water strike the glass and run down it in streaks. Wind whips the palm trees in a frenzied dance. Then suddenly the rain outside stops. Faust shouts, "Your turn, Mary."

"If I were to feel guilty," Mary says, "it might be because I never truly tried to find out what happened to my first husband. Perhaps—I guess this is possible—I might feel guilty because in my heart I really didn't care. But am I destined for hell? No."

Faust raises his arm as if to give Mary a high five but then quickly yanks it back with a smirk, "Whew! A relief, Mohammed? Not headed there either?"

"I'm quite sure. All I had was lost because of an accident. Be that as it may, the crash itself was an accident. I repeat the word: accident."

"Of course it was an accident. But why do you feel the need to repeat it a million times each day?"

"Because in Islam intentions are of the greatest importance. The word is *niyyah*. Intentions. Ultimately it is what Allah judges us by."

Dr. Faust waves his hand in the air mockingly and says, "Hello in there, Mohammed. Of course you did not intend to have a car crash. But have you thought, well, I caused the accident because I was driving too fast. You're still at fault then, you realize—"

"No. I will not take blame for the accident. I too have suffered, more than anyone in this room can imagine even if we are together for eternity."

"Enough of this," Faust announces as a pulls a stack of papers off Dr. Abraham's credenza. "Let's really get this party started with a little test. Sorry there are no seats, but I don't want you comfortable anyway. I have written each of your names on a sheet of paper. You can all lean on Dr. Abraham's desk to fill this out. Now, please write the numbers one through seven."

The patients comply, each writing a neat column of numbers.

"Now, write the names of the seven deadly sins as they are described in Dante's *Divine Comedy*. You might know it by the name Dante's *Inferno*."

The three patients look up from their sheet of yellow paper. Mary, fighting back a tear, is confused by the request. "I'm not quite sure what you want us to do. I think I know what the deadly sins are, but I learned them from church not some book."

Joy and Mohammed look at each other, then Mohammed says, "This is unacceptable. Have you read Dante's *Inferno*, Joy?"

Joy stares at Faust. "No!"

"Nor have I. And I, for one, refuse to be bound by a list believed by Christians."

Faust flashes his eyes at Mohammed. "Point taken, big fella. You can write your own list, or cheat off Mary. Write yours, Mary."

Eager to show the new doctor that she knows the list by heart, Mary uses her best cursive handwriting to write:

pride
envy
anger
sadness
avarice
gluttony

And finally next to number seven Mary writes *lust*.

"Why are we doing this?" Joy asks.

"Just strivin' for completeness, beautiful," Faust replies. "Just tryin' to get some perspective on all the wrong-doing we've heard you all yak-yak about. So write your list."

Joy adjusts the paper on Dr. Abraham's desk and begins writing in Chinese:

Murder.
Lies.
Stealing.

Faust grins. "I can read that you know, honey. Why ya keep trying to hid stuff from the boy here. I don't understand. For everybody's benefit, Joy said Murder, Lies, and Stealing.

Mohammed glares at Faust and then the paper. He writes the words *disobedience to God*, then he tosses his pen to the desk.

"So I want you to buy into my premise that you can't get outta here until you know what sin is. If any sin is on all three of your lists, being different from each other as you are, then it must truly be a sin. Mary says '*pride, envy, anger, sadness, avarice, gluttony, lust.*' That's the official list of deadly sins that the nuns taught her as a naïve, impressionable child.

"Joy came up with only three sins: *Murder, Lies, and Stealing.* Good list. An accountant's view of sin let's call it.

"Mohammed seems to believe that the only deadly sin is disobedience of God and lust. Get away from this desk and stand in your places."

Thunder roars outside, and the gray clouds throw sheets of rain hard against the window, announcing that a powerful storm is rushing through the heavens in their direction. Abruptly, Faust rolls their lists into a ball and sticks it in his lab coat.

"If the three of you can't agree on what sin is, then we are lost. How can I heal you if you do not agree on sin? Sin is God's most basic concept. The concept measures obedience to his will by the absence of sin. Is this true?"

Faust paces before the three patients, keeping his eyes on Mohammed and Joy. "Mohammed and Joy object to using, let's call it Christian, umm… Stuff. But even the two of you should be able to complete this exercise. Who are you?

"Trick question, don't bother answering yet. So few people ever stop to ask themselves one simple question: Who am I? I'm gonna make each of you do it now."

Faust goes to Dr. Abraham's credenza and produces the three thin slabs of polished black marble. He carefully writes their names on three sheets of fine linen paper, places each sheet on a marble slab, then hands one to each patient. "This time, no cheating. Find a private place in the room if you want, or use his desk. At the top of your sheet write the words *Who Am I?* then answer the question twenty times."

All walk back to the desk. Mary stares out the window for a very brief moment, then begins writing furiously. With each word, it takes Mary longer to find the next word. She looks up from her sheet of paper and says to Joy, "I guess you were right when you said I don't know who I am. This is harder than I thought. Do we have to fill in all twenty blanks?"

"No," Faust says. He waits until they all finish writing, then continues. "This is a real psychological test. People usually begin with nouns that are names of the categories they belong to, then end with the adjectives and verbs that reveal their private ideas about who they really are. Read your answer, Mary. I glanced at your paper so I see you can write the words 'I am' without that Irish accent of yours so don't say 'ahm' say I am."

Mary nods obediently and in her sweet voice says, "I've been tryin' to fix that accent, so I will do it correctly now. Who am I?

I am a Woman.
I am a Mother.
I am a Wife.
I am a Catholic.
I am a Survivor.
I am a Cook.
I am Irish.
I am fighting the sadness.
I am protecting Carmella.
I am searching for my soul."

"Protector of Carmella, interesting," Faust smirks. "But at least you proved my point that adjectives and verbs about the real Mary come at the end. You're next, Joy."

"I only needed five. Who am-I?

I am an Accountant.
I am a Woman.
I am a Hindu.
I am a Goddess.
I am my soul. "

Without waiting for instruction from Faust, Mohammed reads in his baritone voice, "Who am I?

A man.
A Muslim obedient to God.

A father.

A Son.

A man guarded by angels. "

After all the lists are finished, Dr. Faust covers his face with his hands and mockingly pretends to cry. "Boo hoo. Boo hoo. All of my patients have failed all of their tests. First failure. You could not agree on what sin is. And now, the worst error of all. Do you know what it is? Mary?"

"No."

"Joy?"

Silence.

"Mohammed, surely you know."

"I understand nothing of what you are saying, Doctor."

"Just now when I asked you who you were, you did not say you were a sinner. Does that mean you have never been disobedient to God, Mohammed? If you are still protected by merciful Allah, why is there rage in your heart?"

"If you are truly without sin, what do you fear, Joy?"

"Why are you so sad, Mary?"

"Yes, yes, yes. You are all sinners, but my exercise just now shows that one of you truly acknowledge it."

Mohammed tenses, stroking his mustache. His clear brown eyes peer at the physician as a child's frightened eyes might peer at their father. "These exercises you make us perform are… I do not see their purpose."

Faust's voice takes on Dr. Abraham's scolding tone. "Eternal healing is their purpose," he says harshly. His eyes pan the three patients angrily. "How often must I say it? We are here for eternal healing. I beseech you to take each exercise seriously. Dr. Abraham said you might already be dead—Is that possible?"

His eyes sweep clockwise around the semi-circle. Faust points his finger like a gun at Mary. "Mary, I have said that we might already be dead. Is that possible?"

Tears roll down on Mary's Mona Lisa smile. "Aye. We may be dead."

"Joy?"

"Yes. The life I was leading may be over."

The physician nods approvingly at Joy then turns his eyes to the man in the black business suit. "And Mohammed? You have never accepted the premise."

"No."

"Will you ever?"

"Perhaps not."

Faust stares deeply into Mohammed's eyes. "Take heed, all of you. Do you know what it will be like when finally you meet your God? Does your faith teach you exactly what that moment will be like? Do you know exactly what it will be like in the same way that you know exactly what beautiful patterns and colors were painted upon that bowl, the one your son broke into pieces, Mohammed? Answer me."

"No. Islam offers no perfect certainty. The Prophet did not spell out the precise conditions of the meeting with Allah."

"So take heed, Mohammed. I may be the almighty ruler of the universe. Look at me. Do you know for certain that I am not?"

"In this place, I know nothing for certain."

"Now, my friend, that's a good answer! That's why you need me. But I can banish you from my presence at any time. Therefore do not regard anything I tell you to do as a foolish exercise."

Faust sighs, "This is getting way too heavy, team. I need a break. Maybe have a smoke or something." He pats the pocket of his lab coat. "Anyone have a cigarette? I thought I had a pack of Lucky Strikes in here, but guess not." Changing his demeanor he smirks. "You know, I don't even know what time is. Joy you have that pretty watch there, what time is it?"

Joy looks at her watch, then grits her teeth.

"Something wrong my dear?"

"There are no hands on my watch. They're gone."

"Oh my," Faust says. "Let me see. Take it off and let me look at it."

"Why?"

"Why? Why not? Those are the two biggest questions of life, by the way my dear Joy."

"You're right, why not." She hands the watch to him, and he puts it in the pocket of his labcoat.

As the patients exchange glances, Faust continues to taunt them. "No problem team. I'll just reach into the old fella's desk and get your—what's it called, that thing that Dr. Abraham took from you, Joy?"

"You mean my Blackberry?"

"Yeah, this thing right here." Faust toys with the handheld device. "Could it give us the time or the date even?"

Mary and Mohammed eye the unfamiliar device warily. Faust stares at the device as if inspecting it then asks, "What are all these words on the front of this thing?"

"It's the hotel reservation for April 13th, 2012. Dennis made in Vegas."

Joy lowers her head.

"And the next thing you knew, you were in this joint, right?"

"Yes," Joy says, lips quivering.

Faust watches Mary sob in confusion. "When did you get here Mary?" Faust asks.

She struggles to say, "About the time of my second surgery."

"Which was when?"

"Ahm so confused right now I can't rightly say."

"Can you just give me the year then, Mary? Maybe something historic that happened?" Faust asks.

"I remember the attack on the World Trade Center. Which happened September 11, 2001, just a week before my operation."

"And then Mary, you showed up here, with these folks, for Isaac Abraham 101 on Day One. Right?"

Mohammed grits his teeth and clenches his fists, "These facts make no sense to me. My accident was in August of 1981 and I came here right after that."

Faust seems giddy with pleasure. "Let's figure this out. I lost my face in a warehouse fire in 1953. The burn unit in the biggest hospital in Kansas City couldn't do any better than this, but what could you expect in…Did I just say 1953? The operation was crap, but let's look at the upside. As we speak I'm ogling pretty little Joy here who shot her man in the early 21st century, or so she thinks. Can we agree that's quite a leap in time?

"How could this be? What manner of trick is this?" Mohammed, enraged, shouts.

"This ain't no trick, Mo. No trick, no games, no horseplay. This is real. How could this be, you ask? We're all here together but our tragedies span 60 years. I'll tell you. We are all dead. Dead. D-E-A-D dead! So time has stopped for all of us."

Faust pauses from his exertions and gauges the reactions of his audience.

"But—wait a minute—we gots a Hindu and a Catholic and a Muslim in da house! They be hosted by a fella who says he be Satan's apprentice. So let's be exact. Those bodies be dead. But we be here, right? What are we then? I'm a-guessin' we are souls! So souls do exist! But none of you are lookin' too happy."

The silence is colder and more brittle than that first faced by Dr. Abraham when they began their journey together.

The smirk leaves Faust's face. "I hope you see that each of you are dealing with eternity now. And thus my ultimatum. If you won't perform my healing process willingly, then you may leave by that White Door right now. Go ahead. Whoever chooses to do so, remove yourself from my presence. Dr. Abraham has been offering you the same choice all along, but now surely you see why he did not want you to do it.

"But it's always been your choice. Take a chance on leaving now and facing the unspeakable consequence. Or maybe it won't matter at all. Take the chance. Roll the dice. But if you do not leave now, you must finish the tasks I am about to give you. I refuse to be defeated as Dr. Abraham was."

Eyes downcast, the three patients stand like prisoners awaiting execution. The sound of the rain and wind drowns out all else as they watch the sky outside turn from grey to black. Then, suddenly the lights in the vaulted ceiling flicker and die. All in the room stare transfixed at the tumult, motionless, silent, like mannequins in a store window. Even their eyes cease to move, staying locked on the scene outside the window.

Shyi Lee Huang

THE DARKNESS AND howling of the heavens fill the chamber until suddenly the scene outside returns to normal and the scene in the chamber along with it. Faust, gaining energy, claps his hands to roust the others out of their stupor.

"Wow, either that was another great illusion by me or something is happening in here. I guess each of you thinks, well, these other folks could be actors and this is all just a high cost, high tech therapy. Or…

"But let's accentuate the positive and keep on truckin'. Joy, do you know the difference between sin and shame?"

Tugging at her locket of Mohini, her eyes rise from the floor. She nods at Faust. "Sin is failing God. Shame is failing the people who taught you, and therefore failing yourself."

Having shouted to be heard above the storm before, Faust's voice is hoarse. "Are you ashamed?"

"Yes."

"Then why is it not on the sheet of paper you are holding?"

"It should be."

"Then write it and read me your list."

She writes carefully on the fine paper, then reads. "I am an accountant, a woman, a Hindu, a Goddess, here to be cured of my fears. And I am ashamed."

"Good. Hand me your tablet. You are done with it. Now I want you to say these exact words: To understand my shame is to understand, then tell your story."

Handing the tablet to Faust, Joy says, "To understand my shame is to understand two cops. You asked if there were a story in the picture of Dennis and the picture of my brother. I was about to say that there is indeed a story, the kind of story you could not possibly understand."

Shrugging, he replies, "Is that so? Try me."

Joy walks to the picture window with the beautiful day shining in again and tugs at a long nylon cord until the blinds slam down to the floor. "I want darkness," she says, ignoring

Dr. Looks-Like-Satan and panning her eyes between Mohammed and Mary.

Moving from the window to stand next to Dr. Abraham's desk, Joy feels suddenly powerful. "Now I am going to take you all, even you Satan, out of this room and back to Hong Kong. Mary, Mohammed, remember how I said I woke up in the morning and saw my mother's nail polish?

"Remember how I said I sat on their bed and carefully painted my nails, hand and feet, with her nail polish? Remember the part where I went down the hall to the bathroom and removed my blouse so I could look at my fingers on myself? Remember?

"Well, I left something out. My brother, the cop, walked into the apartment unexpectedly and called my name. 'I'm in the bathroom,' I shouted back. He walked down the little hallway to the bathroom. The door was half open, but—"

Faust interrupts. "Did you—"

"Yes," Joy says, "I did know that the door was open. And so, it happened. He saw me staring at my breasts. 'Now I know what the applauding was all about,' he said. 'I didn't know you had grown up so much.' I spun around to look at him.

"Wa Cho was my half-brother by my father's first marriage. Our relationship was strange. He scared me because he was so bitter about life. Yet he seemed to be the only one in the family to notice me. When I was very little, a toddler, my mother had him watch me—'babysit' is what Americans would call it. He'd crawl in bed with me sometimes. When I was very little, I wanted it because he comforted me there."

Faust nods. "But this little habit of yours and his lasted well after you were a toddler, I guess. Yes or no, beautiful. Tell the truth."

"When I got older and was in school, sometimes I would wake myself up when I heard him come home. The two of us would sit alone and talk. He would sit in our tiny living room in his blue uniform, so proud of that uniform. He would sip a beer and tell me about the thieves and the prostitutes and the other cops. In his mind, there was not an honest person in Hong Kong. I'd go to my little room and fall asleep, and I think he came there and got into my bed."

"The plot's thickening," Faust says sarcastically. "So he used his friendship that day, didn't he? He abused the one trust you had."

"When I saw him staring at me, I should have slammed the door in his face. Instead I just let him look at me. I started staring back at him. He was wearing his sidearm and he saw me look down and stare at the gun. I looked back into his eyes, and we just stood there saying nothing.

"Finally he looked in my eyes and sneered. He said, 'I do not have time for this. I have to go to work.' I sneered back at him and said, 'Time for what?' Without a word, he came into the bathroom and closed the door. He pinned me against the wall, which was cool against my bare back. He pulled my blouse completely off and yanked my panties down to my ankles."

Joy pauses to recall the moment. "I just stood there. He said, 'You know I've been getting into bed with you since you were a little girl. Tell me you know.' I told him I thought it was a dream. I told him I wasn't sure.

"Then he said, 'You weren't sure I was pulling your little panties down? And how about now that you are growing up? Are you saying you don't know I get into bed with you after those big brother talks we have? You lay still while I pull them down, pull your shirt up. Of course you know.' I could not speak because I did know the things he was doing. My breath and my words stayed in my throat.

"I could feel his breath in my face as he brought his lips near mine. 'Admit it Shyi Lee Han. You let me do everything I want in your bed.' Finally I whispered next to his ear the word 'yes.' His face stayed next to mine, and he said, 'Tell me you like it when your big brother visits your little bed, Shyi Lee Han, my precious beauty.'

"I could barely breathe. But I whispered 'yes' again, because it was true. Then he said, 'I am glad you like my body near yours in your warm little bed. But now, I need the panties off. Pick up your foot.' I lifted my left foot out of my panties. He bent down and kissed my foot, then said, 'Now the other foot.' When I lifted my right foot up, he took my panties off. They were pink. He tossed them in the sink.

The Respite of Ghosts   173

Noticing that Mary is crying, Joy dabs the tears from her own eyes. "Then he said, 'Now let's go to that little bed of yours.' I said 'no.' He said it again and I said 'no' again, this time louder. He watched me pick my panties out of the sink and put them back on.

"And then he did it. He yanked them off, closed the bathroom door, pinned me against it, and... raped me. He whispered in my ear, 'You asked me time for what? Time for this.' He pinned my pelvis against the wall and then he raped me.

"It seemed over in an instant. 'See pretty girl, no time at all,' he said when he was finished. He laughed and said, 'Wish I could stick around, but like I said, I don't have time.' I burst out in tears.

"I was only twelve. I was his half-sister but still I was his sister. We had the same father. I trusted him. How could he do that to me? And worst of all, he left me crying in front of the mirror, vowing to grow up and get revenge."

"He is an unspeakable man," Mohammed shouts. "May he burn in hell."

"Aye," Mary manages to shout through her tears. "May he burn forever under the care of Satan himself."

Joy ignores their grief and anger. "I left there that day and met the Patels. Eventually they let me live with them. Eventually they transported me and my life to America. I did get revenge in a way. When I killed Dennis, in my mind I was killing my brother, too. In my heart, I killed them both."

Dr. Faust's bald head shines eerily in the darkened office as he looks at Mary and Mohammed. They are confused and now hurt. This is not how they expected the session to be. "Impressive strength, Joy."

He pans the faces in the room. "But let's move on. Dr. Abraham instructed me to tell you about myself. My life story is simple. Quite simple and sad.

"To understand my life is to understand my desolate loneliness. I am a psychiatrist; I am single, I do not believe God is a person or that Jesus or Mohammed or Buddha were special in the universe. I studied physics before I studied medicine, and I grasp that eternity is a series of eternities, one within the other.

But if there is a God, then Dr. Abraham is correct—God meant each human soul to exist until the end of time."

Joy, fuming, speaks up: "Right now I don't want to hear about you. I want to talk about Dr. Abraham. He—"

Dr. Faust wrinkles his face in an exaggerated pout. "Not interested in your new shrink, pretty lady? Is it because I'm not the kind of macho man you like? Tsk, tsk, you have pre-judged me. I am a macho man, trust me. Firefighter—takes plenty more balls to do that. They have a higher mortality rate than cops, even taking into account that from time to time a cop's lady friend will shoot him."

Joy looks at Mary and Mohammed then saunters toward Faust. "You seem to know Dr. Abraham well, Dr. Faust. So do I. We each had a chance to talk to Dr. Abraham alone. I don't know what he said to the others, but he told me that I asked Mary and Mohammed questions and helped them. So he told me about himself.

"Mary has battled cancer all her life, but Dr. Abraham's battle began before our very eyes."

"No."

"Had you been looking closely, you'd have seen his energy draining. Were you all so self-absorbed as to be blind?

"Could you not see the irritability, difficulty speaking and swallowing, drowsiness, and muscle weakness on one side of the face? Didn't any of you see it? The trembling hands, the shortness of breath, the growing impatience?"

"Aye" Mary responds softly, "I wasn't sure what I was seeing. I knew somethin' was wrong. Indeed I did know somethin' wasn't right."

"You ignored it of course, Mary. But he would forgive you for that, I am sure," Joy says softly. "But he would not forgive you for holding back the truth here, would he Mary?"

"Indeed he would not."

"Good. Is there anything else you'd like to tell us about that house that you despise so? Perhaps some details of the argument you had that night? Anything more we should know about Carmella, whom you love so? That brooding stone house standing coldly on the hill. Perhaps a conversation took place there that frightened you, traumatized you? Perhaps secrets were revealed there that you have concealed for years, even from your eternal companions in this room?"

Mary begins weeping. Through her tears she says, "Aye, I have concealed a secret."

Joy peers into her eyes. "Tell us the secret now."

Mary's voice is suddenly the voice of an Irish school girl as she says "I won't be tellin' it."

Faust stands next to Joy, who says, "You must."

Mary covers her face with her hands. "No."

Joy peers sideways at Faust then moves a step closer to Mary. "It' is me, Joy, who is saying this now, Mary. You must tell all of your story now."

"Here is the secret, though you seem to know it, Joy. That night at his father's, I told Robert that the baby wasn't his. It was Stephan's baby. Stephan had meant nothin' to Robert. When I said the name Robert asked, 'You mean that dolt of a Spaniard mathematician?' He looked down on Stephan just like later on he looked down on Carmella, and he never noticed her either, never noticin' how much alike Stephan and Carmella looked."

Looking intently at Mary, Joy asks, "What did Robert do when you told him?"

"Robert slapped his hands on the top of his head when I told him. He kept slappin' his palms to the side of his skull. Finally he said he could never forgive me for what I had done. I said I could never forgive him for making me do it. Not two weeks later he made me have an abortion. It was very complicated; I had to travel to France, he had to borrow money from his father and lie that the trip was to celebrate finding a job. It was all very horrible."

Dr. Looks-Like-Satan cocks his brow. "I am sure it was horrible, what with the cancer symptoms you began having right after your tryst with your beautiful Spanish lover. But you say Robert made you take a lover and then have an abortion? I do not understand that. Let's start with the abortion."

"He made me do it because of the complicated plan he had. He told me the plan. He never asked me. He said it was like a miscarriage. I said it was a sin, and he said it wasn't. The sin would be if he had to tell his father why he had to borrow the gun to shoot his goddamn Catholic wife. That's what he said exactly."

"And how did he make you take the lover in the first place? Let's hear that one," Faust urges.

"Robert was so cold, so judging, so brittle. Like his father. Like that house. He was killing me with his coldness. That's why I took Stephan. Stephan was warm; he was kind. He related to me as a woman in a way that Robert never did. Stephan needed me—needed me as a woman, anyhow—like Robert never could."

Faust relaxes in his chair and stares out the window while addressing Mary. "And how did you become lovers?"

"I don't want to talk about it."

Faust shrugs. "You must. That is the agreement. And we are getting close to the place where we will see true healing."

Mary hesitates. Tears rim her eyes. "We were together only once. We—"

Faust interrupts. "I want you to paint a picture for us, Mary. Be vivid. That's what Dr. Abraham would have wanted. Get the picture in your head. Paint it for us. Heal yourself."

"To tell that story vividly as Dr. Abraham had asked, I must tell you about the woman I was in those times."

Dr. Looks-Like-Satan smiles through his bright white teeth. "Sounds almost titillating, Mary. Take us to Ireland to meet the beauty you were back in the day, back—"

Joy steps between Mary and Faust and says, "Do not let him taunt you, but do tell us your story."

Mary looks down at her dull brown penny loafers and shakes her head balefully. "I was thin, lovely, a happy eighteen-year-old with angel eyes and strawberry-blonde hair and that happy, mysterious smile. Robert Fitzpatrick was overweight and studious. His piercing blue eyes peered through his eyeglasses at you. He and I were mutually attracted—at first. Robert's intellect was towering but somehow dark, like the high gables of his father's stone house.

"As we began dating Robert and his mother began planning our marriage. Just as quickly, the brooding side of Robert, that dark, pessimistic, self-centered side of Robert, swooped to the fore and life became unbearable at times."

Faust grins childishly as he leans over to look past Joy. "Mary, please tell your new psychiatrist how you knew Robert was self-centered."

When Mary begins sobbing again, Joy says softly, "Give us an example."

"Once Robert stood over my shoulder and made me write a letter to his mother promisin' that we would marry in the old Anglican chapel where his parents married. They made me promise that I would raise the children outside of the Catholic Church."

Faust looks at Joy but directs his question to Mary. "I know the answer to this question of course, but I want to hear you tell me why they insisted on that."

"His mother was a dowdy woman who claimed her ancestors fought for the Church of England. She was opposed to the marriage because—and she told Robert this—I was too pretty and too Catholic. She still called Catholics Papists, always talkin' about the Pope who she despised. Robert said his father was willin' to tolerate me as long as I promised to raise the children in the Church of England."

Joy asks, "Did they literally say to put it in writing?"

Mary's lips are trembling as she answers, "Did his father say those exact words? I don't know. I do know that he insisted on a letter written in my handwriting."

Still smirking, Faust asks, "Did he literally stand over your shoulder?"

"Aye. Oh God, aye. Robert stood right behind me. He was literally leaning his shoulder against mine every time I would slow down in my writing. He would bump me like a bully on a playground bumps a smaller child. I was leaning over the writing table and my shoulder would bump against the small table lamp when he hit my shoulder from the back.

"The night I wrote the letter I cried so hard that the pen wouldn't write on the paper any more—the paper was soaked with tear drops. Robert held it in my face, tore it up, then said, 'Start again. Promise them. Write.' He really said that to me."

Mohammed jerked upright and peered across at Mary. "And your father allowed this?"

"My father? He did nothing. He seemed… just… so powerless. It was as if I had been taken hostage, and he didn't have the power to free me. When my uncle found out, he wrote a letter from prison. I still have the letter. He said, 'God damn them all. Your Holy Church will have it annulled Mary, mark my word.' Strange, but that's what did eventually happen."

Dr. Looks-Like-Satan grins. "Sounds like your uncle is quite a guy. Staunch Catholic."

Mary manages to find her Mona Lisa smile. "Staunch Catholic? Not at all. He used to joke that he was an old-fashioned Gaelic Pagan. He had this old VCR tape of a movie called—I think it was *Wicker Man*. It was his favorite movie. There's this one island where they pretend to be Christian but really they are not. They have sex out in the open and even human sacrifices. My uncle said that's how it would have been if we'd been lucky. He said if Ireland had stayed Pagan, we'd all have more sex and less violence because Pagans don't need politics for stimulation. So, no, he was not a good Catholic. My uncle was not the honorable man my father was."

Faust's satanic grin broadens. "*Wicker Man*? That uncle of yours is quite a guy! I know the movie well. Anyhow, let's get back to the story of Mary's sex life—I'm sorry, I mean love life."

Mary, eyes downcast, ignores the insult. "We married in September and were livin' in graduate housing while he finished his PhD. I spent my time cleaning our little apartment and reading books that he made me read. I would literally cringe sometimes when he walked in the door in one of his dark moods because some professor of his did not like an equation or a proof or whatever it was he did.

"We ate dinner in silence some nights. Sometimes we ate with our coats on. Robert tried to save on the heat bill, so our place always seemed cold and dark. Each night we would be makin' love in the most listless, joyless way. It was no time at all before I was dreadin' bein' in that bed with him.

"Spring finally came, and then summer. One morning Robert asked me to deliver some books to Stephan. It was on a day that Robert and I had been arguing incessantly. 'Stephan's there all morning but he needs the books by noon,' he shouted to me before slammin' the door as he left the apartment.

"About quarter past eleven I went walkin' the few blocks to the house where Stephan had a room. The air was fresh and trees along the way were green and the sun was bright. When I tapped on the door he was waiting for me with that warm smile of his. I was wearing a green cotton smock with an embroidered low-slung neck, the prettiest of the smocks I wore around the apartment, and a pair of wooden clogs I had received from a Dutch faculty wife for a wedding gift. My legs were bare, I remember, but that was acceptable. It was getting warm outside."

The man in the white lab coat smirks and says, "Tell us more about this fella Stephan."

"I had met Stephan two different times at faculty parties. Perhaps because he was not considered brilliant the way Robert was, he didn't attract the attention and conversation from the more senior faculty. He tended to stand by himself and watch, as I did also. I was always the youngest person in the room. And, of course, the one with no education to speak of.

"I was like Robert's beautiful peasant housekeeper in their eyes. Those wrinkled old professors with the dowdy fat wives, reeking of brandy on their breath and dribbled into their awful beards, they would be leerin' at me from the corners of their tired old eyes.

"Robert knew this—I am sure of that—and seemed to take pleasure in havin' his old professor's leer at me. Stephan noticed too. At the first party where I met him, Stephan saw old Dr. O'Leary lookin' me up and down. Stephan came over later and whispered, 'Sorry about leering O'Leary. Can't really blame him, though.' Stephan would smile at me. Robert never seemed to smile at me.

"At both of the parties Stephan and I fell into small talk about travel and teachin'. He was so very interesting compared to the others. He—"

"Compared to Robert, too?"

"Aye, compared to Robert," Mary says immediately. "Robert made fun of everybody and one day he told me that Stephan's father had been a professional magician, toured

Europe, even came to America. Robert took that to mean that Stephan was beneath him. For me, it made Stephan better. At one of the parties Stephan talked about his father. Stephan said his father taught him the difference, and I can remember the words, between 'show magic and the real, beautiful magic in the world.' We talked about magic."

"My goodness, what a coincidence," Dr. Faust taunts. "You, with that secret fascination with magic. Even the great scientist Larry Josephson believed in it."

Joy glares at Faust. "Just continue, Mary," she says.

"From the parties I remembered Stephan as a beautiful specimen of a man. He was short, well built, always smiling. My heart leapt that day when Stephan opened his creaky old door.

"I said something silly, like 'Book delivery.' He smiled then looked me up and down as I stood at the door of his little apartment. 'The library has inaugurated a worthy service,' I recall him saying. 'Perhaps I can offer the delivery person a cold beer on a warm summer day. It is a bit early, I know,' he said. 'Early for a Spaniard,' I said, 'but not for an Irishwoman.'

"He gestured for me to sit on the sofa of his crowded little efficiency. The sofa was next to the door. Across from it was his unmade bed. There was a small kitchen then a little hallway with a bathroom at the end. I said that if I knew I'd be invited in for a drink I'd have dressed for the occasion. And I remember him replying this way in his slight Spanish accent: 'Not at all, you look like an angel.'

"When he brought my beer he said, 'This is a treat, and let me admit immediately that I have secretly envied Robert for having a woman with pale, angelic skin and such a beautiful smile.' He kissed my cheek and leaned back to look at me.

"We drank one beer and then he said, 'We had one beer for Ireland and now we will have a glass of rioja wine for Spain.' 'That's only fair,' I recall saying. Out of the blue he kissed my cheek. I let his lips rest there for a moment. Then he got up and brought us two glasses of delicious red wine.

"I knew that we were both becoming excited. After one glass of wine he said, 'May I?' and poured another. We toasted and leaned into each other in a soft, warm hug. The hug lingered. Without a word, he took my glass from my hand

and then led me to the bed on the other side of the room. 'Time for some magic,' he said. The bed was a disheveled jumble of sheets and blankets and books thrown open with little notes scrawled on them.

"I didn't care. As I walked there, I slipped my wedding ring off and put it on his little table, piled up with books and papers. I stepped out of my clogs and felt my bare feet against the cool hard wood of his floor. That feeelin' of cold on my bare feet excited me then, and even now it excites me."

"Whooa, Nelly! Some erotic titillation right here in this place!" Faust shouts. "And, is this the famous heirloom ring we speak of now, Mary dear?"

Mary's trembling voice was broken-hearted and defiant at the same time. "Aye. It was their family heirloom."

"Then continue with your story."

Mary closes her eyes, then opens them to continue, "He took off his clothes. He was so dark, so smooth. He began lifting my smock above my head and I whispered no, but raised myself up and removed my panties. We kissed a lover's kiss and almost immediately we were making love. The kind you see in movies, where lovers moan softly and caress. The interlude didn't last even an hour. I put my ring on and left, crying as I walked back to spend another frigid night with my awful husband.

"But it produced a baby, which I killed. But God brought the baby back to me. Carmella, my blessed angel, is the baby that God restored to me years later. So Stephan was right. There was magic that day, indeed."

Silence. Mary's new physician reaches for the ornate ceramic water pitcher. "Water, Mary?"

"Aye. Please."

As Mary drinks, Joy and Faust both look at Mohammed. Faust is about to say something, but Joy speaks first. "So we have learned some new facts about Mary's story. And Mohammed, could you tell us a bit more about that young woman, that American, the one that wore lingerie in front of men and drank strong alcohol in your son's apartment? Can you tell us more about the anger you felt that night?"

Mohammed speaks through clenched jaws. "It is not your place to ask me questions, Joy."

"How do you know it's not," she replies.

"I know nothing in this dreadful place."

Joy smiles to encourage Mohammed. "Then please speak. We are all in this together."

"Very well. Zayd's young lady friend Gloria was a child really. She was a selfish young woman to be sure. Yes, it is a fact: We had sex. And yes, I felt passion. She was supple, soft. She moaned and thrashed about when we made love. But she lacked discipline. She was the kind of woman who would reveal such a fact to your wife and your son, at the worst possible moment. So a man worth millions of dollars, a man of principle, should not meet her in the way it all happened.

"That night of the accident she was also drunk. She woke from her stupor because of the noise of the shouting. She walked out of the bedroom naked, into the living room that had already witnessed so many foul things. 'Well, hey, it's Loverman,' she said, looking at me. 'And Junior, and the missus too,' she said to my wife. Standing there naked, she made such a haughty gesture toward my wife."

Mohammed looks at the floor. "I managed to ignore that girl. I began beating my son, instead. I felt in my heart that his actions had destroyed all that was sacred to me. The bowl suddenly symbolized my life before he brought that horrible American girl into it. Now it was broken.

"As I beat him more fiercely, he slumped to the floor. My fist had made a gash at his lip and another on his eye. He was bleeding. Some of the blood seemed to be rushing in his mouth. He seemed to be gagging on his blood. I began ramming his head against the wall.

"I was stopped by Nia's cries and my lack of breath. I released my hold on him and stood up, slowly. He crawled across the floor on his belly like a lizard or a snake—until he reached the pile of broken pieces. His hands fumbled along the carpet as he picked up two or three pieces then crawled back to me. He bowed his head and sat motionless until, suddenly, he rolled over onto his back.

Nia said, 'There is blood in his mouth. Can Zayd breathe?' She seemed more concerned about her drunken son than our precious family heirloom.

When I bent over to look into his mouth, he grabbed the back of my head and pulled me down to him. He took a sharp piece of the broken bowl and cut a gash across my eye and cheek." Mohammed points to a thin, barely visible scar running from above his right eye down his cheek to his neck. Through the blood in his mouth I heard him mutter, 'Die with your trinkets.'

"And now I was bleeding as well as Zayd. Our blood was mingling on a pool on his white carpet. My eye was on fire. Bright red blood was squirting everywhere, onto the walls, onto my suit and shirt, onto Nia's dress."

"You say blood was on your suit? That night, were you wearing the suit you are wearing today?" Faust asks.

Eyes downcast, Mohammed sulks a bit and admits, "Yes, as a matter of fact I was."

"Please continue."

"Nia ran to the kitchen to make an icepack, acting as if I had not been injured. She began to run back into the living room from the kitchen when she saw the blood running down my face. 'Please bring me a towel; I cannot see.' She ran back to get a towel, but when she returned with it and the ice pack Zayd had lost consciousness. Her face froze when she finally took the full measure of all that had happened. Zayd was sprawled on the floor, blood oozing from his mouth, gasping breaths gurgling blood. I was slumped in the corner, covered in blood, gasping, eyes closed

"She shrieked hysterically. 'You must call 911,' she said. I told her, 'No. Let us not have them involved. We will take him to the hospital; it is very close by.' I dragged him to my car. Nia and I were propping Zayd up, his feet dragging on the floor. Finally we got him to the elevator and then crossed the parking lot to my car."

"What happened when you reached the car?"

"My Porsche has fold-down rear seats. They are small, but they are safe when they are deployed. Nia and I leaned Zayd against the car, and I began to open up the seats so he could be put in one. Then suddenly that grotesque American girl came rushing toward us across the parking lot.

"She had one of his white dress shirts on and was still wearing the towel fashioned as a hajib. Her bare feet were splashing up water from the puddles of an earlier rain. Her naked brown skin could be seen underneath as the white cotton of the shirt bounced and swayed from her running. Nia, and I, of course, saw this. As she ran across the parking lot, her breasts and womanhood were exposed; yet she did not care.

"Gloria rushed up to me and began thumping me on the chest with her fists. 'Do you know why Zayd was so angry at you, his father?' 'No,' I told her. She sneered at me, tears in her coal black eyes. 'Because he found out about us. I told Zayd every detail about how I made love to you.'

"With this, Nia looked at me and then at Gloria. Then Nia looked deeply into my eyes in a way that she had never done before. She turned slowly to Gloria and asked, eyes burning in anger and disbelief, 'What did Zayd find out?'

"A wind was stirring up and a light rain was beginning to fall into Gloria's coal-black eyes. As she and Nia stood facing each other, their raven hair and eyes were so alike that a chill ran down my spine.

"'Yep, dear mother of Zayd. Your son found out that his father, your husband, Daddy Warbucks right here, was sleeping with his fiancé. Me. And paying me for it at $500 a pop, to boot.'

"Nia buried her face in her hands. 'Please do not tell me this, Gloria,' Nia sobbed. 'Mohammed, tell me it is not true.'

"I was shaking from my shame. I could not even speak.

"Nia looked me in the eye. Through her tears she shouted at me, 'How? Why?' These are the questions my dear wife put to me. She and Gloria were staring at me with their radiant coal-black eyes. Their eyes were just so similar.

"My voice was stammering. 'Nia, I confess that yes, there is some truth in what she says. Zayd had told this woman I was wealthy, and I could perhaps help her start a business. One day she called me and it was arranged to meet in his apartment. When I arrived she was drunk and dressed very immodestly.

"I looked at Gloria and said that I disapproved of her dress and her demeanor but agreed to listen to her story. She explained that she and a friend had a business venture that would require five thousand dollars. It was to sell jewelry or something of that kind, which I said was not a worthy investment. Then she offered to have sex with me, 'right here and now, Papa' she said. She wanted to tempt me. Did you not?"

"Gloria ignored me. In her bare feet she stood and stared at Nia. Rain was falling on their hair, on both of them. Their hair was glistening in the rain.

"'Nia, please understand,' I begged. 'This woman could pass for a beautiful Iranian woman, even by her bearing. I have said that although her family was wealthy she had no morals. This was proof.'"

Mohammed looks at the wheat field scene as if seeking comfort, perhaps clarity. "I said to Nia this woman taunted me saying that it is Allah's will that true believers are entitled to many women. She placed her hand on me, and I... finally, I did not recoil.'"

"Gloria let the raindrops sit in her face. 'That is not how it happened. I offered him sex for money and he took it. Then, love began. Yes. I'm a foolish girl because I fell in love with this old man. Then I could no longer bear to be with Zayd in bed. I had to tell him the truth. He wouldn't believe me. I showed hit this as proof.' She handed Nia an embossed business card. Raised gold letters announced MOHAMED IRANI. PURVEYOR OF PRECIOUS ANTIQUITIES. In my handwriting are the words 'Gloria, you are most precious of all.' She had brought it with her, running in the rain."

Faust smirks. "Busted. Big time."

Mohammed ignores him. "Nia looked at Zayd and then at me and once again began crying hysterically. I pushed the girl to the pavement. I heard her head hit the ground. She scrambled to her feet and ran away from us. Suddenly she stopped. She spun on her heels and shouted, 'Damn you Mohammed. I love you so. Tell them both that you love me. Tell your almighty Allah that you love me more than him! Confess it.' Then she came running toward me. She was repeating over and over, 'Confess!'

Faust smirks. "And did you confess it?"

"No. I had to flee for fear of beating her as I had just beaten Zyad. I wanted to kill her. I heaved Zayd into the passenger seat like one would heave a bag of trash. Without a word, Nia climbed in beside him. I sped off."

Faust stares into Mohammed's eyes. "So you ran. Then what? You went ahead and killed your family instead, right?"

Rearing back in stiff recoil at the piercing look in Faust's eyes, Mohammed's jaw tightens, as would a man's when ready to attack. "Anyone who has been in even a minor automobile crash, a minor so-called fender bender, can attest to how fast it happens. They can tell you how final it all seems.

"Even if it is only a dent in the rear bumper of the car, your first feeling is that something is suddenly ruined. So too it was with me. It happened so incredibly fast and, inside that blind instant, I understood in my heart the finality of it all.

"Zayd had a huge bruise above his eye and a cut, made by my punching. Made by this very hand." He waves his fist then stares at it like he is appraising an antique.

"Nia was holding a rag to Zayd's face, the two of them cramped in the bucket passenger seat. My son's blood was everywhere. I felt this incredible anger. My anger was too great for me to bear. I shifted into first gear and literally banged through to fourth gear accelerating my car to the highest speed possible."

Mohammed's deep voice, usually so composed, grows ragged as he talks faster and faster. "I pulled out of the parking lot and made a right onto Ocean Boulevard. My tires were screeching, the engine was whining, my wife was begging me to slow down. 'Go slow. Please! We are all here together—our whole family is in this car! Our whole life is in this car,' she shouted through her tears.

"Suddenly, a large silver car pulled out of one of the driveways. It was really that driver's mistake. She was drunk. Drunk!"

Mohammed shakes his fist again. "She pulled out without looking. No matter. The car struck the passenger side of my car with incredible force. The impact propelled my car into the lane of oncoming traffic and a second vehicle—I can see it now with my eyes—tried to swerve to avoid us but could not. The other driver's tires were squealing and his horn was blasting and I believe I could see him wide eyed, shouting at me to stop. But of course, I could not control the car.

"Before I became unconscious, I remember the sound of my wife gasping, moaning my name. 'Mohammed, I am dying,' she said. There was this horrible sound of metal shearing off again. Even after the side collision and then the head-on collision, our car was struck by a third car. This third car hit us from an angle, from both the front and the side."

Mohammed holds his hands against each other to try to describe the third collision. "The third car and the second car caught us in a vice that made a hellish sound. It was a crunching, crashing sound that simply cannot be described. My son never fully woke from his drunken stupor. When at first we were hit on the side, he called for his mother. His heavy body tumbled when we were first hit and I believe his shoulders were lodged under the front seats, contorting his entire body.

Mohammed casts his eyes to the ceiling. "I heard the horrible metal banging, I saw from the corner of my eyes the banging, lurching of my son's body and that of his mother as the car was hit first from the side and then from the front. I believe, but I am not sure, I saw a piece of metal fly into her neck and sever her head. I beg you, Faust or Joy, whoever is my inquisitor, please allow me to stop here."

"You may," the hideous figure says through his bright white teeth. "After Dr. Abraham's fashion, allow me to pour you a drink of water."

"Thank you," Mohammed says.

Faust permits the room to go quiet after Mohammed relives the moments of his accident. A few moments later Faust yells, "Yess Siree!" breathing tension back into the room. He smiles at Joy. "Whew, that's a lot of truth from Mohammed and Mary. But hey, we've been neglecting Joy."

He shouts toward the ceiling, "So behold, Joy the temptress, the murderess. The unrepentant Joy."

He turns to Joy. "But you feel no need to repent or to conceal."

"You are right," Joy says.

"Why?"

"Because I understand that God knows all, that God sees deep into the heart, that God has fashioned each human soul and knows its journey."

"Ah," Faust says. "Your story is complete. But let me be sure you know who the villain of your story was."

"It was the same man in two forms: my stepbrother the cop and Dennis the cop. I loved them and trusted them. They loved me, too, but they did not honor me. My karma has me searching for a man who will honor me."

Joy walks across the expanse of cold tile to the window to pull open the blinds. As the light pours in, she says, "Evil is the villain in all of our stories. Eventually all souls will discover this, wandering as they do, looking for answers and sometimes finding them."

Joy's eyes cloud with tears. She looks out the window at the white-sand beach and the ocean beyond. Stifling tears, trying so very hard not to be weak, she says, "I am leaving here now."

"As you should," Faust says.

She acts the flirt with the man behind Dr. Abraham's desk, even to the point of exaggerating her accent. "To you, Dr. Looks-Like-Satan, I shall become a great puzzle for you. Yes?"

"Yes. Even with our silly little test, I still don't know who you are. I cannot stop you from leaving. But I would not be comfortable if you left before you knew who you were. Do you know who you are?"

Suddenly there is new light in the room, brighter than the beach outside. All eyes are drawn to the door in the back and it begins to glow, then it shines gleaming white. Joy is transfixed. "Is this a trick, Faust?"

"As I have already said, maybe I am an illusionist. The pictures on the wall came to life unexpectedly, howling winds outside come and go on cue, and now the door in the back of the room is transformed into what looks like an ancient gateway, shining with a perfect white light. White, the color of innocence. White, the absence of color, the absence of soil and filth and dirt.

"You'll decide soon what is real Joy, or perhaps you know but are pretending not to. But answer my question," he says, eyes sparkling with reflected light. "Show the others how you can exit this place. There is a gateway for each soul, Joy.

For each, there is a gate of brilliant white. Pass through it. But first tell us who you are. I really do insist."

Blinking, she studies the light then turns to Faust. "I am a woman whose sin was not lust, but shame. Being ashamed of being judged or called impure. Being ashamed to admit to myself and others that I had been violated. My mind tried to pretend it never happened.

"But now I am cured. I want to get away from that life. In my heart I want to reclaim my lost innocence and be reborn as sweet and immaculate Joy."

She locks her eyes on the red-rimmed, bloodshot eyes of Faust. Her stare is so intense that, this time, Satan's look-alike casts his eyes away to avoid Joy's stare.

Joy turns to the once beautiful woman in the dowdy blue clothes and says quietly, "Goodbye, Mary."

As Mary grasps Joy's hands, a tear rolls onto Joy's wrist. "Goodbye, Joy. God bless you."

Affectionately, Joy ties the little bows on the sleeve of Mary's blue blouse. "I don't know why that little bow can't stay tied," Mary says in her sweetest voice, the one with the faint Irish brogue. "It just keeps a-comin' loose."

Now Joy turns to the man with the piercing black eyes that hide, she understands now, unspeakable sorrow. She loathed him from the first moment they sat down next to each other in Dr. Abraham's chairs. Now it is pity that she feels. Softly she says, "Goodbye, Mohammed."

Mohammed approaches her, moving his prosthetic limb as normally as he can. Soon he and Joy are face to face. "With my farewell I give blessings also," he says.

Joy touches each of them gently on the shoulder and then softly says, "I'll see you later I'm sure, somewhere between now and the end of time."

As Joy speaks, Dr. Looks-Like-Satan closes his eyes as if to draw energy into himself from some invisible source. When his eyes open, he sees Joy turn her back to him. Mary and Mohammed will not look, but Faust watches her make her way toward the glow, then disappear into it.

Mary Joesephson

MARY UNDERSTANDS VAGUELY that a span of time has passed between Joy's departure and the moment when Faust shouts, "Ya-hoo!"

Like a rodeo cowboy who has wrestled a steer to the ground, he grins and triumphantly thrusts his arms skyward. "Yes Siree! Know what happened just then, boys and girls? Dr. Abraham's famous, coulda-been-patented-if-it-existed-in-the-real-world Portal Exercise is finally producing some results with a boost maybe with some special effects care of ol' Faust here. But Mary, where did Joy go?"

For Mary, the scene has the feel of an out-of-body experience. The Mary who is thinking these thoughts believes she is watching some other Mary, some otherwise embodied Mary, recoil at the sound of Faust's voice. She sees Mary adjusting her yellow bandana; she notes the vacant stare in her own blue eyes. The Mary looking at the room from an out-of-body vantage point is surprised that neither Mary nor Mohammed are looking at the streaks of light streaming in from where the door had been..

Eyes ablaze, Faust walks a circle around the two remaining patients. When the energy of his stare locks her eyes onto his, Mary feels present in her body again. She is Mary, standing where her mahogany chair used to be, listening to Dr. Faust say, "So now, Mary—and you also, Mohammed—you are no doubt wondering where we go from here. Well, we are going to be joined by a new member of the group."

He throws his hands out wildly, like a salesman making a final point to close a sale. "Well... not new perhaps, but in a new role. I expect him to join us soon."

Dr. Faust stares pointedly at the shimmering white gate posts where the White Door was. Mary and Mohammed, obedient to an unspoken command, turn and stare also. A figure in a shawl appears, hunched over, moving slowly. Silhouetted against the stream of light pouring into the room, the figure moves like a wooden marionette with huge boney hands and sunken cheeks.

Mary shrieks, "Dr. Abraham!" as the marionette makes its way into the light of the office and moves laboriously into the chair originally reserved for Dr. Faust. He exchanges glances with Mary first then Mohammed.

"Yes," Dr. Abraham whispers through labored breath.

Settling in, he adjusts what appears to be a yellow prayer shawl thrown across his slumping shoulders. "Thank you for having me, Faust, indeed, thank you all." The old man clasps a boney knuckle to his cheek, damming up a stream of drool oozing from the corner of his mouth.

Though shocked by his pitiful condition, Mary takes comfort from the familiar sound of her psychiatrist's raspy voice. She reaches over to touch him and he smiles weakly, head cast down.

Faust rears back. "So. Mary and Mohammed. I see that you are surprised."

Mohammed jerks his body toward Dr. Abraham. "He said you were in a hospice in Israel, Dr. Abraham. That is what this fellow told us."

Mary, her hands still clasped around Dr. Abraham's, begins crying hysterically. She raises her eyes skyward and cries, "Please God, please tell me what's happening to me now!"

A recollection in Mary's mind of Joy slamming down the blinds and challenging Faust, pieced together with a vaguely remembered sense that Joy's act of defiance somehow helped Joy heal, gives Mary an idea. Adjusting her bandana, she glares at Faust then looks at Dr. Abraham sitting in his shawl. She demands, "Someone tell us what is happening here!"

Smiling impishly, Faust plops himself into the chair behind Dr. Abraham's desk. "Calm down Mary, you're making Dr. Abraham uncomfortable."

"Only if you tell us what is happenin'."

"I will tell you when I am ready," Faust shrugs.

"Then I'll be calming down when I'm ready," Mary retorts in a very Irish tone. She folds her arms across her chest and glowers at Faust defiantly.

Smiling, the hideous young man says, "We could stay in this stalemate forever, Mary, but that would do a dishonor to our new patient, formerly your beloved healer. So, therefore, I will do as you wish."

Feeling a surge of confidence, Mary slowly uncrosses her arms and fixes her eyes on Faust's.

As a reward for her compliance, Faust says, "You asked God to tell you what is happening to you. Let me answer the question, nothing is happening to you. Joy has left."

Dr. Abraham nods, his rasping voice strong for a moment at least. "Yes. She and I passed each other, of course. It is good that her healing is complete."

Dr. Faust smiles. "Yes, and congratulations on your success, doctor."

Riveting his eyes on Mary's, he continues. "Now Dr. Abraham is sitting in what used to be my chair. I could explain the logistics that brought him here from Israel, but I won't. If you are interested in that rather mundane point, I invite you to speculate in your own minds. The fact is that he is here now, and he is now my patient in this therapy. His role has changed. For now, he is one of you."

Faust leans backward in his chair, pulling the water pitcher from a shelf of the floor-to-ceiling credenza behind the desk. He places the pitcher on his desk, pulls a glass from the shelf, and pours Dr. Abraham a tall glass of water. Dr. Abraham eyes the operation with a wan smile, focusing on the clean, glistening water and the perfectly formed round ice cubes. "Here, Dr. Abraham."

Dr. Abraham's gnarled hand reaches out from under his yellow shawl and takes the glass; he drinks slowly. Much of the water escapes his lips and trickles down the ashen skin of his cheeks.

Faust looks at Mary, who is still sobbing, still seemingly disoriented. "May I interest you in some water, Mary?"

Mary nods a shaky yes. Faust fetches another glass, fills it with the pure clear liquid and globular ice cubes, and hands it politely to Mary. She takes one small sip and lowers the glass to her chest.

Ignoring Mohammed and Dr. Abraham, Faust says, "Mary, I believe that the subconscious mind is where the human soul really resides. Or more accurately, Mary, the subconscious is where the soul is locked up, imprisoned, chained. Visualize the pretty Irish lass you once were in a jail cell, leaning hopeless against the bars, ankles in chains. You learned about this the first time you met the good doctor Abraham. He didn't tal about chains and jail cell bars, but You learned Sigmund Freud's idea of the subconscious. Remember?"

"I think so but I'm so confused now… Ahm not rightly sure about a single thing."

"I'll refresh your memory. Freud believed that our thoughts and even our actions are guided by a part of our mind that we cannot reach directly. A part of our mind that is, well, below consciousness—hence the word subconscious. I believe it is there that our immortal souls chafe against this earthly life. And so, I believe your subconscious and hence your soul has more to reveal to us."

He glues his bloodshot eyes on Mary. "Am I making sense, Mary?"

Weakly, looking at the floor, she shakes her head no.

Peering intently at Mary's cherubic face, her Mona Lisa smile still vanquished by her bout with tears, Faust continues, "Very well, let me come at it another way. In… let us say, my review of your file, reading your file, I concluded that even after your confession about the abortion of your love child, the murder you believe God un-did by bringing Carmella into your life, there is still more to your story. I do understand why you resented Robert and his family for turning that hot Irish lass into a stone-cold faculty wife, but there seems to be more. I don't quite understand how you can live day to day with Robert's son and not wonder about the fate of his father."

"I don't either sometimes."

"Then let me invite you to do as Joy just did. Say the words to understand my shame, then proceed."

Mary bites her lip so hard that it begins to bleed. When she sips at her glass, a tiny stream of blood oozes from the wound into the water.
Faust looks at the glass. He takes it out of her hand. "Mary, excuse me, but it appears that you have bitten your lip and there is a bit of blood in the glass. Let me take the glass before you get blood on your—hands? Or do you already believe you have blood on your hands so to speak. It that why you bit your lip so hard you made it bleed?"

Mary breaks into hysterical sobbing again. "This is too much. Dr. Abraham, please stop him." She looks down at the man hunched over in his shawl.

Struggling to breathe, with a far-away look in his eyes, Dr. Abraham's voice is a barely audible string of gasps and whispers, "Mary, we must let this process run its course."

"Very well," she says defiantly. "To understand my shame is to understand that my life as a woman has been a lie. I will admit it. To this day, to this moment, I can't bear to think about how often Robert and I argued side by side in the hideous rough-hewn bed his father gave us. I can't bear to think about how quickly I came to hate him. And aye, there is much more to my shame."

"Then tell us," Faust smirks. "After all, the revered Dr. Abraham himself just told us that the process must, how did he say it? Run its course?"

"My father was quite wealthy when I was born. My father was one of the few Catholics who had successfully built a business in Belfast. After my mother died my father drank more and more. Other things happened too, and slowly he lost his major Protestant customers except for one. Robert Fitzpatrick, Senior. Aye, that was my father-in-law. Robert and his father came into my father's office where I had begun working after I finished what Americans call high school. He couldn't stop staring at me and both of our fathers saw it.

"I was eighteen and he was twenty-three. He was a bookish man, a man who spoke constantly about mathematics and his doctoral thesis and how I must attend university someday if I was to be a proper faculty wife for him.

"One day my father said, 'Robert Fitzpatrick rang me up and said his boy's a bit smitten with you.' I told father that I didn't like Robert, much less find him attractive. 'Give the lad a chance,' he said. There was this sense that I was betrothed to Robert. I felt like his daughter's beauty—and I was a beauty— was my father's last remainin' business asset among the Protestants. I love my father so. He is a smart man, a kind man, always laughing and drinking like his good friend Larry Josephson."

"The man you are now married to? We are all interested in the fact that you married a man the same age as your father, that in effect you married your father, but please focus on Robert, your first husband." Faust says.

"I want to do that. Aye' we're speakin' of my first husband now. I knew my father wanted it and I couldn't hurt him so I became involved with Robert. Everything with Robert happened so fast we were engaged two months after our first meeting and married two months later.

"Robert was so impressed that I was a virgin even though I was really only a teenager. I wish Joy had explained why men think that is so important. He made a huge point of persuading his family to give him an heirloom ring that had been in the family for generations. It had an ornate gold setting and two large diamonds. I would think that it was as precious to Robert's family—especially his father—as the bowl was to you, Mohammed."

"But specifically, why is the ring so important?"

"Because the ring finishes the story. I already said that we argued about the ring and Robert walked out. When I told my story, I left the impression that I never heard from him again. That is not true."

Dr. Abraham's slumped shoulders turn to Mary. Mohammed looks over also.

Mary blinks back a tear. "What happened was that I pawned the ring to give Carmella money. She needed money and I wanted to please her with a gift. How Robert figured that out I will never know. Three days after he walked out—it was a Tuesday, I remember—he called me to say he saw the ring in a pawnshop. He said I was the worst kind of thief imaginable. He was right. Until now, I am the only person who knew this secret. And I never told Carmella. I never told Larry. It is a secret I would hide from God Almighty if my silence could make it so."

Mary pauses, her face scrunching up in a sob. "And there is another fact."

"What is it?"

"The fact that he wired his father for money and faced the embarrassment and shame of tellin' what I had done with the family's ring. And the fact that... on the day he went to take the ring out of pawnshop, he was murdered. The police said he died of multiple stab wounds and he had been robbed.

Before, sitting right here in front of everybody, I said that he disappeared and I hadn't heard from him, that wasn't true."

A stunned silence fills the room until Mary speaks again. "When I said that the police came, it was to solve a murder, not to locate him. I deceived all of you. And I am still deceiving my husband. Larry did not know I pawned the ring. I let Larry believe that Robert took it from me, then pawned it himself. He does not know the truth, even to this day."

Mohammed's eyes follow Mary's as she looks up at the ceiling and weeps. "Do you believe it is your fault that your first husband—"

"Was stabbed to death? Aye. And that is the guilt I have lived with. I killed his baby. I disgraced him in front of his family. And in a way, I killed him. He would never been at that pawnshop if I hadn't taken the ring there."

"Very good, Mary. You seem to understand the burden that places on you. But, perhaps there is more … Is there a letter you intended to give Dr. Abraham?"

"Aye," Mary says. She sobs so deeply that for a moment she chokes and coughs, unable to speak.

"Who's it from?"

Mary sobs harder.

"Who is the letter from, Mary? Please tell us."

Mary chokes out, "Robert's mother."

"Care to read it?" Faust urges.

"Aye, but before I do there is one fact I must tell."

"Boy, these facts just keep leaking out. And what new fact do you need to tell?"

"Robert's mother never truly believed he died, because… I did not tell the group this fact about his murder. The men who killed him… they…"

Mary's tear-streaked face freezes, her body shaking. Her jaw is slack, her lips are quivering. She stares blankly ahead, avoiding eye contact with anybody in the room. The room grows still in anticipation.

Through his tight lips with their bright white teeth, Faust says, "Please continue, Mary. We're all eager to hear this new fact."

Finally Mary's eyes come to life and lock onto the eyes of Faust. "The men who killed Robert dumped his body in a swamp. By the time it was found it decayed so much that—"

"That it was hideous and unrecognizable. Correct?"

"Aye."

"Who identified the body for the police?"

"I did." Her composure completely lost, Mary pushes her face down to her lap and throws her arms around her knees.

Observing this, Faust keeps probing. "Are these some of the facts that you removed from the story between versions?"

Mary is weeping too hysterically to speak, but her head, now thrust between her knees, slowly nods yes.

Faust looks away and says, "We will wait until you can continue."

Across the span of minutes, Mary gradually raises her head and gathers her wits about her. Without prompting, she continues her story. "Robert's father decided to have a closed-casket funeral, even t. His mother... she just loved Robert so much; he was even though they did not have his body. She refused to believe he was dead. She tried to convince his father the same thing, and over time it just seems... Let me just read the letter:

Mary – Two evenings ago, I was deep in prayer. For the past several days, I was having visions that I believed could lead the Florida police to Robert. Each day it seemed that my prayers were more heartfelt and my vision of my son was clearer.

Robert was still alive, my visions were telling me. He had been beaten over the head by a gang of awful black men in Florida. They were trying to steal my precious ring. To save my ring he had fought them away—they are cowards, these blacks, when a man stands and fights them—and lived. But his injuries were great, and now he was wandering about with some sort of amnesia. The Americans who saw him mistook him for one of their vagrants, one of their street people or homeless or whatever word the Americans used.

My prayers and my vision were strong in my heart this evening. It was a comforting image I conjured in my old woman's mind, Robert walking down a warm street almost remembering who he was. I had a smile on my face as I sat in front of the fireplace with a roaring fire and a cup of tea.

I was quite surprised to see Father—"

Mary pauses to say, "Both Robert and his mother referred to the elder Mr. Fitzpatrick as Father." Tears in her eyes, she continues reading.

I was quite surprised to see Father walk into the room. He usually sits alone in his study. I wondered if now was the time to tell him of my wonderful vision. Was this the time to give all of the family the hope that I was experiencing?

He stood in front of the fireplace for the longest time without saying a word. Then he took his shotgun down from the wooden braces over the mantel.

I asked him what is this, Father? New Year's eve is a bit away, yet. He said it's a new year in China. Year of the monkey. Half the men in the world are Chinamen. I've decided to celebrate with them this year on this cold purple night with the stars winking down on Ireland. You were right you know, Missus. We never should have let a Catholic girl in the family.

I was surprised yet again. Father wanting to celebrate with those despised Chinamen a half a world away. He had been worrying too much about Robert.

I felt the cold air rush in when he strode out the side door with his shotgun. I decided to clear the cup of cold tea from the table. On the way to the kitchen, I decided that tonight I would tell Father about my wonderful vision. My wonderful vision that our dear son Robert was safe.

Five minutes later, I heard the shotgun blast. I ran outside. The sky was purple and cold. Father was lying there. I couldn't look. Our dear Lord in Heaven would not let me see what the police told me later. The elder Robert had taken a shotgun to his mouth, and with double barrels, blown his brains out.

Thank you for everything you did to destroy me, my son, my family, Mary. Your Papist confessor will tell you that he can forgive you for what you have done, but he cannot. May your soul and his burn in hell.

While reading her final indictment, energy had been draining from Mary's body. She slumps to the floor, and the letter falls to the floor with her. Mary gazes dully at the letter in front of her. Faust seizes upon the moment of her total defeat to grab the letter off the floor. He waves it in Mary's face. "So you've managed to bring about the demise of both the son and the father. Wow. I can't say that I blame Bobby's momma for wanting you to burn in hell.

"But now let me tell Mary's story a la Dr. Faust. Here we have Mary, a pretty Irish maiden whose dad goes broke and next thing you know she's pinned down in a squeaky bed doin' it missionary style with a cold fish of a kid from the wealthy gentry who was briefly smitten with her pretty face but in his heart despised her.

"Luckily, she was able to make real love, passionate, soft love, to a man one time," he smirks, "But it wasn't the aforementioned cold fish. It was a gorgeous, hot-blooded Spaniard. Lucky lass? No. Because tragedy followed. Guilt followed. And why was that?"

Mary lifts her head as Faust continues. "You see, to the end Mary forced herself to forget that her abortion was actually a natural miscarriage. She concocts an elaborate story about a planned trip to abortionists in Europe, then makes herself believe it was a self-induced abortion so she could feel horrible and depressed about her life, and then blame it on Robert.

"The real reason she wanted to believe she had the abortion was that the abortion was worse than having sex with another man. Her imagined crime outweighed the real one.

"Do I have that right? There was never a trip to Paris for an abortion. Yes or no."

"There was no trip," Mary says.

"What did you do to bring on the miscarriage?"

"Nothing. It just happened. I wanted that child."

"Of course Mary wanted to bear that child. And then later on when she's fighting cancer night and day, the one human being who is helping Mary is a girl who lost her mother to the same disease Mary is fighting. Mary thinks maybe God worked a miracle and Carmella is the baby she lost. In an act of kindness she pawns the ring to help Carmella's family. But in her mind she thinks she steals a ring that belongs to her to begin with, gives the money to the child she wished she had, and then the cold fish husband gets himself killed trying to buy it back."

Faust kneels down in front of Mary. "See it like the out-of-body experiences you so cherish. See Mary? The ring belonged to her. It was given to a beautiful little trophy wife by a wealthy Irish family who had a son named Robert. It was yours to do with as you wished, oh former trophy wife. Some stranger, some anonymous drug-crazed knife-wielding dude killed your husband. Still, you lavish this guilt upon yourself. See how your God conspires with your subconscious mind to keep your soul in chains? I'm tellin' ya Mary, it's a bitch."

Dr. Faust ends this rant by waving the letter toward Mohammed, who had been standing as a bystander to Mary's ordeal. "What do you think of our Mona Lisa now?"

"Here is what I say." Lips quivering, Mohammad pauses until finally he addresses the pitiful Dr. Abraham. "Sir, you taught us that the soul begins pristine and in this world it is battered and sullied. What greater proof of that can there be than the story that we have just heard?"

Faust stands. "I agree. Mary, please kneel beside Dr. Abraham and hold his hand. Isaac Abraham, now it is time that you told your story to us. Let's all hear what your mind and that great God of the Chosen People had in store for your pitiful soul."

Isaac Abraham

Dr. Abraham turns to Mary. "To understand my shame is to understand that I wanted to be the brave father that died fighting for America in the Pacific.

"I tried to take his place with his wife, my mother.

"And then I tried to be a killer of men. My father killed Japanese men I killed Muslim men, men like you, Mohammed. The scripture is clear that thou shalt not kill but, like countless soldiers before me, I killed without feeling the guilt or shame that should come with such a grave sin. Except for one time."

He continues in his weak voice, ignoring Faust. "In the 1967 Arab-Israeli War, much of the fighting took place in the desert and in small villages in the mountains. That picture on the wall is the picture of the place where my greatest sin took place: the Golan Heights.

"The western side of the Golan Heights consists of a rock escarpment. In a way it is a beautiful place. It rises almost two thousand feet from the Sea of Galilee and the Jordan River to a more gently sloping plateau It is rugged with brown and grey boulders and rocks and a gnarled landscape. I vaguely recall scrubby vegetation with blooms of various reds and yellows that seemed beautiful and somehow courageous basking in the sunlight of the blue sky there."

He takes a sip of his water. "As we made our way along and occasionally caught glimpses of Galilee and the Jordan, I kept reminding myself that I was an American born in Miami. Yes, my biological father and my stepfather called themselves Jews, but what is a Jew? I asked myself that question, staring down from the hills into the land that the Jews claim God gave to them."

Voice growing stronger, he continues: "And I asked myself: Why was I fighting this war in this far-off place? But more, I asked myself why I was engaged in a killing operation amidst the beautiful names that American children, Jews and

Christians alike, hear as children. The River Jordan. The Sea of Galilee, where Christ calmed the waters. We were bringing smoking carnage and death to the mythical land of the Bible, as the warrior kings of Israel and their enemies had brought it for countless generations.

"My mind was muddled. I could not get it out of my head that my stepfather, the Miami Jew, insisted that my real father's death was meaningless because he was fighting the Japanese and not the enemies of God's Chosen People. My subconscious mind was ping-ponging back and forth between the images of my two fathers and my mother."

Seeming to ignore the passion in the voice of Dr. Abraham, Faust looks at Mohammed to ask, "Do you know the history of this war?"

Mohammed runs his large right hand through his hair. "I do, and—"

Holding his hand up like a traffic cop, Faust says, "No need for commentary, Mohammed. I just want to be sure you understand what Dr. Abraham is about to say next. Catch your breath for a moment, Dr. Abraham, then continue."

Dr. Abraham looks straight ahead like a man in a trance. "The Syrian army consisted of about fifty thousand men. I tried to visualize their soldiers as Old Testament men."

Faust's white eyes brighten. "Ah, Old Testament men. My father the Baptist Deacon was obsessed with the great battles of the Old Testament Hebrews. I like your image, Dr. Abraham. I can smell them. Swarthy, bearded, sweaty, reeking from months without bathing. The men who killed each other in darkling armies a thousand years ago, these are the men First Lieutenant Isaac Abraham told himself he was there to kill. Not good-lookin' fellas like our Mohammed over here."

Dr. Abraham ignores the interruption. "When we finally attacked, we fell mainly on empty territory as the Syrian forces fled. My battalion had swept through a series of tiny villages and lost only a few men to what seemed like random artillery fire. We were working in squads of five, small fire teams. A series of shells found our team and three of my comrades were killed. The other was alive physically, laying face up and appearing dazed, but moving his arms. When I saw blood trickling from underneath him I rolled him over to discover a gaping hole where his spine used to be. He died in just that instant.

"Over the radio I received an order to take my team up into the hills to gather intelligence on enemy positions. The team was dead so I went myself, climbing up an old trail leaving the noise of the shooting and wheezing trucks and tanks below. I came upon a Syrian soldier."

"Describe him," Faust says.

"He was not the swarthy bearded man-warrior you just described, Faust. He was a boy, perhaps fourteen years old. I assumed he must have been left behind for some reason. I assumed he had probably shown cowardice at some point."

"And where was he, Lieutenant?" Faust taunts.

"He was holed up in a small cave, little more than a large hole carved out of the gray-white rock of the hill. There were several such structures, if you would really call them structures that shepherds at one time must have used. I was searching them one by one when I came upon him.

"He had his rifle and, arms trembling, tried without success to grasp it and aim it at me. I took a shot. It struck his ankle. I saw the blood coming out. Writhing in pain, he dropped his weapon immediately.

"I looked at the boy in his filthy uniform, stained with sweat and dirt and grease. He soiled himself at that moment, as he no doubt had been doing for at least a day because the boy reeked of feces and urine. He was a pitiful sight and I felt pity, which, to my mind, is perhaps the purist of all human emotions. If you cannot feel pity, you are not human. I went over and, crouching down, inspected his wound and decided to apply a tourniquet.

"He wrapped his arms around my neck and, shouting wildly, tried to wrestle me to the dusty, rock-strewn ground. We rolled and tumbled as each of us tried to gain control of the other. We were both grunting and shouting and frightened for our lives. His eyes were as wide as saucers, his mouth literally frothing with saliva and sweat. His stench filled my throat with each gasping breath I took.

"Finally I overpowered him and choked him until he began to ease his grip on me. He was still alive. Then from the corner of my eye I saw an ornate dagger on the ground beside him." Isaac Abraham's weary wet eyes look up at the credenza behind what was once his seat of power, to see the young Faust snatch the gold and silver weapon off the shelf and brandish it at an imaginary opponent descending from the lofted ceiling. "That is it. That was the instrument of death.

"When I saw that knife, I imagined that it belonged to his father or uncle or some man who sent him into this battle. Some deep blunt rage was growing in me. I crawled to the dagger on my knees. As I bent to pick it up, the boy seemed to spring to life and grabbed it first. He plunged it into my wrist and my blood was now squirting onto the sand. I began to feel light headed as I rolled on the ground fighting for my life.

"At first after he stabbed me all was vague, dream-like. Then suddenly my mind cleared, I broke the bridge of his nose with my fist, got on top of him, applied my weight to his chest, thrust my knee into his groin as hard as I could and—"

Grinning toward the ceiling, Faust keeps parrying his invisible enemy. "And?"

"And then I cut his throat. Blood rushed from his carotid artery. It spurted red and hot onto the sand as his final heartbeats pumped it there. He moaned. I did not hear. I plunged the knife between his ribs, into his stomach, into his neck again. On my knees over his body, I stabbed not just him but the uncle or the father who gave him that dagger. There was a thrill in it. Yes."

"Dazed, I wrapped a tourniquet around my wrist. There were cans of gasoline there and I poured it on his body and everywhere with the goal of torching the cave. Then I heard soldiers coming from an entrance in the back somewhere. In that instant, even as I grabbed my rifle, I paused to face the mystery. Would the God of the Hebrews, the God of Abraham, my namesake for many generations, save me as he had not saved my comrades below in the valley?

"I though yes. Then I thought no. God's chosen people? Was I chosen to thrill as I cut the throat of a foul-smelling child thousands of miles from my home? My thoughts were a jumble. I heard automatic weapons firing behind me and recall tossing a grenade into the cave and being knocked down by the concussion of the blast, coming to rest on the valley floor near a huge outcropping of rock. Years later I believe I found it and took the picture over there. But it may all be a dream dreamed in this place. I do not know."

The old man pants in exasperation at his own inability to speak.

Faust watches the weak old man struggle to complete the story. "So that is all truth to be told, Dr. Abraham? Can you tell Mary and Mohammed about the dreams you have had over the years as you re-live that moment in your mind?"

Dr. Abraham looks out the window in silence until he says, "I dream and I wonder if the lone soldier did not in fact kill me first. Or perhaps it was the next group. Did I torch the cave in time?"

Mary looks at Dr. Faust. "Are we all dead?"

Ignoring Mary, Faust looks deeply into Mohammed's eyes. "So Mohammed, assume for the moment that our good Dr. Abraham didn't actually die during the fight with this boy he describes as foul-smelling and filthy. You understand that the man sitting beside you cut the throat of a Muslim boy. At a minimum he fantasized of it at the moment of his own death in battle. Do you understand?"

Mohammed, jaw tight and back stiff, averts his eyes to the side. "Yes."

Faust nods then directs his gaze at the old psychiatrist, his colleague, who is now presenting himself as a cold-blooded killer. "You are so close, Dr. Abraham, you must finish telling this story."

His massive head bowed, Isaac Abraham gasps and sputters the conclusion. "I have not allowed these memories to flood into my mind for many, many years. I have succeeded in blocking all but the dimmest recollections of a confused week of battle against an anonymous enemy. But now I know that when I leave through that White Door today, I must make peace with this.

"Most soldiers will tell you that the act of killing a man is a simple, mechanical act. You pull a trigger. You launch a bullet, an efficient little missile designed to fly straight and pierce whatever it hits.

"Fewer kill in hand-to-hand combat but even in close quarters when you smell your victim's breath and his body and struggle against his weight, even when you see his face in agony when you deliver the blow, the act of murder is a mechanical thing, like driving a nail into a piece of wood. Kicking a soccer ball across a field. It is purely an act of physics perpetrated by you against a physical object in your world. In the case of murder, that object is the body of your victim.

"It is afterward that the mind, it is actually the soul I'm sure, looks out into the world to see what has been wrought. That hot afternoon as I crawled away, stood, and regained my composure, my mind spun off in so many directions. When I stepped out of that dim, foul-smelling cave and into the bright sunlight, my mind's eye saw—"

Dr. Abraham's eyelids are drooping now and it is clear to all in the room that a particular kind of exhaustion, the exhaustion of impending death, is taking over his body. His ashen face is crooked, and the muscles are beginning to go flaccid. He breathes in gasps.

Faust still presses him. "And you saw what, Isaac Abraham?"

Dr. Abraham gasps, "As I looked into the dirt that ran off into the distance—my mouth was on the ground and I could taste the dirt, it was mixing with my saliva—I saw the father I never met. I saw his face from the photograph my mother showed me, and I saw him as I imagined him from so many war movies I forced myself to watch as a child. I saw a corpse in a uniform lying face down on a beach in the Pacific, being tugged forward and backward by the waves of an indifferent tide, his yellow face assaulted by the water and the sand and the silt."

Life seems to be draining from the deep pools of his brown eyes. "I saw the Miami Jew staring at me with his paunchy face, regaling me with his tales of King David the Warrior King of Israel and the special place of God's chosen people. And yes, I saw my mother, the beautiful Madonna with the huge sad eyes. But the memory of that brief moment in the cave is with me now. For eternity, I will remember that boy, his blood, his stench."

Looking at his gnarled hands, he whispers. "Yes, with these hands I killed a boy I had never met for a reason I have never understood. I will live with it until the end of time."

Dr. Abraham musters the strength to speak clearly. "Mohammed, do you remember when I asked you what distressing condition I could remove from you?"

"Yes. I said rage."

"And Mary?"

"I said I wanted to be cured of my sadness."

"Well, now I shall tell you the distressing condition I will have removed: Guilt. And now, Mary and Mohammed, I am truly finished."

Faust offers Dr. Abraham another glass of water. The weary creature slurps at it as a thirsty dog might slurp at a fresh bowl of water, the flaccid muscles of his cheeks barely able to control his lips upon the glass. Like Mary earlier, he is drained of energy.

Mary, on the other hand, is roused by the sound of Dr. Abraham speaking her name. She jerks her head forward, eyes open, and shouts, "What is happening here? I still do not know if I am alive or dead. If Dr. Abraham died so many years ago, then he couldn't be my psychiatrist now."

Faust leans forward, flicking his wrists dismissively just inches from her face. Her nose wrinkles and her head tilts back as if smelling something distasteful. "This damn Portal Exercise of Dr. Abraham's is incredibly confusing. He's even confused, maybe. Think so?

"You say you don't know if you are alive or dead. Perhaps the answer is for you to decide, Mary of the Mona Lisa smile. Or perhaps you will never know again. But do you know who you are in this life?"

"Yes. We all took that test where we answered over and over."

"Then who are you?"

"I am my soul. And my soul, 'tis made up of who I am and what I do. I am a woman and a Catholic and a mother. And a sinner. But I am more. I am my soul, and it can be made pristine again."

Faust's reflexive smirk begins to cross his face, but he suppresses it. He closes his eyes and takes a deep breath. "You understand, Mary. I hear it in your heart. There is the door. You and Dr. Abraham are free to leave."

Mary stands. "You have not asked Dr. Abraham who he is."

Dr. Abraham looks up at Mary and shakes his head weakly.

"He's telling you that he knows who he is, but you and Mohammed cannot know… not now, at least," Faust says.

Mary looks at Dr. Abraham. "But why?"

Dr. Abraham's watery eyes pierce hers. "Soon you will know. Please help me up, Mary. You have the strength to help me."

Mohammed takes a step toward his physician, saying, "Allow me."

Dr. Abraham waves him away. "It is for Mary to do."

Obediently, Mary helps the old man up from his seat and slowly they walk toward gates of brilliant white. Without her to serve as a brace, he cannot stand.

When they move off the carpet onto the cool stone floor, they stop. Mary bends her head to Dr. Abraham's face, and they begin whispering to each other. Mary's formless blue blouse and slacks and the yellow shawl enveloping Dr. Abraham's bent shoulder produce a pretty splash of color in the sunlight pouring through the window.

Suddenly Mary bolts erect and looks back to at Faust. "I understand," she says. "Thank God, I finally understand."

Once again the door in the back of the room is transformed into a gateway, shining with a perfect white light. She takes Dr. Abraham by the arm, and they begin to move toward the light. Faust calls after them.

"Yes, Dr. Abraham, behold the Gate of Shimmering White. See it with fresh eyes. It is open for you. And you, Mary, when you walk through that door you of course are welcome to look for a priest or a preacher or anyone who wants to tell you God's plan for you. Or you can seek it in your own mind in heart. It's between you and God. Don't listen to me, that is for certain. Perhaps you should not listen to any man, when you are able to listen for the true healing voice of creation. That is where the healing is."

As Mary and Dr. Abraham near the Gate, Joy steps back into the room, bathed in an aura of light. Without a word she helps Mary steady Dr. Abraham's shaking body. At the sight of Joy, Dr. Abraham's bent and withered frame pulls erect like a crippled man healed in a Pentecostal revival. He looks, silently, knowingly, over his shoulder at the young Faust.

"He knows so little," Dr. Abraham says to Joy.

Mary begins weeping wildly. Joy touches her cheek tenderly. "It is good," she reassures Mary. "He is strong now. Continue toward the Gate."

Joy locks her stare on Faust's red-rimmed eyes. He is visibly shaken.

"How are you doing this?"

"You say you're a magician and illusionist who made a pact with the devil, but you do not understand this place."

From across a distance that feels like a thousand miles, Mohammed and Faust gaze at Mary, Joy and Dr. Abraham exiting. The gate opens, the light pours in, and it closes again. Mohammed puts his head in his hands and weeps balefully. "I alone remain."

"And me of course." Faust taps Mohammed's shoulder. "Don't you see me? I'm still here with you."

Mohammed nods without raising his head from his hands.

Mohammed Irani

FOR A WHILE, the only sound is the cymbal-crashing swoosh of the large waves rushing to the shore outside the office. A particularly loud crash of the surf alarms Mohammed, and his back stiffens.

"It is nighttime now. The waves are louder at night," Faust grins through his white teeth. He studies the man in the black suit like a hunter studies his prey, then whispers in his ear. "Those folks are gone and you don't know where or how, but let's forget that for now. I want to gossip. Some gut-wrenching stories, eh? And how about that uncle of Mary's? What a guy! He doesn't know what Paganism and witchcraft really are, like I actually do, but—"

Mohammed closes his eyes balefully then, after a while, opens them again. He says quietly but sternly, "You must stop making light of all of this."

"All of what?"

"All of…our suffering. All of our pain. And our most cherished beliefs. It is not right that you mock them. You must stop being a Godless buffoon."

"Godless?" Faust pulls the collar of his white lab coat over his head. "I'm a monk, man. I'm a neuroscientist. I've studied what the brain is capable of experiencing concerning God. Eternity. Things spiritual. But even before that, my dad taught me his personal theory of religion. He said there were really only three religions. Know what they are?"

"There is only one religion. There is one God. The Prophet Mohammed assures that."

"Billions of folks who have walked this earth might not agree with you. You're a believer in what my dad called judgmental monotheism. That's Judaism, Islam and Christian. One Big God who is sometimes merciful, sometimes wrathful but always judging. And of course, always right! Maybe a little like our dads? You know what I mean, Mohammed? You and I were raised to believe in that one big almighty God in the form of a man. That makes it easy for sin and shame to merge in our puny brains. We think God's a guy like Pappa who expects us to do right.

"But hey, what about Joy and her avatars and whatever? Know what my dad called Hindus and Buddhists? Anytheists. These folks can believe in any God, or no God. They think a vaguely personified creator set the universe in motion then intervenes in the world from time to time via avatars and mythical interventions. After that, it's up to you to figure out what's right. Dharma, Karma, the middle way, all of that.

"Then there are the nature theists. They believe in the magical spirituality of good and bad forces in the universe without attaching them necessarily to the person of a particular God. That's Mary's uncle, and Mary too. She believes in magic.

"I believe in all of it: magic, demons, angels. Yep! Aren't we seeing it right here? So maybe this ugly fella standing before you ain't so Godless after all. Maybe I see a lot of different Gods.

Looking toward the back of the room, Faust says, "You're probably wondering where those folks are going, but I, on the other hand, just feel like a little bit more gossip is in order.

"Let's talk about Joy. She ends up murdering her surrogate brother the cop who, oh by the way, was in the process of raping her the way her original brother did. She's worried about the fact that she's learned to like fucking so long as she says she's a virgin and the guy gets a little rough but, hey, I'd say she's on the right track. There's nothing wrong with the act that preserves the human race—I won't offend you by using that word, or, for that matter, for saying that there is nothing wrong with it.

"And what about Mary? A pretty Irish chick helpin' her down-on-his-luck dad in the office. Next thing you know she's a frumpy old gal with cancer. Never got what she wanted but found a way to blame herself for everything anyway.

"And the good Dr. Abraham struggling to believe what a father he never met may or may not have believed. Sleeps with his mom, kills a boy in war, and somehow ends up thinking he's dead inside. Not fair."

Mohammed is perplexed. "But is there no judgment? Where does God place his anger and his favor?"

"Judgement smudgment," Faust says. "Why would an all-powerful, all-seeing God judge the creatures he—or she—or it—created?"

"This is not a laughing matter," Mohammed says. "I shall be leaving if you do not stop this mockery."

"Oh really? You're cuttin' out? Don't make any firm plans outside that door, Mohammed, because it's the two of us. Body count: Three survivors have exited a gleaming gate, two left to go. You and me.

"But enough gossip. Question for 'ya. Why are you still here, my friend?"

Mohammed looks at the beautifully woven carpet and wonders if it has only been one second since the room was full of people whom he felt he had known a lifetime. "I do not know why I am still here."

"I can see why that would be," Faust says, "So let me give you a hint. Why do you think Joy and Mary and Dr. Abraham are gone?"

Mohammed smiles. He sighs, as if relieved by a thought. "They have left this place because they have no more stories to tell."

"You are right, ol' buddy. Oh, they left out some details, but none that a companion for eternity would care to hear. So, do you have more to tell?"

"Yes. But it is a simple tale. No rapes or pawned jewelry and unaccounted-for loved ones. Just… a woman."

"From Dr. Abraham's notes I can make a guess. The woman named Gloria. Even after you told so much, you have omitted one detail. A fact you try desperately to conceal even from your own consciousness."

"Yes."

"And the detail is?"

Mohammed looks at his hands and admits gravely, "To understand my rage is to know how I went astray because of a young woman. And my anger wells up each time I am with her, but I see her still. It was she who made me lose my faith in God. There, my friend, I have finally admitted to you that I have lost my faith. She is the true villain of my story."

"You're still seeing the infamous Gloria? I figured that. So did Dr. Abraham. That accounts for why you have trouble visualizing eternity. How could Nia and Zayd and Gloria all be there at once?"

Mohammed shakes his head. "Gloria must not be there."

"Let's drive her out then! You and I can do it!"

"I cannot. I have tried to rid myself of her, but it will never happen."

Faust jumps up and down. "Yikes, Mohammed. Didn't your old man tell you never say never. Mine sure did. So now, you've challenged me to make you a better man. We're going to get this chick out of the picture. Let's start at the beginning. How'd you met this chick to begin with?"

"Zayd told me of a girl he had met in his accounting class. He said she was from a family that had been wealthy in Cuba but now she did not have any money. He also said that she was beautiful in a mysterious way and looked very much like his mother. I said it was impossible for a woman of another race to be as beautiful as Nia."

"What did your born-in-America son say to that?"

"He said 'Yes father, you are right, but perhaps Gloria is still a beauty even if she is not of our race.' Zayd explained that when he told her I was a millionaire many times over, she wondered if she could call me to get help with her businesses."

"Her businesses, eh? What kind of businesses did this mysterious drop-dead gorgeous chick have?"

"Zayd told me she had two or three small businesses she was starting, selling things imported from South America. Perhaps I could help her. And he wanted me to see her with my own eyes. I said yes, she could call."

"And so she calls you."

"Yes. I did not initiate any of this. One day she called me and it was arranged to meet in her apartment, which was close to my antique dealership."

"Why not have her come to your office?"

"I should have required her to come to my office, yes. Perhaps that was my first moral lapse. But I drove there. When I reached my destination, I opened the heavy exterior door and started up the narrow stairway to Gloria's apartment. When a door opened at the top of the steps and Gloria appeared, I thought immediately of how so like Nia she looked. She had dark brown eyes, beautiful long black hair. There was a certain way she held herself that reminded me of Nia. I could tell this from the bottom of the steps."

"What was she wearing? Was she wearing a scarf in your honor, I guess one might say?"

"How could you know that, doctor? Yes, from that first meeting she had a way of wearing a small American-girl scarf—it was a bandana really—when she saw me. Otherwise, she was dressed like an American."

"Which means what?"

"Far too revealing. That day she was wearing a short denim skirt and a pale green silk blouse that was so thin you could the green bra she was wearing beneath it."

"And so, then what happened? How did she greet you?"

"Gloria greeted me formally as a guest with a handshake. Then, she gave me a coy peck on the cheek. I did not recoil, but it was not a proper thing even for a Cuban girl. Gloria placed two beautiful tea cups on the coffee table as I sat down on the sofa. With an exaggerated child's curtsy and 'excuse me', she went into her bedroom and returned with what looked like an accountant's ledger book. She placed the expensively bound volume on the coffee table beside our tea.

She smiled beautifully and said, 'Your son Zayd says you believe you understand the future. Is that true?'

"I told her yes, it is true. But it is not because I understand it personally, it is because obedience to Allah is all one needs and, therefore, the future will be as the past."

"Gloria stretched lazily, exposing to me the bare skin of her legs, and asked, 'Is it true you tell Zayd that a Muslim man is entitled to as many women as he desires?'

"I said, 'Perhaps.'

"She tossed her long black hair back. Even under the scarf, it seemed to flutter in a beautiful wave. She said, 'I can tell you that a Latina woman—that is what I call myself to men like you—can get any man whom she desires. But it is money that I truly desire. I want to be rich.'

"She patted her book and continued, 'Here's where I write my predictions. I do fine for 1- and 5-year predictions— like here, where I predict I'll have a Mercedes before I turn thirty—but I can't even start predicting what will happen ten years from now. So, I'll get my first prediction from you. What will the world be like ten years from now?'

"I found myself lapsing into a serious answer about events in the world, but she interrupted.

"She smiled a coy grin and said, 'Very well, the world is going to hell in a hand basket. I'll accept that. How about you? Are you going to hell in a hand basket? Zayd tells me that you are a student of beauty. You can judge the price of a thing based on its beauty. He also tells me that your wife is having female problems and problems with her back. Is that true?'

"I told her 'Yes,' unsure of where she was going with such questions. She continued by saying, 'That's not too bad for Zayed because she is his mom. But it must be difficult for a virile man like you to have a wife with such problems.' I told her I did not want to discuss this matter.

"She said, 'I apologize for asking the wrong question. Let's try another question. If you're a man who can put a price tag on beauty, can you tell me how much is my beauty worth?'

"I said, 'One cannot judge the beauty of a woman in dollars.' And to my surprise, she responded by saying, 'Of course you can. My customers do it all the time. They pay maybe a hundred fifty for some whore downtown. But I get a premium. It's five-hundred dollars for two hours. Worth it, don't you think, sir.' She stood up and did a pirouette, then sat back down again.

"'Don't tell Zayd I'm selling… may I call it pussy in front of you, sir? He gets his for free. I do it to prove that I can make a man violate any rule, even the rules of a religion followed for thousands of years, established by people who lived in tents and treated their women like dogs and slaves and meat to be bought and sold.'

"Gloria looked closely at my face as she might peer at her father. Her eyes were truly mysterious. She asked if she had offended me. I said I was not offended."

The red-rimmed eyes of the young doctor widened with surprise. "Yikes, Mohammed, I'm surprised. Why were you not offended by that?"

"When I first met her, my faith was a rock. The ruminations of a Cuban girl meant nothing."

The man in the white lab coat casts his eyes toward the window to consider Mohammed's point. After a moment, he says, "Until Gloria came, you were a fortunate man. But let us hear more of your earthly misfortunes."

Mohammed nods and continues, "She said, 'Let's skip that subject for now' and began to explain that she and a friend had a business venture that would require five-thousand dollars. It was to sell jewelry or something of that kind, which I said was not a worthy investment. Plus, I began to believe she was drunk.

"I was very stern in my disapproval of her dress and her demeanor, but I agreed to listen to her give the details of how I would participate. She said I should think it over. It would be simple. I would give her five-hundred dollars every week. When I asked what the return to me would be, she said, 'This is the return,' then parted her knees to reveal nothing under her skirt.

"I told her that was outrageous and stood to leave. She seemed surprised by my sudden anger and said, 'I didn't mean to offend you, oh good father of Zayd Irani. Handsome father of Zayd, I might add. My business goals are complicated, and I guess I didn't state the proposition very well.'

"I told her that I was sorry that my son ever met her. I said, 'I do not know who you are or what you are, my dear little girl', and she seemed to take delight in my remark. 'Who am I? I'm just a little Cuban orphan trying to succeed in Miami the best way I know how. Here is my business card, sir. I hope you will reconsider, sir.'

"She plopped down on her sofa, slipped off her sandals and tossed them gaily onto the floor. She saw me looking at her pretty bare feet. 'Getting comfortable, that's all,' she said. She let her skirt slide up, but not all the way up. 'You have my cell number. I really do think you are quite handsome. You look a bit like my father, you know, though I have only seen pictures of him.' I looked her in the eye when she said that, trying to see if she was telling the truth.

"Then she jumped off the sofa and gave me another—I will use the word 'peck'—this one lingering for a soft, sweet moment. 'You are a handsome man. We'll see if it is true that you are an admirer of beauty.' Holding my hands, she took a step back to force me to look into her eyes."

Dr. Looks-Like-Satan laughs. "How does a young girl force a mature man, worldly, a millionaire, to—"

"Faust," Mohammed interrupts, "my meaning is that her gaze at me was compelling. Do not try to trick me with my own words."

"Point taken. So then what happened?"

"I left her apartment fully believing that the matter was closed. But I called her back the very next morning. I said, 'Your offer is accepted.' It started that quickly."

"That's not a quick start in her business, Mohammed. She's used to getting instant replies from gentlemen such as yourself."

"Please do not taunt me," Mohammed raises his voice, preparing to rise from his chair.

"Not the intention. Realism. Healing requires facing facts."

Mohammed ignores the doctor and let his tense body relax. "Within a month something happened and she began saying 'I love you.' I wrote on my one of my business cards that she was precious. This was my response. She would meet me in Tampa, Orlando, places where I told Nia I had business. It was when we would spend the night it would happen.

"Her father left her when she was a baby. It seems I became her father and her lover. It just happened like that, almost without thinking. I do not know why she told Zayd that we were lovers. Only Allah knows. Only Allah knows why our family had the misfortune of that visit that day. It was like the accident. A misfortune due to coincidence. Too many coincidences..."

Mohammed sighs again. "Gloria looks so much like my beloved Nia. She came to the funeral of Zayd and Nia and stayed a respectable distance from our Muslim friends and family, posing as just a student friend of Zayd. She is quite an actress, I have learned. At the end, she stopped in front of me and said simply, 'Your God may not forgive you but I do. I will call you.'

"When she called we arranged to meet in a restaurant. She cried and asked for my forgiveness. For the longest time she kept whispering over and over, 'Please forgive me.'"

"And did you?" the Doctor asked leaning closer.

"I was not sure if I could forgive her. But she tempted me again, and again I succumbed. I was alone and full of guilt with Nia and Zayd gone. Gloria is… she is so dark; her skin is so perfect. She is enchanting. When we meet she wears headscarves that look to the boys of Florida like the bandanas the girls wear on the beach, but to me they look like hijab. She knows this. Her eyes look into mine with a sparkle that others may not see, but I can. She is so like Nia when Nia was young and full of love for me."

Faust rubs his big fingers beneath his chin. "And you still hook up? When did you meet last?"

Without warning Mohammed's composure crumbles, stone turned suddenly to dust. "Just yesterday." Pounding his clenching fists against each other, his weeping turns to wailing. "We meet in secret, in Tampa. We tell ourselves I am helping her with her business. It will never prosper, but to be near her is a comfort. She sells jewelry as a business, but it turns out that she is also a so-called escort. A special kind of prostitute."

"Did she tell Zayd this rather important fact about herself."

"No. Zayd never knew this. Men pay her to come to their motel rooms. Sometimes she strips; sometimes they have sex, sometimes, so she tells me, the men just want to talk. I pay her when I meet her in Tampa."

Faust, puzzled and amused, cocks his head like a dog listening for a strange sound in the distance. His skull gleams like a marble statue in the sunlight pouring through the window, Faust smiles through his bright white teeth. "Mohammed, my friend, your subconscious mind has been wasting its energy concealing that secret from your waking thoughts. Let's hope that the Gods forgives the sin of paying for a woman. If not, hell will be more crowded than even I would care to imagine. Many an otherwise respectable man will burn in hell if paying for a woman is truly a sin."

He cocks his grotesque head again, thinking for a moment, then grins, "So I hope there is more meat to your story, Mohammad."

"My shame is not that I pay her. My shame is that I crave her. It is an addiction. It is a need greater than my love for Nia, for Zayd, more than anything. It is a terrible thing, but Gloria is an obsession I cannot overcome."

"You cannot overcome it? Why not?"

"When I first told the story of my life in this office, I said that beauty is more than a feeling, more than a thought. I said you see beauty in texture and form and color, but more importantly in the rarity and fragility of the thing. And then I said that the person who desires to own an antiquity, let us say a rare vase, comes to feel that their very happiness depends only on having that one rare, beautiful thing. They will pay any price to own it.

"And that is where I am with this Gloria. I will pay any price, not literally in terms of money—although money is exchanged and her haunting black eyes seem to glow when I hand her two, five, sometimes ten one-hundred dollar bills—but rather I will pay any price in terms of my very life. I cannot overcome my craving for her."

Faust saunters in a small circle, looking up into the vaulted ceiling. "Of course you can. You think it's wrong to crave this woman. True?"

"Yes."

"Then exercise your father's discipline on yourself. Be obedient to him now and use his strength to free yourself of this shackle. It's really quite simple. Tell yourself that you must be free of Gloria."

"It is not poss—"

"Sure it is. Close your eyes and dream. Go back to the last time you were with her, but this time look into her beautiful eyes and say, 'This is done.' If you mean what you say, if you are resolute, she will know that it is truly over. And if she loves you, she will understand why. It will be so easy, if you are truly ready to do it."

Mohammed looks into Faust's eyes, nods as if to obey an unspoken command, then closes his. Only the sound of the surf outside can be heard as time passes.

Opening his eyes slowly like a man waking from a comforting sleep, Mohammed looks at Faust. "Until now, no man has known my secret. Having told that to you, Faust, in this room, in this place, I can swear by God that I have told everything. Do you believe me? Is my story finished now?"

"Are you resolute? Did you say goodbye to her just now?"

"Yes."

"Where did it happen? What did Gloria say?"

"We were on a green hill I had never seen before. The sky was bright and blue but then became orange and crimson as if the sun was setting. A slight breeze rustled in the oak trees and palm trees. The moment was serene and still.

"She was at a distance from me. I could not reach her. Even though I felt speechless, I could be sure she heard what I said.. When I said I would not see her again, she smiled a sad smile. She wore the face of a broken hearted girl.

"She said, 'I am sorry for the loss you have suffered. I am sorry for my part in it. I understand why this is the end, but I will remember you. I hope you find your peace.' She turned to walk away, then vanished before my eyes."

Faust pours a glass of water from the ornate pitcher on the credenza and hands it to Mohammed. "Mohammed, I believe that your story is finished. Your anger and rage is dissipating before our eyes. I think we both believe you are healed. Here is a drink of water. In fact, I'll have one with you."

John Frost, alias Dr. Faust

FAUST WATCHES WATER droplets cling to Mohammed's ashen lips and mustache until finally he looks into Mohammed's sharp black eyes and says, "Mind if I come over and stand next to you? May I?"

"If you wish."

Faust picks up a sheath of papers from the desk, glances off-handedly at some of the pages, then tosses the stack on the floor. As he walks from behind the desk he swivels his hip in a dramatic, comic gesture signifying he is now on the other side of that great mahogany altar.

"Thank you for telling me about Gloria. Or perhaps it is you who should thank me for listening. Now let's gossip some more. So, what did you think of Dr. Abraham's story? Will he burn in hell forever as a murderer? Please bear in mind that the Jewish scripture doesn't talk about heaven or hell."

"I do not know," Mohammed says. "Perhaps he was submitting to God's will."

"Exactly," Faust offers in a chatty tone. "But what kind of God would cause such a thing? What kind of God transports men thousands of miles to kill boys?"

Mohammed shakes his head. "It is not for mortal men to know Allah's will."

"Perhaps God is evil, not good. Have you ever thought of that? Have you ever contemplated that possibility?"

"No."

"Well, golly day, Mohammed, maybe you should. God helped the ancient Hebrews smite their enemies. Yes? Then there's good old Sura Nine Verse Five in the Koran. Jihad. The Sword Verse. God commands you to kill non-believers. Right? But hey, the Hindu God Vishnu drives some dude's chariot for him so he can kill his cousins in battle. Lots of killin.' Yes? No? Yes?"

Mohammed looks at Faust but does not speak.

Faust keeps rattling on. "So many things are possible, actually. Perhaps there are many gods like the Greeks and Romans and Greeks and Hindus believed. Maybe it's what some and the Apaches for Christ sake who saw gods in nature believed. Maybe God is a verb and not a noun, like some professor said one time. He said that would let us deify the laws of nature—like the Apaches I'm just now thinking?? was a bull shitter actually, and maybe the whole thing is bullshit. "

Faust and Mohammed lock eyes. "Mohammed, I can see that you don't approve of this expansive thinking, even after all of this. Very well, back to business. May I tell you my story now?"

"Please."

Faust leans his face nose-to-nose with Mohammed. "Boo!"

Mohammed recoils.

"Remember how I did that when you, Joy and Mary first met me? Seems like eons ago now."

"Yes."

"Remember what I said?"

"Something about going from frightening to ugly."

Faust shouts "Boo!" again and once again thrusts his face at Mohammed. "Do not turn away, Mohammed. Let me tell you exactly what I said when we first met, because I say the same thing to everyone I meet, sort of a pick-up line.

"Please look closely at the skin on my face. It looks a bit like plastic, doesn't it? Some people say...plastic? Putty? Take your choice. I'm disgusting, no matter what word comes to mind. I have no hair on my head, no eyebrows. Ugly when you look up close, eh? Ugly, ugly, ugly. I'm hideous, frightening to look at—when you first see me. Once you get used to it, my face goes from being frightening to being sickening. It's sickening like a place where you know somebody puked and it's been cleaned up, but the stain is still there to remind you. And then finally, I don't scare you or make you feel like vomiting. I just look ugly."

Mohammed sits stiffly, trying not to look away.

Faust ignores the stiffness and fear, and, yes, the loathing he senses in Mohammed, and continues to talk in a chatty tone, waving his hands and smiling through those bright white teeth. "Doesn't it look like a bathing cap? Not literally maybe, but sort of? Or will you admit at least that right now I am a hideous man who does indeed look like Satan, as Joy said? Please answer me."

Mohammed locks eyes with Faust. "Yes. You are hideous. And yes, you look like the stereotypical images of Satan the Americans have."

"Thank you. Know why? Burns. Know how I got them? Of course you don't know, but I am going to tell you the whole story. To understand my life is to understand my loneliness... how I came to be a survivor.

"Dr. Abraham will be proud of me when he sees how I am taking you to be right there with me in that inferno. You will witness my encounter with the ruler of the universe. But first there are words that you must utter, Mohammed, and utter them exactly like this." Faust takes a breath and slowly but sternly instructs, "You must say, 'Allow me to understand your life'—exactly that way."

Mohammed sets his jaws tight. "I will not take orders from you like some pup in the army."

"You must if I am to receive healing in this place. Only you and I are left. Therefore it is up to you to heal me."

Mohammed relents. "Allow me to understand your life, Faust."

"Thank you. To understand my life is to understand that my greatest gift is a sense of wonderment about the contradictions of the cosmos. I said I was a physics major in college, which is true. What I didn't say was that I was also a volunteer fireman. Yep. In a little town called Eureka, Kansas. That's where I grew up. I once wore shit-kickin' cowboy boots and one of dem-dere cowboy hats, Mohammed. Eureka ain't a big town, and for that I thank the Lord. That's what my father would say. He was a deacon at the Baptist church and a captain in the volunteer fire department. You know what a deacon does?"

Mohammed shrugs with as much disinterest as he can display.

Faust looks up at the sky, pauses, then grins sarcastically. "Neither did my father. He told me the Bible didn't say much about what pastors or priests or deacons should do. So, as far as he was concerned, that meant the deacon did everything, even standing in for the pastor at times. My father was always more than glad to take charge of anything.

"I was his only child. His pride and joy. He took me everywhere, or so it seemed, him in his cowboy hat and cowboy boots and me in mine.

"My parents and I were at every church function. At first he dispatched me to play with the preschoolers my own age, but as I got older he would give me useful work to do around the church.

"Meanwhile, my test scores in school said I was brilliant. I became more and more isolated from the other kids. I became interested in creation, so I decided to concentrate on physics. He was all in favor of it. He believed that 'God reveals his creation by many means'—that was a quote he used as a deacon. God reveals his creation by many means. A brilliant quote, really, from a brilliant man.

"By the time I was a teenager, I was leading youth group sessions. That was the only role I was allowed although Dad and I would laugh about the fact that Christ was teaching the rabbis in the temple when he was thirteen. About then I was introduced to Dad's second love, the volunteer fire department.

"Dad was a big man with a big, toothy grin and a big shock of thick, flaxen hair. Like I used to have before I was ugly."

He closes his hands over his face then pulls them away. "Boo! Just reminding you."

Faust shouts. "He had a booming voice like this! So loud that at church meetings the people way in the back would ask him to speak a little more softly!"

He speaks normally again. "It was kind of a joke; all of the old people would laugh because my grandfather had that same huge voice. People in town knew that two generations back, our family farmed the land. But you didn't need to know that to look at my dad and say, 'Now, that big guy is probably a farmer.'

"Dad used to say that God blessed him by putting the farm on autopilot so that he could serve the Lord in church and serve humanity in the fire department. He'd tell people he had good farmer karma, which let him do farmer dharma.

"When he first began taking me to the fire station, I felt like he was everybody's father. Everybody called him Big John. At the fire station he bossed everybody around in that special way he learned from his own father, and also, I think, at the Baptist church. Baptists want to do the right thing, and Big Matt was a man who seemed always to know what was true and right, and he'd do it."

"Problem was, Mohammed, that I started thinking I wasn't anybody particularly special to him, except that I got an extra dose of that fire and brimstone no-sinning-allowed stuff. Funny that Joy talked about pretending she was a virgin... because I am one."

Without warning, Faust interrupts himself and leans back in his chair, eyeing Mohammed. "What was your father like, Mohammed? I know from Dr. Abraham's notes that your first memory is of a beautiful day at the mosque with your father."

Mohammed closes his eyes to make a correct answer. "My father was very much like yours. He believed that to obey God you must know—and do—the right thing."

Faust tosses his hands in front of him in a silly gesture. "Good. See? We have a lot in common. You and your son were in an accident, right? Big John and his son were in an accident, too.

"Fast-forward through years of Junior learning at the hand of his dad Big John at the firehouse and Deacon John at the church. Fast-forward through the time that Junior gets his Physics degree from Yale and becomes a medical student at the University of Miami. Junior is home for the summer eating his mother's cookies while he sits idly, dozing a bit, at the firehouse on a warm Kansas night.

"But now the story turns tragic. If I might use a term of yours, Mohammed, 'by God's will' that night was the one night of the year that the Company's standard firefighting gear was locked up for inventory. Tonight the men were to wear vintage gear from the 1930s." He pauses before continuing.

"Fire is a frightening thing. Except for when you spent time in hell after your accident—just kidding Mohammed—have you ever been in a fire?"

"No."

"Fire is some amazing stuff. Watch this." Without warning Faust pulls two thick sheathes of paper from the credenza, throws them on the floor, then lights a book of matches and tosses them on the papers. Immediately the papers erupt in fire.

Mohammed recoils.

"Afraid now? Watch this." Faust kicks the pile of papers across the floor to the floor-length curtains on the picture window, and the bottoms of the curtains burst into flame.

Mohammed stares at the flames. "What is the meaning of this?"

"Just a little demo of how quick things can happen. This water pitcher will fix things." Faust reaches for the pitcher and the water extinguishes the flames quickly. He smiles, pleased with himself.

"You've probably seen pictures of movies of firemen in the 1930s. They wore tan bib overalls with a flame-resistant coating and, of course, we had our flame-resistant upper body gear and, well, the older helmets without the full oxygen gear. Big John was confident that spending one night wearing gear that had been acceptable when his father ran the firehouse was completely acceptable now. After all, the Company had not been called out to a real fire for months.

"That night there was a five-alarm blaze at an old cotton-goods warehouse. I will spare you the details of the flashing lights and the sirens and the hydrants that did not function at first and the general confusion of water squirting and men shouting and long, thick hoses being unloaded and deployed. And you know what, Mohammed, I won't dwell upon how Big John didn't care if the other fire company with the right equipment would be arriving in five minutes.

"Here is the detail we need: Big John and his son Junior and a third firefighter named Frank 'The Plank' Wilson—he got the nickname because he was tall and skinny as a board—went into the warehouse via ladders and began moving across the third floor toward the flames.

"Big John was in charge, as always. This was actually the first time I had stood beside him in a fire line, and I was surprised to see the tension in his eyes. There was just a bit of hesitation in his voice, as if he wasn't quite sure he had sorted the facts out right. Frank the Plank was on one side of Big John, and I was on the other. We were spaced about ten feet apart.

"We were awaiting Big John's command to begin dousing the floor and walls with our hoses when the fire came at us. Pretend that the fire is coming at us from Dr. Abraham's desk.

"Now is the time for you to put yourself into this picture, Mohammed. Because suddenly a wall of flames shot up through the floor of the third story, right through the floor where we stood and began rushing toward us. They call this a backdraft, an incredible phenomenon of heat, air, and fire.

"The fire was moving toward us from the left side of the desk to the right. As soon as the flames burst up through the floor and the floor began collapsing, the heat knocked Frank the Plank on his back. Stunned, he yelled 'Big John, help!' then he began to sort of squirm to get away from the hose and back onto his feet.

"In the briefest of instants, I watched my father's face begin to burn as he stared helplessly while flames engulfed Frank's boots and began incinerating Frank's tall, lanky body. I was convinced I saw flames come out of Frank's mouth. The fire was moving at an angle from left to right—in other words, in my chair I would be the last to burn—and as I watched my father's face burn, blister and finally catch fire, I believed I saw flames issue from his mouth. He turned his head toward me and the flame seemed to say the words, 'Your God is Satan.'

"It all happened so very fast. A massive backdraft fire is like a wall of incredible heat, light, and noise. Think of it as a massive tidal wave not of water but fire. Just as you would feel if confronted by a massive tsunami wall of water, your heart leaps and then sinks with the pitiful fear of being helpless in the face of certain death.

"That day, there was the massive wall of fire and this rushing noise not unlike a wild surf. The wall of fire had come rushing toward us, and along with it were streams of white-hot fire along the ground, running at us like a pack of rabid dogs. The fire overwhelmed Frank; it consumed my father; and then, miraculously, the main body of the fire diverted toward an open window, and I was left standing. I stumbled backward and had the presence of mind to roll on the floor and smother the fire that was smoldering in my hair and on the skin of my face and neck. I cried out 'Please God, no, this cannot be right!' At that instant, rolling on the floor, I saw my father, still standing, become a stick of carbon."

Faust rises and walks over to the window. He watches the waves of the Atlantic rush onto Miami Beach. "After Big John's funeral and my recovery, my mother moved back in with her brother. My days in Kansas were over. I only went back there one more time. That's when Dr. Abraham took the wheat field picture."

Mohammed rears back in surprise. "Dr. Abraham went back to Kansas with you?"

Yanking his head in the direction of the pictures on the wall, Faust grins and responds, "Yes. Yes indeed! He made me go back to Big John's church. He went with me. That picture of the wheat fields was taken from the graveyard at Golden Corners Baptist Church. More precisely, that picture you see right now on the wall was taken from my father's grave."

"Dr. Abraham went with you to your father's grave?"

Faust walks over to stare at the picture of the wheat field. "Frank the Plank is buried there, too. The volunteer fire department made little monuments for them—bronze replicas of their firefighter hats—yep. Sentimental, eh? The good doc stood there with me and made me read the inscription from Big John's gravestone over and over again. 'He has gone to peace, he has gone to peace, he has gone to peace.' I read it over and over again until I believed it."

Faust tugs at his lab coat and crosses the room to the picture window. "My little Kansas sojourn with the good doctor didn't take place until a lot of bad things happened. So let me get back to my story. After my plastic surgery and my physical therapy, I left Kansas and came back to Miami to finish my residency. But instead, I began to go crazy. You are not the kind of man who goes crazy are you, Mohammed?"

"No. I believe not."

"Agreed. But I am. As I slowly but surely began reconciling myself to the scarring and the fact that I looked satanic, I saw that awful warehouse fire as what some Christians call a sign and a wonder. My father's death and the flames were a sign from God that I was to follow."

Faust's voice turns cold. "My father had taught me that God can take many forms. I never thought of it until this moment, but Big John could have sounded like Joy's revered Mr. Patel and his avatars of Vishnu. My father said God came to Abraham's tent in the form of a man. When God gave Moses the Ten Commandments he appeared as a burning bush, saying 'I am what I am.'

"I convinced myself that God did come to me as fire consuming my father. This was a sign and a wonder, and my scientific mind was supposed to discern that therefore God is Satan. Satan was the flame I thought I saw shooting out of Big John's mouth—and Frank the Plank's mouth, I thought sometimes—and I believed the sign was that I should spread the gospel of fire. Yep, that's how crazy I got. And I feared I would never get better.

"My dad's name was John Frost, the Second. I was John Frost the Third, but my parents and everybody in town called me Junior. Everybody called my dad Big John. After he died I started understanding all of the anger I had toward him for so many years. Anger like you held toward your old man, Mohammed."

"What are you talking about?"

"Remember when Dr. Abraham brought that up when you told your story about the bowl? He was right. You were pissed at your dad, pissed at that God-forsaken bowl, pissed at your own son because of how your father neglected you. You lived a life of rage, really. Inside. Since you were a kid."

"That is not true," Mohammed shouts, slapping his fist into his palm.

"Hey, hey, okay," Faust says. "I don't want to talk about you now, anyway. It's all about me. I changed my name from Dr. John Frost the Third to a much catchier moniker: Faust. Or Dr. Faust. You pick.

"I mentioned this earlier, but do you know the legend of Faust? German legend? The guy who, depending on the version of the story—Goethe's *Faust*, Marlowe's *Faust*—was never satisfied with the knowledge of the universe science could provide. The guy that made a pact with the devil, all of that? Know the story?"

"Vaguely."

"Well, during medical school I played with the idea that I was like Faust but, after the fire, I hunkered down on it! I vowed to be the deacon in the Church of Satan. I joined a witch's coven and attended their rites at night, totally repressing my memory of it during the day. That's how I somehow managed to complete my residency in psychiatry—I totally repressed certain memories. I have access to most of them now, of course."

Gazing dreamily out the window, Faust says, "Do you like sex, Mohammed? Oh—right—you're doin' a hooker, so of course you do. Well, we had so much sex in that witches' coven, like the *Wicker Man* movie that Mary's uncle liked. Pagans understand that sex is a good thing. A Pagan would give you the nod on your relationship with Gloria in a heartbeat."

The young physician's teeth gleam as he clenches his jaw in an ironic smile. "Plus, I hope you realize that Dr. Abraham understood. Remember the final session he presided over when he gave you a chance to buy some nookie from the over-sexed Joy? And you said no? Do you know why he did that?"

Mohammed taps at his red necktie saying, "I do not."

"He did it so you would understand that you love that Gloria of yours. Dr. Abraham knows that much of our sin has love at the root of it. Love—it is so very ironic, isn't it? Love is the root of much of our suffering and guilt. Mary's love for a near stranger, a grad student she met at a party. It extended through her little Carmella and oh, what problems it caused. Your love for Gloria. Dr. Abraham's love for his mother. My love for my father."

"And now, Doctor, you are indeed talking like a crazy man."

"Because of the Pagan bullshit? I already admitted I was pretty crazy for a while. But do not discount the idea of the relationship of love and sin. Luckily, because of the potential survivor's trauma, the medical school had me come to see Dr. Abraham. He was treating me as an individual psychotherapy patient using the same therapeutic regimen as your therapy group. The premise was that neither he nor I truly knew if we were alive or dead, and that we might be spending eternity together sitting across from each other, as we are now, in these chairs, in this place.

"Like all of you, I made progress. First, he got me to reveal the incredible anger I felt toward my father—the more love you feel toward somebody, the more anger you can feel. I had kept the anger locked up for months, my subconscious mind churning the events standing in front of the fire trucks when he gave the order to move against the fire, too self-assured and pig-headed to listen to the other commander who wanted to wait five minutes for better equipment.

"Next, he was able to make me tell him the details of my involvement with Satan worship, Paganism, all of that. I told him the vivid, gory details of the chants and the sex and the small mutilations—all of it. When I left through that White Door, I no longer felt the need to worship Satan or talk to those nutty people.

"And then he talked me into going back to Kansas. But first he took me other places, to Israel and to a Buddhist monastery where he had studied. Those pictures tell you where we went. I would think the whole thing was a dream were it not for the gift a Buddhist priest gave him, that water pitcher on the credenza. It was once a Buddhist offering jar. The lid, a lotus flower, symbolizes perfection. The Buddha and the monks moving among the vines symbolize guidance as we move through the cycles of life. And I got that guidance when we were finally in Kansas.

"We spent time with my mom, spent time at the old firehouse, then finally we went to the grave. We walked through the church first, Big John's old stomping ground. I blinked back a tear when I looked from the back of the church toward the altar. 'You think you can see him in the front of the church waving his arms and holding forth, yes?' Dr. Abraham whispered, half-smiling. I replied with a nod and whispered the words, 'Deacon John, please let me see you.' But I knew finally I never would."

Glancing sideways at the picture of the wheat field, Mohammed asks in his formal voice, "What does a Christian deacon do? What is the role?"

"In a little Baptist church like ours, anything. He said he was a helper for folks that needed help, like old people needed chores done sometimes, and an exhorter for people who needed exhortations in the name of the Lord." Faust's plasticized skin smiles. "Big John had a great sense of humor. He said his chief spiritual role in town, especially the firehouse, was to fight the Scientologists. Know who they are, Mohammed?"

"No."

"'They preach something called Dianetics, which my father said means that the immortal soul lives in the body and operates the mind at the subconscious level. Dr. Abraham believed that there is this battle between God, or more exactly God's will, and the mind. The soul is caught in the middle. My father believed it too."

Faust's elastic smile broadens. "Big John would laugh and say every Christian already knows what they have to say. S in my mind, my dad would say, the Scientologists are sellin' spiritual Amway and I'm gonna run them all out of town!"

Looking closely into the misty eyes of Faust, Mohammed sees tears are forming. He says, "Your father saw humor in serious matters, which my father could not do. You are fortunate for that."

Faust swipes his hands lightly over his face and speaks: "Anyway, Dr. Abraham put his hand on my shoulder and we walked out to my father's grave. Dr. Abraham had a whole metaphysical system about the soul being healed. He explained it to me there with the sun setting over that old Baptist graveyard with the wheat fields moving out to meet the mountains."

"And what was that metaphysical system? What did he explain exactly?" Mohammed asks.

"He said all kinds of things. He started by saying that I could make myself see Big John if I wanted to, that there are not only avatars of God in the universe, but of souls also. 'That is the earthly body,' he whispered in the wind by the grave, 'an avatar of the soul.' Then he surprised me and asked me why many Christians feel better at Christmas, the birth of Christ, than at Easter, which celebrates the resurrection. He answered his own question, 'Because the infant Jesus represents the pristine state of the soul, whereas Christ's crucifixion represents all that the world can do to a soul.' It was odd because Big John had said the same thing to me once when I was younger. Then Dr. Abraham said—"

The young doctor pauses, staring over Mohammed's shoulder and licks his lips. "I must stop; this is not the time for this, we are here for healing, for…"

Mohammed looks closely at Faust's deformed lips as the voice trailed off. "You are growing weary of this, are you not?"

"Yes," Faust replies. He looks at the picture. "You and Rd. Abraham were alike. You treasure beauty. I think the picture captures the sunset that was taking place over to the west of the fields. The wheat is really beautiful, more beautiful in person if you can believe that is possible—it rustles softly in the wind."

Mohammed's mellow voice says, "Yes, it is beautiful."

"Then came our final session. He was scribbling notes, like he always did. Suddenly he got up from this chair, walked around behind the desk and handed me a slip of paper that said, 'My weariness calls me away. You are to meet the therapy group. You will know what to do.' With that, he left through the Blue Door.

"Tell me, Mohammed, when I first appeared before you, did I seem like a man who knew what to do?"

Mohammed closes his eyes and takes a moment to consider the question. Eyes still closed he says, "Yes, you did behave as if you knew what you were doing."

"Thank you. Because I did—at first. I knew what to do when Joy revealed her final secret, that her own brother had raped her. I also knew that when Joy left, Dr. Abraham would· somehow appear here among us. I somehow understood that he would leave and take Mary with him."

Patting Mohammed on the shoulder, he says, "But now, my friend, I am at a loss. I do not know what to do. Here I sit with you, saying that God is Satan and believing that no man can convince me that I am wrong."

Mohammed, jaw tight, casts an angry look at Faust. "Then why have you told me this story? How will that help me heal?"

Staring pointedly at his watch, Faust ignores the question. "We are nearing the end"

"Dr. Abraham said time did not matter. You said you were the master of time. Why are you worried about time, my dear Doctor?"

"I want to be finished with this horrible nightmare! Please help me. Please say something to me!"

Mohammed's deep voice booms with confident authority. "I am only a man. I cannot explain God."

"Understood. But act right now as if yours is the last human soul I will ever be with. Tell me something."

Mohammed casts his eyes to the ground. "You asked me to place myself at the scene with either my son or my father. I did. I performed that mental exercise and, as you might have expected, it showed me what we already know about creation. For there to be good in this world, there must be evil; for there to be right, there must be wrong. Your father's death was wrong, but his life was right. It is that simple."

Faust shrugs. "In the parlance of psychiatry, Mohammed, that is what they call rational therapy. And it is what I call bullshit. I heard the fiery voice of Satan. It is a fact."

Mohammed sits erect. "Is that a fact? Again, I did the mental exercise you suggested, and I am curious about one thing. Perhaps it is an important detail, perhaps it is not."

"What is the detail?"

"I wondered how a mere ten-foot distance between you and your father was able to save you."

Faust rests his head on the desk and falls silent. Mohammed says nothing, then begins to rise from his seat.

Without moving his head, Faust closes his eyes and says, "Please do not go."

Mohammed stands up stiffly, tugging at the sleeve of his suit. "I believe that I am finished here."

"You are finished, but your buddy Faust ain't quite there yet." Faust presses a fingertip into the spongy plastic that is now the skin on his cheek. He asks, "Think this is bad? To be disfigured for life?"

Now Faust presses the palms of each hand to the sides of his skull. "It's nothing compared to what is happening in here. Remember when Dr. Abraham asked you how you wished to be healed? What he could remove? You said rage, Joy said fear, Mary said guilt. Well, guess what. Inside this space of a skull, I have them all. And they are demons unleashed. But most of all, I am lonely. I need to be cured of it. Please stay and talk to me."

"If I am to stay, you must answer my question—How did a mere ten-foot distance from your father save you? I believe there are more facts locked in your mind. Unlock it now. You, a healer, should know that you must unlock the truth if you are to find release now."

Without moving his head, Faust says, "In the din and the confusion, I do believe I heard my father's last words. But perhaps his voice did not say 'Your God is Satan.' Perhaps it said, 'Stay at your station.'"

After minutes pass like an eternity, Mohammed asks, "If indeed he said 'stay at your station,' that would mean you had deserted it."

"Can you hear me, Dr. Faust? It is for me now to ask you the questions. Can you hear me?"

"Yes."

"Then answer the question." Mohammed's baritone voice takes on a tone of pity. "You are finding the truth so that you, too, can pay the ransom."

Eyes closed, Faust whispers in a monotone. "Yes, I began to run at the first rush of fire. In my panic, I tripped and fouled the hose line, which may have been why Frank was not able to get water on the flame. It all happened so fast. We were all fated to die anyhow."

Mohammed touches the physician's shoulder gently and reminds him, "But you lived."

Faust's head remains on the desk. "Did I? Or was everything that happened after a dream I shared with Dr. Abraham?'"

Mohammed says simply, "I cannot answer," and turns to leave.

Dr. Looks-Like-Satan stands up and calls out to Mohammed. "One last question for you, Mohammed. Who are you?"

Mohammed stops. Without looking back toward Faust, he says, "I do not have to answer your questions."

"Sure ya do," Faust says, using his hillbilly accent. "I am just another avatar of your eternal healer, as Dr. Abraham was. You must be obedient to all of us. Answer my question."

Eyes cast toward the ceiling, Mohammed's voice is mellow. His words are not for Faust. They are for his son and his wife. "I am a man who now believes that in eternity, God does not seek simply to judge us, but to heal us also.

"Why he provides for a way to heal from wounds that he allowed, perhaps created, is a mystery. Nonetheless, there is healing. To be healed from the wounds of this world so that we can move with freedom through the next. This is the fate Allah's benevolent creation has in store for our souls, and that is why I must again become obedient to him."

The gleaming gate flashes back into existence with a burst of white light. As Mohammed makes his way toward it, the visage of Joy steps into the room and reaches out to Mohammed. Weeping, he takes her hand.

For a second time, Joy stares across the room, eyes locked on Faust's. There is total silence. Holding Joy's hand, Mohammed looks over his shoulder to take one last look at his healer's chamber, the desk and the chairs in particular, relieved that he will never again have to sit in his chair fashioned in the style of the Second Empire. He is relieved to understand that unlike the play *No Exit*, where people are trapped forever in a finely furnished room, his soul be freed.

Faust watches as the white light from the place beyond the door pours over the silhouettes of Joy and Mohammed. And then the gate is gone again.

Alone with the sound of the surf, Faust studies the office. With the vaulted ceiling and huge picture window, the beautiful photographs, the desk, the chairs—it is a fitting place for healing.

He reaches onto the credenza and finds a page from a yellow pad so old that the paper has the texture of parchment. Recognizing the words Dr. Abraham recites to every new therapy group, he focuses on the final paragraph, reading it aloud with such force in his voice that the walls seem to echo his words:

"Each soul begins its existence unblemished. In this life the soul is battered, torn, sullied in so many ways. The soul must be restored, so that it may spend eternity as it began— unblemished. Thus, healing is the goal. Some religions speak of redemption and forgiveness. The healing I speak of does not forgive, but rather it restores. Restoration: this is what we will seek, together…" And then there is that final phrase that Dr. Abraham keeps to himself. "…inside the mysterious, unknowable conspiracy of minds and Gods."

The White Door across the room catches his attention as he reads. It seems very far from where he stands. Knowing he cannot follow the others, Faust touches his fingertips to the ornate antique desk as he walks around it to the Blue Door. Without looking back, he disappears, closing the door behind him.

No one saves us but ourselves.
No one can and no one may.
We ourselves must walk the path.
Buddha, *Dhammapada*

The Other Side

Mary

She had been to this place before. She was quite sure of that. How could she forget the sterility of it? How could she forget the stainless steel equipment and white tile and the dehumanizing antiseptic smell? And then there were the gauges and instruments, the digital readouts, and the lines silently announcing the condition of the patient's body. She recalls the poem she wrote as a little girl. *Lift me up to the sky; 'tis clear and bright like my good Lord's smile. Take me where sadness floats away, When my own special breezes lift me up for a while.*

The lines on the monitors had been busy, telling the story of a body full of life and breath. Then suddenly the lines had grown jagged and frightening. But now they roll gently and rhythmically, waves on a placid sea. They begin to go flat.

Mary doesn't see the lines any more. She is in another place, not seeing with her eyes and her mind, but rather seeing with her soul. She beholds the scene her soul had anticipate for so long. Before her are the green hills of Ireland. The sun shines brightly on a cloudless sky. Standing there in a brilliant white robe is her Lord and savior Jesus Christ. His smile is soft, serene. There is a smile, serene and also lovely, on the face of Mary's beloved mum, standing beside the Lord. There is nothing to say. Eternity pauses.

And then Mary's Earthly eyes flutter open. This time she does not see her body on the table. Three spectators are standing by her bedside. They all three draw in a breath of relief as their patient stirs. Carmella looks at her adopted father, the great physician.

"She's coming back! She is, isn't she?"

He nods without speaking, watching his patient. He has stood by other beds before, watching consciousness flicker back into the brain. This time, there is more at stake. He takes Carmella's hand and lifts the Little One higher in his arms. His eyes stay riveted on the patient.

And suddenly the blue eyes open. The physician watches them focus. He watches consciousness come back to the woman on the bed, his wife.

She sees them. With an effort she frames a thought. With greater effort still, she speaks. "Where am I?"

"Recovery," her husband says softly. He speaks a bit louder. "You are in recovery."

Tears streaming down her cheek, Carmella looks at him in a silent request for permission. He nods.

Carmella kisses Mary's cheek. "You are back. You are here. They said you were gone, but I said I would not let it happen." Kissing Mary's cheek, she weeps. "God told me you would come back to us. And you came back. And now your eyes are open and you are here. I love you so much."

Mary's husband lowers her son, who smiles into her face.

"Oh my God! Ahm here. We are together."

She draws a breath and closes her eyes. Once again, with an effort she frames a thought. Once again, after far greater effort, she speaks. "But where are the others?"

Her husband smiles.

Looking puzzled, Carmella whispers to him. "Who does she mean? Who are the others?"

"She's just composing her thoughts. Let her take her time. It just takes a while, Carmella."

Mary lifts her head slightly. "But Larry, where are they?"

"Mary, we nearly lost you. You had the finest team medicine could muster, but they are gone now. They are home or making their medical rounds or whatever. Your surgery was finished hours ago."

"No, I mean the others I was with. We were there together. In the end we were coaching each other."

Her husband, her physician, betrays a bit of frustration. "Coaching to do what? Where? Where were you together?"

"At the gate. The portal."

The great neurosurgeon hands his adopted son to his adopted daughter. He concentrates on his next words. "Mary, I'm not sure what you mean."

"We were together and left one by one. A great magician opened the gates for us."

"I don't quite understand."

"It was so horrible. But then it was beautiful. Doc… doc… doctor… Abraham was with me."

The physician hears nothing more than a patient using a name from the Bible. Abraham, the patriarch of the many tribes of Israel would scatter across the Earth.

"That is good. You are here now with me and your Precious One and your Little One."

"Joy came back too."

He hears the name of a wonderful emotion. He smiles at Carmella. "Joy is not a strong enough word."

Mary surprises her husband when she becomes suddenly alert. "No. I mean Joy was a person. And then... there was that awful Dr. Faust, but he was... needed. He knew truth was the ransom that each of us needed to pay."

Her husband smiled vaguely, the psychiatrist in him thought he had the answer. "We understand, Mary. Clinical feelings of entrapment sometimes accompany—"

She looked at the Precious One. "No. I'm not crazy. I was there with the others." With that her eyes began to flutter closed.

Her husband patted her hand. "Let's wake you up, let's talk a minute, then you must rest. How do you feel?"

"Ah simply must find the others. They... helped me."

"Mary, I don't know what you mean. The surgical team finished up hours ago. You had your surgery and now you are recovering."

She looks at Carmella. "My Precious One, please write something for me. Quickly. Do it... now."

Larry pulls a pen from his sport coat and hands it to Carmella, who cannot find any paper to write on.

Mary sighs. "Carmella, just write these names on your hand or something."

With a focus that astonishes her husband, Mary closes her eyes and begins to speak. "Mohammad Irani. Joy Huang. Dr. Isaac Abraham. Dr. Faust... no, it was... John Frost... that was his real name. Just write those four names."

Mary lifts her head from the pillow. "Please. Write those names."

The pen finally begins writing on the skin of Carmella's hand. Larry repeats the names and watches Carmella write them. "Mohammad Irani. Joy Huang. Isaac Abraham. John Frost.

"Yes. Those are the names. That was my group. Read the names to me."

Carmella looks at her hand. "Mohammad Irani. Joy Huang. Isaac Abraham. John Frost."

"Yes. Those were the names. We were… healing each other."

"Mary," Larry says with authority, "it's probably time for you to rest again." His eyes glance beyond her to the rhythmic, steady waves on the monitors. He is pleased and confident.

"Promise me you'll find them."

Husband and daughter grasp Mary's hand. Mary looks at Carmella's hand in hers. She pulls Carmella's hand so close to her eyes that a tear drop falls on the writing. "I'm forgetin' them already, but that's the list. Mohammad Irani. Joy Huang. Isaac Abraham. John Frost. Please find them for me."

"We will," Carmella says. Larry nods in agreement.

"You promise, Larry? They got me back here. They were all so pitiful at first. I was too. We were so different from each other. But because of them my soul is pure now and I can begin again. We helped each other. It was God's plan that we should." Mary closes her eyes.

THREE WEEKS PASS before he receives the phone call. Another week passes before he receives the envelope. Mary, meanwhile, is up and about. She hasn't mentioned her request since the day she made it, and her husband assumes she doesn't remember it.

The private investigator's letter, dated March 22, 2002, is brief and factual. The old newspaper clippings are easy to read. The pictures are sharp and clear. Laurence Josephson's mind briefly ruminates on the small skills that professionals must rely upon to do excellent work. The private eye's assistant is probably quite proud of her ability to make such clear copies of old newspaper clippings.

March 5, 2003
Dear Dr. Josephson,

Thank you for the opportunity to perform this investigation for you and your wife. Let me begin with your inquiry about your wife's medical records and travel. This was a time consuming effort, but I am confident that she did not have a medically supervised abortion in France or any other country, as she did not obtain a passport until she traveled to the United States.

And now to the question of the individuals your wife named as being part of a therapy group. As I told you over the telephone, I was able to locate three of the four individuals you inquired about. They are all deceased. Pictures and relevant newspaper articles, including obituaries, are enclosed.

I actually located two individuals named John Frost. They were father and son. They died in a warehouse fire in Eureka, Kansas, July 10, 1944. Although John Frost Jr. was a medical doctor, if either man used Dr. Faust as an alias, I can find no evidence of it.

Lt. Isaac Abraham died in combat in Syria August 10, 1968; he was an American serving in the Israeli Armed Forces. Isaac Abraham was also a medical doctor,. There is another coincidence that should interest you. Isaac Abraham was born on the same day that John Frost died. So it is impossible that they were ever in the same therapy group.

Mohammed Irani died along with his wife and son in an automobile accident in Miami, Florida May 21, 1980. He was a prominent member of the local Muslim community.

I can find no record of a woman named Joy Huang. I did find a recent human interest story in the Miami Herald *concerning a Joy Huang Patel who came to America with her adopted parents last year. But she is only fourteen years old.*

This was an exceedingly interesting investigation. Please let me know if I can be of additional service.

Yours sincerely,
Foster Herbert, Licensed Private Investigator

Larry Josephson sets the letter aside and studies the pictures one at a time. Each is sad in its own way. The young Lieutenant Isaac Abraham cuts a dashing figure in his uniform, hat to the side in a jaunty pose. It is the face of a proud and capable young soldier. Yet there is a melancholy cast to his large and expressive eyes.

And then there are John Frost Junior and Senior. The picture of the volunteer fire company is full of faces framed against a big red fire truck, but it is not difficult to see the strong resemblance between the Chief and the young man standing proudly next to him. Larry Josephson's love for a son who once belonged to another man is so strong that he can imagine how painful their parting must have been.

Finally, he studies the picture that saddens him the most. The family. Struck by the intensity of the man standing with his son and beautiful wife inside an upscale antique shop, Dr. Josephson cannot help but wonder how they passed their last moments together.

He lays the pictures out in a row on his desk. Mary awoke from surgery believing that these people gave her a new start. They helped her purify her very soul. He smiles as he recalls Mary's definition of magic as when something wonderful happens and you can't explain why. Then suddenly, a sadness overtakes him. Stunned by how their tragedies reach him across time, he closes his eyes and says a prayer for each of their souls. And then he prays for every soul everywhere for all time.

Soon Laurence Josephson's reverie ends and he is listening to Mary bustling about in the kitchen with Carmella. He can hear his son laughing and running busy circles around his mother. His mind wanders again. This time he thinks about how much he looks forward to a flavorful glass of Sangria full of freshly cut oranges and apples.

The brilliant Dr. Josephson stands up from the desk in his study, carefully placing the papers back in the envelope with the innocuous label Herbert Investigative Services. He picks a tape dispenser up from his desk. After studying it for a while, he tears off a long strip and uses it to seal the envelope.

He believes in God and he believes in magic, but the evidence in that envelope, the data some might say, exceeds his capacity to understand. He will show it to Mary later, when she is stronger. But only if she asks again, and he doubts that she will. He hopes that ordeal—and therefore the people she claims to have shared it with—is behind her forever.

Mohammed Irani

The noise and the physical shock of being thrust about in his stylish car kept him from gaining a sense of where he was. There was a business card in his hand but he did not understand what it was.

Bleeding from a gash on his face, the impeccably dressed man at the wheel of the Porsche gasped for breath. His refined sensibilities are assaulted by the acrid smells of engine oil and tires and rainwater evaporating up from asphalt. This, he cannot prevent.

But he does prevent himself from looking at the two mangled bodies on the passenger side. He gasps and yanks his head away. Blood fills his eyes and throat as he wept. "Merciful Allah! Please, this cannot be true. This did not happen. No. Merciful Allah! No!" His brain began succumbing to the shock and the trauma and the loss of blood.

His mind, by equal measure, sinks slowly into a stupor. And then he eyes an embossed business card covered now in blood. MOHAMED IRANI. PURVEYOR OF PRECIOUS ANTIQUITIES. In his handwriting he sees the words that will damn him. "Gloria, you are most precious of all."

"Gloria…" He wanted to say the name, but his mouth could not form the word. His eyes were full of tears. His mind was full of a dulled realization that all he possessed just minutes ago, including, quite possibly, his son, his wife, and his very life, was lost.

His mind was numb, fading. His soul struggled, wishing that the radiant dots he saw through his blood were Angels of Allah's mercy, but even in his shock he knew that they were really the headlights of the other vehicles and the multi-colored indicators of his Porsche's elaborate dashboard. As his eyes grew heavier the points of light blurred and finally merged into one soft glow.

The next sound he heard was the sonorous voice of the Imam of his mosque. Imam Al-Sadid was very old. He had know Mohammed's father and uncle. The Imam leaned so close that Mohammed could feel and smell his breath. The old man's beard stung as it lightly brushed the raw flesh where the skin was burned. The revered Imam spoke in a very soft voice.

"The bodies are prepared. All is ready for the burial. Your doctors say it would be possible for you to be there when the bodies are committed to the earth. What is your wish?"

There was silence.

"My brother, please tell me what you wish to do."

Mohammed's jaw was wired together. He was in great pain. He opened his eyes and managed to mutter one word. "Bodies?"

"The bodies of Nia and Zayd." The Imam's words crushed Mohammed's soul. His eyes slammed shut.

"Can you hear me?" The Imam asked. "Can you understand?"

Mohammed shook his head no, then yes.

"My son, you are in great pain. Perhaps it is better—"

Mohammed found energy. "I must be there." Then he repeated, "Must. Be. There."

"Very well. You shall be."

The well-to-do members of the Islamic community knew the Irani family very well, and worked quietly along with police to sort through the details of the incident. There were no witnesses to the accident, save the Mercedes driver who was still in a coma but expected to recover. One witness to the events preceding the accident came forward, in person, at a local precinct station. Gloria.

The scandalous elements of the story had no legal bearing on the accident investigation, and so the lead police detective and the Imam himself were the only ones who knew the details. They agreed that enough harm had been done already. The local reporters who inquired about the accident were told simply that a full report would be available soon, and that the names of those killed and the survivors were being withheld pending notification of relatives.

The Imam saw it all as a tale of human folly that perhaps would be forgiven by Allah's grace.

The detective, Lieutenant Kelly, saw much the same thing. An intense man in his forties with piercing blue eyes, the seasoned street-cop turned detective also understood human folly. At first he saw a perverse love triangle involving a son and a father and a resourceful prostitute masquerading as their lover.

He met Gloria at Zayd's apartment. He began the interview by summing up the situation. "Thank you for coming forward. The man driving the truck struck by Mr. Irani's car is dead. The woman driving a late model Mercedes that struck Mr. Irani's car is in critical condition. Mr. Irani is also in critical condition. His son and daughter, the other passengers in his car, are dead."

Lieutenant Kelly wasn't sure she grasped that Mohammed was in critical condition but still alive. She didn't ask to see him. Sobbing but composed, she told her story from meeting Zayd at school to meeting his father to the tragic events at the apartment. When he put away his notebook and thanked her for her honesty, she asked, "Now what?"

He put his hand on her shoulder. "Now? Nothing. Nothing for the police. For a priest, maybe yes, and I can recommend mine. But for the cops, this cop, this is over."

She burst into tears. "Thank you. My priest knows all of this. God knows my sins for which I am paying dearly." She shook his hand. "But thank you for your kind thought. You know how I so need some kindness, don't you?" Knowing that this could be a come-on line from a call girl working a Miami bar, but sensing that the young woman was perhaps not masquerading after all, he touched her shoulder again. "Yes, I do."

He neatly printed Father Garcia, St. Peter's Basilica, on his detective's business card. "He's not a whole lot older than you. Trust when I say, I turn to him for comforts from time to time. We all have sins to confess."

Like the Imam and the detective, Gloria also saw a story of human folly. But she saw only hers. Within the span of only an hour she endured the worst tragedy of her already tragic young life. The two loves of her life, men who caressed her and treasured her just days before, were lost. The woman they both loved, Nia, was lost also, an innocent bystander to what had the feel of the sudden and senseless drive-by-shootings Gloria had witnessed in Miami.

Only Gloria, the detective and the Imam would ever sense the weight of the tragedy. Only they know how the priceless antique bowl was broken and how a love note scribbled on a business card brought ruination to so many lives.

As Mohammed wished, it was arranged for him to be present at the funeral of his wife and son. He was on a stretcher of sorts, and two attendants moved him so he could see the bodies being placed in the ground. A murmur of whispered comments greeted the arrival of his stretcher. "He is a broken man but he is alive, merciful Allah be praised," said one man. "Merciful Allah be praised," others repeated.

The sky was bright and blue. A slight breeze rustled in the oak trees and palms. Yet deep, silent sorrow filled the faces of their friends who gathered there.

Gloria had asked the Imam if she could be present, and he allowed it but, knowing the facts, asked her to say little or nothing to the other mourners. She obliged, as she tried always to do. She wore a black hijab, appropriate for mourning. It was to please Mohammed. She stood apart from the others weeping uncontrollable, comforted by no one.

The Islamic funeral prayers were recited silently in Arabic. Mohammed's eyes were closed. His mind and his God and his soul could hear the un-said words with perfect clarity.

Opening his eyes, he believed he saw Gloria standing there, afar, so very alone. Mustering all his strength, he raised his head and thought he saw Gloria bow her head to acknowledge him. For the briefest moment he overcame the conspiracy of his mind and his God, and, breaking their bond, his soul rushed past the bodies of his wife and son, past the downcast faces of the mourners, to look into her dark, beautiful eyes.

The next instant, still reciting the prayer silently in Arabic, one phrase was too much to bear. "Allah forgives all of us who are alive and those of us who are dead." Eyes blood red, he bit his lip in fear and pain and rage.

Soon a crushing pain squeezed his chest, radiating down his left arm. The massive heart attack was but a flash of cosmic time. Mohammed Irani joined his wife and his son in death.

The paramedics attending Mohammed Irani could do nothing. He died beside the grave. As elders began to direct the attendants, Imam Al-Sadid came over to Gloria, who was pacing in a circle, still a desolate figure. She heard the rustling of his robe as he approached, a younger cleric holding his arm for support.

The Imam's deep voice said simply, "Allah desires that the dead be buried as soon as possible."

He glanced at the younger cleric and nodded as if instructing him to speak to Gloria.

"All shall be proper," the young man said with a slight accent she took to be Arabic. "Mohammed's body will be taken to the Mosque, carefully washed and then covered in a clean white linen shroud. Within the hour perhaps, his Earthly body will be committed to the ground along with the others."

She held back her tears. "I understand. I will just stay here. May I?" She addressed her question to the young cleric, but it was the Imam who answered. "Yes. You may remain here."

Standing alone, watching the sadness and the ceremony, Gloria stayed until all was done. After the mourners were gone, she stood a silent vigil. The sky turned from blue to orange and crimson. A breeze came up, and she could see towering white thunderhead clouds rolling in. Walking to her car, she shouted, "No. No. This isn't right. I must say goodbye to you, Mohammed!"

She turned to return to the grave. Running the last few yards, she fell on hands and knees and kissed the ground. Removing the hijab, weeping, she grabbed a clod of the newly turned dirt and rubbed it on her forehead and hair.

She placed the black hijab on the ground, taking great care that it was neatly folded, as Mohammed would have wished it. "I am sorry for the loss you have suffered. I am sorry for my part in it. I understand why this is the end, but I will remember you. I hope you find your peace."

Through so many losses and tragedies, she never felt so alone as when she placed that scarf on the grave.

Mohammed Irani was elsewhere as Gloria spoke her final words to him.

When he died, a curtain of black fell. When it lifted, the noise and confusion of the accident rushed through his brain once more. A blurred menagerie of faces, voices and sounds and books of painful memories rattled by.

Like Mary, for an instant he recalled every word and every name, especially Dr. Abraham and the dreaded Dr. Faust. But, unlike Mary, he was not fortunate enough to have someone among the living to listen. Then came a quiet soft light, a stillness conjured by the whispers of angels.

The curtain fell again, then lifted brilliant white. Soon the angels guided Mohammed to a lush stand of palms and fig trees and flowers bathed in a morning mist. Radiating light, a large black stone sits at the entrance to a path. Could this be the black stone of the Kaaba of Mecca in its original place in the Garden of Eden? This question would have no answer. He kisses it softly to gain entrance to the garden.

The place, and therefore the moment, is luxurious with comfort and warmth and peace. There are no enemies there. For the soul who was once Mohammed Irani, the journey of struggle is over. He moves through flowers red and yellow and green toward a clearing where many people stand. Among them are the people he thought he would never see again. At last, he sees and understands with perfect clarity.

He sees a wife and a son who would now be obedient, as he shall also be, until the end of time. His pleasure at the sight overwhelms him.

Isaac Abraham

Lieutenant Isaac Abraham, weapon at the ready, took a deep cleansing breath and stepped from the bright sunlight into the darkness of the cave. The place reeked of feces and urine and gasoline from half full cans piled around the cave walls. Hearing sounds from inside, he took cover by leaning against the entrance wall until his eyes adjusted to the darkness. Panning his flashlight across the cave, he saw the figure of a man, no, it was really a boy.

The boy held up his World War I carbine and tried without success to point it at his enemy. The lieutenant aimed his vastly superior automatic rifle carefully and squeezed off two rounds. Both hit their target, the right ankle of the boy.

Writhing in pain, the boy tossed his rifle haplessly toward the enemy entering his hideout. It clattered against the wall and landed on the ground near the entrance. After days of killing anonymous foes in an effort not to be killed, the young officer saw a welcome opportunity for an act of kindness. Keeping his weapon trained on the boy, he walked over carefully.

"Who are you?" Lieutenant Abraham asked the question in Arabic. An American totally unfamiliar with Arabic languages or culture, he had mastered the basics of the language in a few short weeks of officer's training with the Israel Defense Force.

The boy answered in Arabic. "I will not tell you."

"Why not?" They began to converse in Arabic.

"Such is Allah's will."

"Are you here alone? Where are the others?"

The boy jerked his head to the side and closed his eyes.

"I am a doctor. I can stop that bleeding and give you something for pain if you tell me your name. Telling me your name will not betray your God."

After a pause, "Abad."

"Your name is Abad?"

"Yes."

After a pause, the boy said, "You are not a doctor. You are a Jew soldier."

In the moment it took Lieutenant Abraham to translate the Arabic in his head, something about the boy's words, uttered in a wretched, foul-smelling cave, conveyed an irony that seemed almost humorous. He could not help smiling.

"An American doctor can be a Jew solder, Abad."

"Enemy," the boy replied.

The lieutenant ignored the boy's words and concentrated on the bullet wounds in the boys ankle that he himself had inflicted.

His Arabic was fluent. "I do not want to harm you now. I will stop your bleeding. Yes? Do you want me to? Yes? Or no?"

The boy nodded.

"Very well. Abad, I am going to lay my rifle down and put a tourniquet on your wound." He made the gesture of pretending to wrap his own leg with imaginary dressing. "Do you understand?"

Abad nodded yes. He then glanced over to his side.

From the corners of their eyes both saw an ornate dagger on the ground. It was barely an arm's length away. For a span of heartbeats they both stared at the dagger, then the boy sprang to his knees and crawled furiously across the dirt and reached it first. With a shriek he plunges the rusted blade into the young officer's wrist sending blood squirting onto the sand.

"God is great," he shouted in Arabic. A self-satisfied grin painted the boy's face.

Well trained in hand to hand combat, lieutenant Abraham grabbed the dagger from his mortal enemy's hand and placed his knee on the boy's chest. He looked at the barefoot boy in his filthy, ill-fitting uniform as he squirmed in a hopeless attempt to set himself free. The lieutenant's blood poured into the face of his victim as the lieutenant leaned his knee on the chest of the lesser creature and, with heartless dispatch, plunged the dagger into the boy's throat.

Propelled by the force of his final heart beats, Abad's blood squirted everywhere. Ignoring his victim and moving as quickly as he could, the lieutenant skillfully applied a tourniquet to his own wound. Next, he poured gasoline everywhere, most particularly on his latest enemy kill, with the goal of torching the cave.

Lieutenant Abraham's hands and eyes were a robot fully engaged in its task. But his mind and his God took him elsewhere. His thoughts were of the father who died in another war and the mother who held him to her breast before she died also, leaving him no less an orphan than the boy now lifeless at his feet.

When he heard the clatter of weapons and footsteps coming, not from the front of the cave where he had entered, but from another entrance in the back, he reached for his rifle and began running out of the cave with the hope that he could scramble down the hill and reach the safety of the Israeli column grinding slowly through the valley a hundred meters below him. His soul was full of faith in the God of his father, the God who brought him to this place.

Gunfire crackled. Hit from behind by three rounds, he stumbled out of the cave into the scorching sunlight and began crawling down the sandy hillside, rifle cradled in his arms. He imagined his father attacking a beach in the Pacific doing much the same thing. In his father's eyes there may have been palm trees and lush hillsides, a beautiful scene just as this desert scene below possessed a haunting beauty.

But in that battle for a Pacific beach, fire and plumes of smoke loomed up behind the palms, and the tide carried dead carcasses onto the shore. One of those was his father. Now Lieutenant Isaac Abraham, Israel Defense Force, was in much the same places as Corporal Jacob Abraham, United States Marine Corp.

Crawling down the hill in a final effort to survive, he shouted for help in English and then in Hebrew. Losing blood from wounds in his back, his mind, beginning to drift, perceived that a squad of Israeli soldiers was scrambling up the rock-strewn hillside, but he couldn't be sure in the bright light reflecting from the sand. His mind was looking for hope, but his soul understood his cause to be hopeless. A second volley of rounds from behind mostly missed their target, kicking sand up into his face. But the three rounds that did penetrate his shoulders crippled him.

He was lying face down, motionless, when a man in full combat gear shouting "Allah Akbar" rolled him over to face up at the sun. Gasping for breath, he somehow managed to savor the moment staring into the sky. "So be it," he whispered in Hebrew.

Spitting in his captive's face, the soldier brandished the ornate dagger, the Jambiya, the Israeli had used minutes ago to kill a boy. He pressed it against Lieutenant Abraham's nose as if forcing him to closely examine what would be the instrument of his death. Shouting "Allah Akbar" once again, he waved it in the air and then slowly slit Lieutenant Abraham's throat. "God is greater" shouted in Arabic were the last words Isaac Abraham heard in his Earthly life.

A curtain of black fell, but when it lifted another battle was revealed, harsh, jumbled. Not just his suffering, but the suffering of all humanity played out in faces and voices and books of painful memories. The scenes rattled by. Then came a quiet soft light. A soul was ready.

The curtain fell again, now a pure white, and lifted. After the instant of death, everything changed. He was in a better place. A perfect place. The place, and therefore the moment, was luxurious with comfort and warmth and peace. There were no enemies there. The soul that was once Isaac Abraham knows many things. He knew that the one called Mohammed was at peace. He knew that Mary has been given back to her Little One and Precious One. She still belongs there because her love for those who needed her was so strong.

His job is complete. He knows that Joy and the one who called himself Faust are elsewhere, on a special journey together. Perhaps he will join them later. Perhaps not. All that matters now is that he sees a kindly mother. Her once sad eyes now sparkle with peace. He gazes at her briefly and then all vanish from the place.

Dr. Faust and Joy

The surf and the air were unusually quiet. A breeze whisked by his face as he strode out onto the beach and stepped gingerly into the surf. A cloud drifts down from the heavens, the morning mist sits on the water as far as his eye can see. Warm waves draw eddies of sand about the ankles of the man standing barefoot and wearing a floppy straw hat. He recalls a child's poem he composed but never wrote down for fear that it would sully the purity of the first verses of Genesis.

> *The sun, the sea, the flowers and the air,*
> *How lucky we are!*
> *All of creation is there.*

At an angle to the beach, a gleaming wall of windows reflects sunlight back onto the palms hugging the edifice. The sun rising in the east throws its rays against the glass, where they dance a frantic dance, shafts of light bouncing everywhere. Shading his eyes with his hands, he looks up and considers the power of the wall of light. He is now on the other side of it.

The hat protects his skin. Dark sunglasses protect his eyes. Through the fog of his reverie and the mist on the water, he sees the figure of a woman—a beautiful woman with raven hair wearing a white cotton shift.

The light bounding against the water, along with the disarray of his thoughts, combine to blur his vision. At first it appears as the silhouette of a woman, and then it is a figure seeming to possess many arms until at last she is upon him and he sees her clearly.

"Hello. I am here because I decided to continue my journey with you, Dr. Abraham," the woman says, embracing his shoulders softly.

"You have come back. Thank you," the man says from under his hat, teeth gleaming. "But if you came to journey with Dr. Abraham, you are mistaken," he says. "Dr. Abraham is now where he prefers to be. I am Dr. Faust, a stand-in of sorts. So sorry to disappoint."

"Not disappointed at all. It doesn't matter who you say you are, at least not this instant."

"Do I get a peck on the cheek?"

"Why not? Of course." She cups his jaw in her hand and kisses him softly on his cheek.

"So I guess my skin doesn't scare you any more or make you want to puke."

"When did you scare me? Where?"

He smiles. "So very coy, my enchanting Joy. We both know that time and place are lost to us, so your question is a trap."

"Not a trap. But you are right. Time and place are lost, as is self. Do you know who I am, Dr. Faust?"

"You are, or more precisely believe you are, an Avatar of Vishnu. Perhaps I am one also. Is that possible, my enchanted one?"

She looks deeply into his eyes, compelling his stare to follow hers as she looks down to her necklace with its Hindu goddess, its beautiful face and many arms shimmering in the sunlight. "Where we are, all things are possible. There are so many garments we can wear. Your soul has just shed one garment, allowing me to witness it. Thank you, my dear Dr. Abraham now Dr. Faust. Or do you want to at least change that name to John Frost?"

"Who cares about names. Let me be Faust. You be Joy. Where are we? Why are we here? I don't know, do you?"

"I don't know, at least not with any certainty."

She twirled around playing little girl, bare feet sinking into the cool sand. "But let's try thinking like children. When you were a little boy you loved to hear your father read from the *Gospel of Matthew*. 'Do not store up for yourself treasures on earth, where moth and rust destroy, and where thieves break in and steal. But store up for yourself treasures in heaven, where moth and rust do not destroy and thieves do not break in and steal. For where your treasures are, so there your heart will be also.' Remember, little fella?"

"Yes."

"It is a beautiful thought and fitting for this very moment. Can we agree for the moment that we are where our treasures are, no matter what else is true or not true or beyond truth?"

"Agreed."

Joy peers off into the sea. "Perfect. Now you be a child who once rode a fire truck. I'll be a child who used to sell carpets. So forget the man who fancies himself to be Faust, the doomed soul of the dark German legend. Be John Frost, the kid with a dad who tried to teach him about life and about God."

"I'll go with this. We're innocent kids at the beach. But Joy, please tell me how did we get here?"

"For myself, I have been summoned back. You saw that I had the power to cross back and forth in the Portal. I have returned from the many," she says softly, "to serve the many. This is our role in this vast, mysterious conspiracy of minds and Gods. But I am also here to serve you. You helped to heal my shame. I am here to heal you of your loneliness. And we can both help others pay the ransom of truth that makes souls pristine again and set them free for eternity."

Playfully, Joy stands back and takes on the image of Mohini the Goddess with many arms.

Faust smiles. "Nice. Oh, by the way, remember this?" He holds her watch in his hand, the one he took from her at the Portal. Before she speaks, he tosses it above her head, and a rainbow aura of Vishnu appears to fill the sky. "Vishnu is timeless, if I understand correctly."

"Time is irrelevant in the story of creation."

"Yes. But you and I have our powers, of course.. The power to bend time. Powers of illusion that enabled Dr. Abraham to transport the dagger used to cut his throat to the credenza of his psychiatrist's office."

"How is that possible?"

"I'm not sure it matters," Faust answers. "Our powers over time and illusion have no real use. Our true power is the knowledge that the conspiracy of minds and Gods, the chains that hold the soul in bondage until truth brings release, is as it should be. Truth is the pristine force in all of creation, how it begins and ends."

"Yes, truth is the force," Joy says, returning to the form of the young accountant from Hong Kong Faust first met in Dr. Abraham's office. She is wearing a sundress and the necklace with the form of Mohini.

Faust reciprocates, returning to a form she has not seen before, the handsome young medical student who set out one night to fight a warehouse fire. Dressed for swimming like he did in those days, he does a summersault on the sand.

"Stay just that way," Joy asks.

"For you I will be whatever you want," he replies. Rubbing his finger tips across his cheeks, he says, "How did I get so handsome? Ah, so questions. The big one, of course, is that, if minds invented gods to imprison souls, if God did not exist, then how could we be here, spirits without bodies? How could there be disembodies souls, unbound by the physical world of time and space? I'm stumped. All questions, no answers."

"I'm stumped too," Joy shouts, running into the surf. Faust watches. As larger waves crest and break on her, her clothes vanish. He watches her nude form, then follows. As he reaches her, she turns, the water rising so that only her shoulders and face are exposed. He too is now nude, waves cresting on him, shoulder height.

Joy rubs the sea foam and bubbles through her hair. "Maybe the water holds the answer. Right now it seems to want to cover us up. Eve and Adam after the fall from grace, do you think?"

"More left unexplained," he replies, splashing her with water. "This reminds me of how my dad and a pastor friend of his baptized teenagers. Sort of like this." He splashes her again.

"Like this?" She cups water in her hands and pours it slowly over his forehead.

"Kind of like that."

"Tell you what, Dr. Faust. Let's start over as children who met on this beach and say that what came before doesn't matter any more. Start over again. Agreed?"

"Agreed." The surf, the tide, rolls out. Two children walk a long path parallel to the beach, naked as at birth, laughing and kicking and splashing in the waves.

In a realm where time has no meaning, the interlude may have lasted for a minute. An hour. An eternity. After a period of silence, two adults walk out of the water, dressed once again. Sopping wet, they climb the hill, returning to the respite, stepping effortlessly through the gleaming wall of light and into the place where their powers can be of use once again.

About the Author

Van Douglas is the pen name of a writer and technology entrepreneur working in Washington DC. He is the author of other works of fiction as well as non-fiction, including two college textbooks. His training in social psychology and group dynamics are a source of concepts for this psychological thriller.

To learn more, visit www.Vandouglaswriter.com. His email address is Van@vandouglaswriter.com.

www.ingramcontent.com/pod-product-compliance
Lightning Source LLC
Chambersburg PA
CBHW060129130626
46556CB00006B/2279